Dear Reader,

Buildings speak to us. They have heart and history and whispered secrets within their creaking floorboards. They have a feel about them as soon as you walk in the door that you cannot explain.

When I was looking for a backdrop for my new novel, *The Lost Child*, an old black-and-white map of Chichester that I saw by chance at the Goodwood Hotel in Sussex and the faint image of a building labelled 'County Lunatic Asylum' gave me goosebumps.

As soon as I got home, I called my mother-in-law, a former police detective. She kindly agreed to drive us to Chichester and take a look at the building which was once Graylingwell Psychiatric Hospital and is now luxury flats. She had taken a few 'lost souls' to be admitted to Graylingwell in her days on the beat in the seventies and knew her way around.

It was a beautiful sunny winter's day as we drove around the grounds, drinking in the atmosphere and taking pictures of the untouched derelict outbuildings. In spite of the smart new veneer of the flats, you could still feel the history of the place. I could picture patients walking around and visiting the chapel – that was still intact.

However, despite drinking in the atmosphere, I still didn't have my story. But as we drove away from the imposing Victorian building my mother-in-law said, 'Did you know that until about the fifties, if a wealthy man was bored with his wife, he could have her put in there so he could marry his mistress?'

I nearly crashed the car. A sane woman could be locked up for life at her husband's discretion? It turned out to be true. The Matrimonial Causes Act 1937 extended the grounds for divorce, which, until that date, had been only for adultery, to now include unlawful desertion for two years or more, cruelty, incurable insanity, incest or sodomy. As divorce was very hard to come by, many husbands resorted to fake pictures of infidelity or, indeed, 'arranged' for their wives to be declared insane and locked away as a means to escape any scandal or repercussions.

I was shocked, horrified . . . and inspired. I had my plot and my building. Now I just needed my characters and, as soon as I started my research on that incredible, and hidden, part of our recent history, these came magically to life.

I hope you enjoy reading *The Lost Child* as much as I have loved writing it.

Emily x

The Lost Child

Emily Gunnis previously worked in TV drama and lives in Brighton with her young family. She is one of the four daughters of *Sunday Times* bestselling author Penny Vincenzi. Emily's first novel, *The Girl in the Letter*, was an international bestseller and has been translated into twelve languages.

You can find out more information about Emily Gunnis and her books by visiting her on Twitter @EmilyGunnis and on Instagram @emilygunnis.

The Lost Child

The Lost Child

EMILY GUNNIS

REVIEW

First published in Great Britain in 2019
by HEADLINE REVIEW
An imprint of HEADLINE PUBLISHING GROUP

This edition published in Great Britain in 2020
by HEADLINE REVIEW

1

Cataloguing in Publication Data is available from the British Library

ISBN 978 1 4722 5506 8

Offset in 13.94/16.53 pt Adobe Garamond by Jouve (UK), Milton Keynes

Printed and bound in Great Britain by Clays Ltd, Elcograf S.p.A.

Headline's policy is to use papers that are natural, renewable and recyclable
products and made from wood grown in well-managed forests and other
controlled sources. The logging and manufacturing processes are expected
to conform to the environmental regulations of the country of origin.

HEADLINE PUBLISHING GROUP
An Hachette UK Company
Carmelite House
50 Victoria Embankment
London EC4Y 0DZ

www.headline.co.uk
www.hachette.co.uk

For my husband Steven,
my love, my life, my reacher of high things;
I didn't know I was lost until I found you.

———

Ever has it been that love knows not
its own depth until the hour of separation.

Kahlil Gibran

Prologue

Saturday, 19 November 1960

'Please let me out, sir. I don't feel well.'

Rebecca looked over the table at the policeman with wire-framed glasses who hadn't let her leave the interview room since they had arrived two hours before.

Detective Inspector Gibbs took a deep inhale of his Woodbine then blew the thick grey smoke into the airless room.

Rebecca stared down at her hands: tiny specks of her mother's blood were spattered on the back of her right wrist and she began scratching at them with her nails. She was still wearing the white nightie she had slept in. Trails of blood dragged along the hemline. She wanted to tear it off, get in a bath, sink underneath the water and never come up again.

'We're nearly done. I just need to get a few more details straight in my mind before we have your statement typed up.' DI Gibbs reached forward, his black eyes glaring into hers, and crushed the Woodbine under his nicotine-stained forefinger. 'I'll get you some water.'

As he stood, his chair scraped across the tiled floor, letting out a high-pitched screeching noise which startled her. She pulled the scratchy woollen blanket round her. She was shaking, and cold. So cold.

DI Gibbs let the door slam behind him. Rebecca's eyes

stung as she looked up at the clock: 4 a.m. She had never stayed up this late before. She and Harvey sometimes hid in the bomb shelter together late into the night, to escape her father's fury, but his desire for whisky-fuelled oblivion usually took over his rage by midnight.

As the yelling began, she would signal to Harvey from her bedroom window with a torch he had given her and he would sprint across the cornfield to her, open the hatch to the bomb shelter under Seaview Cottage. By then she would be waiting for him, having accessed the shelter via the trap door in the under-stairs cupboard. A small underground cave, which her father had filled with tinned food and books and candles in case the German enemy returned to slaughter his family. Father's never-ending paranoia, which made her and her mother's life hell, unwittingly provided her with an escape.

Rebecca sat and watched the seconds ticking on the clock, the passing of time taking her further and further from the last time she had seen her mother. The last time she would ever see her mother. She could still picture her: her mouth gasping for air, her beautiful lips, which had kissed her so many times, her skin losing colour, then taking her last breath, the life leaving her.

The silence of the smoke-filled room throbbed in her ears. Her body was exhausted yet her brain played over and over in her mind the scene that had greeted her when, hearing her mother's wall-piercing screams, she had run from her bedroom into the sitting room at Seaview: her mother, lying on the pale rug Rebecca had watched her beat clean of dust so many times on the sun-dappled steps of the cottage.

A rug now dyed red with the blood that had poured from her ears and her nose. Her eyes so swollen shut from her father kicking her with his heavy black boot she couldn't see her daughter in the doorway.

'So, Miss Waterhouse.' DI Gibbs made her jump as he walked in through the door. 'Let's go over this one more time.'

It already felt like another lifetime, lying in her bed only hours before with the storm blowing in from Wittering Bay hissing at her window. Despite the extra quilt she had pulled from the cupboard, her extremities had throbbed with the cold.

She had pictured Father groaning as he tended the fire, muttering to himself as the dust made him cough. Mother would be looking over at him, her straight, mousey hair swept up in a bun, her tired legs stretched out on the stool in front of her, silently waiting for his temper to light along with the kindling. The fire lit, Father would take his key from the desk drawer, walk over to the locked cabinet and remove his Luger pistol, as he did every Monday, meticulously taking it apart and cleaning the grips with linseed oil while Mother watched anxiously. 'We can't all afford to be as naive as you, Harriet,' he would say. 'A man needs to be able to protect his family.'

Rebecca had felt the tension through the floor. It was deathly quiet, as it always was when her father was brooding. It had been a fraught day, since her parents had been called in to see the headmaster about her. Her father hadn't spoken to her since, except to say that they were leaving Seaview first thing in the morning and that she would never be seeing Harvey Roberts again.

The thought of Harvey slammed her back into the present. 'Please let me see Harvey,' she pleaded now.

'All in good time. Harvey Roberts was making rather a nuisance of himself so we've had to put him in the cells.'

The nausea was coming again, Gibbs's presence overwhelming her. He reminded her of one of the rats scuttling about the lambing pens at Seaview Farm. His teeth were yellowing and sharp; the ends of his thick black moustache twitched as he spoke, like whiskers.

Rebecca gulped down the rush of tears. Soon after she had been taken to the interview room, she heard Harvey crying out for her in the corridor outside. She had heard several policemen talking over one another, shouting for him to calm down, threatening to lock him up for the night. He had pounded at the door between them, his voice fading as they dragged him away.

'What about Harvey's dad? I'm only thirteen. Shouldn't I have an adult with me?' Rebecca's voice trembled, and DI Gibbs glared at her.

'Ted Roberts is inebriated – he doesn't even know his own name at the moment, so he's not much use to you, I'm afraid. We'll call social services once their office opens, and you'll be made the subject of a care order.'

'What does that mean?' she said, her heart flooding with panic.

Gibbs glared at her. 'It means you'll be placed in the care of the local authority and you'll have a social worker attached to you who is responsible for you.'

'But I want to live with Ted and Harvey.' Rebecca couldn't help the tears coming now. 'Please let me use the bathroom, I really don't feel well.'

'Well, the sooner you can be a little clearer about what happened, the sooner we'll be done here.'

'But I have been clear, I've told you everything. Please don't make me go over it again.'

She didn't want to recall the sound of her father's raised voice piercing the storm howling at the house. The bellow that had come through the floorboards, and the sound of her mother's voice, trying to calm him. She could picture her mother trembling in her chair now, her fear of what was to come evident. Something in the room below had smashed. Rebecca's heart had thudded painfully as the wind and rain pelted against her window and she had pulled the covers over her head.

'So I'm going to write it down this time and then the secretary can type it up when she comes in at the start of her shift.' He sighed, exhaling smoke. 'Tell me again, what was it your mother did to anger your father this evening?'

Rebecca angrily wiped away a tear. Her head was shattering: she had no way of making this man understand what it meant to live with a man like her father. 'She didn't do anything. We didn't need to do anything. I could leave a pencil out, maybe my mother didn't fold a towel the right way. My father suffers with chronic battle neurosis. He was treated at Greenways Psychiatric Hospital but he's never fully recovered. He's got a violent temper and the smallest noise or upset can trigger a flashback.'

'But today something did happen to make him angry? You said you played truant from school.' The policeman stared at her, his pen poised.

Rebecca closed her eyes and thought back to the day before, when she was a different person, still a little girl with a family, sitting in the corridor outside her headmaster's office staring at the orange, swirly carpet as voices resonated inside.

'It's that Roberts boy, he's a bad influence.' The headmaster spoke loudly and Rebecca had pictured him pacing, his hands clasped behind his back as her parents sat inside.

'They live on the farm bordering Seaview Farm and Ted Roberts employed my wife while I was being treated at Greenways.' Father's voice had been quiet, as it always was outside their secluded home. 'As a result, Rebecca and Harvey grew up together and, unfortunately, I wasn't around to stop the unhealthy amount of time they spent together.'

'Well, I would trust your instincts, Mr Waterhouse. While I thought Rebecca had her sights set a little higher than being a farmer's wife, I fear her relationship with the Roberts boy is having a detrimental effect as her grades have started to slip.'

'Her grades?' her mother had said, anxious. 'Her studies are very important to her – she wants to be a doctor.' She stopped, as if suddenly embarrassed by her outburst.

'It's a bit late to be fussing now. I warned you about those people, Harriet.'

'Well, the ambitions of most ladies fall by the wayside when they fall in love, I find,' the headmaster had said matter-of-factly.

'Love?' Despite himself, her father's voice had become louder. 'She's thirteen, for God's sake.'

'Can I ask, have there been any issues at home?' the headmaster said, treading carefully.

'No, nothing I can think of. Can you, Harriet?' Rebecca had held her breath. Both knew full well why she had played truant that day, why she had been desperate to see Harvey.

Her father was taking her away, from Seaview and Harvey, the only things that made it possible for her to survive.

Her grades were not slipping because of Harvey, they were slipping because she was exhausted from living in fear. Because her nightmares ended only when the day of treading eggshells began. Because she lived in a house where she was scared to walk into a room in case her father was in it; where she had wet the bed until she was eleven because she was too afraid to get up in the night in case she bumped into him. Because watching her father beat her mother had become almost a relief from the endless tension of waiting for it to start. And, every time, her mother would apologize for him, make excuses, dab at her bleeding mouth, try to mop up the blood on her face over the ceramic sink in their tiny kitchen.

'Why did you feel the need to leave school today without permission?' asked DI Gibbs, jolting her back into the present.

'I went to say goodbye to Harvey,' Rebecca said quietly. She was shaking now, her whole body starting to go into shock.

'Because you were moving away?' Gibbs waited for her to nod before scratching her words out on the paper.

'He was baling at Greenways Psychiatric Hospital. They have a farm the patients work on. Harvey and his father stay at the local pub in the week so I knew I wouldn't see him before we left.' Rebecca closed her eyes and let out a slow breath, trying to ease the nausea.

'We are smitten, aren't we?'

'Ted and Harvey are like family to me. They took my mother in when I was a baby and my father was sent to Greenways. We would have been on the streets without them.'

DI Gibbs nodded slowly. 'And how did you get to Greenways after sneaking out of school?'

'I got the bus.'

Rebecca's stomach throbbed. The sanitary pad in her knickers was irritating her skin and she was sure it needed changing, but she had nothing with her other than the nightie on her back. She hated what her body was doing to her – the mess, the pain of it, not just in her tummy but in her back, her legs. She hated the hairs between her legs, her growing breasts, sore and ever present. She didn't want her body to change and had no use for any of it. She knew that, unlike the other girls in her class who were already giggling over the prospect of marriage and children, the idea of it filled her with horror.

'Don't get married, Rebecca, it's a mug's game,' Mother had whispered one evening as they peeled potatoes for dinner. 'I've put some money in an account for you for medical school.' She had looked out of the kitchen door to where Jacob was reading the newspaper, then back at her. 'There's no need to tell anyone about it. Promise me, whatever happens, you'll finish your studies.'

She had startled as her mother pulled a post-office booklet from the back of the kitchen drawer and pressed it into her hand. She felt herself beginning to cry, all the tension that forever filled the house pressing down on her.

'Promise me.'

'I promise.'

It had started the day he came home from Greenways and she had looked over at her father, his dark, brooding eyes glaring at her, a forced smile etched onto his scarred face.

'Why, Mummy? Why does he shout at you and hurt you?' The knot in her stomach this stranger had inflicted was already having an effect on her sunny fearlessness. A black cloud now followed her everywhere she went. She loathed being alone with him and cowered behind her mother's legs whenever he emerged from his bedroom, bleary eyed and foul tempered.

'Things are going to have to be different at home from now on, little one, because Daddy's a bit sad and frightened from fighting in the war. And you have to be there for the people you love, even when they're not being as kind and nice to you as you'd like them to be. He'll be better soon.'

At the age of five, life as she had known it had ended. Their carefree, fun-loving home became a prison over-night. The sounds of laughter, the smells of the sea breeze through the open windows, the sand pockets over the kitchen floor, the music on the wireless. As he came in through the door, her mother's heart went out.

'And what happened when you got to Greenways?' asked DI Gibbs, leaning forward to picking up a now-cold cup of coffee.

Rebecca thought back to the previous afternoon. The biting cold had snapped at her when she stepped off the bus, as if warning her to turn back. With butterflies in her stomach, she had walked towards the three-storey Gothic building at the edge of Chichester. The high wrought-iron gates a threatening reminder that once you were in, it was near-impossible to get out.

Soon after the gates had slammed shut behind her, a clean-shaven man had walked up to her, blocking her path, his eyes averted.

'What is your date of birth?' he asked rocking gently from one leg to the other.

'Don't be shy. Tell George your date of birth and he'll tell you the day of the week you were born.' With relief she had turned to see Harvey smiling at her in his mud-soaked dungarees, his blond hair flopping in front of his blue eyes.

'Okay. I was born on 8th January 1947.'

To her amazement, George, without a moment's hesitation, blurted out, 'Wednesday.' Staring at her, he added, 'You're the girl in the painting.'

'That's incredible. How does he do that?' said Rebecca. 'What painting is he talking about?' she added, frowning.

Harvey shrugged. 'George has a brilliant mind, but he's totally institutionalized. He would never survive outside these walls now.'

'It isn't how I imagined it would be – I thought everyone would be locked away.' She had tried not to stare too much, but her curiosity got the better of her. The biting cold was making her shiver.

'Well, the ones wandering around are the ones the doctors think should be kept occupied with physical activity, but the ones who are psychotic, who are a danger to themselves or others, they're locked up in Ward B, up there,' said Harvey, pointing to the dozens of arched windows staring down at them from the façade of the main building.

'Anyway, what are you doing here? Shouldn't you be at school?' Harvey led her out of the bitter wind through the door and stood at the end of a seemingly never-ending corridor which looked like the stuff of nightmares. There was a tension in the air, and she could hear what sounded like a woman screaming for her life.

'I found Harvey and told him we were leaving,' Rebecca said quietly now to DI Gibbs.

10

'And what did he say?' He looked up from his notes and glared.

Rebecca paused. 'He said he would come to Seaview tonight and we would run away together.'

She could see him now, staring at her with his baby-blue eyes. 'But Seaview Farm is your home. Your dad would be lost without you.'

'He can cope. He knows how much I . . . I care about you.' Harvey kicked the soil at his feet.

'Where will we go? What about school? If I go with you, I'll never finish my studies and I'll end up just like Mother.' Tears of panic stung her eyes.

'And what did you say to that idea?' Gibbs leaned forward, glaring at her intently, his cigarette breath sucking at the oxygen in the room.

'I said I couldn't leave my mother,' said Rebecca as another tear escaped. She was afraid to cry; if she started, she would never stop.

'So you left?' asked DI Gibbs.

Rebecca nodded.

'But when we arrived at the house tonight, you said you heard someone at the door, before you came downstairs and found your mother and father. And that this person you heard started the argument that led to your parents' deaths. Do you think that person was Harvey?'

'No.' She could still hear her bedroom windows, shaking in the relentless gale as if they might smash, the rat-tat sound of the door knocker which must have been the howling wind.

'How can you be so sure?'

'Because when I went downstairs there was no one in the

house. I must have imagined it. He and Mother argued all the time. There was a storm, battering at the windows, I couldn't hear properly.'

'But you said you heard your father speaking to someone, and that an argument broke out. Wouldn't it make sense that this person was Harvey, if he said he was coming for you?' Gibbs leaned in further and Rebecca felt her body tense and her stomach spasm again.

'No.' Rebecca shook her head. She had to get out of this room. She couldn't breathe. She could smell the burning fumes from the Luger pistol when it went off.

'Why?'

'Because Harvey would never have left my mother dying on the floor like that. He loved her.'

'Could he have shot your father to save your mother?'

'No.'

'How do you know?'

'Because I know. He couldn't do something like that. Please, sir, I really am going to be sick.'

'Well, luckily for him, his father is an alcoholic, so there are witnesses to say they were both at the King's Head tonight.'

'So why are you asking me this? Why won't you let me go? Please, I feel very unwell.'

Rebecca felt vomit rushing up from her stomach.

'Because I'm not sure you're being entirely honest with me, young lady. I think you're holding something back. And that you have an idea of who was at the door.'

The tears started now. She began to panic that she was going to choke on the vomit burning at the bottom of her throat. 'Please sir, there was no one there when I went downstairs. No one else was in the house.'

'And your father kept a pistol?'

Rebecca nodded, putting her hand over her mouth as the sounds of the night screamed in her ears.

She had put her head under the covers, as the storm picked up its pace, echoing what was happening downstairs. The sound of yelling, smashing glass, her father's fury thudding through her veins, feeling it as if it were her own. She had lain in her bed, paralysed with indecision, until her mother's screams came through the floor, forcing her to act, to go to her. 'Mother!' She had shouted to her, opening her bedroom door and launching herself down the stairs towards the horrific scene unfolding in the room below.

Her mouth was filling with vomit now and, as it began to pour through the fingers covering her mouth, the acid in her stomach burning, she gagged and bent double.

DI Gibbs shot up, but it was too late: it was all over his notes, the table, the floor. As bits of the last meal she had eaten with her mother – their final supper, at which no one had said a word – covered the detective's black shiny shoes, and the last of the air in the room became wretched, their interview finally came to an abrupt end.

Chapter One

Harvey

Harvey Roberts walked over to the window of his farm-house kitchen and looked out beyond the ice-covered courtyard to the South Downs. He had only been up for a couple of hours but he could still barely walk from exhaustion after spending the past two days holding his daughter's hand through her labour. When he had finally got home to his bed he'd barely slept, spending most of the night worrying about her. He took a glug of coffee and resolved to gather his strength for another long shift at St Dunstan's Hospital.

It had been a harrowing couple of days. His daughter had gone into labour three weeks before her due date and, as Jessie's boyfriend, Adam, was in Nigeria on a photoshoot, it was Harvey's phone that had rung at 2 a.m. on Sunday morning. He had dressed quickly and driven into Chichester, where the last of the Saturday-night revellers were still making their way home. When Jessie opened the door to her and Adam's two-bedroom period flat, she was already out of her pyjamas and dressed.

'I think it's started, Dad,' she said, looking less like the thirty-nine-year-old features writer she had become and more like the little girl he used to comfort after a bad dream. Her shoulder-length highlighted hair, normally blow-dried into a sleek bob, was scraped back into a ponytail, her porcelain skin free of make-up and her green eyes framed with tortoise-shell glasses.

They had stood by the large sash windows in Jessie's lounge, staring at one another in shock. 'I haven't even left work yet,' Jessie had finally said. 'And the nursery isn't ready, there's no food in the flat.' Her eyes slowly filled with tears. 'Adam isn't due home for another week. I can't get hold of him. I can't do this without him.'

'It's all right, sweetheart,' he had offered. 'I'll track him down. He'll be here in no time – it might even be a false alarm.' Instinctively, he had said the words she wanted to hear, even though he knew it was probably a lie. 'Maybe we should take you into the hospital, just to get you looked at. Have you packed a bag?'

'It's all gone wrong, Dad. We haven't even set up the birthing pool yet,' Jessie said, looking over at the box still sitting in the hallway. 'I just rang my midwife and she said, because it's so early, I have to go in. We had it all planned – we wanted to have the birth at home, we didn't want to go to hospital.'

After that she seemed to go into a state of heightened anxiety from which, Harvey felt, she hadn't yet come down. He put his arm around her and told her it was okay, that if she could just sit on the bed and point to where things were, he could grab a few bits.

But everything he suggested was wrong: dresses and cardigans rather than pyjamas and sweatpants, her iPad rather than her birth plan, which she and Adam had spent hours over and which Harvey now couldn't find. And she was in too much pain to sit still. She paced up and down, snapping at every suggestion, until they finally cobbled together the things they needed to take.

'What about your toothbrush?'

'Okay,' she managed, before putting her hand out against the wall to let out a wail of pain. Harvey had rushed into the bathroom and grabbed it. The cabinet was open and his eyes fell on the box of Citalopram, the antidepressant Jessie had been taking since her stepmother died two years ago.

'I'll throw these into the bag, shall I?' he said, walking out of the bathroom towards her.

Jessie shook her head. 'I stopped taking it – my midwife said I couldn't breastfeed on them.'

Harvey's stomach plummeted. It had been a rollercoaster of grief for both of them, and Jessie had only made it through because of a great deal of counselling and the lifeline which was Sertraline. 'Right,' he managed, knowing it was too late to say anything else. 'Did your midwife talk to you about bottle feeding? It didn't do you any harm.' Harvey attempted to hide his rage with a smile.

'No, Dad,' Jessie snapped. 'I want to breastfeed. It's best for the baby. I'd been thinking about coming off it anyway. Adam says I don't need it any more.'

Harvey stood in front of his daughter in stunned silence. He felt that Adam had no idea of the depths to which Jessie had sunk after Liz, the woman who had been like a mother to her since she was a baby, had died, and to encourage her to come off her medication when her baby was nearly due and he was away with work only served to prove it.

But as he went to say more, to implore her to reconsider,

he could feel Liz's hand on his arm, pulling him back, stopping him. So instead he said nothing. In the absence of his wife's guiding hand, he felt paralysed.

Indeed, from the minute Jessie had opened her front door to him he had felt his wife's death rush back to him. It was as if he was being told the news all over again. He knew Jessie was feeling it too: anger over their loss hung in the air between them; anger that they were having to cope without her; that, as always, he was clearly not up to the job.

As they left the flat, in silence, it had occurred to him that Jessie would have told her stepmother if she was thinking about stopping the Citalopram. It would have been mentioned over a cup of tea or during a Sunday-afternoon walk and Liz would have found a way to talk her out of it. Sertraline had made Jessie forget how bad she had been – the anxiety attacks, the OCD; all the things that had been at their worst before Adam came along a year after Liz's death. Now, the potentially catastrophic decision had already been made and it was too late for Harvey to do anything about it.

'Owww!' Jessie had cried as they passed the out-of-order sign by the lift and began walking down. With each wave of pain, she stopped, clutching the wooden handrail of the three flights of stairs to Harvey's car.

As Harvey looked on helplessly he thought back to the night he'd tried to broach the subject of she and Adam moving somewhere more practical. They had invited him round to dinner in Adam's immaculate flat which Jessie had moved into when she fell pregnant only six months after meeting him. After telling him they were having a girl and a great deal of congratulatory hugging and crying, he had suggested that, perhaps, if they wanted to look at a house, so that Jessie wouldn't have to struggle on the stairs with a buggy, or deal with noise from the nightlife in Chichester town centre, he could remortgage and help them out with the deposit.

Jessie and Adam had looked at each other and, within seconds, Adam had dismissed his offer. They loved their flat, he said as Jessie cuddled into him on their cream sofa with its matching, perfectly arranged cushions. They didn't want to be one of those couples who moved out of the area they loved and were miserable because of it. The baby could fit in with their life, Adam had added. Jessie was planning to go back to work before too long; nothing needed to change. Jessie had looked at Adam and then smiled at him, the same smile she gave as a child when Harvey asked her how her day at school had been and she tried to hide the fact that the class bully had upset her again.

Harvey had looked round at their elegant flat, each wall and surface white, nothing out of place. Pictures Adam had taken in his work as a travel photographer had been framed, blown up and hung on every wall. Everything had been arranged and mapped out as carefully as their lives. He couldn't picture it: the baby food, the mess, the sleep deprivation. Adam's work meant he was away a lot but when he was home they pleased themselves – ate out, wandered around the shops, sat on the beach. Then, when they started to niggle one another and it all got too real, it would be time for him to go off again to far flung places. And Jessie would throw herself back into her work which – if she had an event or a client dinner – could mean twelve-hour days. To him, she never seemed to stop, lugging her bump on the train up to Victoria and back every day. There had been little effort to stop, slow down even, and take in the life-changing event that was about to happen to them both.

He had wanted to be happy for them but a depression had descended on him since Jessie and Adam told him about the baby. It was more than the intense sadness that Liz wasn't there to share it, it was a sense of foreboding that seemed to increase in strength alongside Jessie's growing belly.

Something didn't feel right to him, and he suspected it was the fact that this was Rebecca's granddaughter too, yet no one had dared to mention the elephant in the room.

Adam had never even met Jessie's birth mother and, though Harvey had several times encouraged Jessie to introduce Adam to Rebecca, Jessie had been reluctant. Until five days ago Rebecca hadn't even known about the baby, but last Friday Jessie had announced, to Harvey's shock, that she had been to see her. The meeting had clearly been a disaster and only added to Harvey's concerns about Jessie's increasing anxiety.

'I just don't want her in our lives, Dad, it's too hard. I don't want her around when the baby is born.' Jessie's eyes had filled with tears and Harvey's guts had twisted with worry.

Now, Harvey set down his coffee and pulled on his muck boots again. After dragging himself from the shower he had taken the dogs for a bracing run around in the freezing morning surf at Wittering Bay, the beach of his childhood, which he could now bear to visit only in the winter because of the gridlock that plagued it in the summer months. He could barely even cope with the two buses

20

a day blocking the narrow lane in November, and in his sleep deprived state found it hard to bottle his rage at having to back up for a bus he met head on in the lane that morning.

The FOR SALE sign next to Seaview Cottage had caught the morning light as he reached the mouth of the footpath which led to its door. As far as he knew, Seaview was still owned by the family who had bought Seaview Farm from him nearly forty years before.

Over time, people had forgotten what happened there, but in the weeks and months afterwards it was all anyone had talked about. 'So dreadful,' they'd say, leaning into one another with glee. 'Did you hear, the coroner said he had battle neurosis. Their little girl, Rebecca, was in the house at the time. Found them both. Horrific.'

Yet the trauma of that night for both him and Rebecca continued to this day, manifesting itself most visibly in the shattered relationship between Rebecca and Jessie, the daughter they shared.

As he fed the dogs, the mirror by the back door reflected his sorry state: with his grey, unkempt hair, the heavy bags under his eyes and washed-out skin, he looked every day of his sixty-eight years. But then the sun broke through the clouds and hit his face as he crossed the courtyard and it was so warm on his skin that for a moment he relaxed and a smile broke on the edges of his mouth.

He had a granddaughter. She was Adam in a babygro, with his long forehead and dark eyes, but she was beautiful. And he had been there for every moment of it, two days and nights.

Jessie had refused an epidural for too long. As Harvey rubbed her back and held her hand through every excruciating wave, she said that she had promised Adam they would have a natural birth, that she wanted to make him proud of her. Her father had tried desperately to persuade her, but she wouldn't hear of it. Then when her pain limit came and she couldn't take any more they said it was too late. By the time she came to push she hadn't slept or eaten for over forty-eight hours, and she couldn't do it. The baby was stuck and Harvey had looked on in horror as the doctors used what seemed to him brute force to finally suck, cut and pull the limp baby girl out of her.

Jessie had called her Elizabeth Rose. He had expected – hoped – that her middle name would be Elizabeth, but it had been almost too much after months of Jessie barely uttering her stepmother's name, and a stark reminder of what was bubbling below the surface.

Harvey unpadlocked the door of his workshop and tugged the frozen catch open. In an attempt to keep busy before he was allowed to return to the hospital, he sought out the tools he needed from his cobweb-covered work surface to mend the gate onto the driveway which Jessie always struggled with. A shard of light broke through the small windows and fell on Liz's gardening gloves. Slowly, he picked them up, squeezed his long fingers into the stretchy fabric and put his hands up to his face the way she used to. He closed his eyes.

Pull yourself together, old man. He could hear her voice as clearly as the dogs barking outside. *You've done well so far, but you need to keep it up. Jessie needs you. Your granddaughter needs you.*

And she did. As they sat together soon after Elizabeth's birth, the midwife seemed to be sucking Jessie into a vortex of stress that the baby wasn't latching on. It was four in the afternoon and starting to get dark and Jessie was approaching her third night straight without sleep when a midwife thought it sensible to tell Jessie she had 'awkward nipples'.

'You need to try and feed her, Jessica.' A midwife with cropped black hair and onion breath had appeared next to Jessie, holding the baby while they were still stitching her up after the birth.

She had turned to him, wide-eyed. 'When is Adam getting here, Dad? It's getting dark, you aren't allowed to stay here with me tonight, only the babies' fathers are. I need him to help look after her. I'm scared someone will take her in the night.' Jessie had the same haunted look in her eyes as Rebecca did, the same conviction that someone was out to hurt her baby.

'He's booked on a flight tomorrow morning. He'll be here tomorrow evening, sweetheart,' he said gently, hiding the fact that he had just called Adam's editor for the fourth time, demanding to know where the hell Adam was. 'Don't upset yourself about tonight, honey,' he said. 'Hopefully they'll let you go home soon. I'll stay with you as much as I can until Adam gets here.'

'Why doesn't she like me? Why isn't she feeding?' Jessie said, looking deathly pale.

'Jessica, I know it's hard, but it's important you keep trying. We need to feed her within the first hour or it could be bad for the baby. If you move her round a bit closer to you, that's it, support her head, so you're both more comfortable. Does that feel better?' the midwife had said as the baby screamed blue murder and tears poured down Jessie's cheeks.

'Could we not give the baby a bottle to keep her going?' Harvey had suggested, trying to bury his rage, but the midwife pressed on.

She shot him a steely look. 'The baby needs Mum's colostrum,' she snapped when Harvey eased her out into the corridor. 'It could be there's a reason she's not feeding properly.'

'What about what Jessie needs? Do you know she suffers with depression, that she's come off her Citalopram because of this obsession with breastfeeding?'

'I appreciate your concern, Mr Roberts. We are aware of the situation with Jessica's medication and we are keeping a close eye, but there is a small window for her baby to get her colostrum. There will be plenty of time for Jessie to rest after that.'

'She's going to die, Dad.' Jessie's eyes were wide when he went back to her after popping outside for some much needed air in an attempt to calm down. She seemed highly agitated and she hadn't touched her lunch. His daughter was acting just as Rebecca had – the same panic in her eyes, the same sleeplessness. It was like reliving a waking nightmare over and over again.

'She's not going to die, darling,' he said, lifting Elizabeth out of Jessie's arms, whereupon she immediately stopped crying now that she wasn't being forced to Jessie's breast. A breastfeeding poster glared down at them both: BREAST IS BEST. A mother shown contentedly kissing her baby's foot while it breastfed happily. *Breast milk lowers baby's risk of ear infections. Breast milk lowers baby's risk of diarrhoea. Breast milk lowers baby's risk of pneumonia.*

He walked over to the window with his granddaughter

in his arms and looked out over Chichester as a group of noisy relatives armed with balloons arrived at the next bed.

'It's so noisy here, I really want to go home.' Jessie started to cry and he tried to hold her hand, the baby lying awkwardly in the crutch of his arm.

'Why don't you try and rest now?' he said, as firmly as he could. 'Just lay down and try and close your eyes. I'll have a word and see when they're going to discharge you.'

'Promise me you won't take your eyes off her so you know if she stops breathing. Promise me, Dad.' Jessie's knuckles were white as her nails dug into his arm.

'I promise, darling.' But while Jessie tried to sleep a young female consultant came to tell him that because the baby wasn't latching on and feeding they had taken a heel prick blood test, and it was showing that Elizabeth had a raised white blood cell count.

'What does that mean?' he had snapped.

'It means the baby is showing signs of an infection. We're starting a broad-spectrum antibiotic until we have time to grow a blood culture, which takes twenty-four hours. When we have the results of that we'll know if she's on the right antibiotic and whether she needs to continue it.'

'Is she going to be okay?' Harvey stood up, still holding baby Elizabeth in his arms.

The doctor nodded. 'I suspect it's Group B streptococcus, which is a common infection. She'll need seven days of antibiotics.'

'Do they have to stay here? I mean, could the baby be given the antibiotics at home? My daughter desperately needs to get some peace and quiet so she can rest.'

The doctor shook her head. 'We're going to take the

baby and put a cannula in her hand now so she can have the antibiotics by IV. She needs to complete the treatment, I'm afraid, or she could become seriously unwell within a very short time.'

He had tried to stop them, said that he'd promised Jessie he wouldn't let the baby out of his sight. But they had insisted. So, with Jessie finally in a rather fitful sleep, he had reluctantly put Elizabeth back in her cot and watched them wheel her off. He had hoped Jessie would carry on sleeping, perhaps even until they brought Elizabeth back, but the ward was so noisy she was awake again within minutes. She had looked at him, seen he was not holding Elizabeth and then looked over at the space where her baby's cot should be.

'She's dead, isn't she?' she had gasped in panic, sitting up and trying to haul her broken body out of bed.

'Darling, she's fine, they needed to give her some antibiotics. Please, Jessie, don't upset yourself.'

'Antibiotics? What for? Where is she?' Jessie was hysterical within seconds and stayed that way until he fetched someone and they took her, in a wheelchair, to Elizabeth. And then they both stood and watched two paediatricians try for half an hour to find a vein in Elizabeth's tiny hands while she relentlessly screamed blue murder.

After that Jessie seemed to Harvey to disappear into herself entirely. She wasn't eating, she couldn't sleep and she wouldn't let anyone else touch her baby.

'They're trying to poison her, Dad. It's not medicine, they're hurting her.'

'Sweetheart, they wouldn't do that.'

'I want to take her home, I don't want to be here. I don't

want them putting that stuff in her little veins. We don't know what it is. Please, Dad, I want to get out of here.'

'I can't let you do that, honey, you haven't been discharged. I'll stay as much as I'm allowed and in a day or so Adam will be here. Before you know it you will be able to go home.'

'Please, Dad, they're killing her. You need to take me home before they come to take her away again. She's poorly – can't you see what they're doing to her? She's my baby. Why can't you take us home if that's what I want? I hate it here.'

'Darling, we'd get into a lot of trouble if we left now. We need to let them give Elizabeth these antibiotics and then you can go. Just a couple more days.'

And they had talked like this, on a loop, as the night descended on the first day of little Elizabeth's life. He had sat there trying to calm her, until 8 p.m., when they told him visiting hours were over. Then, he left, having made the distracted, overworked midwives promise to keep a close eye on Jessie. They said a private room would soon be available so she'd be able to move there and get some rest, but it had done nothing to alleviate the sense of doom engulfing him as he walked away.

Now, crossing the yard back to the house, he saw a police car pulling up outside.

He stood rooted to the spot, wishing he could stop time. A hundred scenarios of what had happened to Jessie spun through his mind but he knew for certain they were there about her. A man and a woman climbed out, let themselves through the broken gate then walked towards him.

'Harvey Roberts?' Harvey nodded at the tall man with

the long, narrow face who had addressed him. 'I'm DC Paterson and this is DC Galt from Brighton CID.'

'What's wrong?' Harvey's throat felt dry. The words were stuck; he didn't want to let them go.

'We wanted to talk to you about your daughter Jessica Roberts.'

'What about her? What's happened?'

'I take it that means she's not here.'

'Of course she's not bloody here, she's in hospital.'

'I'm afraid Jessica left the hospital with her baby just after eight o'clock this morning. I take it from your reaction you've not heard from her?'

Harvey stood staring at him, unable to respond.

'Could we possibly go inside and talk?'

Chapter Two

Harriet

VE Day, Tuesday, 8 May 1945

Harriet Waterhouse sat at her pine dressing table next to the small draughty window on the top floor of her employer's townhouse and pulled the diary she had bought that day from her shopping bag. It was still wrapped in brown paper, which crackled like newly lit kindling as she unwrapped it, the scent of the post office wafting out from the parcel and making its mark on her musty room.

The smart leatherbound book had the words 'Five Year Diary' embossed on the front in gold letters and a small brass lock fastening its cover tight. Harriet realized that she was holding her breath.

She didn't know what had made her spend a month's salary on something she had never coveted before. She had only gone into the post office to escape the crowds. Every man, woman and child was ecstatic at the news that the war was finally over. They were desperate to be together, united in their euphoria, singing and shouting from every doorway, window, rooftop, lamp post. She had stood in the queue for an hour in Wilson's grocery store to get Miss Clara's and Miss Ethel's weekly rations, surrounded by people she had known all her life looking at her expectantly, demanding an ecstatic reaction from her.

'I can't believe it,' she had said after being asked how she felt about Jacob coming home, forcing a smile as they frowned at her, waiting for more, until, to her great relief, someone came along and swept them back up into the celebrations.

It had been a day like any other Tuesday. She had taken Miss Clara and Miss Ethel a cup of tea at seven then laid the fire in the sitting room. After breakfast, she had made the beds, tidied the bedrooms, dusted and polished the silver before serving lunch. It was around three o'clock when she was starting on the laundry that they had called to her and she'd found them sitting in a highly unusual state of stunned silence by the wireless as Winston Churchill made his broadcast to the nation.

The sounds of cheering and singing began to echo through the streets outside and Harriet stood, her legs shaking, her heart hammering, unable to take her eyes from Miss Clara and Miss Ethel as they clutched one another and sobbed.

'Isn't it wonderful, Harriet!' said Miss Ethel, beaming at her, her ruddy cheeks shiny with tears. 'Our boys are coming home.'

In the safety of the kitchen, she had locked the door and sat down on the cold stone floor, closing her eyes and trying to feel some emotion that Jacob was coming back to her. The same image kept playing on repeat in her mind's eye, the last day she saw him, saying goodbye at the station, his canvas bag slung over his shoulder, his Chestnut eyes warily darting around, his beautiful smile absent.

They had watched the other couples kissing goodbye

and, tears in his eyes, he'd turned to her and said, 'I can't do this, Hattie, I'm not strong enough.' He had been home for just one week's leave and she had been shocked by the change in him: his sunny nature was gone, replaced by a short temper and a lack of appetite. He had recoiled if she touched him and had barely slept, sitting up all night drinking, too afraid to fall asleep for fear of the nightmares that lay in wait for him. 'Please help me,' he had said on their last night, crying himself to sleep in her arms then minutes later kicking her violently out of her bed because she had turned over in her sleep and startled him.

As she wiped away her tears and dragged herself up to make Miss Clara and Miss Ethel's afternoon tea she thought of Jacob's letters, folded neatly in her dressing table. Bundles of writing paper sent over the years which she'd ironed painstakingly and brought back to life. Jumbled snapshots of hell written in his childish handwriting on borrowed or stolen paper and pushed into envelopes of different shapes and sizes. Letters which when she read them she could picture him writing, by candlelight, in makeshift camps; cold, scared, alone, pausing over the words, not wanting to worry her but desperate to get the memory out.

D-Day landings were rough. Having found ourselves finally on land, there was no time to gather ourselves as we set off to the scene of the battle. I shall not tell you about that for fear of planting the pictures that haunt me into your head, but I will say that I had no time to eat or drink for an entire day. We broke through the beachhead and we are now advancing rapidly. No sleep. Lost all my kit and money. The clay and the rain were our greatest enemies. Some of the toughest

31

fighting of this war is taking place now as the Allies battle to gain a foothold in France. Feel very far away from you and as if I have left a part of me behind on that beach.
 All love, Jacob

The clay and the rain were our greatest enemies. At night she had dreamed of his face and the tracks of his tears through the thick clay on his skin, she saw him injured and cold, blood and clay sticking to his face, in his eyes and hair, trickling out of his ears from the relentless shelling she'd heard about from those who came home. Every letter was a dissolution of the hope that he would walk away from the war with any of his fun-loving, gentle soul intact.

Today is only our twentieth day in action, yet it seems like years. What has happened to me and my battalion would be viewed by most as being impossible. Sending us into battle with our best friends is torture. I've seen as many of them blown to pieces beside me as I can stand. I just can't believe it is all really happening. Landing deep in enemy territory and trying to hold a position assaulted and shelled from all sides until friendly troops break through is something I would rather take my own life than have to repeat. I crawled for hours with bullets whistling past my ears, thinking each second was my last. I can't tell you what else I saw and shall never speak of it. Suffice to say I never knew man was capable of inflicting so much pain on his fellow man. I shall never recover from what I have witnessed.

After taking Miss Clara and Miss Ethel their tea, she had asked to go into town to fetch their rations then gone

32

up to her room to change. She had walked over to her dressing table and brushed her lank hair, staring at her haunted reflection in the mirror with a heavy heart. She had patted some rouge on to her pale cheeks then sat on the bus into town, a smile painted on her face, as everyone spoke of getting the train up to London, where thousands of people were gathering in Trafalgar Square and at Buckingham Palace to watch King George, Queen Elizabeth and Winston Churchill make their appearance.

The bus had been hot and crowded, everyone singing and dancing, just as they were on the street when she got into town and fought her way through the crowds to the entrance door of the post office. It seemed a fitting place to hide, having been a lifeline to Jacob for so many years. The first day of the war, she had made a point of sending her first letter, and now she was back, on VE Day, having come full circle. She tugged at the handle and almost fell through the door, the gentle bell ringing as she closed it behind her with a sigh of relief.

Inside, it was cool and empty of people, the counter from which she had sent all Jacob's letters tucked away in the corner. The elderly lady who ran it always smelt of lavender and the shelves were cluttered with envelopes and parcels, notebooks and rolls of brown paper. As with everyone else the proprietor was in a state of excitement as Harriet took a deep breath and, for something to focus on, looked inside a glass cabinet next to the till.

'Hello, Harriet, how are you? What can I help you with?' The lady with grey hair in a bun and an abundance of freckles smiled at her warmly.

Harriet felt thrown by the question and, as she looked

again in the cabinet, the thick, brick-like diary caught her eye, 'Can I look at the diary, please?' she asked.

The woman lifted it out and placed it on the counter. 'Are you looking for a present for Jacob's homecoming?'

Harriet reached out and touched the leather cover, flicking through dozens of pages taking her into the future, days stretching ahead of her expectantly. She imagined her scrawled writing recording a life without war, where she hadn't lost their baby during the Blitz and Jacob was still himself, days filled with picnics and swimming and bike rides and adventures, the two of them and their baby; a little family that felt like an impossible dream.

She hadn't even told Jacob she'd fallen pregnant again. And she knew she never could. To anyone. How could she be so selfish as to talk about a baby that had never existed to any one of the people who had lost a son, brother or husband on the front line?

Miss Ethel had been so kind. Calling the doctor when the pain and bleeding got too much. This time, she could see it was a girl before the doctor took her away. She had bled for ten days afterwards and the pain was like never before. But she had needed it. Needed the agony that came with it, needed to see the blood to know she hadn't imagined her.

Yet, months later, she couldn't forget and still didn't know how to feel in this pit of grief over a person who had never even existed. She needed to tell someone, someone who would not chastise her for her selfishness, someone she could talk to when she couldn't sleep.

'Have you had word when he's coming home, Hattie? It's a beautiful gift, so perfect for your future together. There is so much to look forward to now.'

'Yes, there is!' she said, lifting the diary from the counter and smiling. 'I'll take it.'

That night, once all her duties had been taken care of, Harriet pulled open the top drawer of her bedside table, opened the first page of her diary and picked up her fountain pen.

Tuesday, 8 May 1945

Dear Diary,

The day everybody has dreamed of is finally here. The war has ended, but I fear it is not over. There is a sense of exhaustion overriding the street parties and victory parades.

Britain is no longer the country it was before the war. We have lived, eaten, slept and dreamed war and though it is declared over, we only have to look at our empty larders, empty store cupboards and half-empty coal cellars to know we still have a long way to go. For everyone I know, the war has brought the loss of someone they loved and for those who have survived there are blinded eyes or amputated limbs.

How then can I mention the loss of my baby girl? I still don't know how to feel in this pit of grief over a person I never even held. Where to put all my hopes and dreams for her.

I was so close this time, nearly six months gone – I really thought we had made it, that Jacob would be coming home to two of us. Now my arms ache for the baby I will never hold and I cannot share my grief with my husband, for he has too much to bear already. How can a woman ever understand what a soldier fighting on the

35

beaches of Normandy has experienced? How can a man returning from war comprehend what a woman has been through in the Blitz and in holding the fort at home? When Jacob was last home, I felt that there was a sea between us that we will never be able to cross.

I know caring for my husband and keeping my job are my priorities, but I can't stop thinking about my baby girl. I don't know where they took her. When I went to see him the doctor said he didn't want to upset me by talking about it and that I should move on. I'm worried she is buried alive somewhere. I saw her but they took her too quickly for me to make sure she was dead. What if they made a mistake? I can't accept why my body keeps doing this to me, why a baby who is strong and kicking and alive is suddenly dead.

I am glad that I have someone to talk to about the troubles I mustn't bother anyone else with. I must sleep now, for I need my strength to welcome home my poor husband. I cannot bear to think what a state he must be in. Thank God, at least, the bloodshed is over, but I fear it will be some time before the full effects are spent.

Chapter Three

Iris

Iris Waterhouse watched her husband walk into the office of the solicitors in Clerkenwell she'd instructed to handle her divorce and inwardly gasped at how gaunt he had become in the two years since she had last seen him.

James had always been athletic, just over six foot, and a keen cricket player when they met at medical school. He had never had an ounce of fat on him. But today he looked different: he had gone from slender to drawn-looking and for the first time since they met, sixteen years before, he seemed world-weary.

If it weren't for the fact that her heart, which was finally starting to heal, had been ripped open again at the prospect of losing her beloved home, his downtrodden appearance would have prompted her to jump up on to the shiny walnut conference table and perform a merry dance.

As things stood, all it did was confirm her suspicions that Lucy Brewer, the twenty-three-year-old ex-receptionist at her husband's practice, hadn't stolen her husband because she wanted to look after him. Quite the opposite. She had needed a cash cow and after trying and failing to get one of the other chiropractors to leave his wife – something she and James had laughed about at the time – Lucy had moved on to James. And, to her horror, he'd fallen for it.

'Does she know you haven't got any money?' Iris had said as they sat in their small sun-dappled garden on their last morning together when he had come to get his things. There was no screaming or crying from her this time, no telling him to get out, to leave, that she hated him, that she wished they'd never met – the bravado of a broken heart. She had no tears left. All she felt was an indescribable pain.

'Iris, I know you want to hate Lucy but it's not about her. This is about us. We've been broken for a long time.'

'Oh right, thanks for telling me,' she had said, biting down on her lip.

'I'm just tired of everything being about us not being able to have kids,' he had said after packing up the last box and slamming the car boot. 'It has been like living with a black hole slowly sucking the joy out of our lives and I can't do it any more. And before you ask, no, Lucy's not pregnant. She doesn't even want kids.'

That had been two years ago, two years of such uncontrollable grief she wished James were dead, rather than out in the world and happy with someone else. They had been together since she was eighteen and it was the first time she had felt the true meaning of loneliness. Her mother and her girlfriends had saved her, but she still found it hard to come home to an empty, dark house. No one to discuss her day with, to bicker with, to keep her awake with their snoring. He was such a large character, like a small child who never stopped talking and crashing about, interrupting and creating endless dramas at the practice which she had to smooth over. It had driven her mad, his energy, always on to the next thing, the investment that would make them rich, yet now she was like a sad old lady, keeping the TV on all evening just for company because of the silence that seemed follow her around everywhere.

But while she had known she would grieve for James, what she hadn't been prepared for was the tsunami of grief she had suddenly felt for her childlessness. 'It will happen, honey,' he had insisted. 'There's nothing wrong with us, the specialists have said so, we just need to be patient.' So she kept getting pregnant, having the shots they gave her to stop her miscarrying, going for regular scans to watch the heart-beat on the screen: *thud, thud, thud*. Until, at four months, five months, six months, the inevitable dreaded silence.

'Excuse me for a moment,' the sonographer would say before disappearing to seek a second opinion. Every time the same routine. They'd be sent home and, eventually, she would start to bleed. Then they would climb into the car, make the sad journey back to the maternity hospital where she would have to give birth, all the while listening to the agonizing wails of other women in childbirth and the pier-cing cries of their newborns.

She had known this day was coming, when he would come after her for more money. He was so allergic to any kind of saving or budgeting that it was inevitable that he would burn through their savings in no time. Their whole married life she had been the one on the steady pay check as a health correspondent at *The Tribune*, paying the mort-gage, while he moved from clinic to clinic, having extended periods of leave in between jobs to work on the house. Work which never materialized while he spent all day looking into ways to invest money they didn't have in the stock market.

But to stop him would mean officially divorcing him, something she couldn't face – and she never thought he would go so far as to try and force her to sell her beloved cottage in Southfields.

'Am I correct in thinking that nothing was put in writing when you made this agreement about the house and your savings?'

Iris looked over to her solicitor, Katrina Keep, a softly spoken woman with a fringe as blunt as an axe and an attitude to match.

'That is correct, yes,' said Miss Keep. Miss Keep now looked over at her husband's solicitor who was leaning back in his chair with an air of arrogance which was making Iris feel very nervous. 'Well, my client is arguing that as she has paid the mortgage most of their married life, including long periods when he was out of work, and her husband walked away with roughly £100,000 in savings, and his pension which is also worth £100,000 at a time when the house was worth roughly £250,000, they agreed between them it was a fair split.'

James's solicitor, a balding man in an expensive-looking cobalt blue suit straining at the waist, spoke. 'My client informs me that his ex-wife staying in the house was only a temporary arrangement, and that it was never formalized.' He paused for effect before continuing. 'He's also saying that he's under significant pressure as his partner, Miss Brewer, is pregnant.'

Iris felt her whole body tense. Her heart began to hammer in her ears. She was aware her face was burning and as she reached out for a glass of water her hands began to shake. From the day he left, she had known a young girl like Lucy would want a baby, that James was an idiot for thinking otherwise.

Now it was suddenly a reality, she couldn't stop her heart from breaking while they sat around the shiny walnut meeting-room table discussing whether she was liable to foot the bill for their baby.

Miss Keep settled back into her black leather chair. 'As you know,' she began, 'your financial statements have now been exchanged and we are meeting to discuss the situation in a bid to keep this out of court and come to an arrangement between the four of us.'

James's solicitor leaned in, his piggy eyes sparkling. 'As this would be classed as a long marriage, the starting point would be equality. My client feels that the house has increased in value to such a degree over the past two years it would be manifestly unfair were he not to receive an equal share of its current value.'

Iris forced her eyes up towards James. He was doodling mindlessly on a pad of paper, listening to his solicitor speak, unwilling to meet her eye.

'Right, so,' said Miss Keep, and Iris felt her stomach lurch, 'we need to look at the major issues. My client has been living for two years in the house on the understanding that she would stay there and that it would be her nest egg. Mr Hennesey told my client that he would keep the savings they had accrued over the twelve years of their marriage, just shy of £100,000, and his pension, and that Miss Waterhouse would keep the house, which at the time was worth roughly that amount, just under £250,000.'

'What happened to all the savings, James?' Iris burst out, and Miss Keep put her hand on her arm.

41

James's solicitor spoke again. 'Unfortunately, my client invested a lot of capital in setting up a business venture and it hasn't broken even as of yet. Given this situation, I am afraid we can no longer accept what was only ever an informal arrangement. Your client is living in a two-bedroom cottage now estimated to be worth £300,000 in one of the most desirable locations in south London, while my client is renting a one-bedroom flat in Tooting. With no deposit and his partner unable to work, his income stream is insufficient at present to change his situation and we believe that we are legally entitled to a share of money from the house, be that from remortgaging, or the sale of the property.'

'Can I ask about your new partner's earning capacity, Mr Hennesey?' asked Miss Keep softly.

James still hadn't spoken and now shook his head, not looking up. His solicitor filled the silence. 'My client's partner worked as a secretary for a while, but her job is not very well paid and she is about to have a baby, so let's keep that out of the equation for now.'

'She might be pregnant now, but she can't expect to be a one income family if money is tight,' said Miss Keep curtly.

'Why is she suddenly left out of the equation when it's all her doing?' Iris was annoyed her voice was trembling. Katrina put her hand on her arm again.

Iris fought back tears and stood up. The room was stifling and she had to leave. On shaking legs, she made for the door, tugging it open, hearing her solicitor's voice, as if through a tunnel. *'I think let's adjourn for the day.'*

Iris heard James's solicitor address Katrina as she left the room: 'If we can't sign a heads of agreement today, we're willing to go to court.'

Dizzy, Iris headed through reception, pushed the revolving doors and launched herself into the cold November morning, taking large gasps of air. As she squatted down, hugging her knees to her chest, Katrina Keep appeared beside her.

'I don't understand this,' gasped Iris, sucking back tears. 'I thought I was the wronged party, that the law was on my side.'

'I'm afraid that's a huge misconception. I hate to say it, Iris, but I'm afraid the law is on his side because you made the mistake of not having anything put in writing at the time.'

'I trusted him, even after what he did. We were married for twelve years! I thought that counted for something.'

Miss Keep squatted on the pavement next to Iris. 'I'm afraid that if you take this to court, looking at the current situation, they will certainly find in his favour. Award him money based on his needs.'

'He's not taking my house.' Iris wiped away angry tears.

'But this is a needs-based case and your ex-husband will need to be rehoused with a baby on the way. You can push this all the way to court, but even then you might be penalized and asked to pay his legal fees if the outcome is in his favour. I would advise a fifty-fifty split.'

'I can't agree to this now, I need to think.'

'Of course. Can I suggest we meet again in two days? I know Mr Hennesey is prepared to go to court if we can't sign a heads of agreement today. His partner's due date is looming. He knows he has a strong case, but I think I can buy us a couple of days.

'Fine,' Iris heard herself mutter. 'Two days.'

Katrina nodded as Iris watched a young couple walk past, gazing at each other, oblivious to the pain they were capable of inflicting on one another. Iris's mobile started to ring.

'Hello?' said Iris, her voice shaky.

'I'm sorry to bother you darling, I know you've got your meeting with James this morning.' Her mother's voice was quieter than usual.

'You sound funny. What's wrong?' Iris looked at her watch. She had told Miles she would be back at her desk at *The Tribune* by eleven at the latest. She was not in her news editor's good books at the moment, and she couldn't afford to be any later than that.

'Iris, I didn't want to blurt it out like this. I was going to call you tonight and talk to you—' Her mother sounded on the verge of tears.

'What is it? Are you okay?' Iris asked.

'Yes, I'm fine. It's Jessie. She's missing,' Rebecca said.

'What do you mean, missing?'

'Jessie gave birth to a little girl yesterday. I only just found out myself that she was pregnant.'

Iris's stomach lurched at the news that her half-sister, whom she barely knew, had just had a baby. That Jessie, not her, was making her mother a grandmother for the first time.

'But how is she missing? Didn't she go to hospital to have it?' Iris's overcrowded brain struggled to take in the news.

'She walked out of St Dunstan's Hospital this morning, without being discharged. The baby needs antibiotics, and Jessie's taken her away so it's all extremely worrying. The police just called me to say there is a police liaison officer

44

on their way to me. I want to drive down to Chichester but I'm sure Harvey wouldn't want me down there. He probably blames me.'

'How can he blame you? You haven't seen Jessie for nearly a year.'

'That's what I wanted to talk to you about, Iris. Jessie came to see me on Friday. I'm sorry, I wasn't trying to keep it from you. It was just all rather difficult.'

Iris felt her defences snap. How had it come to this? She felt a wave of guilt that she felt so hostile towards Jessie, when she was clearly going through some sort of crisis. She had lost count of the number of times she had had to pick up the pieces after her mother had had an upsetting visit with Jessie and her overbearing stepmother, Liz. And on the rare occasions her half-sister had come to stay, Jessie got away with murder. Their mother would tiptoe around her, desperately trying to make up for her absence in Jessie's life. Still, Iris tried to understand as best she could, and she wanted nothing more than for Jessie to be in her life.

'That's awful. How could she just leave? I thought hospital security was tight,' said Iris.

'I don't know, but she's found a way. I'm terrified she's got psychosis, like I had. It sounds like everyone's in a panic, thinking she's going to do something stupid. They wouldn't tell me anything on the phone, and no doubt Harvey will keep me completely in the dark as always. I've tried to get hold of someone at the hospital, but no joy, they're in a panic and on lockdown. I was wondering if there might be anything you can find out?'

'Okay.' Iris frowned. 'Does anyone from the press know about this yet?'

'Well, the officer that called me said there was the possibility of a press conference later, but other than that I have no idea. Presumably there must be some CCTV footage of her walking out of the hospital? How much do they tell the press in a situation like this, if they need you to help inform the public?'

'They'd normally just brief us before the press conference. But it may be that my boss has heard something from one of the local press agencies.'

'If you could just ask I'd be so grateful. I'm just desperate to know if they've been seen at all since. You're always saying your colleagues on the newsdesk at *The Tribune* seem to know what's happening before the police do.'

'Okay, I'll call my boss and see if he's heard anything. I won't say we're related, just that I've heard a rumour about a new mother walking out of St Dunstan's Hospital.' Iris felt her heart throb with jealousy. Jessie was a mother, but from what she could gather she was putting her baby at terrible risk.

'Thank you, darling, I just wanted to call before the police liaison officer gets here. Are you okay?'

'Yes, I'm okay, Mum. I better go. I'll call you if I hear anything.' Iris took a deep breath and, after a fleeting glance at the solicitors' office she dialled the newsdesk and set off towards Victoria Station.

Chapter Four

'Can you tell us your name?'

The muffled female voice pulls me to, though my eyes are heavy and I can barely open them. I hear the loud crashing of the sea next to me and feel cold, wet sand under my shaking legs. Broken shells scratch at my skin like claws. I am at the opening of the sea; it is rushing under me, then drawing away. The icy wind is strong and the tide is pulling me towards the water, to where I want to be.

A woman crouches down and wraps a blanket around me. 'Can you hear me?' I turn and look at her. She is wearing a green uniform and tells me her name is Claire. I am too cold to answer.

'We need to get you away from the water and warmed up. Can you try and stand up?'

A man appears and they take an arm each. 'One, two, three.' My limbs ache and I let out a moan.

'Do you know how long you've been here?'

I don't answer, but I left soon after lunchtime and now it's getting dark. I'm frozen through and my tummy is so empty it's groaning, but I don't know when I arrived or how I got here. I stand and stare out at the sea, my legs throbbing mercilessly, and when I look down I see I'm not wearing any shoes. I think I took them off when I walked down to the water, but when I look over at the bench at the edge of the bay they aren't there.

'That's it. You're doing great. Can you remember if anyone brought you here today?' The woman pulls the blanket more tightly around me. The sea air thrashes at my face.

It is a dark, cloudy day, and the sea looks the same shade of grey as the day I left her. The air feels the same too; intensely cold, like it's carrying droplets of ice. I close my eyes and try to remember her. I've been trying to remember her all day. Her smell, her hair, her skin. My heart hurts from trying to remember.

'We need to get you into the ambulance, warm you up a bit. Can you put your arms around us so we can help you walk?'

I turn and look at the woman's face. Her lips are moving but my brain can't connect with what she is saying so, again, I don't answer. My thoughts are on a loop, entangled like the seaweed at my feet.

'I should never have left her,' I whisper, but the rush of the sea drowns out my words.

'There you go, just take it slowly. You're probably going to feel a bit dizzy,' says the woman. She is blonde, her short, wavy hair pinned back with kirby grips, no make-up. She keeps smiling at me, her brown eyes creasing at the edges, but I don't smile back.

I came back here to feel closer to her and I don't want to leave. This where I last held her.

They are taking me away and I don't have the strength to stop them. I'm shaking and my legs cannot hold me up. The man wraps another blanket around me. It doesn't help. I didn't know it was possible to feel this cold. 'Okay, see the

48

ambulance up there?' he says. 'That's where we're headed. We'll take most of your weight. There you go.'

An overwhelming feeling of fear and dread washes over me as we start to move. I know that this is it. After today, I will never come back here. I will never so clearly remember those precious few days when she was mine.

'I didn't leave her. I just wanted to swim,' I say. Again, the roar of the sea crushes my words.

'It's too cold today, love, you can't go in,' the woman says, misunderstanding me. She looks so young, barely out of school. The walk is long and hard and I sink into the sand.

I look back at the sea and it whispers my name. Just as it did that day.

We reach the open doors of the ambulance. I'm hauled up the metallic steps, laid on the bed. They put the side up so I don't fall out; like a baby in a cot. I close my eyes and listen to my heart in my ears.

The woman is tugging at my hands. 'You're too cold for the finger probe so I'm going to hold your hand to warm you up.'

I don't want her to hold my hand. I pull away but she persists, puts something on my finger and around my upper arm. I try to pull them off, but she stops me and I start to feel angry. I want to be alone on the beach so I can remember her. The last moments with my baby, just the two of us. I don't want to leave.

'Please let me stay,' I say. 'I don't care if I die.' But her back is turned and she doesn't hear.

'How's she doing?' The man is at the door.

'She's getting a bit agitated. She's bradycardic and hypothermic, temperature low – thirty-four. Oxygen level sixty. Blood pressure ninety over fifty-five. Let's get her in.'

'Blues and twos?'

'Yeah, it's coming into rush hour.' She turns her attention to her notes. I wish I had the strength to run.

I look back and watch the sea as the man closes the doors. It's calling to me.

I've been here before.

They were wrong. They've always been wrong. I didn't take my baby into the sea.

I left her in the cave. I was going to go back.

The ambulance rattles along the road. I sleep then jerk awake when stop, abruptly. The doors open. The voices of the paramedics are more hurried now, they move quickly.

'Her temperature's down – thirty-one. Can we get some help here!'

They lift the stretcher, carry me down the ambulance steps, wheel me through a bright entrance. Accident and Emergency. The words are an angry red and hurt my eyes.

I turn my head slowly; a nurse is running towards us. The lights in the corridor they wheel me along are too bright. I long to be back at the beach, in the dark, alone with the memories of my baby girl.

'We were called to Wittering beach by a passer-by. When we got there she was sitting at the water's edge and seemed confused. Her temperature has dropped from thirty-four to thirty-one; pulse forty. We've asked her name and age, but she's not responding.'

'Cubicle three.' A nurse in white scrubs leans down to me. 'Hello? Can you hear me? I'm Helen, one of the nurses. Can you tell me your name?'

I close my eyes and turn my head away. A tear escapes. I wish they would all go away.

'She's very pale and her lips are looking quite blue. I think we'd better put her in resus. I'll get a doctor to come straight away.'

The stretcher is moving again; there are more people around me now. It's so loud, too bright. I feel frightened, surrounded. I wasn't frightened on the beach, I wanted the sea to take me this time. I don't want this. I don't want to be here.

'Let's get her across. One, two, three, slide.' They lift me onto another stretcher. I tell them to leave me alone but they don't listen. They tug at me – 'Let's get you out of these wet clothes.' Everything hurts.

I hear the rip of the blood-pressure cuff. 'Ninety over sixty,' someone says.

Please let me die. I feel the stretcher move gently, as if I'm on a boat. I feel myself rocking and close my eyes, longing to be back at the sea's edge. I wish I'd had the strength to go in.

The stretcher jerks, the side bars crash down and I hold on to the sides in case I fall. I feel queasy and try to turn over to get away, but I don't have the strength.

Another voice. 'Hello? Can you hear me? I'm Dr Hardy, I'm one of the A&E doctors.'

He pinches the muscle on top of my collarbone. It stings and my eyes open briefly.

'Do we know what her name is? Did anyone come in with her?' His voice is urgent. I start to feel nauseous. And suddenly, my body starts to warm.

'She was spotted wandering on the beach by a passer-by. She's not told anyone her name.'

Slowly, the heat creeps through me. I start to feel unbearably hot. I try and push the blanket off. They pull it back on.

'Put her on high-flow oxygen.'

More unbearable noise. They put a mask over my face; I hear it hiss in my ears. I try to take it off but they stop me and tell me to breathe. In, out. In, out.

It's like the tide. You cannot stop it.

I try and think myself back there. Try to remember my last moments with her. I hear a baby's cry and look around me.

My eyes fill with tears and I feel pressure on my chest. I want to scream at them to go away but I have no voice.

'Air entry throughout her chest. Pulse rate forty. Blood pressure ninety over sixty. Temperature? We need to put a cannula in, take some bloods and give her some warmed intravenous fluids.'

'I can hear a baby crying,' I try to say through the mask, but I just swallow the words back down.

'Sorry?' The nurse stops what she is doing and leans down to me. She lifts my mask. 'What did you say?'

'That baby needs help.' My shivering is uncontrollable.

'It's okay. Don't upset yourself.'

'What are they doing to her?' The baby's cries take me back.

'Can you tell us your name so we can contact a family member? I'm sure there are people who are worried about you.'

'My baby cried like that. I didn't leave her. I was going to come back.' The nurse strokes my hair and puts the mask back on.

'She's very confused,' she says.

I close my eyes and let my mind return to the beach. The place where it ended. And where it all began.

Chapter Five

Rebecca

Friday, 14 November 2014

Rebecca Waterhouse looked along the road outside her Victorian townhouse for any sign of her daughter's red Fiat, then up at the clock on the wall, for the third time in as many minutes.

It was nearly 10 a.m. Jessie was half an hour late, but it had been so long since they had arranged a meeting together with just the two of them Rebecca had no idea whether it was out of character or not. She let out a heavy sigh and tried to calm her nerves. Jessie was fine; their chat – as Jessie had referred to it the night before – was going to happen. After all, Jessie had been the one to call her to arrange the visit, so why would she change her mind? She had clearly just inherited her father's *laissez faire* attitude towards timekeeping.

Rebecca walked over to the kitchen counter and poured herself a large black coffee from the percolator. Her eyes stung; she had barely slept after her daughter's call had woken her just before midnight. She had thought it was sleep tricking her when she turned to her buzzing phone and the name 'Jessie' was flashing on the screen.

'Jessie? Are you okay?' She had grabbed the phone and answered in rather a panic.

'Yes, I'm fine.' Her daughter had sounded slightly on edge, but it had been so long since she'd spoken to her. 'I'm sorry, did I wake you? I'll call back,' Jessie had said.

'No, don't worry! No, it's fine. I was just dozing. I'm not asleep. It's lovely to hear from you.' She knew she sounded slightly needy, as she always did when she spoke to her thirty-nine-year-old daughter.

Sitting up in bed and fumbling for the light switch, she felt a stab of grief for her husband. He had been gone nearly a decade and would have done nothing but roll over and continue snoring, but his presence would have calmed her.

There was an awkward silence, Rebecca anxious not to say anything that would frighten Jessie off, as if she were a robin perched on the sill by an open window.

'I know it's been a while now, but I don't think I've had a chance to say how sorry I was to hear about Liz. I do often think about how much you must miss her,' she said finally, knowing that the death of her daughter's step-mother from breast cancer needed to be acknowledged, and hoping that Jessie didn't think her words insincere. 'I hope you got my card at the time?'

'I did, thank you,' Jessie replied, but offering nothing more about her grief over the woman who had raised her since she was a baby. Jessie had barely contacted Rebecca since Liz's breast cancer diagnosis and in the two years since her death. Rebecca guessed that – knowing she and Liz didn't get on – she perhaps felt it would be disloyal to do so.

Rebecca's mind had flashed back to the last time she had seen Liz, nearly ten years before. Close to the time John died.

She, Liz and Jessie had met in a café in Brighton, which

Liz had suggested as a good halfway point – though Rebecca would have driven to the ends of the Earth for any time with her elder daughter. The atmosphere had been painful, plates and cutlery clattering around them while Liz lectured Rebecca about homeopathy and harnessing the power of the menopause, her oversized bangles jangling on the table between where she and Jessie sat.

That meeting had signalled the beginning of the end of any semblance of a relationship between mother and daughter. Rebecca, grieving for her husband and overflowing with frustration at having her precious and rare meetings with her daughter dominated by Liz, had called Liz afterwards to ask whether it might be time for Liz to step aside and give Rebecca's relationship with her daughter a chance. Liz had flown into a rage. 'She's a lot more traumatized by these meetings than you'd ever know, Rebecca,' she'd said.

'Well, I *should* know – I want to know – if you'd just give me the chance to talk to her.'

'None of this is my fault. I had to push her to come today – she wouldn't even come out of her room.' Liz spoke as if Jessie were twelve, not twenty-eight. 'But if that's the way you want it, that's fine. I won't have anything to do with it, and we'll see how far that gets us, shall we? A thank-you would have been nice, Rebecca, after all I've done for your daughter.'

As time dragged on and Rebecca's letters and phone calls remained mostly unanswered, Liz's prediction that their relationship wouldn't survive without her intervention turned out – rather fortuitously for Liz – to be correct.

'Anyway, how are you?' tried Rebecca now.

'I'm okay,' said Jessie, then, after a long pause, 'I'm . . . pregnant, actually.'

Jessie's words, so sudden, so unexpected, had taken Rebecca's breath away and left her utterly speechless. She could feel herself starting to cry, the emotion and over-whelming sadness an uncontrollable tirade. How had it come to this? The most significant moment in her daugh-ter's life, and she was probably one of the last to know. Rebecca wiped away the stream of tears that had sprung to her eyes and cleared her throat, scrambling around in her stunned brain for the right thing to say.

'That's absolutely wonderful. How far along are you?'

'Thirty-six weeks, so nearly there.' Jessie's voice had sounded so matter-of-fact, so grown-up. Her daughter was having a baby and she didn't need her mother, any more than she ever had.

Why hadn't Harvey said anything to her? Jessie, her first born, was four weeks away from having her first grand-child!

'Don't be cross with Dad. I told him I wanted to tell you myself,' said Jessie, reading her mother's mind.

Rebecca tried to shake the emotion away and cleared her throat. 'I'm not cross, I'm over the moon. I'm so happy for you and it means the world that you called me.'

Since John died, their once-happy unit had felt increas-ingly small and lonely. James and Iris's split, and Iris's longing for a baby that never came made them feel Jessie's absence from their lives even more acutely. Perhaps, she dared to let herself hope, this baby was going to change everything.

'Thanks, Mum.'

Rebecca allowed herself a smile, trying to enjoy this momentous event, one that had already changed everything. It had been over a decade since Jessie had said those two words: 'Thanks, Mum.' Rebecca was terrified this was all a dream from which she would wake any moment.

'Can I do anything? I'd love to help you, or be involved in any way you'd like me to.' She tried not to sound too overbearing. One step at a time; don't scare her off.

'There is something, actually,' Jessie said after a moment.

'Anything.'

Rebecca had clocked the nervousness in her daughter's voice and understood that Jessie was about to ask her something she wouldn't like. She felt the hairs on the back of her neck prickle.

'I've been feeling quite anxious about it all. The pregnancy, I mean.' Jessie paused before going on. 'And Dad said you were the same when you had me. I've just never really spoken to you about any of it, what happened when you had me and why you couldn't cope. I thought it might . . . well, help.'

Rebecca closed her eyes and tried to gather her racing thoughts. *Dad said you were the same when you had me.*

How much had Harvey told her? Had he sat her down and spoken to her honestly about the abject horror she had felt when she found out she was pregnant, just after qualifying as a doctor? Had he shared the brutal truth with Jessie about Rebecca's ever-increasing anxiety about returning to work six weeks after the baby was born – as she would have to, in order to keep her job as senior registrar? Working all day, leaving the baby in the crèche at the hospital between seven-thirty in the morning and six in the evening, going

57

down to breastfeed her, being on call at night? Did he share real memories of her psychosis, which had started within hours of Jessie being born and turned every day into the most terrifying, inescapable nightmare? Had he told his daughter how, at night, Rebecca pleaded with him not to fall asleep because she was too scared to be alone with the policeman who had appeared at the end of her bed soon after Jessie was born and who nobody but her could see: Detective Inspector Gibbs, the man who had questioned her for four terrifying hours the night her parents were killed as she sat in her nightie, still covered in her mother's blood?

Of course he hadn't. Saint Bloody Harvey strikes again. Why hadn't he at least called to warn her about the bombshell that was heading her way? She couldn't go back there, she just couldn't.

'Darling, have you told your midwife how you're feeling?' she said, trying to buy herself some time to think.

Jessie went very quiet. It was a dangerous silence and one that made Rebecca very nervous. She could hear her little girl's brain ticking over. *You're fobbing me off, you don't want me, you want someone else to deal with me, like you always have. You've never wanted me.*

'I can tell you're not keen,' Jessie said. 'I understand. I'll let you go. Sorry to call so late.'

Rebecca's veins flooded with adrenaline. This was it – this was her opportunity to fight to get something resembling a relationship with her daughter. If she let this go, it was over; she would lose Jessie for good and any chance of a bond with her grandchild. And she would have only herself to blame. 'No, darling,' she said, trying to sound calm. 'It's not that. I'm just a little thrown and I want to make sure that you're getting all the care you need from your midwife. Of course I want to help. I'd love to talk to you. It's just it was a difficult time. But you have every right to know. I realize it was hard for you to ask.'

Rebecca dug her nails into her knee. *Please don't hang up, please don't.* Finally, Jessie spoke. 'I don't want to do it, though, if you don't want to. I mean, if we can't be honest.'

Rebecca could hear Liz's influence on the language her daughter used. We should all be honest, share our feelings. Women should be there for each other. She could picture Liz clasping Jessie to her ample breast: *Come here, poppet, it's all right to cry, you have the right to talk about how you feel, it's not selfish to put yourself first. If you don't feel strong enough to see your mum for a while, you have a right to have some space.* And all the while omitting to turn any of that honesty on herself and – with no children of her own – her real motivation for encouraging their estrangement and keeping Rebecca at a safe distance from both Jessie and Harvey. And all the while, Harvey continued to bury his head in the sand, as he always did, taking Liz's side, the easy option, rather than standing up to her.

'I know some of your breakdown was tied up with what happened to your parents,' Jessie continued, 'and that it affected you very deeply. I've just never felt strong enough to ask you about it, but it's all stored up inside me and I don't think it's healthy to leave it there. It's not helping how I'm feeling.'

Breakdown? Rebecca cringed at Jessie's turn of phrase. Was that Liz or Harvey's interpretation of what had happened to her after she had Jessie? Still, she hadn't helped Jessie to understand what happened to her, because it had been too painful to go back there. Why was it that that night was determined never to let her go?

'I think you're absolutely right,' she said. 'Whatever helps. Would you like to come here, maybe? And we can have a chat.'

'Yes, please. Would tomorrow work?'

The next day, Friday, was Rebecca's first day off for a fortnight and she had planned to meet a friend for lunch, then go to the National Portrait Gallery. Of course, that could all wait. 'Tomorrow would be lovely,' she said.

So they had agreed a time and as she finished her call to Jessie Rebecca's thoughts had immediately turned to Iris. Her younger daughter, whom she had with John, five years after Jessie was born, and to whom she was very close. Iris, who, like her, had struggled to form any real relationship with Jessie, despite desperately wanting to.

She had toyed with phoning her younger daughter and telling her about Jessie's call – and the baby – but stopped herself. It would be selfish of her to unburden herself on Iris, particularly when it concerned Jessie's pregnancy. Iris had experienced so many nasty miscarriages it was going to be difficult for her to see her mother with a grandchild.

So she had spent the rest of the night alone, digging out old press cuttings from deep in the recesses of the loft and embedding a splinter in her palm in the process.

WAR VETERAN KILLS HIS WIFE THEN TURNS GUN ON HIMSELF

A man suffering from wartime battle neurosis killed his wife before committing suicide last night.

Jacob Waterhouse, 45, who had been treated for psychosis, beat his wife, Harriet Waterhouse, 43, to death in a fit of blind rage, before shooting himself.

Locals in Wittering, Sussex, described Mr Waterhouse as a reserved, private character who was very rarely seen in the village. Seaview Cottage, where the murder–suicide took place, is a remote cottage overlooking Wittering Bay. Locals describe hearing police sirens late last night and witnessed the bodies being taken away by ambulance.

Their daughter, Rebecca Waterhouse, 13, was believed to be at home at the time of the horrific scenes but is thought to be unhurt and has been taken into the care of family friends.

As her tired eyes hovered over the words that still felt as raw to her now as they did then, every part of her ached not to go back there. But she had no choice. She had to focus, for her daughter's sake, and remember the night she had spent a lifetime trying to forget.

Chapter Six
Harvey

11:00 a.m. Wednesday, 19 November 2014

'So, Mr Roberts, you haven't heard from your daughter since she left the hospital at approximately eight o'clock this morning?' DC Paterson was sitting next to him on the sofa, staring at him with his grey eyes, his pen poised over his notebook. Harvey could hear the training in his voice, his careful, well-rehearsed sentences. He moved slowly and had a long, expressionless face, which reminded Harvey of the monolithic statues on Easter Island.

'No, I've told you already, the last time I spoke to her was yesterday evening, when I left the hospital. I texted her about an hour ago to say I would be there today about eleven – so now.' Harvey looked up from his watch out to the hallway, where DC Galt was pacing while talking on her phone. He strained to overhear what the detective constable was saying. It was obvious she was trying to keep her voice down, but Harvey was able to decipher the odd word: '. . . Station . . . sighting . . . witnesses.'

'And did you get a reply to that text?' DC Paterson looked up from his notebook.

'What?' Harvey snapped.

'Has Jessica replied to your text this morning?'

Harvey looked over at his mobile on the coffee table. 'No, not yet. I don't understand. How can this happen? There's security at the hospital – I had to be let out last night.'

'That's what we're trying to work out. She left just after visiting hours began this morning so it's possible she snuck out when someone else was coming in. But the receptionist must have been distracted . . .' said DC Paterson.

'Well, that's not hard to believe. Everyone was distracted – the place was bedlam. Do you know that the baby has an infection?' Harvey put his head in his hands and tried to shake off the fog of exhaustion which was making it impossible to think.

'Yes, we are aware of that, Mr Roberts, which is why we are particularly concerned.'

'They said the baby would get seriously unwell, within a very short time, if she didn't complete the course of antibiotics they put her on.'

'Yes, we're working closely with the medical staff at St Dunstan's Hospital.'

'And what did they say about the medication? How much time do we have to find them?'

'It's hard to say. Mr Roberts, it's important to stay positive.'

'How much time before we lose Elizabeth?' Harvey snapped. 'Please be honest with me.'

'About twelve hours from her last dose, which she was given just before Jessie walked out at eight o'clock this morning. The doctors I spoke to said she will start to become very poorly after that. So we need to work together to find them both safe and well as quickly as possible. Approximately what time did you leave the hospital?'

Harvey nodded. 'Visiting hours ended at 8 p.m. I tried to stay longer as her partner is working abroad, but they wouldn't let me.' Harvey pictured Jessie staring into the distance as he left. He'd hugged her, whispered goodbye and told her he'd be back in the morning. Then, a sense of foreboding eating away at him, he had kissed baby Elizabeth's forehead while she lay in her cot, her tiny hand wrapped in the thick tape securing the cannula.

'And do you have any idea where she might have gone?' DC Paterson's breath smelt of coffee. Harvey stared at him, visualizing the two police officers sipping at their takeaway cups as the call came in to come to his home to break the news about Jessie. To sound him out. Another day, another house call. 'Let's finish this quickly, could be a long day,' they would have said before heading out of Chichester across the South Downs to the village of West Wittering, where Jessie had spent her childhood.

Harvey felt his legs jump. They always jolted when he was exhausted. It used to annoy Liz intensely as they sat together on the sofa in the evenings, Liz reading one of her dreadful crime novels while he fell asleep in front of the ten o'clock news. 'Just go to bed,' she would say, sighing as he nodded off. He could see her now, curled up next to him, gasping at the twists and turns of the book in her hand as she propped her feet on his lap. 'I knew it,' she would say. 'It's the boyfriend, I thought he was hiding something.'

Harvey knew DC Paterson was watching him, assessing how he was reacting to all his questions. Paterson had probably done a background check on him, possibly even knew that he'd been held in a cell as a fifteen-year-old the night Rebecca's parents died, and given an official warning.

Making him feel like the criminal, when he had done nothing.

'There was someone at the door that night, Harvey. I heard Father talking to them. I thought it was you, that you'd come for me.' Rebecca's voice had been shaking as she recalled that night several months later, when she had come to live with him and his father.

'But you said there was no one there when you came downstairs and found your parents,' he had said, worried about what the trauma of that night had done to her. 'Who could it have been?'

'I don't know, I suppose I must have imagined it,' she'd said. He had tried to hold her and comfort her but, as always, she had recoiled. 'You don't believe me.'

Her emerald green eyes had filled with tears, and he tried desperately to find the right thing to say. 'Of course I believe you, I don't know what to say to make you feel better,' he said, stumbling for the right words. 'You're so upset all the time, I feel like you blame me for not being there.' He had watched her change after that night, retreat into herself, no longer turning to him for comfort. And nothing he could say seemed to reach her and get her back.

Now, Harvey glanced towards the hallway, trying to hear what DC Galt was saying on the phone. 'Okay . . . will do . . . we're with Jessica's father now.' The policewoman was short and petite, with dark hair in a bob to her shoulders and dark brown eyes that seemed to sense him watching her and darted away whenever his gaze came too near.

DC Paterson tried again. 'Mr Roberts, would you have any idea where your daughter might have gone?'

Harvey turned his attention back to DC Paterson and

realized he was holding his breath. His senses felt heightened. The winter sunlight pouring through the window into the lounge was hurting his eyes, the clock in the hall seemed to tick louder than usual, burning indigestion crept up his chest. Everything hurt; his whole body ached.

'Have you tried her mother? Rebecca Waterhouse?'

'Yes, we have informed Dr Waterhouse. There is a police liaison officer with her now, I believe.'

'Well, I've had custody of Jessica since she was a baby and I don't want Rebecca here, complicating things.'

'That's fine, Mr Roberts, but I should tell you that we are thinking about holding a press conference at lunchtime, if we haven't found Jessie by then. It might be a good idea for her mother to make the appeal with you.'

'Absolutely not,' barked Harvey. 'That's out of the question. If anything, it would upset Jessie more.'

'Okay, so I take it Jessie and Rebecca's relationship is under some strain at the moment.'

'They have a very complicated relationship. Jessie went to see her a few days ago and she was very upset afterwards. I wouldn't be surprised if that was what triggered all this.'

DC Paterson nodded slowly and began scribbling in his notebook again.

'Could you tell us a little more about what Jessie told you with regards to the meeting with her mother?'

Harvey let out a heavy sigh. 'Not really. My wife, Liz, Jessie's stepmother, died two years ago, and Jessie's taken it very hard. They were very close and with the baby coming she was probably looking to fill that void. But, as always, their meeting didn't go very well.'

'In what way?' DC Paterson's eyes widened.

'I don't know! Ask Rebecca,' snapped Harvey.

'We will, Mr Roberts. I understand your frustration, we are *all* very concerned, but we need to get as much information as we can to try and work out what's happening with Jessica so that we can find her.'

'What's happening with Jessica is that she has been through hell. She has lost the woman who was like a mother to her, she's just been through a very traumatic birth, her boyfriend is away and she hasn't slept for days.' Harvey felt his face burning, but went on.

'Jessie was being bullied into breastfeeding while her baby starved. Jessie was catatonic when I left, but nobody listened to me. Rebecca, her birth mother, was the same when she had her. And now they've let her just walk out. And it's bloody freezing out there. Do you not have any idea where she's gone?'

'We have officers looking at all the CCTV footage now, Mr Roberts. The last images we can find of Jessie show her walking towards Chichester train station. Obviously you would assume she got on a train but there are no images of her on any of the platforms so it may be that isn't the case. Of course we have informed train and bus stations and also all of the taxi companies in the area.'

DC Paterson excused himself and went to speak to DC Galt. Whispering, conferring – the usual story with the police, Harvey thought; you tell us everything, and in return we tell you nothing.

He could see Liz sitting on the arm of the sofa, arms folded, shaking her head disapprovingly, the way she did when he lost his temper. He could hear her calm voice behind him now, feel her warm breath on his neck. *They*

are just trying to find Jessie. You need to cooperate with them.
But his wife's experience of the police extended to a speed-
ing ticket and a ticking-off for peeing in an alleyway on a
drunken night out. 'Why are you always so hostile towards
them?' she'd ask when he scowled at any copper he walked
past.

Watching DC Galt and DC Paterson now was like
being dragged back to that winter of 1960.

DC Paterson returned. 'Someone fitting Jessie's description has been seen, with a baby, in Chichester town centre.
There's also been a possible sighting of her getting on a
train to London.' The man spoke so infuriatingly slowly it
was as if his batteries were running low, and Harvey felt
an urge to slap him on the back to jolt him into life. Where
was the urgency?

'Right, so do you have police officers following this up?
I should go into Chichester, join the search,' said Harvey,
pulling his shoes on.

'We have officers out searching for her in Chichester and
on standby for the trains coming into London. I think, for
now, you're better helping us with our enquiries here, Mr
Roberts.' Harvey let out a sigh, waiting for him to continue. 'We've seen on the hospital CCTV that Jessie walked
out wearing a dress, but did she have any other clothes with
her – a coat of any kind? It would help us to give a fuller
description of what she might be wearing so we don't miss
her. What we also need to know from you is what's going
on in her life right now – any mental health issues, any
financial worries, issues with her partner?'

DC Paterson's words sounded slurred and far away.
Harvey watched his lips, trying to decipher what he was

saying as he began to lose himself to the image of Jessie battling through the freezing cold November gale with his beautiful granddaughter in her arms.

'We also need to contact as many of Jessie's friends, family and work colleagues as possible – in the next hour, ideally – in case she has been in touch or is on her way to any of them.

'We understand from the hospital that her boyfriend, Adam, is in Nigeria and apparently he has been in contact with them. He is due to depart on a seven-hour flight back to Heathrow at midday tomorrow our time, which will take us to seven p.m. So there is no point delaying the press conference for him. We'll also need to go to Jessie's flat, check through diaries, notebooks, emails, to work out who she is closest to.'

'She was closest to her stepmother,' said Harvey quietly. 'My wife, Liz, is buried at Shoreham cemetery. Jessie sometimes goes there.'

Harvey thought back to the day they had put Liz in the ground. They had driven home in silence and made tea, with little idea of the force of the grief that was thundering down the tracks towards them.

'Okay, we'll get someone to check that out.' DC Paterson turned to his colleague, who nodded and left the room, 'I realize this is frustrating, but we need to get as much detail about Jessica's life as we can.

'It would be a great help to us if you could drive DC Galt to Jessica's flat as we came in one car. I'm going back to the hospital to speak to the team that were looking after your daughter and granddaughter. We are aware the situation is urgent. I've just had word that we are going ahead with a press conference which is being set up now and, if you would be willing, we think it would be beneficial for you to make a personal appeal on that. It will be broadcast on all the news channels.'

Harvey looked up. Two hours ago, he had been walking the dogs on Wittering Bay, reflecting on the birth of his new granddaughter. Now, they were missing and he was expected to go on national television and keep it together while he begged Jessie to come home.

Harvey pushed his anger at Adam's absence to the back of his mind, 'Of course,' he said. 'Whatever you need.'

'Do you have a key to Jessica's flat?' said DC Paterson. 'We should probably get going.'

'I'll get it. One thing I have to know. And I'd really appreciate an honest answer.' Harvey paused, composing himself. 'If you do find them, will the baby be taken away from Jessie because she's done this?'

'It's in everyone's interest to keep Jessica and her baby together.'

'But are social services involved?'

'Child protection have been in touch with the hospital social worker and they have referred the case to social services for backgrounds checks.'

'So is there a chance the baby will be taken away?' Harvey asked again.

'Nobody wants that, Mr Roberts. Child protection is all about keeping families together. Now, if you wouldn't mind, we do need to get to Jessica's flat as soon as possible.' And with that, DC Paterson ushered Harvey out of his house, into the bitter November air, the two officers flanking him on either side, as if he were already in the dock.

Chapter Seven

Harriet

Boxing Day, 1945

'I'm sorry about this, Harriet. You have been a great asset to this house for the past five years and we will be very sad to see you go.' Miss Clara stumbled over her words as Harriet stood in the doorway waiting for Jacob to appear at the top of the stairs.

'Please don't worry yourself, Miss Clara, we'll be all right. It was very Christian of you and Miss Ethel to let Jacob stay here at all.' Harriet heard the nervousness in her voice and cleared her throat. She felt close to tears to be leaving this house, which had been more of a home to her than a workplace.

'We have tried to be understanding, but we just don't feel safe with your husband in the house. We're not as young as we were and it has been rather unsettling.'

'Of course. Really, you don't need to explain. I'm sorry again about yesterday.' Harriet flushed red.

An awkward silence hung between them, the memory of the events of the day before still fresh in their minds.

'Where will you go?'

'Jacob has heard there's a groundsman's position going at

Northcote Manor, so we are going up there today to see what we can find out.'

Harriet glanced over at the stairs and saw Jacob. He looked like he had tried to make an effort with his appearance, having shaved and combed his hair back with oil. But still he seemed a little bedraggled: his clothes were unpressed, he was deathly pale and the heavy bags under his eyes gave away the nightmares which plagued his sleep.

Miss Clara looked up at him too. 'Well, good luck, Harriet. I wish you both well. Your references and wages are on the hall table.' She leaned forward and kissed Harriet on her cheek, patted her arm awkwardly then scuttled off before Jacob reached them.

Harriet's eyes filled with tears, but it was almost a relief that it was over. The strain of trying to hide Jacob's behaviour from Miss Clara and Miss Ethel was taking its toll on her health. And she didn't blame them for feeling frightened of him.

It had been a constant, unbearable strain since she had welcomed him home at Chichester Station six months earlier. She'd had to hide her horror at the state he was in when he eventually emerged from the train carriage and she had fought her way through the crowds to get to him.

He had lost so much weight he was barely recognizable. His once-ruddy cheeks were sunken, his tall frame cowering, his confident stride gone. His right hand was bandaged up to the elbow, and she'd had no warning that two of his fingers had been amputated after becoming infected after a burn. When he kissed and held her, his lips were cold and his hug limp. It was as if all the light and strength had left him, leaving just an empty sack of bones and skin.

Miss Clara and Miss Ethel had welcomed the war hero home, kindly letting him stay in Harriet's small single room in exchange for some help in their garden. But all too soon the warm atmosphere in the small townhouse began to unravel and their nervousness took root. Jacob drank to excess, was short-tempered and unable to cope with any tiny changes of plan or nuance in the day.

Her diary had been her only outlet, and she would scribble in its pages in the early hours when Jacob finally fell into a drunken stupor in his chair by the window.

19 December 1945

Dear Diary

I miss my husband terribly, and feel most lonely at night, when I have to sleep on my own as Jacob is too frightened of the nightmares that haunt him to come to bed. Instead, he stays up, drinking cheap whisky and talking to himself. If he does nod off in his chair, he wakes, crying out like a wounded animal. I rush to him and he is drenched in sweat, there is no one behind his eyes, but it is the only time he shares any of what happened to him with me. He tells me he is back on the beaches of Normandy, in the moment when his childhood friend, Michael, was blown to pieces in front of him. He sobs as I rock him like a child, telling me things I wish I had never heard. That he picked up what was left of his friend's body and tried to put the pieces back together. That he will never forgive himself that he couldn't save him. Clinging to me, he eventually falls asleep at dawn, but we are both thoroughly exhausted and Miss Ethel often complains at breakfast about the noise. I try to quiet Jacob, but he is strong and his shouts are uncontrollable. He is like a man possessed by the devil when he wakes at night and I can do nothing to calm him.

My warm, fun-loving husband is suspicious of everyone and talks of German spies hiding in the countryside still, waiting to invade our town. I have been feeling increasingly isolated of late and pressed him to go into town for a Christmas Eve drink at our old local pub, hoping it would help to see some old friends. I asked tentatively if any of the other wives were experiencing a change in their husbands, but I was made to feel that my questions were in rather bad taste, as the men had been told by their superior officers on the ship home not to dwell on the past, that it would be unpatriotic to talk about what had happened to them.

As the evening wore on, I noticed that Jacob was very morose. The other men laughed and chatted, but he sat, glaring at me, and I could tell the other girls were starting to feel quite uncomfortable. By the time we came to leave Jacob wouldn't talk to any of us.

When Pete complimented me on my new coat I smiled at him. In a flash, Pete was being dragged across the table, all the glasses were sent flying and smashed on the floor and it took most of the bar staff to haul Jacob off him. The landlord went to call the police, but Jacob and Pete go way back, so Pete just headed home with his bloodied nose. I apologized desperately to everyone, but this just infuriated Jacob more. He said it was my fault, that I had been flirting all night with everyone and was drunk.

When we got home he started asking me if I was having an affair with Pete. He told me that I was in love with

Pete because I was disgusted by my husband. That I thought he was a coward for letting his friends die. That I didn't love him any more. He was shouting so much I couldn't calm him. Suddenly, his fist came from nowhere and he punched me. I cried out as my mouth filled with blood. I was so terrified I buried myself under the covers to shield myself from any more blows, at a loss what to do. He's never laid so much as a finger on me before. Miss Ethel heard the commotion and came knocking on the door, and I told her I was sorry, that all was well. But she was horrified by the state of my face and I knew then that their good will was at an end. Had I known what was going to happen on Christmas Day, I would have packed our bags right then and there and slept on the street.

On the long bus ride out of Chichester and into the countryside Harriet and Jacob sat in silence, the memory of Christmas Day haunting them both. Harriet looked out of the window and recalled preparing the Christmas turkey and putting it in the oven, then laying the fires while Jacob went into the garden to cut more logs. It was when he came back and checked on the turkey that their fate had been sealed.

She had heard Jacob shouting from the kitchen, dropped what she was doing and rushed to find him kneeling next to the Aga, pulling the turkey out of the oven with his bare hands, the fat hissing and burning his skin as he yelled at her that his friend was burning.

She'd tried to calm him, but it was impossible. He'd thrown the turkey in the sink and poured water over it as he yelled and cried for her to do something to help.

With all her strength she had managed to drag and pull him away. And as she put him to bed he had wept as he told her that when he opened the oven, the sizzling skin on the turkey had triggered a flashback of the skin on his friend's torso burning in front of him on the beaches of Normandy. She had managed to rescue what she could of Christmas lunch, but before long Miss Ethel had appeared at the kitchen door, breaking the news that they would have to go. She and Jacob hadn't mentioned it that morning, she couldn't really bear to think about it, and when she looked down at Jacob's hands burnt and blistering from the heat of the cooking meat he had pulled out of the hot oven, she had to turn away to stop her tears.

The bus juddered to a stop outside Northcote, bringing Harriet back to the present. 'Come on, let's go,' Jacob said, dropping her case at her feet as she stared in awe at the huge iron gates and the long, ice-covered driveway that led to the Georgian mansion.

Jacob started off across the stone-covered ground, snapping at her to follow, but she felt rooted to the spot, despite the harsh December wind swirling around her, lacking the strength she knew it would take to work as a servant in a house which, rumour had it, held thirty bedrooms, four drawing rooms, two libraries and a state banqueting hall.

But she forced herself on, towards the manor, where, soon, they would be ringing the bell and asking for work – and closing the door for good on the life she'd had before Jacob came home.

Chapter Eight

Iris

11:30 a.m. Wednesday, 19 November 2014

Iris ran for the train to Chichester and, as she jumped through the doors just as they were closing, she heard her phone ring.

'Newsdesk' was flashing on the screen and she picked it up. 'Hi, Miles.'

'Hi, Iris. Apparently, the baby is on medication, or needs to be in the hospital for some reason.' Miles was tripping over his words. 'I think this is going to turn into quite a big story as the day goes on. The police obviously think she's going to jump off a bridge, or in front of a train with the baby. How did you hear about it again?'

Iris tried to fight back the image Miles had just planted in her head, of Jessie and the baby, and fumbled for the right words. She hadn't expected such a reaction to the story. She would have to come clean soon enough, but she didn't want Miles to pull her off the story and send someone else. It was too important.

'I've got an old friend – a contact – at St Dunstan's Hospital, he tipped me off,' she lied.

'Right, well, see if you can meet him today. The police are with the baby's grandfather now. He was with the mother when the baby was born, I believe, as the baby's dad's not around. Not sure why, but hopefully you can shed a bit more light on it all. This has all come from a tip-off from another mum on the ward who spoke to the first reporter at the hospital, but the police have got to her now so she won't say any more. That's what I was hoping you could help us out with. Might this contact of yours know anyone who works in the Maternity Wing?'

'I'm going to make some calls on the train so I'll try and get hold of him but he might be nervous to say more. There's also the element that the hospital may have screwed up in some way so the staff will have been told not to speak to the press – or anyone. When I get there, I might try and speak to any other new mums coming out, or any other patients who may have heard something and be willing to talk.'

'No point. The police have now spoken to all the women being discharged today and told them not to talk to the press. We need to get hold of someone on the inside, some-one who works at the hospital, ideally.' She could almost feel Miles's adrenaline.

'Well, I'll try this contact again, he works at A&E at St Dunstan's so I don't know if he'll know much. It's a big hospital, so he may not know anyone in Maternity—'

'Well, he must know something to have tipped you off!' Miles cut her off. 'Just get on it. We need a name of a mid-wife at St Dunstan's Hospital we can doorstep, preferably the one who was responsible for Jessie. And also, you need to get hold of a specialist in this field, get their take on postnatal depression and psychosis. Royal College of Psy-chiatrists, Royal College of Paediatrics.'

'Yup,' Iris said as a sea of commuters pushed past her at the next stop. 'We need to look at medical ethics. If she's walked out with her baby because she doesn't want it to be treated, the court would need to make an application to go against the mother's wishes, so could we get hold of Legal and find out the situation there, if we can write about that?'

She could hear Miles barking orders across the office.

'Does this woman have a name, by the way?' said Iris when Miles finally returned his attention to her.

'Yes, Jessica Roberts, she's thirty-nine. First baby.' Thank goodness Iris was not responsible for the name getting out. Miles went on, 'From her Facebook page, it looks like she lost her mother fairly recently, Liz Roberts. Also, there's an obit in the *Telegraph* from October 2012. The mother died of breast cancer; does Jessica have any siblings we can get hold of and interview?' Iris stayed quiet at Miles' assumption that Liz was Jessie's mother, it was all much too close to the bone, and she couldn't tell Miles yet, he'd pull her off the story.

'It all adds to the profile of a woman on the edge,' Miles went on. 'This is going to be huge, it's the lead story on the lunchtime news, and they're planning a press conference with her dad. Everyone thinks she and the baby are on borrowed time. It's just a matter of when and where. Call me when you've got something – this is your chance to get back in my good books, Iris, okay? Don't screw it up.'

'Okay,' said Iris, and hung up.

What was going through Jessie's mind to walk out of hospital on a freezing November day with her poorly newborn baby? Where could she be? If they'd had any kind of relationship, Iris would have been there, visiting her in hospital, looking after her. Instead, she'd had no idea that her half-sister had even been pregnant. It broke her heart to think about it. She pictured Jessica standing on a train platform somewhere, in a cold station, chronically sleep deprived, in pain from the birth, desperately trying to get as far away as possible and find somewhere to hide. She would have cowered at every loud noise – the crashing ticket barriers, the train conductor's whistle – while her broken body would wince at every bustling commuter who knocked into her and her tiny baby.

Her mobile rang again.

'Hi, Mum. Thanks for calling back. Miles, my news editor, is sending me to Chichester to try and find out what's happening.'

'Oh, right.' Rebecca's voice was quiet.

'He wants me to try and meet up with a contact I was at university with, Mark Hathaway, he's an A&E consultant at St Dunstan's.' Iris stood by the doors so as not to be heard in the train carriage. 'Do you mind telling me what Jessie talked to you about, Mum? What might have upset her, I mean.'

'You sound like the police.'

'Sorry,' said Iris, slightly taken aback. 'So are they at the house now?'

Rebecca spoke quietly so as not to be heard. 'Yes, they arrived half an hour ago, and Harvey has obviously planted the seed that Jessie and I had a falling-out when she came to see me. That somehow this is all my fault.'

'That's nice of Harvey to try and blame you,' said Iris shaking her head.

'Yes, and of course they're not giving me any updates, other than to tell me they're holding a press conference that Harvey doesn't want me at.'

'Okay, well I'm doing my best to find out what I can.

80

Like you asked.' She frowned, annoyed at her mother's change of heart. She had failed to mention to her mother that, on a quiet news day, her news editor had positively leapt on the story. It had been a long time since she'd brought anything to the table, and he hadn't been subtle in showing his disapproval.

'I know, I just thought you might have heard something in the office. I didn't realize he might send you on Jessie's trail.'

'It's a good thing, isn't it? I'll be at the heart of it, and I'll be able to update you. He wants me to attend the press conference too.'

'Oh dear. Won't Harvey notice you there?'

Iris let out a sigh. 'I think he's got a lot on his mind, Mum. And he knows what my job is. Besides, who cares? You have a right to know what's going on – you shouldn't have to resort to this subterfuge.'

It always staggered Iris that her mother, who had worked her way up to being a senior paediatric consultant, always kowtowed to anything that involved Jessie or Harvey. Her daughter was missing. She should be in Chichester with Harvey, being told everything he was. Not getting snippets of information from a police liaison officer.

'So, what was it you talked about? Why did Jessie get upset? I won't share it with anyone.'

'I don't really want to talk about it, darling.'

'You always do this, Mum, and it's not fair.'

Iris felt her hackles rise. It was unlike her to argue with her mother, but seeing James that morning, the possibility of having her house taken away from her and, then, finding out her half-sister had had a baby and no one had told her about it, was putting her on edge. She was risking her job to try and find out what she could; the least her mother could do, she felt, was to tell her what she knew. She was tired of always tiptoeing around the subject of Jessie. Her sister and her newborn niece were missing. They needed to pull together.

'Do what, Iris?'

'Shut me out of anything to do with Jessie. Dad used to fill me in on this stuff, but now he's not around I never have a clue what's going on with her.' Iris knew she was being childish, but it was at times like these that she missed her father desperately. She had a good relationship with her mother but Rebecca could be a closed book, and the two of them had often relied on John to ease any friction.

'That's not true, I talk to you about her all the time,' her mother said curtly. 'And I know you miss Dad. I miss him too. I so wanted to talk to him about Jessie, I wanted to talk to you about her visit and the baby but I didn't want to upset you.'

'But you're upsetting me now!' Iris surprised herself at her honesty as she looked out of the window at the Sussex countryside hurtling by.

'Well, I'm sorry, Iris. I get it wrong sometimes, well, most of the time, as Jessie was very quick to point out.'

'Mum, this is not your fault. I love her because she's my sister, but I hate what she's done to our family. I can't believe she was pregnant and didn't tell me. Why does she hate me so much?' Iris angrily wiped at a tear. 'She's always pushed me away.'

'Iris, I'm sorry I've upset you. I really don't think it's a good idea, you going to Chichester. It was stupid of me to ask for your help. I don't think it's appropriate.'

'Mum, who cares what's appropriate! Jessie's had a baby, you're a grandmother, I'm an auntie. They're missing and I want to try and find out what's happened. Why can't you tell me what you talked about?'

'Because it's upsetting, and it's got nothing to do with the fact that she's missing. I don't understand why everyone needs to dwell so much on the past.'

It was then that the penny dropped. Jessie had gone to talk to her mother about the night her parents were killed. The shadow that hung over their broken family, the subject that was never broached, that she'd never been allowed to mention.

'But Mum . . .'

'Darling, I have to go. The police liaison officer here wants to talk with me again. I'm very sorry I've upset you.'

'Okay,' said Iris. 'I'll speak to you later.'

She felt a desperate yearning to speak to her father. Ten years had passed since his death, and yet still, at times like these, there was no one who could smooth things over better than him. Her separation from James had hit her all the harder without her father there to pick her up and tell her that there would always be a man in the world who loved her unconditionally.

As the train pulled into the next station a throng of commuters poured on. Iris found a seat and looked out of the window, her mind darting to the articles she had found as a fourteen-year-old, only a year older than her mother had been when her life was torn apart.

It had been almost a relief to find them, in a scrapbook in the bottom of a box in the attic, after years of wondering and worrying about this big secret. She felt wretched for her mother, to have witnessed such horror so young. But as time wore on and Iris's teens turned into her twenties, it became increasingly hard for her to understand why her mother, despite their closeness, would not discuss it.

Iris sighed and logged on to Jessie's Facebook page. She sometimes looked at it, for lack of any other contact with her half-sister, and seeing it now she wished she'd looked at it sooner. A picture of Jessie and her boyfriend Adam on the beach at Wittering, Jessie's bump just showing under her sundress. It was dated August 2014, and it was a clear summer's day, Jessica's hair was cut in a neat blonde bob around her pretty, smiling face and her sunglasses were propped on top of her head. She looked happy, Iris thought, but so thin it was hard to believe she must have been five months pregnant. She reminded Iris of a fawn and was sun-kissed in the photograph and wearing a loose summer dress, so you would have barely known but for her boy-friend, who Iris had never met, pointing at her stomach and biting his fingernails like a character in a cartoon. The caption read, 'And in other news, we're due in December!' A stream of likes and comments followed, all offering con-gratulations. Iris scrolled through. Several mentioned Jessie's stepmum, Liz, and how proud and excited she would have been at the news of her first grandchild.

Iris scrolled through the other pictures of Jessie at vari-ous work events and pub lunches with friends and turned her attention to another photograph. It had been posted in December 2011, and in it Jessie and Liz were wearing Santa hats and beaming at the camera. The hats were at a jaunty angle and you could see that Liz had no hair, pre-sumably because of the chemotherapy. Despite the smiles, the intensity of their embrace gave the impression they were clinging to each other for dear life. Across the bottom of the photograph in blue italics was written, 'Death is nothing at all. I have only slipped away into the next room. How we shall laugh at the trouble of parting when we meet again.'

Of course Liz was going to mean a lot to Jessie, she had looked after her since she was a baby, but it saddened Iris to the pit of her stomach that Liz had always kept Jessie's birth mother at bay. But Liz had been gone for two years now and they had seen no more of Jessie than when Liz was alive. There was so much pain to contend with, so much hurt and misunderstanding. And her mother wasn't one to put everything out there for discussion. Least said, soonest mended. At least Jessie had tried to reach out to her mother.

As the train pulled into the penultimate station before she got off at Chichester, Iris scanned the frozen commuters as they filled her carriage with the cold air they brought with them.

Where are you, Jessie, Iris thought to herself, and why did you go to see our mother? As she thought back to how defensive her mother had been on the phone about her and Jessie's meeting, Iris became increasingly convinced that her half-sister had quizzed her mother about the night in 1960 when her grandparents were killed.

And if she was right, Iris had to find out why.

Chapter Nine

I wake in a small room with a large window overlooking Chichester. I don't know what time it is, but it feels like the evening, there is a trolley of food being wheeled around. I turn my head slowly to see the hustle and bustle beyond the window in the door out to the nurses' station, but the light from the corridor hurts my eyes and I look away again. I cough hard and my chest rumbles. My eyes scan the room. There is a chair in the corner, a sink on the wall opposite, a cabinet next to me with a jug of water on it and a door to a bathroom.

I don't want to be here. But I know I don't have the strength to leave.

I have stopped shivering, but my body feels broken. My arms ache, my head pounds, my back throbs and, as I look down, I see a drip attached to my forearm which leads up to a clear pouch of fluid hanging from a stand next to my bed.

I try and swallow, but my mouth is dry and I feel desperately thirsty. I look longingly at the cup of water on the bedside table but I don't have the strength to push myself up. As I lie listening to the nurses' chat in the corridor, I pick up the faint sound of a baby crying and try to work out where it is coming from.

I need water. I see a red button and reach out to press it,

but my arm is too heavy. Tiredness overwhelms me and I close my eyes. I hear the sea in my ears and it calms me.

'How are you feeling?'

When I open my eyes again a girl in a nurse's uniform is standing over me, smiling.

She cannot be more than twenty years old, and her long, wavy brown hair is pulled back in a half-ponytail. She has sea-blue eyes and a big smile which creeps up the sides of her kind face and takes over. It is the smile of a girl filled with optimism.

'Where am I?' My throat hurts.

'You're on Churchill Ward. I'm the night duty nurse. They brought you down from resus a couple of hours ago once you'd warmed up a bit. Can I get you anything?'

'I'm thirsty.'

'Okay, let's sit you up and get you comfortable.' She reaches out for a button and presses it and slowly the bed raises until I'm upright. She hands me a cup of water and I take it gratefully.

'I need to take your obs, if that's all right?' I don't reply, just nod, and she reaches behind her to a monitor which has a clip attached to it for my finger. While we wait, the machine beeping noisily, she smiles at me again. I notice a small diamond on her engagement ring finger.

'Your oxygen levels are good, and your body temperature is right back up, but we need to keep an eye on you. The consultant thinks you might have a chest infection, so they've given you some IV antibiotics and fluids as you were dehydrated. I think they were quite worried about you when you came in.' She moves carefully; she is self-assured and calm.

I watch her as she takes my blood pressure. The cuff

pinches my sore arm and when I wince she apologizes, still smiling.

'They said you were at Wittering Bay for quite a while, it can be really harsh down there at this time of year – no wonder you got so cold. I love going for walks there in the winter, but I spend a lot longer by the fire in the King's Head afterwards.'

I say nothing, just watch her as she slides the monitor away then sits on the edge of my bed and presses two forefingers into my wrist. She has long eyelashes, which with her long limbs and graceful movements make me think of a gazelle.

'I didn't want to leave the beach. I don't want to be here.'

'I know, but you're quite poorly so we can't discharge you yet. Could you give me any contact details for your family? We need you to tell us your name and where you live so we can let anyone worrying about you know that you're okay. Is there a family member I can get in touch with so they can come and see you?'

I look over at the door behind her, picture visitors bundling through it with flowers, handmade cards, tears, hugs. Love. I don't know how to answer her. I start to cough and cannot stop. When it is finally over she hands me some more water and a tissue.

'I have been trying to find my daughter,' I whisper. I haven't said those words out loud for twenty years, because nobody has ever believed that she is still alive.

'Trying to find her? Did you lose each other when you went to the beach?'

I want so much to tell her, but I don't know how. My body shakes as the fear in my heart takes over, as it always has.

88

I shake my head but say nothing. She looks at me then away again as she writes my heart rate in my file. I cough and swallow hard in an effort to gather myself.

'Do you know her number? I'll call her for you.' She clicks her pen closed and returns it to her top pocket.

'I don't know where she is. I don't want to hurt her. But I really want to tell her I'm sorry. Before it's too late.'

My voice is quiet and I stop, but she waits for me to go on. I think of this morning, which started the same as any other – a fight to wake up, get dressed, eat, get through the hours without thinking of her and what could have been. I had given up long ago, resigned myself to never seeing her again. And then I saw his face. Harvey Roberts.

'And when did you last see her? Your daughter?'

I start to cough again but manage to catch my breath so it doesn't take over. My chest burns. 'When she was five days old. I went back today, to where I last held her, to try and remember.'

I know I have to tell someone what happened to me and my baby. I can't keep it inside any longer, it has eaten away at me for so long that there is nothing left, but I don't know where to start. I don't know if this girl is the angel I've been praying for or if I'm just wishing her to be because I know she is my last hope. Because I know I am never leaving this room.

Another nurse appears at the door and asks her a question. I panic she will leave and not return. That this conversation, which has barely begun, will never have existed. My body floods with relief when the other nurse goes and she looks at me again.

'And you stayed at Wittering Bay until it got dark? On your own?' she says, frowning.

'I couldn't leave. I realized that I would rather die than face another day without her.'

I watch for her reactions, silently wishing I hadn't said anything. I feel frightened that she will take my words and act on them. And equally frightened that she won't.

I think back to this afternoon, stepping out of the taxi at the top of Seaview Lane as I made my way towards the seafront. The prickle of hairs on the back of my neck as I came to Seaview Farmhouse.

I stopped at the gate to look at the small Georgian farmhouse set back from the road by a courtyard as memories flooded back.

I walked down to the cove where I left her, the white stone cottage jutting out from the headland, and there I stayed until my blood froze from the bitter wind.

I close my eyes and drift off until the sound of a baby crying wakes me again. But as soon as I open my eyes it stops. I see it is night now and the darkness is heavy in the room. My chest hurts more than it did earlier. I start to cough again and a stabbing pain throbs in my chest.

I see the nurse I like through the glass. She's talking to one of the other nurses, and I remember what I told her about my daughter with rising panic. I don't know why I did it. I think every part of me has accepted that I will never see her again, but somehow I still find myself believing in a miracle.

She looks up and sees me and starts to walk towards my room.

'How are you feeling?' she asks when she reaches me. She looks a little tired now, her eyes less bright, her neat ponytail loosened so wisps of hair escape around her pretty, oval face.

'My chest hurts,' is my reply.

'The consultant is coming to see you later. I won't be here because my shift finishes soon, but I'll do a handover so they know how you are. He may decide to do another X-ray and see how you're responding to the antibiotics.' She takes my temperature and blood pressure.

'You've got a visitor.'

I frown. 'Who?'

'Someone called Rosie, one of the carers at Maycroft. The police called us, everyone at your care home has been worried about you.'

'Don't the police have better things to do? I don't want to be any trouble,' I say, though my heart lurches with hope. Rosie. I like Rosie. She is kind to me. I have always wanted to talk to her about my baby but I've never had the courage.

'Rosie would like to come and have a chat with you, if you'd like that?'

I nod. She smiles and writes down the readings.

I smile, unsure of how to express how indebted I feel to this stranger. I cough, and this time the pain is intense. The nurse leans me forward as I struggle to catch my breath. I feel like it is never going to end. The pain feels like tiny knives stabbing in my lungs.

'Thank you,' I manage, breathlessly. The nurse hands me some water.

'You're welcome. I think you may need to be on oxygen – your levels have dropped. I'll mention it to the day team.'

As soon as she goes I will Rosie to arrive at my bedside. I'm terrified to be alone in this place. On this ward. Hearing patients cry, being unable to get out, is bringing it all back.

That when they took me from the beach against my will then pulled me out of the ambulance into the hospital I was suddenly back there, being dragged, screaming for my baby, through the entrance of the Victorian Gothic building.

Along the endless red stone corridors and on to a locked ward where weird women in various states of undress cackled and pulled at my clothes and hair with their scrawny hands. Where I was left, for weeks, staring at the barred windows in a never-ending cycle of sedative-induced nightmares and half-awakeness, utterly alone, as I am now, with no idea if I would ever get out. 'You can get in easy enough,' one of the women would say to me, twisting her raven-black hair through her dirty fingernails, 'but you can never get out.'

'Hello. I brought you some tea,' says Rosie. She is wearing a baby blue coat, with a flower pinned to her lapel. She sets two tea cups down next to my bed.

'Thank you for coming,' I say slowly. She has long blonde hair which is always falling out of her ponytail. And she is wearing a light pink cardigan which looks so soft I want to touch it.

'We were all very worried about you. We didn't know where you'd gone. How are you feeling?' She leans in and takes my hand.

'A bit better,' I lie.

'Why did you take yourself off like that so suddenly? If you'd waited until the end of my shift, I could have come with you.' Rosie winks at me, in the way she always does when Bart is making crude jokes.

'I wanted to be alone,' I say, simply.

She nods and smiles gently. 'The nurse who has been

looking after you said you've been talking about your daughter. You've never mentioned her to me.'

'I wanted to, it's hard talking about her,' I say, as Rosie leans in.

'When did you last see her?' Rosie asks.

'When she was five days old.' I feel my voice shake.

She pulls up the chair next to my bed and takes my hand in hers. 'I'm sorry.'

My chest tightens and I feel breathless again. 'I find it so hard to remember her. I didn't hold her for long, but she was inside me for nine months so I knew her, even for that short time. I try so hard to recall her tiny body, her smell, her sea-green eyes. But all I really remember is the fear.'

'Fear? What were you fearful of?' Rosie picks up her tea and blows into it before she takes a sip.

I look at Rosie, her innocent eyes frowning, concerned. I don't yet know how to trust her with the truth. 'From the moment I discovered I was pregnant, I just felt intense fear that something bad was going to happen.'

I take a deep breath and look away. How do I begin to explain to this girl how I lost my mind? I am ashamed, still, and afraid. But she is my only hope of ever seeing my daughter again and I know somehow that I have no choice but to trust her.

'Fear of the birth, was how it started.'

Rosie nods encouragingly and so I continue.

'For as long as I can remember, I always had feelings of intense panic just reading or hearing women talking about childbirth. As a young woman I remember thinking if my husband wanted desperately to have children, then I could see only two possible outcomes for me: I would die during

93

childbirth or I would become "mad". As it turns out, it was the latter.'

I try to smile, though I know it's not appropriate. She doesn't return it but gives a slight nod. I am talking too much and another round of hacking coughs take over. Rosie stands and leans me forward, giving me a glass of water when I finally finish.

I twist a stray thread from the blanket on my bed around my finger until it turns white and try to focus on the words rather than the memories.

'When the contractions really began in earnest I couldn't cope with them and I began to panic. It was the first time in my life that I faced the terror of being certain that I couldn't go on and yet there was no way back. It just kept getting worse and worse, for hours and hours, no baby came, the pain tore through me. And as day turned into night I knew that before the morning came I would go mad.'

I cough again. The pain in my chest is getting worse and, when it finishes, tiredness takes over. Rosie pulls my covers up and when I fall asleep I dream that I am standing at the water's edge, holding my baby, and a wave higher than the cliffs behind me is coming for us and there is nothing I can do.

Chapter Ten

Rebecca

Friday, 14 November 2014

Rebecca heard the door buzzer and hurried to the window. A red Fiat was parked on the road opposite her house. Her heart lurched. Jessie had finally arrived.

As she hurried along the chequerboard tiles of her hallway, her eyes fell on the photo albums on the hall table which she had dug out that morning. Just flicking through the black-and-white images of her and Harvey in the garden at Seaview Farm holding baby Jessie in her arms, she was struck by the haunted look in her eyes. She hadn't been able to bring herself to look at the photos for decades, such was the strength of the emotions they brought back, but this wasn't about her. Her eldest daughter was having a baby, and she needed to understand what her mother had been through having her – however hard it was for Rebecca to go back there.

'Hello, Jessie!' she said, opening the front door. A gust of cold air swept in. Jessie stood on the doorstep holding a small bunch of tulips. Her blonde hair was neatly blow dried, and her green eyes sparkled as she handed over the flowers. She wore a navy wrap dress around her bump which was smaller than Rebecca would have expected for someone who was eight months pregnant, and also looked alarmingly thin, and rather pale, but Rebecca managed a warm smile as she took the flowers which Jessie held out. 'Come in, it's bitter out there.'

'Thank you for the flowers.' Rebecca leaned in to kiss her daughter on both cheeks, immediately feeling awkward, as she always did around Jessie. An image of Iris flashed into her mind's eye, a complete contrast to Jessie, sweeping into her house on a wave of chatter and laughter, her arms filled with bags she'd throw on the floor at her mother's feet. Jessie and Rebecca always danced around one another, their conversation stilted, their chemistry out of synch. She longed for just a fraction of the easiness she had with Iris for her and Jessie, but perhaps now things would begin to change. Perhaps that was what today was the start of. She could only hope.

Rebecca smiled at her daughter. 'You look beautiful, darling. Can I get you a cup of tea?'

Jessie smiled shyly and began following her mother into the kitchen. 'Do you have any decaf? I'm trying not to drink caffeine as it doesn't help with my anxiety.'

Rebecca immediately started to worry about what she had to offer her elder daughter. Jessie hadn't been to her house for over a year and she was losing touch with what she liked. She chastised herself for not going shopping and instead spending the morning pacing and panicking about Jessie not turning up. 'I don't have any decaffeinated, but I might have some chamomile somewhere. Oh dear.'

'That's fine. I'm not a big fan of chamomile. I'll just have a glass of water.'

'I'm sorry, Jessie, I should have thought. I can pop to

Tesco, it's just round the corner.' Rebecca started towards the door.

'Honestly, it's not a problem. I don't really drink tea.'

Rebecca took a breath and tried to stop herself from fussing. It was just a cup of tea, but it seemed to represent everything that was off in their relationship. She and Iris couldn't function without tea; they'd sit for hours on the sofa, their legs curled under them, putting the world to rights. Often they would talk about Jessie, if either of them had heard from her or seen her, and how much they wished she was in their lives.

'Water it is. Still or sparkling?' said Rebecca, smiling and trying to warm the slight frost between them as Jessie followed her into the kitchen.

'Tap water is fine, thanks.' Rebecca noticed her daughter look around the room, pausing at the various photographs on the wall, black-and-white images of Iris and her father, John, in various holiday locations. One, pinned to the fridge, of her and Iris in fancy dress, pulling faces for the camera, seemed to catch her attention.

One lone photo of Jessie stood on the kitchen window-sill, from their day trip to Brighton, the last time Rebecca had seen Liz. She had asked Liz to take the photo so that she would have some memory, some moment to cling to that wasn't dominated by Jessie's stepmother. They had stood in front of the angry grey sea on the cold January day, Rebecca with her arm awkwardly around her daughter, Jessie's limp by her side. Rebecca had beamed at the camera while her daughter had managed only a weak smile.

'There you go,' said Rebecca, handing Jessie a glass. 'Shall we go into the sitting room?'

Passing the hall table, Rebecca lifted the photo album and propped it under her arm.

'I dug out some pictures of when you were a newborn. I thought you might like to see them.' She kicked herself for the insensitivity of her words. Why was she having to 'dig out' pictures of Jessie when there were pictures of Iris everywhere?

But she knew why. The pictures of Jessie as a newborn took her back to a time she hated being reminded of. A time when she had been frightened she wouldn't be able to get through the day and was filled with so much terror, every waking moment felt as if she were about to fall off a cliff. When she could barely open her eyes from the sheer exhaustion of existing, thinking any moment she was going to die, yet too terrified to fall asleep because of the nightmares that lay in waiting.

'Did you want to sit on the sofa? You're probably tired. I didn't offer you any food – sorry, would you like a biscuit?'

'No, I'm fine, thank you. Your house is very cosy,' said Jessie. 'I've never really noticed before. Probably because it's so bloody cold outside.' She looked at the room where Rebecca spent most of her time at home, collapsing with a gin and tonic after long, brutal shifts at the hospital. It wasn't a stylish room – it was rammed with cushions, over-sized lamps and shag-pile rugs – but she loved it and it was home. But far from taking her daughter's comment as a compliment, it only served to fuel her sadness that she hadn't spent any time here with Jessie.

Jessie sat down on the sofa and let out a little sigh.

Rebecca hovered for a moment, wondering if she should sit next to her, then, not wanting to crowd her, opted for her favourite armchair opposite. Jessie smiled wanly and Rebecca thought she might be about to cry. Her heart ached for her. The few steps between them felt like an uncrossable chasm. She longed to walk over to her little girl, to wrap her arms around her. But it wasn't what Jessie wanted. What her daughter needed from her was answers, and honesty, not superficial physical contact. Whether she had the strength to give them to her remained to be seen.

'So, do you mind me asking who the lucky man is?' asked Rebecca cautiously. 'I don't want to pry.'

'Adam, his name is. He's a travel photographer. We haven't been together that long, about eighteen months. The baby was a bit of a surprise – a happy surprise.'

'It's so wonderful, and I'd love to meet Adam one day.' Rebecca wanted to say more, but waited for Jessie to take the lead.

Jessie took a sip of her water and smiled awkwardly. 'I don't think Dad likes him much.'

'Really? What makes you say that?' Rebecca tried not to pounce on the confidence Jessie had shared with her.

Jessie shrugged. 'Dunno, it's just a vibe, really. You can just tell, can't you? It's a chemistry thing.'

'I'm sure he likes him really,' said Rebecca, cringing at her superficial attempts to stick up for Harvey.

'Adam's away a lot with work. I think Dad worries he won't be around for all the tough bits – you know, if I'm not coping too well.'

Rebecca frowned. 'Has he said that?'

'No, you know Dad, he doesn't say anything outright

but his silence speaks volumes. He's just never given me the impression he likes Adam much.'

Rebecca knew exactly what her daughter meant. Any attempt at openness brought Harvey out in a rash, which was why his marriage to Liz and her obsession with 'getting it all out in the open' had at first baffled her. Over time, however, she had realized that Liz was, in fact, one of those dangerous people who would jump at the opportunity to discuss anyone else's faults at length but would storm off if you dared to confront any of hers.

'And you're due in about four weeks?'

Jessie nodded. 'We're having a home birth, in our flat in Chichester.'

'Good for you,' Rebecca managed, the memories of Jessie's birth, which she had worked so hard to suppress, slowly starting to creep back in. 'So have you got a birthing pool?'

'It's coming tomorrow. Adam's gone on a photo shoot to Nigeria for a few days. He'll put it up when he gets back.'

Rebecca could see why Harvey would be worried about Adam going so far away so close to the birth. She could imagine him disapproving of Jessie's partner jetting off all over the world for his work and leaving his daughter alone with the baby. As far as she knew, Harvey had never left Seaview Farm, at least for all the years she'd known him. 'The cows don't milk themselves,' he would say if she suggested even a night away.

'How lovely that he gets to travel for his work. And are you still working at the press agency in London or have you found something local to Chichester?'

Jessie smiled. 'No, still trekking up to London. I'm not

very good at making life easy for myself. I guess it's in my genes.'

Rebecca smiled cautiously, unsure if this was a dig at her.

Jessie went on. 'I'm still at the same press agency. I like it, I'm hoping to go back to work after a few months and put the baby in nursery. But I'll see how I'm doing.'

'I'm sure you'll do brilliantly.' Rebecca's smile went unreturned as Jessie looked down at her hands. She looked exhausted and weighted down with worry. Rebecca was concerned that Jessie had already decided she was going to struggle terribly after the baby was born. As if it was a foregone conclusion. She hesitated. 'I'm not sure what your dad has told you, but I'm sorry if he's worried you. Just because I didn't cope too well, doesn't mean you won't be able to. I was fine with Iris.'

'Yes, I know. Everything was perfect with Iris.'

Rebecca felt a stab of defensiveness and bit her lip. There was so much bubbling below the surface, but she needed to take anything Jessie threw at her today if they were going to make any progress at all.

Rebecca chose her words carefully. 'I didn't mean it like that. I just meant that it won't necessarily follow that because I struggled, you will.'

Jessie shrugged, and Rebecca felt suddenly ashamed of herself. Jessie had come to her; she needed to just listen, not shut her down. She was clearly worrying, and her body language was alarming Rebecca. Her movements were slow; her body, though slim and frail looking, appeared to be a huge burden to her. Yet her eyes and words were darting, her mind clearly working on overdrive. Now Jessie was in

101

front of her, it was obvious to Rebecca that she was very subdued. She was nervous and anxious.

'Sorry, Jessie. I don't want to dismiss how you're feeling. I just don't want you to take it as a definite that you're going to have any kind of postnatal depression. My mother didn't.'

'How do you know?'

Rebecca baulked, surprised, and shook her head. 'I would have known if she'd had depression when I was born, Jessie, or anything like it. We were very close.'

'That doesn't mean she didn't keep things from you – to protect you. Look at you and Iris,' she said quietly.

'What about me and Iris?' said Rebecca cautiously.

'You're close but you don't talk to her about the night your parents died. Everybody has secrets,' said Jessie quietly. 'Anyway, it was psychosis, not depression.' Jessie looked up and locked eyes with Rebecca.

'How do you know that? What has your dad told you?'

'I know a lot more than you think.' Jessie continued to glare at her in a way that made Rebecca feel uneasy. 'Who was it said that history is a set of lies agreed upon? Napoleon?'

Rebecca rubbed her temple and tried to push down the acute sense of foreboding she was feeling. She wished she could have talked to Iris about Jessie's call, but that would have felt disloyal somehow. It felt as if she had jumped into this head-first without checking with anyone the best way to manage it. It was too much, too soon, as if she was holding something extremely fragile in her hands.

'I've come here because I want us to have an honest conversation for once, Mum.' Jessie looked close to tears.

'Well, I was never officially diagnosed.'

'Why not?'

102

'It's complicated. I don't know if it's helpful to go into it.'

'I knew this would happen. I shouldn't have come.' Jessie stood up and walked towards the door.

'Jessie, please.' Rebecca walked over to her daughter and took her hand. 'I want to help you, I really do. I'm really happy that you're here. More than happy, I'm overwhelmed. It's just this is all very sudden. I haven't had a chance to think.'

'For God's sake! This isn't about you! I don't want you to think, I want you to feel something – anything – for me. I just need to know what happened so I can try and understand why you left me behind. It didn't just happen to you, it happened to me too.'

Rebecca stood in stunned silence, unsure what to do next. However many times she tried to tell or show Jessie how much she loved her, nothing ever seemed to be good enough.

Rebecca looked over to the pile of black-and-white photographs, took Jessie's hand and sat down on the sofa. Slowly Jessie lowered herself down next to her.

'See this picture, see how I'm smiling but it's not reaching my eyes. I remember so clearly your dad taking that picture, telling me to hold you up so that he could see you better. I didn't know how to find the words to tell him how scared I was, how I didn't want anyone else to hold you because I was so frightened of something happening to you. I loved you so much, Jessie, I was too scared to sleep. And the fact is, I'm feeling just like that now. I'm so frightened that I'll say the wrong thing and upset you, and you'll walk out of here and I'll never see you, or your baby, again.'

Jessie looked at Rebecca, then reached out for the photograph, and as she took it, she began to cry.

Chapter Eleven

Harvey

12:00 p.m. Wednesday, 19 November 2014

'Harvey's on board. We're coming in now.' DC Galt was sitting next to Harvey in the back of the police car as Harvey looked down at the speech on his lap.

He'd had no idea where to begin, what to say to put into words how desperately guilty he felt, how much he would give to go back in time and not walk out of the hospital. To have not let them down. Every time he tried to find the right words they sounded like excuses he was telling himself for abandoning his girls when they needed him most.

After watching the police ransacking Jessie's beautiful flat like burglars, looking for any clues where she might have gone, DC Galt had suggested he take himself off for a minute and think about his words to Jessie for the press conference.

He had walked into Jessie and Adam's bedroom, which smelt of Jessie's perfume, and seen that the duvet was still crumpled at the end of the bed where Jessie had sat, having contractions, while he rushed around trying – and failing – to fetch what she needed for the hospital.

He had closed the door behind him, sat on the floor, and laid his head on the space where she had sat, as if resting it in her lap. And then he had spoken to her as if she were still there. About how all he could keep thinking of was the times he had told her off for not tidying her room or leaving her shoes in the hall as a child. For not walking the dogs or doing her homework as a teenager. All those afternoons she and Liz had spent together on the beach at Wittering, trips he refused to go on because he hated sitting in the summer traffic, and the crowds on the beach, and being a spare part around the two of them, with their in-jokes.

He couldn't shake the feeling of certainty that there was no point to the press conference, or the search, or the appeals for information. The words he wrote down to read out to all the reporters felt futile: she would never read them or hear them. Because wherever she was, she was unreachable.

Just like Rebecca.

As he looked out of the window, his phone rang, 'Adam Mob' flashing on the screen. Harvey stared at it for a time, anger burning inside him that Adam had not been there for his daughter when she needed him. Tears stung his eyes as he cleared his throat and pressed the green button.

'Hello?'

'Harvey? It's me, Adam. I'm just about to board a flight to Heathrow. It's slightly delayed but should be leaving soon. Is there any news?'

No apology, no remorse. It was a bad line and Adam's voice crackled in Harvey's ear. Harvey fought the urge to hang up.

'No, not yet. Where have you been?' Harvey tried not to sound as enraged as he felt.

'I was out in the countryside, there was no reception, I didn't even get your message until last night.'

'You shouldn't be uncontactable this close to the birth.'

'I got to the airport as soon as I could. Is there any news? The police said she may have got on a train?'

Harvey bit down hard on the inside of his mouth. 'Well, the last CCTV showed her walking towards the station. We're about to do the press conference. The police are hoping that might help get some more witnesses.'

'Sorry, Harvey, you're breaking up. They're calling my flight. Did you see my little girl being born? Is she beautiful?'

Harvey tried to reply. 'So beautiful,' he whispered as Adam's call cut off.

'How are you feeling?' said DC Galt kindly. 'It really won't take long, we aren't taking any questions and as soon as you've read your statement we can get you out of there. It will just really help to focus people's minds. Anyone who may have seen something suspicious, but doesn't think it's worth calling, we're trying to reach those people. And Jessie of course.'

Despite the freezing November day, the police car was stiflingly hot. Harvey kept staring out of the window into the harsh November day. People going about their lives, doing whatever they did on a normal Wednesday – getting their lunch, running errands. The car stopped at traffic lights and he watched a young couple with a child cross. As the little girl passed she looked back and stared at him with her big green eyes, just like Jessie's, and his stomach lurched.

DC Galt turned to him as her phone rang. She answered. More hushed tones. 'Right, okay, can you let me have an update in, say, an hour?'

'The sighting in Chichester wasn't Jessie,' she said, then before she could say more, the phone rang yet again.

He looked out on the endless grey pavements, pictured Jessie walking along holding her baby in nothing but a pink blanket. No pram, no sling. Surely they would stand out? Surely someone must have seen them? Where were they hiding? The entire Sussex police force seemed to be looking for her. Scouring CCTV, trawling Chichester, Worthing and Brighton town centres. They had spent the whole morning at Jessie's flat, going through her laptop, her diary, her private letters, her bank statements and her address book. Discussing every outfit she could be wearing so she might be spotted on CCTV. Calling every friend he could think of, every work colleague she mentioned in all the emails they ransacked. The place was a mess by the time they finished with it, Jessie's beautiful flat, to which he was beginning to fear she would never return. Not one clue.

As Harvey wrung his hands he could still feel little Elizabeth's fingers wrapped around his, clinging tight as he kissed her forehead. He could see the signs. It was obvious that what had happened to Rebecca was happening to Jessie. Why did he always bury his head in the sand? Why hadn't he shouted and made them listen?

Harvey looked down again at the words he was about to read out on national television and cringed at their futility.

'Are you happy with your statement?' DC Galt said, scrolling through the emails on her phone.

Harvey shrugged. 'I think Jessie would have done a better job with this. She is the one who is good with words in our family. So how many people will be in the room?'

'Around sixty I'd say. The news crews with cameras will

be standing at the back, they tend to sort themselves out in tiers, the journalists normally squat at the front. The conference room isn't huge, though, so everyone is squashed into quite a small space. We'll get you in and out of there as quickly as we can, I promise.'

'Will they be asking me questions about Jessie?' Harvey asked.

DC Galt shook her head and put her phone down. 'No, we'll say no questions before you go in, and we'll give out a press release with all the up-to-date information we have, what Jessie is wearing, that the last CCTV footage was her walking towards Chichester train station, the picture of her and baby Elizabeth you gave us.'

Harvey looked down at his notes, his pathetic, desperate words to his daughter that had come too late and that the entire country was about to hear.

'It'll be quite a sombre atmosphere, the press are very respectful. They're aching to hear what's going to be said – it's silent apart from cameras clicking. It's unbearable and intrusive but it will be over quickly and then hopefully we'll start getting calls straight away from the public.' DC Galt reached over and put her hand on his. 'It's a good statement, you'll do great.'

Harvey felt sick. The heating in the car was on too high and his shirt collar was too tight.

He needed to focus on what was happening, and he scanned his statement. 'I just want to double-check this bit if that's okay – you said to say Jessie's done nothing wrong. So, she's not in any trouble for taking her baby out of hospital when she needs treatment – is that true?'

DC Galt smiled gently. 'The main message we need to

convey is that we want to make sure Jessie and her baby are okay.'

'I understand that but I just want to check she's not breaking the law in what she's done,' said Harvey looking over.

DC Galt paused before speaking. 'We can't be sure of anything at this stage. Perhaps if it's worrying you, you should keep it vague. Say that you're missing her, to please get in touch. That you're proud of her and what a wonderful mother she is. Maybe add that baby Elizabeth needs medication and we want to make sure she gets what she needs to stay well.'

'She didn't want her baby to have the medication – that's why she ran away. So I don't think we should be saying anything about that.' Harvey took a deep breath. 'But okay, I'll keep it vague. I'd prefer it if you didn't mention the medication either. Because it won't help.'

DC Galt drew a line through her notes.

'But,' Harvey hesitated, 'I want you to be honest with me. Is my daughter going to be in trouble for putting her baby at risk? I don't want to feel I'm luring her into a trap.'

'We aren't sure what we're dealing with yet, Mr Roberts. Our priority is to get her back as soon as possible so that both she and the baby can get the help they need. As long as Elizabeth is okay then no, Jessica hasn't committed an offence. She will probably be admitted, with her baby, to a psychiatric unit until she's well again. And mother and baby will stay together.'

'I'm trying to believe you, but presumably Jessie's in the system now, so she'll have to prove herself before she's able to take care of Elizabeth.'

'I wouldn't describe it as having to prove herself, and perhaps keeping an eye on her for a while would be a good thing. We are about keeping families together. That is what is best for everyone.'

DC Galt reached out her hand and put it on Harvey's shoulder. 'I'm sorry if I've been distracted, but we have a family liaison officer you'll meet later today who will be looking after you from now on. You are not letting Jessie down by doing whatever it takes to get them back safe and well.'

Harvey nodded.

All too soon they were pulling up at the back of Chichester Police Station. Harvey stepped out into the freezing November air as DC Galt hurried him through the back door.

'The detective chief inspector leading the missing-persons investigation will be sitting in the press conference with you,' said DC Galt. 'He will make an appeal to Jessica and anyone who might know where she is to get in touch. After the DCI speaks, he will give a number the public can call, the incident room will then hopefully start getting members of the public calling in and we have a team of people ready to log the calls on our system.'

'How many people?' he asked.

'We've set up an incident room of thirty, some of which are extras from call centres. And there is a dedicated number for it.'

'And if someone calls in and says they've seen Jessie, how do you deal with that?'

'Any sightings are flagged up straight away to the officers on the investigation. There would be a very quick response if someone phones to say "I've seen her in the centre of Chichester, by House of Fraser." You get a lot of time-wasters, people claiming to be clairvoyants, but these people know what they are doing, they sort the wheat from the chaff very fast.'

They were ploughing down the corridor now, and reached a door, outside which four or five people were standing, waiting for him. A tall man with white hair in full police uniform stepped forward.

'Mr Roberts, my name is Detective Chief Inspector Bell. I'm heading up the investigation into your daughter's whereabouts. We'll be going in shortly, and I just want you to remember, you're talking to Jessica, you're trying to tell her that time is running out for us to help her baby. She's the person you need to convince. No one else matters.'

Harvey looked up at the door with the sign saying Major Incident Conference Room.

'I hope DC Galt has briefed you, but is there anything else you want to ask before we go in?'

Harvey shook his head. His body was shaking so violently that he felt his teeth chattering. He gripped his speech to steady his hands.

'Okay, the noise from the cameras is quite overwhelming when we go in, but they've been told no questions and they'll respect that. The press are only ever bad, in my experience, when they're not given anything. Right, shall we do this?'

Harvey nodded as adrenaline flooded his body, his stomach making him feel as if he were about to face a baying crowd in the Colosseum as DCI Bell stepped forward and reached for the door handle.

As an image of baby Elizabeth flashed into his mind's eye, Harvey held his breath, and as he stepped over the threshold into the tightly packed room, the camera shutters began to roar.

Chapter Twelve

Harriet

May 1946

Harriet Waterhouse sat at the small table in her and Jacob's bedroom in the servants' quarters at Northcote, watching the sun come up.

She looked over to the empty chair by the fire, where Jacob usually slept, a musty woollen blanket wrapped around his shrunken frame, snoring by the glowing ashes in the fireplace on yet another broken night. He had stopped showing her any affection and coming to her bed for any comfort. Only occasionally did he want sex, taking what he wanted without any regard for her. The last time had been a week ago, when he had woken her, and lain on top of her, pulling down her knickers while she was still foggy from sleep, pushing himself inside her so hard that it hurt her, breathing his whisky breath into her face until he was satisfied. She was no longer his wife, just something to be used when he was drunk.

But not last night. Harriet rubbed her tired eyes and pulled the leatherbound diary from under her mattress, her eyes lingering over the bed in which he had never slept with her. Opening it, her eyes fell on her entry from their first day at Northcote, when they had dragged their suitcases up the long driveway and rung the bell at the servants' entrance.

Boxing Day, 1945

Dear Diary

As I write this, we are spending our first night in the servants' quarters at Northcote. I have secured work as a
lady's maid to the lady of the house, Mrs Charles Barton.
Jacob will be assistant groundsman.

My interview with Mrs Charles Barton took place in a
huge study, which I did not take to be hers, and she seemed
not the least bit interested in my skills but more preoccu-
pied with my ability to keep secrets. Although they can
be occasionally tricky and stubborn, I prefer working for
older women. They have seen it all and know who they are.
Whereas Cecilia Barton is barely twenty, stunningly beautiful in the way of a newly born colt, newly married and
rather apprehensive about the world in which she has found
herself. She talks rather fast, darting around in conversation, her big, green, smiling eyes locking on you so intensely
that you daren't blink, her infectious warmth lighting you
up so that when she is distracted by something else, which
happens often, and she is gone, you feel rather in the shade
again.

Her apparently much older husband came in at one
point to collect some papers, and she launched herself at
him, so that I didn't know what to do with myself while
they were carrying on by the encylopaedias. He is a very
handsome man, tall and fair. He spoke and moved slowly,
with an intense stare and long pauses between his well-
thought-out sentences. She teases him and rushes about
him so that he gets rather dizzy and has agreed to anything she asks by the time he leaves the room again.

113

It seems from her demeanour around him that she has married for love, yet unfortunately for her, the role of Mrs Charles Barton comes with weighty expectations. She will need to play the part of devoted wife and hostess, entertaining dignitaries and politicians – no doubt – in her palatial home. I had barely spent five minutes with her and she was confiding that she was in much need of some support in her new position and that her husband's family have already made it clear to her that she is not up to the job. Not even being sure if I wanted the role of lady's maid, I spoke rather boldly and told her that in time her confidence would grow and not to take their words too much to heart.

There were two other young ladies waiting to be interviewed by Mrs Barton when I came out. A lady's maid is a most sought-after position, but it does require a great deal of life experience. Taking great care of a lady's clothes, picking her wardrobe, dealing with her dressmaker, caring for her jewels and looking after her hair. Everyone covets the role of lady's maid – they get the best tips, the cast-off dresses; they are the only person the lady of the house talks to. She comes back late after the ball and tells you all her secrets. The lady's maid is the only person who knows absolutely everything, but there is a danger in that of which I am nervous.

There is something in Mrs Barton's manner that has made me feel that she is hugely out of her depth. It doesn't seem to concern her much, but I have worked in a house of this stature before, and I fear there may be scorpions at bay wishing to break her wonderfully warm, but rather naive, spirit and force her to conform.

Harriet let out a heavy sigh and looked down at the pages in front of her, thinking back longingly to her life with Miss Clara and Miss Ethel. The work had been hard, but the house had held within its walls a warmth and genuine love which she could feel. Northcote, on the other hand, felt to her like a graveyard.

She had sensed it the first day as she walked along the stone hallways: there was a nervous atmosphere in the house. The servants moved quickly, not catching your eye, and the house was cold in every way. There was a strange musty smell about the place and, despite the owners' tactile behaviour during her interview, there was a feeling of unease which appeared rooted in a lack of respect for Cecilia. A Georgian mansion with fires and flowers in every room, but it lacked warmth and homeliness and held a sense of discontent which was infectious. Harriet picked up her pen and began to write.

Dear Diary

It has been five months now since I became Mrs Barton's lady's maid at Northcote Manor and, despite its vast size and household staff of twenty-four, it has the feel of a tiny rowing boat at sea in a fierce storm.

Mrs Barton is the most unusual mistress I have ever worked for. She hasn't a snobbish bone in her body and appears utterly blind to class difference. She takes very strongly towards or against people, despite their background, and cares genuinely for me and all the servants. She is totally indiscreet and often tells me things about her husband that make me blush and wish for the ground to swallow me up.

Charles often comes in from riding while I am doing a dress fitting or drawing her bath and makes it patently clear what he has been thinking about all afternoon. I can barely get out of the room quickly enough before they're on the bed in a state of undress, and I often trip over Mr Barton's riding boots in my haste to get out.

It worries my lady greatly, however, that despite the enormous amount of time they spend fawning over one other, my lady isn't yet with child. She grills me most days about my childlessness and, though I try not to share too much with her, I have become incredibly fond of her and I do not wish to lie to her. She was in tears when I told her about my last miscarriage and insisted on clutching me to her bosom for an uncomfortably long time. I come from a family where affection was limited to handshakes, so Cecilia's passion for clinging to people is something I have yet to adjust to. I have insisted that she is in wonderful health and that, when the time is right, she will fall pregnant, and that I will make the greatest fuss of her, which makes her start up again with her tears.

She is very keen on asking me about Jacob also, and I know she spends a lot of time talking to him about the war. It breaks her heart what he has been through and, though I am grateful for her concern, it worries me when the other servants notice them talking. I know that her heart is nothing but pure, that Cecilia loves her husband with every breath she takes, but there are dark forces at work at Northcote. There are those who do not like the way Cecilia runs the house and wish to cause trouble for her.

They come in the form of Charles Barton's two sisters, Jane and Margaret, and though Cecilia makes me laugh heartily with her impressions of them eating like pigs out of troughs and asking for my help to squeeze their 'huge' frames into dresses too small for them, the two women make me very nervous.

I have heard them talking, and Cecilia is unaware how much they detest her. Their power over Charles makes me very uneasy. Blood, after all, is thicker than water. They have huge influence also over the servants, some of whom have worked for the family all their lives and, despite Cecilia's genuine love for her staff, that love is seen as weakness.

It is a mistress's role to be strong and firm with her staff, not to be cruel but to instill a respect which commands a sense of stability. Cecilia gives no such sense of stability to the house, and her affection for those who work for her is often mocked in the servants' quarters. I chastise those I overhear, but I know the Barton sisters encourage it, and so it bubbles away under the surface. They feel she is a joke, a plaything for their rather immature brother until he finds a more suitable wife.

And as long as Cecilia doesn't fall pregnant, she cannot give him the heir which will give her security.

Mr Barton, I can tell, is slowly picking up on these undercurrents. Indeed, he has confessed to me that his sisters are formidable creatures of whom everyone is terrified, and that he is used to the women in his life taking control. I can see that Mr Barton married for love and to bring some tenderness into his life but, unfortunately, a young girl with little life experience and a carefree disposition was perhaps not the best choice to deal with all matters to do with Northcote while he spends his days hunting and roaring around in sports cars.

In between his violent outbursts Jacob has become totally withdrawn from me. He no longer speaks of the demons of war still haunting him, although from his sleep-talking I know that they do. He sits by the fire every night drinking whisky until he falls asleep, never coming into our bed. Mr Barton seems to be very pleased with him, mostly because he never rests. He is convinced that the Germans are trying to get on to the property, and he obsesses about booby traps in the garden and dangerous radio waves in the house picking up every conversation the Bartons have. I seem invisible to him. When I try to speak to him, he just looks through me.

In Cecilia Barton, however, he seems to have found a kindred spirit. I have seen them talking in the gardens. I watch from the window until I am noticed, and Cecilia waves up at me cheerily. Jacob stares at her, the way he looked at me before the war.

'Could I trouble you to help me with this blasted clasp, Hattie?'

Harriet, who had been sewing at the French windows, watching Cecilia and Jacob talking intensely to one another in the grounds, turned to the open door of Cecilia's bedroom, where Charles's sister Jane stood.

'Of course, Madam.'

'You are wonderful, Harriet. Everyone is so pleased with your work here,' Jane said, smiling in a way that Harriet didn't trust.

'Thank you, Madam.' Harriet's stomach knotted as she wrestled with the clasp at the neck of Jane's dress. In contrast to Cecilia, who had porcelain skin, Jane's was like a lizard's despite a film of sweat always permanently oozing from her skin. She also had a slight spattering of hair above her lip which moved when she spoke. Harriet could feel Jane watching Cecilia and Jacob.

'Cecilia was rather lost before you came to Northcote, and you have done wonders for her. You and your husband.' Jane stood at the window and stared down at Cecilia and Jacob as Cecilia reached out her hand to touch his arm. As they spoke it started to rain and one of the maids ran across the garden but the two of them stood rooted to the spot, oblivious.

Jane turned and smiled, showing her slightly yellowing teeth. 'I do commend the way you don't suffer with jealousy. You really are a good sort.'

Harriet felt her chest tighten, panicked at the warning bell that Jane was giving her, that Cecilia and Jacob's behavior had been noticed. 'Madam,' said Harriet, curtseying, desperate to escape the trap Jane was trying to set for her. 'Will there be anything else?'

'No, thank you.' Jane put her hand briefly on Harriet's arm before walking slowly from the room.

Harriet nodded, unable to speak for holding the tears back. She pulled on a coat and boots and ran out into the rain. Cecilia and Jacob had vanished. Harriet ran to the outbuildings calling out Jacob's name, until she eventually found him in the hay loft of the old barn.

'What are you doing out here?' she asked, out of breath, pulling her coat tightly around her against the cold.

'This is where I'm sleeping from now on,' he said matter-of-factly. 'I can't be in the house.'

She looked at him, his hair bedraggled, his clothes dirty and wet, his face drawn. 'Jacob, what do you mean?'

'The house is bugged. The Germans are watching us. I've seen them in town, the people that tried to kill us in Normandy. They followed me back here. I need to sleep here so that I'm ready when they come.'

Harriet covered her mouth and fought back the tears, then took several breaths, trying to calm herself. 'Jacob. You can't stay here. You'll get ill from the damp. What about when winter comes? You'll die of cold.'

'Then you'll be glad,' he said simply, looking up at her.

'Jacob, what do you mean? I love you. I would never want anything to happen to you.'

'You're one of them. I've seen you talking to them in town about me, the people watching me. You wanted me to go to war. You would have stopped me going otherwise.'

'Jacob! I never wanted you to go to war. You're my husband, I love you. If you hate it here, let's leave. How are we ever to have a baby if we do not sleep in the same bed?'

Jacob stared at her and frowned, then stood and walked over to her. His breath smelt of alcohol.

'Why is all that matters to you to have a child? To have a son who will be sent off to be blown apart in another war? Or a daughter who has a life of servitude like yours?' He paused then and as he walked closer to her, his eyes narrowed. 'There's no baby because there is no love between us now. You only wish that they would come and take me away now so you can be rid of me. I see the way you look at me.'

'Jacob, that's not true.' Harriet stepped forward and took Jacob's hand which he pulled away. 'I love you. I would do anything to go back to the way we were and be happy

120

again. If you could take your eyes from Cecilia for one moment, you would see that.'

In a flash of rage, he struck her. She tried to right herself but he had hit her so hard that she spun round and with nothing to grab hold of she lost her balance and fell into the stable door. She felt a sharp pain splinter through her temple where she landed against the wrought iron hinge and she felt her heart thudding hard in her ears, pushing her blood out through the break in her skin. She stood up in a daze and put her hand to her head as the blood oozed slowly out across her palm.

When she looked over at Jacob he was staring at her with cold steely eyes; no remorse, no concern and as he walked towards her, she flinched, terrified that he would hit her again.

But instead he kept walking, a small smile of satisfaction on his face as though he were pleased that she had finally been taught a much-needed lesson.

And she had.

As small droplets of blood splashed onto the pale hay of the stable floor, she knew with absolute certainty, that their love was gone. That the old Jacob had died on the beaches of Normandy and was never coming home to her.

And if her beloved was dead, so too was any hope of her one day becoming a mother.

Chapter Thirteen

Iris

12:30 p.m. Wednesday, 19 November 2014

As Harvey Roberts left the room in which the press conference had been held and the roar of camera shutters finally died down, Iris Waterhouse clicked the stop button on her Dictaphone and looked down at her notes.

It had been almost ten years since she had last seen him, but Harvey was clearly a man in a great deal of turmoil. Even though it had been a fairly short statement, he had still had to compose himself twice, the first time as he talked about what a natural mother his daughter was to baby Elizabeth, the second after telling her she had nothing to fear by letting someone – anyone – know where she was. Iris had made sure she had stayed at the back of the room, not wanting to be spotted by Harvey, but she needn't have worried. He seemed to be in another world entirely and, despite the way he had treated her mother over the years, her heart went out to him.

He was still a handsome man, tall and slim with broad shoulders, but his silver hair was thinning, his face weather-beaten, and heavy crow's feet lined his blue eyes.

She wasn't sure if it had been the police's intention to make him look dishevelled, but if it was, they had succeeded:

shirt unpressed, cheeks gaunt and stubble visible. Liz had died two years ago, and Harvey Roberts certainly looked like a man who was desperately missing his wife – and now his daughter and granddaughter too.

A young photographer with a goatee and a large grin asked her, 'So Adam's the baby's father? Where's he been, then?'

Iris smiled awkwardly. 'He's a travel photographer, I think, and he's away with work,' she said, adding that it was gossip she'd overheard in the toilet.

The young man nodded but said nothing. Iris hated being with the pack, mostly because of her inability to banter. She would stand in silence, her mind blank, watching the new recruits with envy as they darted about in conversation, making everyone laugh and getting titbits of useful information in the process.

It was the side of journalism she loathed, preferring instead to hide away at her desk in her role as health correspondent, doggedly doing her research, attending medical conferences and meeting with obscure contacts. All things that took time and commitment, neither of which she'd had much of lately. As such, she hadn't come up with any strong, leading stories for the best part of a year. And her refusal to cave in and revert to the new way of doing things – regurgitating press releases and calling it journalism or camping out on some poor soul's doorstep until they gave in – was what had caused Miles to run out of patience.

He must have called her two dozen times, asking for an update. Word from the pack huddled in the cold outside the hospital was that not one member of the hospital staff – medical or otherwise – or any of the discharged patients who had left the maternity ward at St Dunstan's Hospital that day had given an interview to the press. On top of which, all the sightings of Jessie and her baby had turned out to be dead ends.

Meanwhile, public interest in the story was gathering pace with radio stations running the story all morning, and social media awash with the CCTV images the police had released of Jessie walking out of the hospital into the bitter cold with baby Elizabeth wrapped in nothing but a blanket. The press conference had been rammed with news crews from all over the south of England, and by the time the lunchtime news aired, Iris had no doubt that the entire country would know Jessie's name.

Although no one dared say it, it felt as if the expectation was that there would at some point be an announcement that their bodies had been found in some dreadful setting.

The focus at the newsdesk didn't seem to be on finding Jessie but on assigning blame; scapegoating whoever was responsible for letting Jessie walk out of the hospital and hanging them out to dry.

And Miles was relying on her – and her contact: Mark Hathaway, an A&E consultant based at St Dunstan's Hospital.

The problem was that she hadn't spoken to Mark for months, since they'd snuck out of the British Medical Association annual representative meeting and gone for a rather drunken dinner together – after which Mark had kissed her. Despite the fact that her husband had left her for a woman half his age, and Iris definitely fancied the tall, fair-haired, blue-eyed doctor whom she had known since university days, she had bolted and sobbed the entire journey home in a train carriage full of chanting Chelsea fans.

And it seemed that Mark had been – understandably – confused, as they had spent several months flirting outrageously with each other and exchanging indiscreet banter over email – all of which fell deathly silent after the unfortunate encounter, despite Iris' best efforts to resurrect them.

She missed him. They had been friends since attending their first post-mortem at medical school in Bristol when he had clocked her turning green as the rotting corpse had his kidney pulled out, and he'd slipped her his hip flask which she'd gratefully taken a slug from in the toilet.

After that, they had bonded, often bumping into each other in the student bar or the library, until one fateful day Mark had introduced her to a latecomer to the course who had been kicked out of University College London and had decided to try his luck on the Bristol course instead – turning her world upside down in the process: James Hennesey.

The police press room was emptying fast. Most of the news crews were already gone and footage would be winging its way to newsrooms, to be broadcast on the lunchtime news within the hour. After that, the phones in the incident room would be ringing off the hook with possible sightings and tip-offs.

Iris pulled out her phone and saw that she had four missed calls on her mobile: two from Miles at the news desk, one from her solicitor and one from Mark. Rushing to get away from the noise as the press packed up, she made her way out into the hallway and past the incident room, where rows of call handlers were being briefed by DCI Bell

125

before the onslaught began following Harvey's appeal due to air on the lunchtime news.

She sat on the steps outside the station and raced through the other messages until she reached the final one from Mark. Her heart jolted into life when she heard his voice, although he sounded slightly cautious. 'Hi, Iris, thanks for your message. Hope you're well. Sorry, I only just finished my shift and then they called us into a meeting about this missing girl and her baby. We've been given strict instructions not to speak to anyone from the press.' Mark paused. Iris felt her heart sink. 'But as it's you, obviously, I will meet you briefly. But please don't tell anyone. It will have to be strictly off the record.'

A small smile broke on Iris's lips. There was hope, after all. She tapped into her phone the name of café Mark said he would meet her at in less than an hour and just as she finished it rang again. 'Mum Mob' flashed up.

'Hi, Mum. You okay?' she said.

Silence.

'Mum? Are you there?' Iris pressed the phone to her ear as the traffic roared past.

'I've just seen Harvey on the news,' said Rebecca. Iris could tell her mother had been crying. 'I should have been there beside him. What if Jessie thinks I don't care about her?'

'Mum, she would never think that.'

'The policeman here with me is asking me all about my parents and the night they died. I hate talking about it, Iris.' Iris could hear her mother's voice breaking.

'Why are they bringing that up? What's your parents' death got to do with Jessie?' Iris held her breath, waiting to hear if her suspicions were correct.

126

'Because she asked me about it, when she came to see me. I had to tell them, and I wish I hadn't. But he kept pressing me, just like Jessie did when I saw her last week. He knew I was holding something back. Why won't the past ever leave me in peace? I can't stand it.'

'Oh Mum, I wish I was there to give you a hug.' Iris felt a desperate need to protect her mother, to drive to her house and be there for her, but the need to grill her about what she actually told Jessie was overwhelming.

'So I know you don't want to talk about it, but did you tell Jessie anything about that night that might have surprised or upset her?'

'No!' snapped Rebecca. 'Just because I hate talking about it, doesn't mean I'm hiding anything. It's all there for anyone who wants to see. I've told the police the inquest report is in the coroner's office, along with the cuttings painting every gruesome detail. Why are they fixating on something that happened over fifty years ago rather than finding Jessie? They aren't telling me anything, Iris! Where is she? Where has she gone? I always knew something bad was going to happen to her, and I was right. I knew it from the day she was born.' Rebecca was crying quietly and Iris could picture her tucked away somewhere in her house where she couldn't be heard by the family liaison officer.

'Mum, listen to me. You've done nothing wrong. Harvey and Liz made it impossible for you. You're the best mum in the world, and we're going to find Jessie. Okay? Can you get one of your friends round to sit with you? I hate to think of you at home on your own.'

'There's something else.' Rebecca paused. 'The baby has

an infection, Iris. They think it's Strep B. She was on intravenous antibiotics.'

'How do you know?' said Iris.

'The police liaison officer just told me. It's not good, Iris. That baby won't survive long on her own if she's got Strep B. Until morning, I'd say. I'll never forgive myself if she dies.'

'Mum, this is not your fault. How many more times do I have to tell you? I'll do what I can, okay, see if I can find out anything from the pack. Promise me you'll call a friend to come round?' Iris ended the call and let out a heavy sigh.

She had always respected her mother's wishes not to talk about the night her parents were killed, but now she had a legitimate reason – a duty, even – to try and find out what she could. Jessie had obviously grilled her mother about it and Iris needed to know why.

Iris googled 'Coroner's Office, Chichester', dialled the number and promptly explained her situation to a very helpful woman.

'If you're a relative, you can see the file here at the records office. We'd need a copy of your ID and a request in writing, then we'll get back to you within five working days.'

'Is there any chance it could be sooner? I hate to ask but it relates to an urgent family matter,' Iris added, already bubbling over with curiosity about seeing a file which she had never dared seek out before.

'I can try. The coroner is in today, but she's very busy. I can't make any promises. Strange, this is the second request we've had in a week for this file.'

Iris felt her heart lurch. 'Really? Do you know the name of the person who asked for it?'

'I can't share that information, I'm afraid, but it was a relative, so the coroner approved the request. Hopefully, that will work in your favour, as it's not been sent back to the main archive so we'd still have it at the County Records Office.'

'Okay. Thank you for your help. I really appreciate it,' said Iris, and hung up. She tried to process the information. If it was a relative, it had to be Jessie, but why? And had she read something in the inquest file that had prompted her to go and see their mother about it?

Iris's phone beeped again. Miles, chasing. She quickly typed a reply.

Contact has been in touch, hopefully meeting him shortly. Will let you know update asap.

Iris looked up to see a taxi, its light on, making its way up the road towards her, and with both fear and excitement coursing through her at the thought of what lay in wait for her at the County Records Office, she ran towards it.

Chapter Fourteen

When I wake, Rosie has gone. It feels like night-time and the pain in my chest is even more acute. I am sore and exhausted from coughing for hours. I look out of the window and see a small crowd of people huddled together outside the hospital.

I look around. I am scared to move because I know, if I do, I will start coughing again. I want to sit up, but I can't reach the red call button and I start to become breathless again. I feel panic and try to calm myself, but the coughing starts anyway. I try and turn on my side, and manage to press the call button. A nurse I don't recognize comes over to my bed and, as she sits me up, I vomit green phlegm over myself.

'I'm sorry,' I say when I'm able to take some shallow breaths.

'Don't apologize, you're okay,' she says, handing me a cup of water. I take a sip. I have nothing inside me and I can picture the water swishing around my empty stomach. This nurse is dark-haired and when she smiles it is as if she's on autopilot. She is brisker than the other nurse, banging at my pillows and pulling at my blankets sharply so that it makes me jump.

'Who are those people out there? With the cameras?'

'Journalists. A woman and her baby have gone missing from the hospital. It was on the news. I'll just go and get you a clean gown, then I'll do you a bed bath.'

Her words shock me. I think again of the man on the lunchtime news, Harvey Roberts. My mind races. Perhaps he was here. Perhaps he is still here now.

The nurse comes back and cleans me up. After I have coughed most of the way through it, I realize that I am struggling to breathe all the time now. It feels like I am trying to live on another planet; I am a long way from home but I have no idea where home is. I'm more tired than I've ever felt in my life. I'm barely able to keep my eyes open. I start to doze off but a tall, slender man in a checked shirt with a stethoscope around his neck appears at the end of the bed.

'Good evening. I'm Dr Evans, the medical consultant. How are you feeling?'

'Tired,' I say tentatively, scared to speak in case it sets off another fit of coughing.

The dark-haired nurse speaks. 'She had an unsettled evening because she is coughing so much. Her saturations were a bit low so we gave her some oxygen, but I think she might need a nasal cannula because she kept pulling the mask off in her sleep.'

'Sounds like a good idea,' says Dr Evans, studying my chart. 'How's your chest?'

'Painful,' I say.

'Your temperature is 39.3, so it seems that your chest infection may be getting worse. Let's get another X-ray done. Ideally we need forty-eight hours to see if the antibiotics are working but if things don't improve overnight I'll substitute one. We'll keep a close eye on you and monitor your oxygen levels. I'd recommend eating something, if you can, then try and catch up on some sleep.'

I try to sleep but every time I doze off I am back on the beach with the wave looming over our heads. But it never breaks, and I am standing, holding my baby, staring up at the skyscraper made of water, knowing there is nothing I can do. I cannot run. I cannot hide from it. There is no escape. It is going to break over us and all I can do is wait for it to happen.

The sky outside grows orange, the crowd of journalists dwindles, and the endless coming-and-going in my room begins to slow. I hear the day drawing to a close: visitors stop walking past my room, the chatter at the nurses' station quietens, the starlings begin their evening flight outside my window. Every time someone appears at my door I pray that it is Rosie. I don't know if I will see her again; perhaps she has to work late or cannot come again today. I am too scared to ask the other nurse when she is coming back, because I will be embarrassed how I will react if she is not.

A plate of food is put in front of me, but I tell the nurse I don't want it and turn to watch the starlings twist and turn in one swirling, liquid mass. It soothes my agitated mind and my eyes begin to feel heavy. As I fall asleep I hear a baby cry and it jerks me awake. I begin to cough again and cannot stop. I cannot catch my breath and, for the first time, I feel truly frightened. I try and reach for the alarm, but I can't. I am dizzy now and am struggling for breath.

I am starting to lose my vision as the door opens again. I hear footsteps rushing towards me and someone eases me forward and puts the oxygen mask over my face. They rub my back as the oxygen rushes into my system and gradually I can breathe again.

'You're okay.' I know that voice but I'm too scared to open my eyes in case it's not her. I'm putting too much pressure on Rosie. I don't know what I expect from her. What can she really change? She eases me back and when I see that beautiful face that has always showed me such kindness, I know that I and my baby may still have a chance.

'I hear you haven't been eating. You won't get better if you don't eat.' Rosie smiles that lovely smile, her blue eyes gleaming, reminding me of aquamarine. I am sure, more than ever, that she is my angel. The relief that she is here makes me feel like a lost child who has been found.

I smile and take her hand. She sits down next to me. 'I'm going to ask if I can sit with you tonight,' she says. 'I don't think you should be on your own. It's either that, or you go on a ventilator in the intensive care unit, and they don't want to send you down there until it's really necessary.'

Panic streaks through me as she says this. I squeeze her hand hard. I try and speak through the mask, which makes me cough again. She gently takes it off.

'I don't want that. I don't want to go on a ventilator. Promise me you won't let them,' I say.

'That's a conversation I'd really like to have with your daughter. Which is why I want to spend some proper time with you, to see if I can help you find her.'

Tears fill my eyes, but I can't reply so I just nod. She feeds me and I manage a few mouthfuls and feel a little better.

'Did you see the journalists outside?' I ask.

'Yes, it was a right pain getting through the entrance. Apparently, the girl who has gone missing with her new-born baby was at this hospital.' Rosie puts her coat on the back of her chair and throws today's *Chichester Evening Herald* newspaper on my bedside table.

'Jessica Roberts,' I say, scared to utter the words, pushing myself to tell her.

'Yes,' says Rosie, frowning. 'How do you know her name?'

'I saw the news. I recognized her father, Harvey Roberts.' Slowly, I point to his picture on the front of the paper.

'What?' says Rosie, leaning in. 'Are you sure?'

I nod. 'It was a long time ago, but I know his name and his face is much the same. My father used to rent Seaview from Ted Roberts. We spent our summers there.'

'Seaview?' Rosie says, 'What's that?' She picks up the paper, staring at the image of Jessica Roberts intently.

I look at her. 'It's the link, between me and my baby.'

And then I tell her.

Chapter Fifteen

Rebecca

Friday, 14 November 2014

Rebecca stood in her living room watching her eldest daughter break down in front of her and felt utterly helpless.

'Jessie, I know we didn't have the best start. It haunts me every day, and I want to try and be honest with you about what happened. But it isn't straightforward, it's extremely complicated. You just need to try and be patient with me. Please?'

'I shouldn't have come here,' said Jessie as Rebecca handed her a tissue.

'Yes, you should, and I'm so happy that you have,' said Rebecca, sitting down next to her and taking her hand. 'But there's so much ground to make up. I've wanted to explain to you for so long, but I've never really been able to get to you.'

'What do you mean, you haven't been able to get to me?' Jessie snapped defensively, pulling her hand away.

Rebecca looked at her nervously. 'I suppose what I mean is I feel I've tried very hard over the years to build a relationship with you, but I think Liz felt –' Rebecca stopped herself, knowing that any criticism of Jessie's stepmother would drive her daughter away, 'quite rightly, very protective of you.'

'Well, someone needed to,' Jessie said quietly.

Rebecca shifted in her seat. Her shoulders were so tense they were starting to ache. 'Of course. I'm happy that you had her to do such a good job of looking after you.'

'You don't mean that. You never liked her. You couldn't have been more obvious about it.' Rebecca looked at Jessie, her face the same as it had been as a teenager on the weekends she had gone up to Wittering to visit her daughter, or on the rare occasions Jessie had come to stay with John, Iris and her, when she had spent most of their hours together seemingly sulking, in her room.

'Look, Jessie, if it helps you to sling mud at me, that's fine, but I don't think it helps us to try and get to the truth.'

'The truth?' Jessie scoffed. 'You're allergic to the truth. You just want to bury your head in the sand and pretend me and Dad don't exist.'

'That's not true. I love you, Jessie. Iris and I talk about you all the time, how sad we are that you're not a proper part of our lives, but I don't know how to reach you.'

Rebecca stumbled over her words, looking at Jessie, afraid she would walk out at any moment.

'Well, you could try,' Jessie said quietly.

'I have tried, Jessie. I promise you.'

'How? With a few phone calls and birthday cards?' Jessie quipped.

Rebecca let out a sigh of exasperation. 'Jessie, I fought to keep you every day. I cried myself to sleep every night over you, for years. What did you want me to do?'

'I don't know. Sleep in your car outside the house. Write

to me every day telling me how much you love me. Find a way to show me you gave a shit.' Jessie threw her arms up in exasperation.

'Look, I don't think this is helping,' said Rebecca flatly.

'It's helping me. We've spent our whole lives pretending with one another. It's nice to be honest for once.' Jessie glared at her mother.

'It was just very hard trying to have any time just the two of us, or a proper conversation even, when Liz was always there.'

'Well, she's not here now,' Jessie said, biting her cheek.

'I know, and I can't imagine how hard it has been for you. She has been like a mother to you since you were a baby. I tried very hard to have a relationship with her, I promise you I did. But she was a very strong character, and your dad employed her as a nanny without even asking me. It was a tough situation,' Rebecca said gently.

'What?' said Jessie. 'Dad employed her? Not you?'

Rebecca shook her head. 'He saw an advert in the post office window. Liz was looking for work. I know he didn't mean any harm, but I was getting better. I was still exhausted and on strong antidepressants, but I was doing it. We were starting to bond, I was feeling stronger, we were in a routine.'

Rebecca leaned in to Jessie, encouraged that her daughter seemed to be listening to her side of the story – for once.

'I got you up at six, fed you, then we drove to the hospital together – you were at the crèche all day from about four months old. But it was a very long day, and your dad was worried about us both. I remember I'd had a bad week. One of the doctors at work made a complaint about me as

I had to leave on time every day to collect you so I wasn't able to do any overtime. I was starting to feel very anxious again. Your dad interviewed Liz while I was at work one day. I came home and he said that he had a plan. Liz would live in and take care of you so my work didn't suffer in the week. And then we would spend weekends together as a family.'

Jessie tried to process what her mother was saying. 'So you were never there. And then Liz and Dad fell in love?'

Rebecca shook her head. 'Me and your father should never have been together. It was one night, an explosion of emotion, of everything we'd been through.'

'I should never have happened, you mean!'

'No, that is not what I said. Our relationship is very hard to explain. We grew up together – we were joined at the hip. I ran to your dad on the nights my father beat my mother, and his father took me in when my parents were killed. We've always had an incredibly strong bond, but we were more like brother and sister. He wanted someone like Liz. He needed a woman like Liz. Someone who wanted to be at Seaview, at home, a homebody. To help him run the farm. Seaview was a place so wracked with terrible memories that even being there made it almost impossible for me to function. But having Liz did make things trickier between us, between you and me, because of course you spent so much time with her. And, before long,' Rebecca paused at the painful memory, 'you didn't want me any more.'

Rebecca looked over at her daughter. Jessie was lost in thought, trying to take it all in.

'Look, what I'm trying to say – badly – is that if you

want to know what happened when you were born, I need to be honest, and I can't really do that without, maybe, contradicting what you've been told. Which could be upsetting for you.'

'I haven't been told anything. That's the problem. I can't believe what you've just told me about Liz. I thought it was all your idea to get a nanny, so you were free.' Jessie shook her head.

'No, and you seem to think I left you behind,' Rebecca said gently.

'Well, you did, that's true! Whatever way you spin it, you put your job before me.'

Rebecca shook her head. 'That's not true, Jessie. But telling you the truth involves hearing things about your dad and Liz that might not be easy for you to hear. I'm not saying I'm blameless, but it was a very difficult time and, in the end, I had very little choice.'

'You always have a choice. My baby's not even born yet and I already know I could never give her up.' Jessie spoke quietly, her head down, playing with the tissue in her hands.

'It's a girl?' said Rebecca gently, a glow of happiness infiltrating the pain of their discussion.

Jessie nodded.

'That's wonderful.' Rebecca edged towards her daughter and put an arm around her. 'I can't wait to meet her.'

'I feel so worried about her all the time. Like I'm going to do something that's going to hurt her, or . . .'

'Hurt her?' Rebecca frowned.

'I don't know. Did you feel worried all the time? When you were pregnant with me? Is that how it started?'

'To be honest, I can't remember how it started.'

'Can you at least try?'

Rebecca looked into her daughter's deep emerald eyes. They pierced through her now, staring at her expectantly, as if Rebecca had all the answers to her burning questions. Just as they had on the day she was born.

She could still hear the deafening sound of babies crying on the ward, the overwhelming lights that had scorched down on her as they stitched her up, the crashing hospital trolleys, a voice in her head which she had started to hear during Jessie's birth.

As Harvey had fussed around her, taking photographs of Jessie, the male voice got louder, terrifying her, until she had felt the strangest sensation of something snapping in her head.

And then suddenly he was there.

Detective Inspector Gibbs, the man who had questioned her over and over until dawn on the night her parents died, who wouldn't believe her, and haunted her dreams ever since, had appeared in the corner of her hospital room, arms folded, watching her silently as she held her newborn baby in her arms.

And despite her terror and her tears, and him being as real to her as Harvey was, nobody but her could see him.

Chapter Sixteen

Iris

2:30 p.m. Wednesday, 19 November

Iris sat in the corner of the small café off Chichester High Street anxiously watching the door. She looked down at her watch, then at her phone, then back at the door. Mark Hathaway was half an hour late and hadn't responded to her text.

The first issue of the paper went to print at 4 p.m., and Miles was having a stroke about the fact that she hadn't come up with anything yet. She had taken a huge gamble in not telling Miles that the only reason she'd heard about this story was because the missing girl was her half-sister. She'd had no idea when she'd first called the newsdesk that this would turn into such a huge story.

All she did know was that time was running out for baby Elizabeth and she cared a great deal more about Jessie's welfare than she did about filing a story. The fact was, her only chance of holding it all together and not losing her job was if Mark gave her something to get Miles off her back.

But for now, all she could do was sit and wait. Her eyes fell on a woman in the corner of the café feeding her baby and she found it hard to tear her gaze away. It had started to rain and she pictured Jessie out there somewhere with her newborn and suddenly felt a wave of anger. She knew what was happening to Jessie was not her fault, that she needed help, but as she watched the doting mother stroking her baby's flushed cheek, she couldn't help but feel the cruel irony that Jessie had the one thing she wanted more than anything in the world, and yet was putting that precious gift at risk. She looked at her watch again.

Iris felt a cold blast of air as the door opened and she looked up to see her old friend walking through the door, with little droplets of rain on his flushed cheeks and a long black coat over his tall, slim frame. His blue eyes scanned the room and settled on Iris. She smiled gently, trying not to show the overwhelming relief she felt that he had turned up.

'Hi, Iris,' said Mark, kissing her slightly awkwardly on one cheek before pulling off his coat and setting it on the back of a chair. Drops of water trickled on to the floor underneath it.

'Hi, Mark. Thank you so much for coming,' she said, smiling in spite of the butterflies in her stomach.

'No problem,' he said. 'I'm afraid I've only got twenty minutes, we're really short-staffed today.'

'Of course. Can I get you a tea or anything?' she said, surprised at how good it felt to see him.

'I'll get it, would you like one?' he said. She shook her head and he walked over to the counter and ordered. Iris felt her cheeks flush self-consciously as Mark looked back at her and smiled. 'It's so bloody cold,' he said as he collapsed back into his seat. 'I can't stop thinking about that girl being out there with her baby. Senior management are

142

really freaking out at the hospital about this one. I've never seen a group of journalists outside the hospital before. It's making St Dunstan's look bad that she managed to get out. They've called all the senior staff in to work out whose head is going to roll.'

Iris could still feel the cold radiating from Mark. His nose was slightly pink and he clutched his mug to warm his hands.

'What I don't understand is how it was possible for her to leave the hospital without being noticed? Isn't there any security?' said Iris.

'Yes, there are security measures in place, but no one has any idea what it's like being a midwife on a busy postnatal ward,' said Mark, shaking his head. 'It can be horrendous, exhausting and, quite frankly, bloody dangerous when it's short-staffed – which is the case most of the time because they've made so many cuts. They keep playing that image on television of the poor woman walking out of the hospital with her baby. They're clearly just waiting for the news that she's jumped off a bridge or under a train.'

'Listen, Mark, there's something I should tell you,' Iris said, her voice shaking slightly. 'I didn't want to say anything on the phone, but Jessie is my half-sister.'

Mark stared at her wide-eyed. 'Well, now I feel like a complete shit. I'm so sorry, Iris.' Mark put his hand over hers.

Iris felt herself welling up. 'I'm sorry, Mark, you don't need this. I'm just so worried about Jessie and I've dug myself into a hole not telling my boss that me and Jessie are related. I had no idea the story would end up being so big. I just wanted try and get the inside story for my mum.'

The woman with the baby pushed past them with her buggy, interrupting them. Iris stood to move out of her way and suddenly felt dizzy as the heat from the steamed-up café became claustrophobic. It was so good to see a friendly face after the day she'd had, but it was throwing her off guard. She had missed Mark more than she had admitted to herself, but knowing him well she could tell that he wasn't his usual self around her.

'Presumably the police are telling you more than they're telling us?' said Mark, frowning.

'Not really, she seems to have just vanished. They've received hundreds of calls to the incident number but that all takes time to follow up I suppose,' Iris added. 'And they've got to trawl through hours of CCTV footage. They said at the press conference the last images of her show her walking towards Chichester train station. But she wasn't seen on any of the train platforms. Nobody's seen her since. None of her bank cards have been used, so if she and the baby are still alive, they must have been taken in by someone. There's no other explanation, they can't survive out in this weather.'

'And you're having to report on this for work? Isn't that a bit much?' said Mark, taking a gulp of his tea.

'I haven't said that she's my sister. It was my idea to come here and try to find her. But I'm not sure it was a good one.' Iris took another sip of hot tea and added a sugar. She hadn't eaten all day, but watching people eating in the café turned her stomach. 'My mother phoned this morning to tell me Jessie had gone missing and to ask if I could find out anything. It's a long story, but things aren't good between her and Harvey, Jessie's dad.'

'The man who spoke at the press conference? I wondered where her mum was. So the great Doctor Rebecca Waterhouse is also Jessie's mother?'

'Yes, and she was asked by Harvey not to attend the press conference, so she's at home with a police liaison officer, tearing her hair out. Things were never great between her and Jessie. Our family's always been a bit screwed up.'

'Every family is a bit screwed up.' Iris understood Mark was referring to his own messy divorce and his ex-wife making it as difficult as she could for him to see his twelve-year-old son.

'She had Jessie when she first qualified, and it was all quite a struggle, I think,' said Iris.

'Yes, well, your mother was one of the first female paediatric consultants in the country, wasn't she? You don't get to be a trailblazer like that without making some personal sacrifices.'

'Well, my dad was a hundred per cent behind her, they were a good team.'

'And what's your relationship with Jessie like?'

Iris just shrugged. 'I don't know. It's complicated.'

'Does your sister have a history of depression?' he asked.

'I don't know, but it wouldn't surprise me.' Iris ran her finger round the edge of her mug, lost in thought. 'I don't know much about it, but my mother had very bad postnatal psychosis when she had her.'

Mark nodded. 'Well, postnatal psychosis is familial. And the fact that Jessie chose to leave is making me think she is psychotic rather than depressed. Obviously it's not my area of expertise but she must have been convinced that her baby's life was in danger if she stayed. And she would have had to wait for the right moment, when the doors were open for a second and the midwives were distracted. It wouldn't have been easy.'

'They think the baby's got Strep B, she needs to be on antibiotics, it's not good,' said Iris quietly. 'I wish she'd come to me. I've been thinking all day about how I wish I'd been a better sister to her. My mum always pandered to her when she came to stay, and it made me really jealous, but of course I know now that it must have been really hard for Jessie – having an annoying younger sister to look after.'

Mark smiled cheekily. 'Did you follow her around when she came to stay?'

Iris nodded. 'Yup, everywhere. I even made her a mix tape once with all the songs I could find with the word sister in them.'

'Oh dear, did she like it?'

Iris shook her head. 'Nope, she gave it back to me and said it wasn't really her thing.'

'Harsh,' said Mark, taking a sip of tea. 'Come on, she's your sister, you must have one happy memory of her.'

'I do remember this one time that we got lost in the woods. It was a rare weekend that we had together and we took the dog for a walk. I suppose I was about twelve and she was seventeen. It started to get dark and really cold and I remember I was panicking. Every path we took seemed to take us deeper and it started to rain and I began to cry.' Iris paused, frowning at the memory. 'She'd been snapping at me to keep up until that point, and suddenly she changed completely. She held my hand and we sat under a tree, and she put her coat over our heads to make a shelter, and then she told me a story. It was all about this little girl called Iris, who was the apple of her parents' eye, who played the piano, and made the best apple crumble and loved ghost stories and would give anyone her last Rolo. I thought she didn't know me at all, and she didn't care, and I suddenly realized she was just sad, because she thought my mum loved me more than her. And the sad thing is, my mum doesn't love me more. She really doesn't.'

'You have to find her, Iris,' he said, matter-of-factly, as if he was the first person that day to have thought it.

'I know I do, but how?' said Iris, wiping away a tear with a crackly café napkin.

'I'd like to help more, Iris, but all I can do is give you the name of the midwife who was assigned to your sister,' he said, scribbling on a napkin. 'I can't give you an address, but presumably you can find that. She won't talk to you as press, but she might talk to you as Jessie's sister.'

Iris looked across the table at Mark. It was so typical of him to stick his neck out for her. She felt the overwhelming urge to throw her arms around him, but the noisy, stuffy café didn't seem the right place and somehow she didn't feel he would welcome it.

'Thank you,' she said, her voice trembling. 'And Mark, I'm really sorry about what happened last time I saw you.'

'You've got nothing to be sorry for. Good luck with it, Iris. I really should get going now, before I'm missed.' He pulled his coat from the back of the chair.

Mark left the café, leaving Iris alone with a napkin bearing the scribbled name of the last person to speak to her sister before she disappeared: Jane Trellis.

Chapter Seventeen

Harvey

3:30 p.m. Wednesday, 19 November

Harvey Roberts sat in the back of the police car, waiting for two police officers to push back the dozens of locals who had gathered at the gate of his house so the car could drive through.

DC Galt turned to him. 'Your liaison officer is here already, waiting for us. He's one of the best. I think you'll like him.'

Harvey said nothing, slightly irritated by her cheerful tone.

'He'll hopefully be able to bridge the gap between you and the investigation and answer any questions you have. As I mentioned at the station, the search team is still inside your house now, but hopefully they'll be finishing up soon.'

Harvey looked out of the window at the villagers waiting to be told what they could do to help. He'd known these people his whole life – been to school with them, drunk in the pub with them, worked with them on his farm – and now they stood gazing at him pitifully, as if he were off to be burnt at the stake.

Approaching the house, he overheard a snippet of

conversation. An old friend, Fred Samuels, who owned the grocery shop in the next village, was bearing down on one of the police officers who were trying to keep the crowd back. 'We've been here for three hours now, waiting to be told what to do. We want to help!'

'We don't need any more people to help with the search for the time being,' replied the officer. 'Best if you go home for now as we can't search in the dark. We'll let you know if we need any more help tomorrow.'

As he entered the house, he was greeted by a tall, blond man dressed in jeans and brown brogues, his small belly straining out of a light blue shirt. Behind him, in his living room, in his hallway and on the upstairs landing, he could see half a dozen police officers, all dressed in black, ransacking his house. One walked past him with Harvey's laptop, not even acknowledging him.

Harvey's eyes fell on a picture on the hall table of Liz and Jessie, a close-up of their smiling faces. He pictured them walking along, arms interlinked, deep in conversation.

'Harvey, this is DC Rayner, your family liaison officer,' said DC Galt, smiling gently. 'DC Rayner has a great deal of experience of working with families in these situations.'

'I still don't understand the point of going through my house? Am I suspected of something?'

'As you know, we've searched Jessie's flat and, as your daughter spent a significant amount of time here, we are just making sure we have done everything we can to understand her state of mind and work out where she might have gone.'

'Wouldn't your time be better spent actually looking? There are a lot of locals wanting to help, old friends who seem to have been standing out there for a while, waiting for you to coordinating a search,' said Harvey, looking at DC Galt. 'I don't understand why you are telling dozens of people who want to help that you don't need them?'

'I'm sure any offers of help are being managed appropriately,' said DC Galt.

'It doesn't sound to me like they are. I just heard one of your guys telling them all to go home.'

DC Rayner stepped forward. He was in his early fifties, Harvey guessed, and moved more slowly than Galt. He smiled gently at Harvey and put his hand out. Harvey shook it.

'Mr Roberts, shall we take a seat? It's been a long day, and I'd like to fill you in on what we are doing to find Jessica and her baby. I'll try to answer any questions you may have.'

'I've got a question for you. How was Jessie just allowed to walk out of hospital with a vulnerable newborn baby and not be stopped? And then just vanish into thin air?'

'Unfortunately, we don't know the answer to that yet, but the hospital will be conducting a review of what went wrong. And as for finding them, we've got twenty police officers on this, so we are doing everything in our power to try and work out where Jessica and Elizabeth have gone.'

'And what about the press conference? Has anyone called in? She's got a newborn for God's sake, someone must have seen her.'

DC Rayner gently put his hand on Harvey's elbow to lead him towards the kitchen table. 'You did a great job at the press conference, and in response to the broadcast we've had over a thousand calls to the incident room, and among them are two possible leads which we're following up now.

One, we're not permitted to share with you at this stage. As for the other, I can tell you that a lady called in to say that she found a baby's sock on a bus that goes from Chichester bus station, to Dell Quay, Birdham and West Wittering. Unfortunately, she picked it up and handed it to the driver so it's been contaminated, but it's with Forensics now and, from the blood tests the hospital did on baby Elizabeth, we have her DNA. We're doing tests on the sock to see if it matches. We'd also like you to take a look at it to see if you can identify it.'

'Of course. And what about the driver? Did he remember seeing Jessie?' Harvey leaned towards DC Rayner.

'Unfortunately the driver was on nights, the bus which the baby sock was found on this morning was the last route on his shift. We've been unable to contact him as yet, but we have a police car on its way to his house now to try and track him down.'

'I don't understand how Jessie could have got on a bus? There wasn't any CCTV of that, was there? Just her walking towards the train station.'

'It's possible that she walked through the station and got on a bus there, where there isn't CCTV. It would make sense, as there are no other CCTV sightings so we all assumed that she'd got on a train but she wasn't seen on any of the CCTV footage on the platforms.'

'So she may have headed towards Wittering?'

'It's a possibility. Does she have any connection with Wittering?'

'I used to own Seaview Farm in Wittering Bay. I inherited it from my father. But I sold it nearly forty years ago, when Jessie was baby.'

'Seaview Farm,' DC Galt repeated from the other side of the room, writing it down in her notebook.

'And did you ever go back there?'

'Not very often – it's a long, narrow and often traffic-choked road to the Witterings. It's one of the reasons I sold it. Jessie used to go with Liz in the summer holidays so it would make sense for her to go there. But you said this morning? Surely there's no way they could have been there all this time? It's bitter down there in the winter, harsh and exposed. I was there this morning with the dogs, before I knew Jessie was missing. I backed up for that bus! Are you telling me Jessie might have been on it?'

Harvey stared at DC Galt wide-eyed, his mind racing. 'But it's dark now, we won't be able to see them. If they are in the dunes, that baby will be freezing to death. You need to send out search parties along every stop of that route, she could have got off anywhere.' Harvey was pacing now.

'Well, we need to try and establish if she was on the bus, and the route covers a huge area. As you say, it's dark now, so we will probably start again at first light, once we've heard from Forensics and coordinated a search.'

'But the doctors said the baby didn't have long. That she would become seriously ill if she wasn't found within twelve hours.'

'It takes time to organize a search party, Mr Roberts. You need equipment, a search grid, and we need to coordinate everyone so that we're not wasting time covering the same ground.'

DC Rayner looked up at DC Galt. 'Could we arrange for a car to go over to Seaview Farm now, have a look around, speak to the current owners?'

'Sure,' said DC Galt, and left the room.

Harvey shook his head. 'We can't just sit here and wait for it to get light while they die out there. We might as well just wait for the call to say their bodies have been found. You're handing out Elizabeth's death sentence by doing nothing.'

'It is certainly not the case that we are doing nothing. We will send some officers down there with torches to search the dunes, if you think there's a possibility they could be there.'

Harvey let out a heavy sigh. 'Well, I'm putting some more layers on and heading down to that beach,' he said. 'And I'll be getting some of my friends out there to join me if that's all right with you.'

'I think it would be better if you stayed here, Mr Roberts, in case there are any developments.'

'I'll be on my mobile if anyone wants me.' He left the room, as DC Rayner watched him go and heard the thunder of Harvey's shoes up the stairs and onto the landing.

'Has anyone been to interview the elderly lady at St Dunstan's Hospital that the nurse called in about?' asked DC Galt as she walked back into the room.

'It wasn't a nurse, it was one of the staff from her care home. Rosie Jones I think the name was. We weren't sure if we were going to be able to speak to the elderly woman as they are talking about sending her down to ICU. Reading between the lines, they don't think she's got long,' added DC Rayner.

'And what is it that she said again which was of particular interest?' said DC Galt.

'She saw Harvey Roberts on the news at lunchtime, and said that he knew where her baby was.'

'Her baby, not Jessica's baby?' queried DC Galt.

'No, her baby. But the old lady knew Jessie. Or rather Jessie knew her. Jessie tried to get hold of her a couple of weeks ago, according to Rosie Jones. She came to the care home, but the old lady was asleep and Jessie didn't want to wake her. Rosie recognized her from the lunchtime news.'

'Who is this woman? Why would Jessie know her?' DC Galt scanned her notebook for any clues and then nodded her head. 'Okay, send a car to the hospital now. Can you update me once someone's spoken to her? Is someone on their way to Seaview now?'

'Yes,' said DC Rayner as Harvey's shoes came thundering down the stairs again.

Harvey watched one of the policemen who was carrying a box full of his belongings out of the front door grab the picture of Jessie and Liz which was sitting on the hall table.

As Harvey followed him out, he looked down at the photograph of the two women smiling into the camera, and in the background, on the cliffs behind them, Seaview Cottage.

Of course she would go to Wittering Bay. How could he have been so blind?

Harvey stopped in front of the policeman, blocking his path, and reached in to take the framed picture of his wife and daughter out of the box, before making his way out into the descending night.

Chapter Eighteen

Harriet

January 1947

Harriet Waterhouse stood on the driveway of Northcote House watching the ambulance take her sedated, restrained husband away to Greenways Lunatic Asylum. Feeling eyes on her she looked up to see Cecilia Barton staring down at her from her bedroom window. She was as white as a ghost and shaking, her hands pressed hard onto the glass of her balcony window and Harriet watched as she let out a silent scream.

'Are you all right, dear?' Harriet turned to the head housekeeper who was hustling back inside the servants who had come out to see what the commotion was.

'Yes. I just need a minute if that's okay?' Harriet managed, before rushing through the cold stone corridors to her bedroom, and curling up in a ball on the bed. Her head in her hands, she closed her eyes, and tried to make sense of the morning's events which she knew she would never be able to live down.

She had been laying out Cecilia's clothes for the day when she heard running footsteps along the stone corridor. Knowing that running in the hallways was forbidden at Northcote she'd had an immediate feeling of dread that

155

all was not well in the household. When a frantic knock came at her door, it was with trepidation that she opened it, to see one of the servant girls standing there, looking very pale.

'Sorry to bother you, Mrs Waterhouse,' she had said, out of breath from rushing. 'But Mr Jameson said to come and fetch you. There's been an incident in the kitchen involving your husband.'

Despite getting to the other side of the house as fast as she could, by the time they had reached the kitchen door, Jacob had managed to push the chopping block in front of it so that no one could get in or out. All they could hear was Cook screaming from the inside.

'What's happening?' she had asked Mr Jameson, the head butler, who was hammering at the door and shouting to be let in.

'Your husband has shut himself and Betty in. Apparently, he's convinced there are Germans occupying the house, and that Betty is to blame for fraternizing with them. He's torn the telephone out of the wall so we can't call the police and when he shut the door, he had a knife to Betty's throat.'

Harriet had stared at the head butler, then placed her hand against the cold, stone wall to steady herself just as Cook's piercing screams echoed again through the corridor where they stood.

She had then turned to the young servant girl who had fetched her from Cecilia's bedroom. 'Mary, run to the stables and tell Sam to cycle into town and call the police. He must tell them there is an emergency at Northcote and they've to come immediately. Go now, and hurry. Don't come back here saying you can't find him. If he's nowhere to be found, you go.'

'Yes, Mrs Waterhouse.'

She'd walked over to the kitchen door, asked Mr Jameson to step aside, and gently tapped on the door. 'Jacob? It's me, Harriet. Please open the door. You're frightening Betty. Let her go, Jacob. I know you don't want to hurt her.'

She had pleaded and begged for him to come out – all to no avail. And as she stood at the door, trying to come to terms with the horror that Jacob would most likely be incarcerated in an asylum, she began to pick apart the past months in her mind, trying to work out what she could have done to prevent it.

Despite Jacob totally withdrawing from her, she had still tried to visit him in the barn where he had lived for the past six months. But it had reached a point where she felt every visit angered him more, whilst the nest he had built for himself high up in the animal barn, with a view over the countryside, a paraffin lamp, his books and blankets seemed to have created some form of peace for him. So she had started recently to give up and leave him to the feral existence which appeared to make him calmer – as long as she stayed away.

Betty's screams had stopped now and Mr Jameson had begun hammering on the door again. Harriet pictured the scene in the kitchen, her husband's brown eyes black with rage, the kitchen turned upside down from the commotion, cook locked in Jacob's tight grip, terrified for her life. And it was all her fault. Knowing they needed to keep their jobs, she had tried to hide Jacob's behaviour, praying that, with time, he would start to recover.

In part, they had got away with it thus far because Mr Barton had no complaints. On the contrary, Jacob, plagued by insomnia, worked up to twenty hours a day and had been promoted to head groundsman. According to gossip in the servants' quarters, he was the most hard-working groundsman ever employed at Northcote. In addition to this, Jacob's absence from Harriet's life meant that Harriet was available round the clock to be with his 'tiresome' wife, as she was now known, which also pleased Mr Barton greatly.

After what felt like hours, when Harriet was hoarse from calling through the door to Jacob, they finally heard the sirens and Harriet had staggered in a daze to the main entrance and watched three vehicles hurtling down the drive: two police cars and an ambulance.

The passengers had got out and rushed past her. Within seconds, the policemen had forced the kitchen door open, pinned Jacob to the floor and plunged a huge needle into his buttock. Barely conscious, he had been led past her, a brown blanket wrapped around his shoulders. In his drugged state, when she had reached out to touch him, he had not recoiled for once and with tears in his eyes had told her that he was sorry for what he had done.

She had known Jacob would never fully recover, she had convinced herself that lately he was finding a way to cope – in his work, living in the countryside, being away from the battlefield for over a year. He had never shown his violent side to anyone other than her before that day and this episode, to Harriet, seemed to have come out of nowhere.

A tall man with dimples and a tweed jacket, who had been in the ambulance, held out his hand to shake hers.

'My name is Phillip Poole. I'm one of the welfare officers at Greenways Asylum, and I'm here to make sure your husband is well looked after. We have an acute battle neurosis unit at Greenways, and your husband is obviously experiencing some difficulties so we'd like to take him in and assess him over the next few days.'

She had looked up helplessly at the man, who was considerably taller than her and cast a huge shadow over her. 'What will you do to him? He would never have hurt Betty. It's the war that's done this, it isn't him.'

'We won't do anything for a while. I suspect he hasn't slept properly for a long time, so we'll give him something to help with that. Then we may consider some other options.'

'Please don't give him electric shock treatment,' she pleaded, moving closer to him so as not to be heard by the others. 'He just needs rest. I don't want that for him.' Though she tried to control herself, panicked tears escaped at the thought of what they might do to her husband.

'It will most likely be something called modified insulin treatment. But we will call you in when we have a better idea of where we are, and we won't do anything without your consent. Try not to worry. It's the best place for him at the moment.'

Lying on her bed now, the covers wet from her tears, she saw her diary sticking out from under the mattress. The image of Cecilia at the balcony window, watching them take Jacob away, flashed into her mind's eye. The look on Cecilia's face did not seem to Harriet to be concern for Jacob, Harriet reflected now, but more like abject terror. As she tried to work out the trigger for Jacob's breakdown, Harriet found herself pondering the last time she had seen

Cecilia and Jacob speaking together in the grounds. Their friendship seemed to have evaporated as quickly as it had begun, right around the time that Cecilia's nerves had got the better of her. With a feeling of unease creeping over her, Harriet flicked through the pages, racking her brain for a picture of the past months, trying to find an explanation for what had caused Jacob to go so suddenly downhill. She started to read.

May 1946

Dear Diary

I have done my best to hide it but, unfortunately, it is no longer a secret that Mrs Barton has become rather unwell. Her nerves over matters concerning the house have become so acute that she is incapable of reaching any decisions. She tortures herself over the tiniest of details, to the point where she sometimes loses two nights' sleep over one conversation she had with a house servant. Though he tries to be patient, Mr Barton is spending increasing amounts of time in London entertaining business acquaintances and guests he would normally see at Northcote but now cannot due to his wife's troubled state, and their love affair appears to be cooling rather over past weeks.

She speaks longingly of escaping oppressive Northcote and returning to her childhood summers at Seaview; long, hot days with her mother, swimming and picnicking in the cove.

Indeed, she talks of it so often I feel as if I know Seaview, an old stone cottage that sits not fifty feet from the beach at Wittering Bay and backs on to a neighbouring

160

farm, so is surrounded by nothing but barley fields and ocean. A cobbled path up to it from the beach, white wood windows dressed in lace curtains that blow in the sea breeze, a beautiful open fireplace in the living room and a balcony from which you can see for miles.

When Mr Barton is away for long periods, my lady swings between periods of great apathy when she refuses to get out of bed and will not wash or make any effort at all with her appearance to days of delusion when she adopts deep obsessions about throwing grand fancy-dress parties with all her husband's business acquaintances to get herself back in her husband's favour. During these times she barely sleeps, preparing invitations, lists, menus and costume fittings for parties that will never happen – exhausting me, the servants and herself entirely. Last week she was in such emotional turmoil that the doctor was called and my lady was prescribed very strong sedatives. These help her sleep for an hour or so, but then she wakes screaming that her mother is drowning and that she must go to her. As I cannot convince Jacob to return to our bed-room, I have taken to sleeping on the chaise longue in my lady's room so that I can calm her when she wakes, as Mr Barton is away so much my presence is not an annoyance to him.

Rather than helping her, Mr Barton's sisters take great delight in her suffering. I often hear them talking, rather too loudly and cheerfully, about how Charles is no longer in love with her and that if she continues her descent into madness – as they describe it – so that she ends up in the asylum, it will be rather a fortuitous way to get her out of the way so that Charles can marry more suitably.

A knock on the door brought Harriet back to the present, but she felt too faint to answer it. 'Yes,' she managed to call.

'I'm sorry, but Madam is asking for you.' It was Violet, one of the young servant girls. Even though the under butler and the housekeeper had been kind enough to let Harriet have some time to herself, Cecilia was no doubt worrying about Jacob.

'Please tell her I'll be there presently. Then go to the kitchen and prepare the baby's milk and bring it back here to me,' she managed, forcing herself to sit up on the bed.

'But Madam doesn't like anyone else but you to prepare the baby's feed, Mrs Waterhouse.' Harriet could hear the nervousness in Violet's voice.

'Just do it, please, Violet.' Harriet felt sick at the thought of Jacob alone in that ambulance, sedated, frightened. Waking tomorrow morning to find himself incarcerated in an asylum. Her love, with whom she had shared her life, now broken, unreachable. She could hear Cecilia's baby crying and she wanted to go to her to feel the comfort of her tiny body next to hers. She had grown so close to Cecilia, and to her baby girl. She loved spending every second with the child and, as Cecilia's anxieties grew, she had needed help desperately and Harriet, broken-hearted over Jacob and desperate for a child of her own, had been only too happy to oblige. But her love for Cecilia and the baby meant that she had neglected her husband terribly, and the guilt haunted her as she pored over the pages of her diary, desperately trying to find evidence that she had tried to help Jacob. She felt sick with guilt. He was right to think she didn't love him. She hadn't fought hard enough.

162

Dear Diary

As dawn breaks over the Sussex countryside and I sit here watching the contented breathing of the beautiful baby girl who has given me untold happiness, it is hard to think about the pain she caused when she came into the world four days ago. The small miracle that is the rightful heir of Mr Charles Barton was born here at Northcote – three weeks before she was due – on the morning of 8 January 1947.

From the first second I saw her, screaming blue murder as her mother's blood was washed from her fair skin, I loved her as if she were my own. And, contrary to Cecilia's fears, she is a healthy baby. Over the past two days Cecilia has become convinced that the doctors are trying to kill her and the baby – citing as the reason that Charles no longer loves her and wishes to remarry. Whenever the doctors come near, she will not let go of the baby. And she will not let anyone but me feed her or hold her so I have to sit in a chair with the baby while Cecilia sleeps in case something happens to either of them. I am to keep watch all night and I am exhausted.

When we are alone she whispers to me that the doctors meant for her to die in childbirth, but because she survived she is convinced they are now plotting an alternative way to get rid of her. In a way, I do not blame her for thinking they did nothing to try and alleviate her suffering. I didn't know being in such pain, without dying, was possible. Within two hours of her pains starting, Cecilia was unable to cope. Every contraction made her sick, and it was a constant battle to stop her fainting from the pain. After being telephoned twice, the midwife finally arrived on her bicycle, gave my lady a pubic shave, a bath and an enema and offered her a mild sedative of chloral hydrate. But this didn't seem to touch the pain at all and just left Mrs Barton feeling even more woozy and unwell.

I felt early on that something was very wrong and went to telephone the doctor, but Mr Barton was in London, as the baby had come early, so his uncaring sisters were in charge. They intervened and said I was making a fuss and that Cecilia needed to learn to toughen up. It was a rite of passage, they said, which would help her become a woman. After that, they wouldn't let me into the room with her. I heard Cecilia calling for me time and time again as I sat outside her bedroom while day turned into night. Only when they at last grew bored and tired of the noise was I allowed to go in. As they walked out they told me – in all their childless wisdom – that my lady was not of strong character and that her weakness shouldn't be encouraged by me.

The room was dark as I rushed in and my lady was in the corner of the room, thrashing about on the floor and begging me for help. The sight of her brought tears to my eyes and, when she looked at me, her haunted eyes made me think of an animal caught in a trap. There was nothing I could do and the helplessness of the situation only grew greater as the hours went on.

In truth, I felt ashamed at myself for not overruling the sisters sooner and fetching the doctor. All my tireless preparations in the end did nothing to alleviate her suffering. I had read every book and guide I could lay my hands on, and in the weeks before the birth distracted myself from my deep-rooted fear for my lady by making nightgowns, baby flannels, nappies, maternity pads and maternal nightgowns. I ventured into town and bought Lysol and glycerine and Vaseline. I filled lemonade bottles with cooled boiled water and found an old sheet for the birth, which I padded with a thick layer of newsprint and baked in a warm oven to kill any bugs. I spent my evenings knitting, making the clothes I have so longed to make all my life: little bootees, dresses and cardigans – for I was convinced it was a girl.

But for all my hard work, when it came to it I let her suffer dreadfully for nearly two days before I acted. Finally, I could not bear to see my lady suffer any longer and asked the head butler to drive me to the hospital in Mr Barton's Daimler to fetch the doctor. By the time we returned the sisters were nowhere to be seen and Mrs Barton was begging the midwife for one of her husband's guns so that she could shoot herself. The doctor very quickly concluded that she was suffering from an obstructed labour. Mrs Barton is very narrow in her hips and her pelvis was too small for the baby to pass through so the birth had become blocked. She was delirious with pain as the contractions overworked in an effort to push the baby out. Within minutes, the doctor had knocked my lady out with chloroform and, using forceps, grasped the infant and, putting his leg on the bed to steady himself, tore the baby from her. I think it will be a month before Mrs Barton is able to walk again, and she has a rubber ring to sit on as she had a great many stitches. The baby has a very pointed head because of the forceps used by the doctor to pull her out.

Cecilia woke several hours later to find out that she had a little girl, whom she has barely let out of her sight since, though Mr Barton has yet to return to meet her.

Mrs Barton has also struggled terribly with feeding. The nurse who tended to my lady straight after the birth was very strict. A baby born in the morning, she said to Cecilia as she lay barely conscious on the bed, is entitled to two feeds on its first day in the world. Her beautiful baby, however, came into the world in the afternoon and was, therefore, only to be fed once before morning. Babies, as I understand it, are limited to five feeds, spaced four-hourly, with nothing overnight. The last feed should be at 9 p.m. so the mother can be in bed by 10 p.m.

But I began to worry almost immediately that the baby was not feeding well. She is a peaceful soul who sleeps a great deal, and yet when she is offered the breast she screams mercilessly. If she does latch on, it is for a very short time, and she immediately falls asleep again when her stomach is still empty.

When the nurse weighed her yesterday, she said she wasn't gaining weight, and I asked if it was possible to give the baby some formula. Knowing that Cecilia was in poor health, I have been buying and storing formula milk for months now. The nurse wasn't best pleased, but I know that Cecilia is extremely weak and whatever the baby needs it will take from her. So, I have started giving the baby a bottle in the morning and at night to help alleviate her hunger. She gobbles it down. Her little hand rests on mine as I rock her backwards and forwards in front of the window and she gets most annoyed if I talk. She likes it quiet, just she and I.

Another frantic knocking on the door brought Harriet back to the moment. 'I'm sorry to bother you again, Mrs Waterhouse. I have the milk here. Louise just came to find me in the kitchen. Madam is very distressed, and the baby is inconsolable. She's asking please can you come.'

'I'm coming now, Violet,' said Harriet, slamming her diary shut and pushing it under the mattress. She checked her swollen eyes in the small mirror on the dressing table, dabbing them quickly with cold water, then unlocked her bedroom door and opened it to see Violet standing there, as white as a ghost. 'Thank you, Violet. I'll go to them now.'

The long corridor felt oppressive as the servants scuttled past her, each one of them knowing about the scene with Jacob and trying not to stare at her face which was swollen from crying. She could hear the baby's cries growing stronger and fiercer as she reached Cecilia's bedroom door. She took a deep breath, knocked and then opened it.

Cecilia was standing near the open window holding her baby. One of the younger servants stood on the other side of the room, looking utterly terrified. Cecilia was dressed in a long white nightie, her blonde, wavy hair falling in front of her green eyes, her high cheekbones and collar bone jutting out from her emaciated frame.

'Harriet! Where have you been?! I was so worried about you and Jacob. What's happened? Why have they taken him away?' Cecilia's eyes were red from crying and she stared at Harriet like a deer in the road about to be mowed down and killed.

'I'm sorry I was delayed, Cecilia. Would you like me to take the baby and feed her?' Harriet walked over to Cecilia, who was holding her daughter in a vice-like grip.

167

Cecilia backed away, clutching her baby to her, walking towards the balcony window, which was letting in the harsh January air. 'But I saw the ambulance – what happened?' said Cecilia. 'What did Jacob say to you when he walked past? I saw him say something. What was it?'

Harriet looked over at the young servant girl cowering in the corner. 'You can go now, Louise. Please don't speak of this to anyone, or you'll have me to answer to,' she said quietly.

'Yes, Mrs Waterhouse,' said the girl, shooting from the room like a hunted fox.

Harriet turned to Cecilia, who was moving closer to the window. 'Jacob was taken away by ambulance this morning. He has suffered terribly since he came home from fighting in Normandy, but he is in the best place for the moment. I apologize for all the disturbance.'

Harriet looked at Cecilia as she stood by the balcony, clutching her crying baby and shaking her head. 'Did he tell you? Is that why you can't look at me, Harriet?'

'I don't know what you mean,' said Harriet, but before she'd finished saying it, realization started to dawn. Goosebumps prickled up her arm as she stood by the fire and the cold room suddenly became unbearably hot again. All the clues over the weeks began to present themselves neatly in a row in her head as she watched Cecilia's face and struggled to keep her composure. It was all there, plain to see: Jacob and Cecilia's closeness, his hatred of Harriet visiting him, Cecilia's inability to have a child then suddenly conceiving, Jacob and Cecilia's friendship coming to an abrupt end. Jacob coming unravelled four days after the birth of Cecilia's child. *I'm sorry, Harriet, for what I've done.* The first kind words he had spoken to her in over a year.

Harriet tried to block out Cecilia, who had backed out onto the balcony now, and focused on the tiny baby crying out for her feed. 'I have her milk here, Cecilia. I'll sit down on the chair and you can hand her to me, like you always do.' Harriet walked slowly away from where Cecilia stood and sat herself in the rocking chair by the fire. Her whole body was shaking. Please let it not be true. Please God.

'I don't trust anyone but you, Harriet.' Cecilia went on, 'You were the only one who helped me when I was giving birth to her. They all wanted me to die. But you saved me and I know why.'

'Please don't say any more, Cecilia. The baby is terribly hungry, let's just focus on feeding her.' Harriet tried to smile at Cecilia, desperate to calm the dark mood in the room as Cecilia pressed the baby into her so tightly it seemed the child was struggling to breathe.

'It wasn't his fault,' Cecilia said.

'Mrs Barton, please give me the child so I can feed her. I'm worried you're hurting her arm, holding her so tight.' Harriet heard her voice falter.

Cecilia stood on the balcony, her eyes locked on Harriet's. To Harriet, she seemed beyond reach, with the same haunted look Jacob had had that morning when they took him away. Harriet fought back tears as she tried to push away the thought of how much the baby looked like Jacob when she was first born. How she had noticed something familiar about her, but pushed it into the back of her mind. *I'm sorry for what I have done.* His words kept repeating themselves in her head.

Though Harriet tried to stop her from saying more, it was impossible. She could sense Cecilia's relief at finally being able to share this immense burden she had been carrying for nine months. 'I didn't know that could happen, that he could do that to me.' Cecilia paused for a moment, struggling to go on. The baby had stopped crying so hard now, and was just whimpering in Cecilia's arms.

'Have you ever had somebody grab your wrist, Harriet, and hold on just a little too tightly? And for a moment you realize that you're not strong enough to pull it away? Imagine that feeling over your whole body. Once I realized there was nothing I could do, I just lay there and waited. And when it was finally over, and he freed me, my body wasn't mine any more, it was contaminated, destroyed.'

Harriet looked at the baby's pale arm hanging from Cecilia's grip, completely still now, having given up the fight to be released. Harriet sat, too scared to move in case Cecilia did something to hurt her. 'I just wanted a little bit of attention because Charles hadn't paid me any for weeks.' Cecilia started to cry. 'I know I'm owed no sympathy but the worst pain has nothing to do with the bruises and the cuts and the blood or the threats Jacob made to my life when it happened. The pain is in the fact that I can't trust the world any more. I can't trust my judgement. I can't tell any more who is good or bad. Except you. You are the only person I can trust, Harriet.'

Harriet hung her head and Cecilia began moving across the room towards her. Slowly Harriet held out her arms and, after a long while, Cecilia lowered the baby into them.

As soon as Harriet gave the little girl her milk, she took it. The only sound in the room was the baby gently and contentedly sucking on her much-needed bottle. A calm came over Harriet as she held the warm bundle in her arms, the baby's skin touching hers, her eyes fixing on her gratefully. She felt her body relax into the chair as she ran her fingers over the child's soft arms.

'Harriet, do you think Charles knows?' Cecilia asked quietly.

Harriet felt a sickness in her stomach again and pulled the baby to her to give her strength, focusing on her contented breathing. In, out; in, out.

'Jacob told everyone what he did, didn't he? That's why they took him away?' said Cecilia.

'No, Cecilia, nobody knows. We have to keep this secret. For your sake, and the baby's. Please.'

'No. It's too late, Harriet. Charles knows,' said Cecilia, her green eyes fixed on Harriet's. 'Everyone knows that Rebecca is Jacob's child.'

Chapter Nineteen

Rebecca

Friday, 14 November 2014

Rebecca glanced down at her daughter's bump and resisted the urge to reached out and place her hand on it. Instead she took her daughter's hand. 'I'll try to remember and tell you all I can about what happened when you were born, darling, but can you promise me one thing?'

Jessie shrugged, but didn't pull her hand away.

'Please, just hear me out. I may be wrong, but I feel that whenever things get tough with us, you tend to want to shut me out. Could you just promise to stay this time? This is going to be painful, but you're asking me to do it, and I want to, but in return I need you not to leave.'

Jessie said nothing, but Rebecca took it as a yes. She suddenly felt very hot and stood up to open a window. She took a few deep gulps of air then turned back to her daughter, whose green eyes were fixed on her.

'Until the night my parents died, I loved Seaview, but my mother was determined I would do something with my life. Not be trapped as she was, in a life of servitude, with no choices, and married to a man I hated. I worked so hard at school, focused all my energy on doing the best I could so that I could go to university. And it was never a hardship, it came naturally to me, school had always been an escape. I remember, on my first day, I stood outside the little wooden building with my satchel over my back and a desperate desire to get into the classroom, where there were books, and maths puzzles, and an orange story chair. There was a little boy in the playground with red hair sobbing, clinging to a pillar, while his mother tried to peel him off, and I remember wondering, why would anyone be frightened of school? What could be more frightening than home?'

'And why did you want to do medicine? Why was that so important to you?'

'Well, what I said to anyone who interviewed me for university or any of my placements was that it plays to all my strengths. And of course, that I wanted to help people.'

'And the real answer?'

Rebecca shut her eyes before she spoke. 'Because when I lie awake in the dark, I can still hear my mother's screams and picture her eyes when I got to her. She was still alive, but she was bleeding to death and I couldn't do anything to save her. He beat her until he broke her jaw, and stamped on her beautiful face until her teeth came loose. When I got there, she was barely breathing. I watched the blood pour from her ears, her eyes, her mouth onto the living room rug. The blood coming out of her pulsed, like her heart was bleeding out of her. She had this look of resignation, like a broken animal. She wasn't crying out in pain. I think she was trying to be brave for me. But we both knew her unhappy life was over. It was probably too late, but in that moment I decided that had I known what to do, I could have saved her.'

Jessie finally spoke. 'Why did he do it to her?'

'He was traumatized from his time serving in the Second World War. And I believe he was jealous of the bond that my mother and Harvey's dad had formed while he was in the psychiatric hospital.' Rebecca hesitated before going on. 'I've never told anyone this before, but my mother was holding a necklace when she died.'

Rebecca looked at Jessie for a long time, then stood and crossed the room. She opened a drawer and pulled out a small box from the back, then returned with the small gold locket.

Jessie looked at it. 'It's beautiful. Who do you think gave it to her?'

Rebecca handed it to her. 'I think Ted Roberts gave it to her, and I think Father found it that night and that's why he flew into such a rage. I hope he knew. And I hope it haunted him as he died. I think about my mother's diary sometimes.' Rebecca added, 'I would give anything to read it.'

'How do know you can't?'

Rebecca frowned at Jessie. 'Because I have no idea where it is. She used to go down to the bomb shelter when he was drunk and I suspect it may have been down there but I've never been back to Seaview since that night. There's no chance it would still be there now.'

'You don't know that.'

Rebacca looked up at Jessie.

'We could go back there together and look?'

'It's someone else's property, Jessie, and has been for years.'

'So,' I think Liz mentioned once that you could still get down there. Rebecca tried not to bristle at the bait which never failed to reel her in. Liz claiming to know more about Seaview, about Jessie, about everything, than she did. Liz

174

was gone now, so why did she continue to get jealous about the hold she had over Jessie? She was the lucky one, Jessie was with *her* now, she still had time.

'Why didn't your mother leave him?' said Jessie.

'Women didn't then. It's hard enough now, but back then then it was almost impossible. She had no money and nowhere to go. And her husband had fought in the war – it would have been unthinkable to abandon him. A lot of women felt the same when their husbands came home. Everything had changed. They had to cope with so much while the men were away – run the country, essentially – and afterwards they were expected to go back to their role as submissive housewives.' Rebecca's mind wandered back to barefoot walks on the beach with her mother, when Rebecca had encouraged her outside into the fresh air to escape her father's dark moods. As the tide danced over their feet, Harriet had shared all her great ambitions for her daughter until it was time to force themselves to return to the tensions within the four walls of Seaview Cottage.

'I think most women stayed with their husbands, however unhappy they both were, but they poured all their heart and their ambition into their daughters. Like my mother did. I always remember her standing at the sink one night saying, "Don't get married, Harriet, it's a mug's game."'

'That's unbelievably sad,' said Jessie. 'That was her whole life, thrown away because of a sense of duty to a man that didn't love her. How could he, if he could do that to her?'

Rebecca nodded. 'I remember she went to the police once, after a particularly bad beating from my father. It took all her courage – she was still shaking when she told me about it that night when she came home. She asked them to help her. All they did was give her a good ticking-off, told her she needed to get on with it, that it was her duty, after what he had been through. As did the priest, when he spoke to her at confession. Her hell was not just my father, but having nowhere to turn.'

'He went into a psychiatric hospital, didn't he?' Jessie was still now, her hands in her lap as she locked eyes with her mother.

'Yes, he did, just after I was born. He was there until I was five. It was just my mother and me until then. His violent temper had a profound effect on me, growing up. Watching her trapped every day of her life and living with him, it rubbed off on me. He had battle neurosis from the war, and I had it from living with him. I was jumpy, anxious. I wet the bed until I was eleven. I made a promise to myself that I would live my life and not marry until I had achieved my ambitions. That I would earn enough money of my own that I always had choices.'

'It makes me really sad to think of you as a thirteen-year-old girl, seeing your mother hurt like that. Why don't you ever talk about that night to anyone, Mum?' Jessie rested her hand on her bump.

'Would you?' Rebecca frowned at her.

'I would if my daughter asked me about it. Surely having secrets is never a good thing.'

'It's not a secret!' said Rebecca. 'It's my pain, it's personal to me, and I had to lock it away in order to cope. I find it hard that you can't respect that, but I'm trying to understand. Why do you think knowing about it will help you?' Rebecca felt her defensiveness rise.

'Because I feel like I don't know you. Something like

176

that would shape who you are, and it might help me to understand you more,' said Jessie.

'But it's not just you, Jessie. I didn't talk about it to anyone – not to John, not to Iris. No one. I wish you wouldn't take it so personally.'

'But if you're keeping a secret as big as that inside you, how can you really be honest about anything?'

Rebecca let out a heavy sigh. 'I said, it's not a secret, Jessie.'

'If you say so.' Jessie shrugged, then continued quietly. 'Dad said my birth was quite traumatic. Do you think the trauma of that night was locked inside you until you had me?'

'Is that what your dad said?' Rebecca looked over at the small scrapbook of newspaper cuttings she had found in the loft.

'He's told me bits and pieces, but I really need to hear it from you.'

'What did he tell you?' said Rebecca, standing and fetching the cuttings.

'He said that when I was born you became very anxious. He said you thought you could see the policeman who interviewed you the night your parents died. That he was following you.'

Rebecca nodded, sitting down on the seat next to Jessie. 'When the birth was finally over and they had stitched me up, I was sitting up in my bed at the hospital, holding you, and . . .' Rebecca cleared her throat and pushed herself to go on. 'I remember I felt something click in my head. It's so hard to describe. I just felt this very strange sensation come over me. I started to hear this male voice, talking about me.

177

I asked Harvey what it was, but of course he couldn't hear it. I was frightened. I didn't know what or who it was.'

'What was the voice saying?'

'He seemed to be talking about me to the medical staff around me, saying that he knew what I'd done, and that they were coming to take me away from you and they were going to put me in prison.'

Jessie stared at her mother, transfixed.

'After that I started to unravel very quickly. I was convinced this man was following us everywhere. I didn't sleep because I thought he was going to take you away from me, because he didn't think I was fit to be a mother. He was there, everywhere I went. In every room, in the road outside Harvey's farm where we were living. Just watching me, all day and night, smoking the Woodbines he was smoking in the interview room the night my parents were killed. When they made me sit in an interview room for four hours, with my mother's blood still on the nightie I was wearing. I could smell the smoke, from his cigarette. It was that real.'

'That's awful,' said Jessie, turning to face Rebecca.

'I have dreams still. Dreams where my father is climbing the stairs in our house at Seaview to come and find me.'

Rebecca pulled out the police cuttings slowly from the file and handed them to her daughter.

'He's holding his gun, the wooden stairs creak as he steps on them one by one, closer to me. I am under my blanket. I can hear him come into the room, and just as he gets to me I turn and look him in the eye as he pulls the trigger.'

Chapter Twenty

Iris

4 p.m. Wednesday, 19 November 2014

Iris looked around the emptying café from which Mark had just made a hasty exit and pulled her notepad from her bag. She wrote down the name Jane Trellis, adding, *midwife, Maternity Wing, St Dunstan's Hospital*. It hadn't been hard to find her on the hospital website, with a picture. She looked mid-twenties, Iris guessed, with a broad smile, and the tips of her hair were dyed pink.

Iris's phone began to ring and Miles's number flashed on the screen. Iris looked down at it with dread. She needed to own up to Miles about being Jessie's sister, but as time ticked on it seemed more and more impossible to come clean. There was still a chance she could hold together this mess she had created and thanks to Mark she had Jane Trellis' name, now she needed to find her.

'Hope is fading this afternoon for a young mother on the run with her newborn. Jessica Roberts and her baby, Elizabeth, have not been seen since Jessica walked out of the Maternity Wing of St Dunstan's Hospital in Chichester at eight o'clock this morning.' Iris looked up at the small television in the corner of the coffee shop, unable to take her eyes from the pictures of Jessica holding her newborn baby as they walked out into the bitterly cold November morning.

Her phone began to ring again and, when a local number she didn't recognize came up, she answered it.

'Hello, is that Iris Waterhouse?'

'Yes, who is this?' asked Iris.

'My name is Helen Tate. I'm calling from the County Records Office.'

'Oh, hi,' said Iris, slightly thrown.

'We've just heard back from the coroner regarding your request to access the file on the inquest into the murder–suicide of Jacob and Harriet Waterhouse in November 1960. As you are related to the deceased, it has been approved, so if you'd like to look at it, it's currently at the County Records Office in Chichester. You'd just need to bring some ID.'

'Oh, okay, great. What time does it close today?'

'They're open until five o'clock, so just under an hour from now. You'll need to bring some ID with you.'

'Okay, thanks.' If she was going to make this work, she needed to buy an hour to get to the records office and photocopy the files.

Iris tried to gather her thoughts. She had no idea if that fateful night in 1960 was connected to Jessie's disappearance in any way. But her instinct was telling her the past was rearing its head. Having barely spoken to their mother for the past year, she felt certain that Jessie had gone to see Rebecca to ask her about something specific. Rebecca wasn't willing to discuss that night; she completely shut down if Iris even tried. So it was up to her to find a connection.

Iris tapped out a text message to Miles: *Managed to get*

the name of Jessica's midwife, Jane Trellis, St Dunstan's Hospital, Chichester. No contact number or address. Can you help? Will send picture, from hospital website. Doing some background checks on Jessica now will call asap.

Within seconds Miles had texted back: *On it, will let you know as soon as we have something. Good work.*

The journey out to the records office was slow, the pelting rain slowing the traffic down as rush hour began to bite. By the time the taxi pulled up outside, it was nearly half past four.

'Hello, my name is Iris Waterhouse,' she said to the woman behind the desk.

The woman took in Iris's bedraggled, rain-sodden appearance and glanced at the clock. 'You will need to register, I'm afraid, and it will take a while for them to bring the file down, so you won't have long to look at it. We close in half an hour so it may be better if you come back tomorrow.'

'I can't, unfortunately, I work up in London and I've got rather a heavy day tomorrow. The inquest was a murder–suicide,' said Iris. 'Jacob and Harriet Waterhouse, 1960.'

'I see.' The woman had the disapproving look of a person with a great deal of time on her hands. 'Well, if you start to fill this in, I'll call and see if they can bring it down.'

'Thank you so much,' said Iris, forcing a smile. She pulled a pen from her bag, her hair dripping on to the form, as she pretended not to eavesdrop.

'Luckily, the file is waiting for you,' the woman reported. 'The Coroner's Office emailed earlier to say you were on your way.'

'Wonderful. Is it through here?' said Iris, signing the form and walking towards the door.

'I need to issue you with a card,' the woman said curtly, 'and you'll need to sign in. Also, if you want to take any pictures of the file, you'll need a photo permit, and that costs twelve pounds for the day.'

By the time Iris sat down with the file on the inquest into her grandparents' deaths, she had signed most of her life away to get her laminated card and had exactly twenty minutes until the office closed.

She took a deep breath, looked down at the light blue file tied like a birthday parcel with coarse white ribbon and realized her hands were shaking. Despite her desperate rush to get to it, the inquest report which detailed the events of the night of 18 November 1960 now felt like Pandora's box. It wasn't a thick file, but she could feel the weight of her mother's past within its pages. A past her mother had never shared with her.

As her hand hovered over the cover page in the quiet open-plan room she felt as she had when she was fourteen, sitting in the loft of her childhood home, feeling the rush of blood to her face as she spotted the small scrapbook while she cleared out old boxes of books on a rainy day. She hadn't hesitated then, sensing its importance and that it had been an oversight on her parents' part, leaving it in a place she might discover it. She had known that her grandparents had been killed when her mother was young. And that her grandfather Jacob Waterhouse was a violent man who had killed his wife, and then himself. But what she hadn't known, and discovered as she sat alone in the dusty loft of her childhood home, was that her mother, aged thirteen, had been in the house at the time.

After years of never being allowed to ask questions about her mother's parents, of her father giving her weighted looks across the dinner table if the subject ever came up, reading the first article, faded to light grey and dated November 1960, had, despite the abject horror of what had happened to her mother, almost felt like a relief.

For as long as she could remember, Iris had known that their family was different. That her mother wouldn't be at the school gates or at school nativity plays or assemblies, and because it was all she had ever known, she was okay with it. Because her kind, patient, funny father always bridged the gap with great enthusiasm and made her feel like she was special for understanding.

'She's saving lives, Iris, and by supporting her we are helping those families too.'

Her father was enough. More than enough, and over time she had begun to feel sorry for the other girls, as their mothers fussed over them endlessly, suffocating them in their teenage years, until it ended in explosive rows. She had an element of freedom and independence in her life that she learned to love. She and her father had bumbled along, all the world to each other, until his sudden death from cancer when she was twenty-three threw her and her mother into a situation where they had to cope without him. But they managed it, sharing their grief, their heartache and their secrets. Except one: the night in November 1960 that her mother would never discuss, the details of which Iris held in her hand now.

Iris felt a stab of guilt digging into her mother's past, when she knew she was against it. But the thought of Jessie

183

and her baby drove her on. Her hand hovered for a moment before opening the cardboard folder and reading the opening page. At the top, in bold heavy wording: **County of West Sussex: POLICE REPORT TO CORONER CONCERNING DEATH.**

Then, below it, several boxes filled with questions and, in answer to them, the distinctive typeface of an old-fashioned typewriter. She could picture a policeman stabbing at it with two forefingers. Her eyes ran down the first page, slowly, carefully, struggling to take in the last moments of her grandfather's life.

Full name, age, occupation and address of deceased: Jacob Robert Waterhouse, 53, Ex-Services, Seaview Cottage, Wittering Bay, Wittering, West Sussex.

State where and when (day and hour) the deceased died, or was found dying or dead: Seaview Cottage, Wittering, 1.10 a.m. on Saturday, 19th November, 1960 Found dead.

What is the opinion of the Medical Practitioner as to the nature of the illness and cause of death? Gunshot wound to the temple.

If any known illness or injury existed before death, state if possible, the nature of it, and its duration: Chronic Battle Neurosis, admitted to Greenways Psychiatric Hospital in January 1948. Discharged back into Community Care April 1953.

State the supposed cause of death, if known or suspected, and the circumstances relating to it: A 999 call was received from Miss Rebecca Waterhouse, age 13, daughter of Harriet and Jacob Waterhouse, at 1.30 a.m. on Saturday 19th November

1960 requesting an ambulance for her mother, Harriet Waterhouse, and her father, Jacob Waterhouse. The police were notified and arrived at the house to find Miss Rebecca Waterhouse in the front room of Seaview Cottage in a highly distressed state, next to her mother. On the other side of the room was the body I now know to be that of Jacob Waterhouse, with a gunshot wound to the head. It was apparent to me straight away that he was dead. I attended to Mrs Waterhouse, she was breathing, but it was very laboured. She had severe bruising to her face and neck, and her left eye was bleeding heavily. She told me that her husband had shot himself. Mrs Waterhouse then lost consciousness and stopped breathing. I attempted CPR on Mrs Waterhouse, but soon after the ambulance crew arrived and declared Harriet Waterhouse – and Jacob Waterhouse – to be dead. A small Luger pistol was lying on the ground next to his right hand. I took possession of the Luger pistol.

Iris sat back in her seat and closed her eyes. She could imagine the clacking of the typewriter keys as the policeman filled in the form back at the police station, the form Iris now held in her hand: *'I found Miss Rebecca Waterhouse in a highly distressed state, next to her mother.'*

Iris began trying to piece together the scene after Harriet and Jacob had died. What had happened to her mother? Had the police officer comforted her, taken her from the room where her parents had suffered brutal and violent deaths? Put her in a police car and taken her to the station? She knew her mother had lived with Harvey and Ted Roberts before going to medical school, but presumably she hadn't been placed with them on the night her parents were killed? Iris's eyes swam with tears at the thought of Rebecca as a child, sitting helplessly as her mother lay dying in front of her.

She looked up at the clock: twelve minutes until closing. She moved on to the next page.

East Sussex Constabulary

Statement taken at: Chichester Police Station
Time: 6 a.m.
Date: Saturday, 19th November 1960

Name: Miss Rebecca Waterhouse
Address: Seaview Cottage, Wittering Bay, Wittering,
Chichester, West Sussex
Occupation: n/a
Age: 13 years

My father, Jacob Waterhouse, came home to live with me and my mother, Harriet Waterhouse, when I was five years old. Before this it had been the two of us at Seaview. I had not met him before this as he was admitted to Greenways Psychiatric Hospital for Battle Neurosis when I was born on the 8th January 1947. He always had a violent temper, flashbacks and night terrors – he was very depressed at times, possessive of my mother, and often hit her. She went to the police, as she feared for her life but they were unable to help her. There had been an upset between my parents that evening as we were due to move away from Seaview Cottage the following day and my mother and I didn't want to go. He was angry because I had played truant from school and went on the bus to visit Harvey Roberts at the farm at Greenways Hospital in Chichester where he was working. There was a storm that night and as I lay in bed, I thought I heard a knock at the front door and someone else in the house. My father's shouting became louder and I heard my mother screaming. I was normally too frightened to go downstairs when my father was angry but when I heard the gunshot I ran downstairs. I found my mother lying in the front room. Her face was very swollen, she was bleeding from her ear and eye. I called 999 and sat with her. She died a few minutes later. I did not go to my father . . . I could see that he was dead. There was no one in the house. Perhaps I imagined it from the knocking and whistling sounds the storm made at the doors and windows.

The above statement was made in the presence of Detective Inspector Gibbs.

'We'll be closing in ten minutes, just to let you know.' Iris startled as the woman from the desk appeared.

She took a photo of her mother's statement, then moved on, just as her phone buzzed again. Mum Mob. *How are you getting on?*

Iris tapped out her reply: *Okay, managed to get hold of the name of the midwife who was looking after Jessie. My boss is getting her address so I can try and talk to her asap. Will keep you posted.*

Iris watched the dots as her mother composed her reply, then: *Okay thank you Iris.*

Iris looked up at the clock. Eight minutes to closing.

WEST SUSSEX COUNTY COUNCIL

Greenways Psychiatric Hospital
Chichester
West Sussex
22nd November 1960

Re: Jacob Robert Waterhouse (deceased). Aged 53 years.

Mr Jacob Waterhouse was first admitted to the Battle
Neurosis ward here at Greenways in January 1947 when he
was employed at Northcote Manor as head groundsman. He
was under our care for a period of five years, during which he
was given insulin therapy, electro-convulsive therapy and a
number of occupational therapies, including art therapy,
which he found to be beneficial.

Jacob Waterhouse was sectioned originally suffering with
acute states of neurotic disturbances or Battle Fatigue, aka
Exhaustion, and he had to be heavily dosed with lithium
carbonate. Electro-convulsive therapy proved to mechanically
lift Mr Waterhouse's depression, and after a year he was able to
leave the locked ward and spent the rest of his stay on the open
ward, during which time he was able to go for a half a day or a
single day excursion before returning to the safety of the ward.
In his final year he would return home for weekends, a week
or two on leave before his formal discharge. His wife, Harriet
Waterhouse, had a young daughter at home so we wanted to
be sure that she would have community support for her
husband before he was fully discharged.

Upon returning home, Mr Waterhouse appeared to be
coping well at first, but over time his symptoms returned.

Mrs Waterhouse had confided in me during a consultation with her at Greenways that she was finding it increasingly hard to cope with his escalating moods and violent outbursts. At his consultation in June of this year, I found Mr Waterhouse to be suffering from acute depression which had at some point made him want to attempt suicide. During his stay at Greenways he attempted to take his own life and he intimated in fits of depression that life was not worth living.

I have seen the opinions of the medical practitioners who examined the deceased after death at St Dunstan's Hospital, and I would agree with their verdict that the death of Jacob Waterhouse was caused by a single, self-inflicted gunshot wound to his right temple.

Signed

Dr Philip Hunter

Iris took a photo of Dr Hunter's letter and, with no time to digest, turned to the next page.

Chapter Twenty-One

Harvey

4:30 p.m. Wednesday, 19 November

Harvey pulled up next to the police car in the Wittering Bay car park and looked down at the framed photograph of Liz and Jessie lying on the seat next to him.

With their blonde hair, beaming smiles and sun-kissed cheeks, they could have been mother and daughter. It had been two long, painful years since losing Liz, and it occurred to him now, staring at the photograph of his daughter's beautiful face, that in all that time that beaming, contented smile of Jessie's had never resurfaced.

He had known she was suffering, known she wasn't herself, but he had been so immersed in his own pain he'd been unable to take hers on board too. He had convinced himself he was there for her, that because she and Adam had a baby on the way she was moving on – coping.

But she wasn't, and he knew in his gut that she was doing too much. Her job was highly pressured and she hadn't let up at all since she fell pregnant. She was still getting up before six every day for the hour-and-a-half commute up to London, still going to evening events. He'd expressed his concern a couple times, knowing Liz would have been horrified, but on his visits to their flat Jessie always assured him she was fine.

'If there's anything you need me to do,' he'd offered. 'Any odd jobs, or maybe painting the baby's room. I'd love to help. I know my decorating won't be up to your standard but babysitting might be my forte – I'll introduce her to *Farmers' Weekly*.' He'd sit on their pristine cream sofa in their beautifully decorated flat, being stared at by six-foot photographs of Masai warriors and Peruvian coffee farmers. He always felt slightly out of place, his muck boots banished to the communal hallway, his muddy jeans leaving flakes of mud on the pale grey rug beneath his feet.

'I know you're there for us, Dad. It's very kind of you, but we're fine. Do you want to see the nursery? It's not finished yet, but you wouldn't believe all the stuff we've had to get for such a tiny person!'

He had followed her into the small spare bedroom, now painted in a seagrass green with Peter Rabbit transfers on the wall. A white crib which had yet to be assembled was propped up against the wall and a rocking chair sat in the corner, still in bubble wrap. There was baby paraphernalia everywhere: a baby bath, breastfeeding pillows, boxes of nappies and neatly folded piles of babygros.

'Why don't you let me put the cot together? I promise I won't bodge it.'

She had laughed. 'It's okay, Dad. Adam will do it, there's plenty of time. It's getting there, though, don't you think?' She pulled out a drawer and began putting the baby clothes in it.

It was going to be beautiful, thought Harvey, like everything Jessie touched.

'Right, Dad, I'm sorry, but I've got to get some work done for an interview tomorrow.'

'But it's past ten. You need to get to bed, don't you?' he said, looking at his watch.

'It's just an hour or so. I need to do some research, otherwise it's going to be a car crash.'

He had hesitated, knowing what he was going to say would fall on deaf ears, 'Obviously, I'd hate it, but wouldn't it be easier if you lived in London, sweetheart?'

'Adam likes being near the sea. He hates London, he'd suffocate,' Jessie had said, and Harvey smiled politely, holding his tongue, as he always did when it came to Adam. Why they needed to live where was best for Adam when he was always swanning off to far-flung places, leaving her to deal with a crippling commute alone, was a mystery to him.

'I know, darling, but you're about to have a baby, and if you're going back to work, that's going to be really tough. You'll be exhausted.'

'Dad, it's fine. We've talked about it. I'll drop the baby off at nursery on the way to the station and he'll collect her.' Jessie smiled at her father, shaking her head.

'But what about when he's away with work?' Harvey tried to keep the concern out of his voice.

'We might get a childminder. Dad, please don't worry. Adam's very good with babies. You should see him with his sister's kid – he'll probably be better at it all than me.'

Harvey stopped himself from saying any more as an image flashed into his mind of Adam doing his hair at the mirror while the baby screamed at his feet.

Adam. Even the mention of his name made him bristle. Their relationship had moved so fast. He and Jessie had met just a year after Liz's death and six months later Jessie was pregnant and she had moved into his flat. Harvey was wracked with worry that they hadn't built the foundations to weather the storms of having a child, but Jessie seemed to have rose-tinted glasses permanently on around him, whereas Harvey's bullshit detector always went onto high alert whenever Adam walked into the room. He could picture him now, packing up his camera gear, reading his photography magazines in a nice quiet aeroplane, leaving Jessie, sleep-deprived, to deal with a screaming baby and a full-time job.

Indeed he had tried to like him, really tried, for Jessie's sake, but it was clear very early on that Adam's favourite subject was Adam, and he didn't seem to look at Jessie in the way her other boyfriends had. Jessie had always had such kind boyfriends in the past, sweet lads who were in love with her, most of whom she had dumped and left broken-hearted. Adam was different, a model turned photographer, and appeared to be far more in love with himself than he was with Jessie. And, it seemed to Harvey, he had slowly and carefully moulded their lives so that everything was set up in his favour while Jessie made all the sacrifices and did all the running around.

Over time, he found being with them and witnessing the imbalance in their relationship uncomfortable, then unbearable, and before long, despite being desperately worried about his grieving daughter, he had found himself making excuses not to see them.

And now, because he had put his grief and his feelings towards Adam before being there for Jessie, she hadn't turned to him.

Instead, it seemed possible that she'd followed in the footsteps of the past and come to Wittering Bay, where she and Liz had spent every summer since she was a baby. Were she and baby Elizabeth out here in the dunes surrounding him as it started to get dark? On the beach? He felt sick at the thought of Jessie and her baby taking a bus out to this bitterly cold beach after the trauma of the birth. She had barely been able to walk. An image came to him of Liz and Jessie in summers past, running towards the sea, holding hands, laughing. And Jessie now, standing at the edge of the sea, holding her baby, feeling utterly alone and desperate.

As dusk set in, Harvey looked over at the plain-clothes policeman standing on the doorstep of Seaview Farm and let out a heavy sigh. The small Georgian farmhouse that five generations of his family had grown up in looked exactly as it had in his childhood; the wisteria snaking around the windows, the black wrought iron light hanging over the front door. He could envisage his younger self walking through the front door, his cheeks burning from a day in the fields, his father in a whisky-induced slumber by the crackling fire.

It had taken everything he had to try and hang on to the farm, not to let the night Rebecca's parents were killed change the course of his entire life, but in the end it had.

The police knew that it hadn't been him at Seaview Cottage that night, but the rumours of an affair between Harriet and his father persisted. And his father, guilty at the part he may have played in Harriet's death – that Jacob may have noticed how much he loved her, even though nothing had ever happened between them – had drank himself into an early grave.

Harvey had tried to keep going, but crippling death duties and supermarkets' stranglehold on the market cutting into his profit margins meant there came a point where he could no longer keep his head above water. After weeks of clearing decades' worth of paperwork, photographs, furniture and keepsakes, he and Liz had handed over the keys to Seaview.

Harvey slammed the car door shut. As the light faded he walked towards the sound of the crashing surf. The frozen sea air whipped angrily around him as he made his way to the beach. However much he tried to move on from Seaview, the past wouldn't let him go and, now, forty years after he had handed over the keys, Seaview Farm was back in his life.

The tide was out and he made his way down the boardwalk and across the waterlogged sand, to the water's edge, and stared out at the grey sea. As the darkness descended, the wind skidding off the surface of the November sea told him the sea was fierce. Had Jessie been there that day? Had she walked into the sea with baby Elizabeth? Were they hiding in the dunes somewhere behind him?

'Jessica! Jessica!!' He chanted her name over and over. Knowing it was no use, knowing there was nothing he could do. He felt exhausted, as if his legs could barely hold him up, and the freezing sea rushed towards him, seeping into his shoes and up his legs. He started to cry, great, wracking sobs. Begging his wife to help him find Jessie, pleading for Liz to take care of Jessica's baby.

He didn't know how long he stood there, but when he lifted his head again it was dark. A flashlight caught his eye. Turning, he saw the light moving along the coastal path hugging the cliff edge to Seaview Cottage. When the beam reached the cottage, there was a moment before the lights at Seaview Cottage turned on and he watched two people step over the threshold. Harvey stood, staring up at the cottage on the cliff edge, watching the two people move from room to room, looking for Jessie as the night wind stung his cheeks until they went numb.

As he stood looking up at Seaview Cottage, he could picture that fateful night playing out like one of the flip picture books he had as a child. In each window a different scene. Rebecca upstairs in bed, the storm at her window, the fight in the living room, the gunfire, Rebecca bent over her mother's bloodied body, the police hammering on the door. And the visitor, who Rebecca always insisted was real. Had it been her imagination? Or a reality?

That night had taken hold of his life then and had never let go.

As the lights in the different rooms at Seaview Cottage turned on during the search for Jessie and the baby, Harvey's phone began to ring, dragging him back to the present.

'Mr Roberts? It's DC Gale.'

'What is it? Have you found Jessie?'

'No, but there's a woman at St Dunstan's Hospital in Chichester we think you should talk to.' DC Gale's voice was faint; the mobile phone reception was terrible.

'Who is she? Does she know where Jessie is?'

'No, but she is looking for her daughter.'

'I don't understand, what are you talking about? Her daughter? Who is she? I'm going to have to call you back.'

'Her name is Cecilia Barton. She's asking to talk to you about her daughter – Rebecca.' And with that, the line cut out.

Chapter Twenty-Two

Harriet

13 January 1947

Harriet Waterhouse sat on the painfully slow train out to Wittering Bay feeling as if her heart was going to stop at any moment.

It was only four o'clock in the afternoon but it was already getting dark, and the ice-cold rain was hammering against the train window as the train carriage rocked along.

Her eyes stung. She was exhausted, having been up all night after Cecilia had become paranoid that Rebecca's milk was laced with arsenic. It was only when the doctor came to sedate her that Harriet was able to take the baby from her iron grip and feed her.

There was no hiding Cecilia's illness any more, and as Cecilia slept, Harriet had spent the entire night in the rocking chair by the fire, holding Rebecca and feeding her with as much milk as she could. Cecilia had screamed the house down as they held her down and plunged the needle into her behind, saying that Charles wanted her and her baby dead because Rebecca wasn't his. She no longer cared who knew, but Charles – who had stayed well away with his parents in their London townhouse – had been terrified of the scandal getting out.

The baby and Cecilia asleep, Harriet had crept along the corridor to the room adjacent to the library, where the family GP and Charles's sisters were sitting by the fire. She held her breath and listened.

'The adoption agency is coming in the morning to take the baby away.' It was Margaret who spoke, Charles's elder sister. 'Charles thinks it best if she is sent to America to be adopted and he wants to ensure there is no paperwork leading back to him. He doesn't want Rebecca turning up in eighteen years' time and causing a scandal.'

'And Cecilia?'

'For now, he's keen to keep her out of the asylum. Don't ask me why – he's too soft-hearted, that's what's got him into this mess in the first place. It's the quickest and easiest way for him to get a divorce. But he's adamant that we try and treat her here first. I think he's hoping that, once the baby is gone, she will start to get better, and then they can live separate lives but avoid divorce. There's never been a divorce in this family, and he doesn't want to upset Mother, and particularly Father, when he's in poor health. Where's that brandy got to? These provincial staff really are utterly useless.'

Harriet had crept back to Cecilia's bedroom then and lifted the sleeping baby out of her cot. She inhaled her smell, kissed her soft cheeks, talked to her about how sorry she was that she was being sent away to a country she didn't know, to live with people who were strangers to her, about how much she loved her and would miss her. With tears in her eyes, she had slowly lowered her down and resettled her in her cot.

And all the time Cecilia slept peacefully – and oblivious – for the first time in weeks.

Harriet had no clue how long she slept for, but when she

woke it was with a start. The fire in Cecilia's room had gone out and the balcony window was open. She had immediately had the feeling that something was amiss and when she turned her aching neck slowly to look into Rebecca's cot, it was empty. She had shaken herself awake, and walked into the bathroom, which was as lifeless and cold as the bedroom. She had not known Cecilia to leave the bedroom once since Rebecca had been born, but she pulled a blanket around herself, opened the bedroom door and dashed into the cold stone hallway.

It was dawn, and the house silent, as she dashed from the library, to Charles' study, to the drawing room, knowing in her heart she wouldn't find them. Scared to call out to Cecilia in case she woke anyone before she'd had a chance to think what to do. After fifteen minutes she had run through every downstairs room, and when she reached the back door she pulled on a pair of boots and dashed out into the freezing January dawn just as the cockerels started to crow.

As she stood, her eyes still foggy from lack of sleep, blinking in the sunlight that had come up over Jacob's beautifully manicured lawns, she had known for certain that Cecilia and the baby were gone.

The train jolted to a stop outside a station, bringing Harriet back to the present. She had known immediately where Cecilia had gone. But it had been six painfully long hours before she herself could leave. After discovering they were missing, she had called the police, and as the day ticked by and Cecilia and her baby got further and further away, Harriet had to sit and be interrogated about Cecilia's whereabouts.

'I find it very hard to believe, Mrs Waterhouse, that you

know every intimate detail of Mrs Barton's life but yet had no clue that she was planning to run away with her baby.' The detective inspector had a black moustache and smelt strongly of body odour. He paced around her chair and leaned in far too close to her.

'If I had known that she was planning to run away I would have informed Mr Barton of my fears,' Harriet had said quietly. 'Mrs Barton is very unwell and it troubles me deeply that she is out there, in this weather, with no suitable clothing, no money and a vulnerable baby I have grown to love.'

'And you really have no idea where they might have gone? If you do, and it turns out you didn't tell us, you will go to prison for obstructing a police investigation. And if any harm comes to the baby . . . All Mr Barton wants is to have his wife and baby safely home.'

Harriet looked up at Margaret, who sat opposite her, staring intently at her, tapping her fingers on the table.

On the train, Harriet tried to distract herself from the painfully slow progress it was making through the Sussex countryside towards Wittering. Harriet pulled her diary from her handbag and began to write.

13 January 1947

Dear Diary

I am frantic. My lady is gone. And she has taken baby Rebecca with her.

I am writing this on a cold train to Wittering and I am sitting at a table opposite a lady who keeps looking over at me disapprovingly. She is dressed immaculately, in a white blouse with a tight red belt, and she is clutching her bag as if she fears I might snatch it. I know I must look a fright. I've barely slept, my hair is unkempt and my dress unpressed.

As we jolt along, the ice-covered fields become a wispy blur and I am trying to fight the images in my mind of Cecilia and Rebecca at Wittering Bay. I have never been there, but it is a bitter January and I know from Cecilia's fragile state that Rebecca will not be suitably dressed. I can almost imagine the cold wind draining the heat from Rebecca's little body, Cecilia too distraught to notice that Rebecca's tiny hands and feet have lost their colour. That she is succumbing to the cold.

It is nearly impossible to sit still. But I have to distract myself, as I have no other way to cope with my nerves. Writing everything down seems to be the only way I can stay calm, keep myself from standing up in the middle of the carriage and screaming.

As soon as the police finally left Northcote this afternoon, I told Cook that I had to run some errands in town. Not wanting to ask for a lift in case I needed to answer any questions about where I was going, I borrowed the stable boy's bicycle and cycled to Chichester train station. It is a thirty-minute train ride to Wittering and then I must get a bus to Wittering Bay. There are twenty minutes more until the train gets in to Wittering, then I have to get a bus to Seaview Cottage. I have no idea what I will find there. I have spent the day with the police, being pressed for hours on end about where Cecilia might be, so anxious is her husband – and his family – to contain the scandal. Indeed I took a call from a very anxious Mr Barton to his sister, to say he was on his way down from London. I spoke to him briefly before I put him through to his sister Jane, to say that I had no idea where Cecilia had gone. I listened in to their phone call in the next room: Jane was insistent that when they found Cecilia she must be committed to the asylum, now that she cannot be controlled. From the way Jane was speaking it sounded to me as if Mr Barton is in agreement.

I know I am taking a risk by not telling them about Seaview, for when I arrive it may be too late. But if they find her first, they will take Rebecca away and Cecilia will be incarcerated, and I will never see either of them again.

I wish the woman opposite would stop staring at me. I don't want to be noticed, I don't want anyone to see me or remember me. Despite the cold, sweat is trickling down my neck and my palms are slippery. A baby bottle, full of milk, sits in my pocket, its lid poking out, visible. I put my hand over it to cover it. I'm sure she's seen it. I'm sure she knows.

My head throbs from the lack of air so I stand and open the narrow window, but it makes no difference. I still feel gripped by the fear that plagued me when I woke this morning to find them gone. I do not know if Cecilia heard me talking to Rebecca last night, telling her that she was being sent away in the morning. I do not know if all this is my doing. I feel like I no longer know or trust myself.

The train staggers into the next station. The woman stands up and walks past me. I try not to look at her but can feel her eyes boring into me. My mind is racing. She can read my thoughts, she's getting off the train early so she can raise the alarm. I am wracked with uncertainty about what I have done. I should have told the police about Seaview. I'm risking Rebecca's life by taking matters into my own hands.

Please God let them be there. Please God let them be safe.

It was nearly pitch black, apart from the intense full moon lighting up the sea, by the time Harriet reached Wittering Bay and climbed off the bus and on to the winding lane.

'You all right, love? You know where you're going?' said the bus driver, frowning at her with obvious concern.

'Yes, thank you, I'm fine,' said Harriet unconvincingly.

The gale blowing in from the bay was pushing her off balance and the icy rain stung her cheeks. Harriet stood looking out at the bay, feeling the baby bottle in her pocket while a sense of utter despair began to course through her.

She had been so desperate to reach Cecilia and the baby she hadn't thought about arriving in the middle of nowhere in the dark. Cecilia had told her that you could see Seaview from the beach, and that a stone footpath led from the bay directly to its front door. As she walked on, a small Georgian farmhouse came into view. Approaching it, she saw a sign: SEAVIEW FARMHOUSE. It took everything she had in her not to open the gate, hammer on the front door and beg for help. But no one could know who she was or why she was here. If they did, they might call the police and she might never see Rebecca again.

Not knowing what else to do, she walked towards the dark, angry sea in search of the footpath that would lead her up to Seaview Cottage. The wind was bitterly cold and she pulled her thin black woollen coat around her. Her brown leather lace-ups sank deep into the cold sand with every step. Several times she nearly fell as the dunes leading down to the beach rolled and banked.

The dunes gave way to the flat beach and her feet plunged into several freezing puddles of seawater. Before long her shoes were soaked through. She could no longer feel her face or her hands. She knew that she was close, Cecilia had spoken of a path linking Seaview Farmhouse to Seaview Cottage, but above her the jagged cliff obscured her view. She knew she needed to push herself through the bitter gale, further towards the sea so that she could look beyond the cliff face and find the cottage.

The sea sounded like rumbling thunder as she forced herself to walk towards the water, the image of Cecilia and Rebecca floating in the violent, rolling waves haunting her. After ten minutes of pushing herself towards the sea, she reached the edge of the water, as far as she could go,

As the light from the moon danced on the frothed waves at the edge of the shore, she saw them – a pair of black brogues she recognized as well as her own. Harriet let out a cry and ran towards them as the sea lapped at them, preparing to sweep them away. Reaching them, she sank to her knees as she thought of the part she had played in Rebecca's death, imagining Cecilia carrying the helpless infant in her arms out to sea.

Kneeling down at the mouth of the sea, her shoes and coat sodden through with ice-cold seawater, she tried to compose herself, turning away from the water as if she could no longer face what it had done. As the full moon broke through the clouds, she saw it, the tiny white cottage, a beacon nestled in the hardness of the land, calling to her. Her heart broken, the pain in her body from the stinging rain began to totally consume her so that she felt as if she were drowning. Harriet forced herself to her feet and began trudging slowly across the sodden sand in the direction of the cottage. Jacob's voice began to taunt her: *'There is no baby because there is no love.'* She could see Cecilia clutching Rebecca, pleading with her: *'Please help us, Harriet. I trust only you.'*

As she neared the bottom of the path, the piercing, howling wind gave way to another sound. A sound she knew so well she was convinced she was imagining it. The sound of baby Rebecca's cries. Harriet stood, looking all around. The faint cry came again and she stood listening, desperately trying to pinpoint where it was coming from. Rebecca was somewhere on the beach.

She began to follow the faint sound, as she desperately tried to block out the sound of the howling wind blowing Rebecca's tiny voice away from her. Eventually a cave emerged from the blackness and as she stood at its entrance, the sound of Rebecca's cries began echoing off the walls. Harriet rushed inside, going deeper and deeper, Rebecca's cries growing louder now that she was out of the freezing wind.

'Tell me where you are, my darling!' she called out. 'Rebecca! Rebecca!'

Through the pitch blackness, the baby let out a long, desperate wail. Harriet began running, stumbling and falling on the sharp, jagged ground, and reaching out, felt a little, cold hand in the darkness.

Chapter Twenty-Three

I cough and cough and cannot stop. I begin to retch. I cannot breathe, I am frightened. Rosie presses the alarm for help and soon there are more of them. They put a mask on my face and push me forward so I can breathe, but I fall back on to the bed and the room goes dark. I feel as if I am under water. Seaweed wraps around my head and I am sucking in salty black water.

I am drowning again, sinking down and down. Deeper and deeper into hell. I close my eyes and wait for it to be over. For a moment, there is silence, then I feel a stab of pain in my shoulder.

My arm is being yanked and I am being pulled to the surface. I feel freezing air on my face and suck air into my lungs.

'Hold on!' a man is shouting at me, but I can barely hear him. My ears are filled with salt water.

He puts his arm around my neck and starts to pull me through the water. It comes at me from every direction. Every time I try and catch my breath a wave crashes over us. I want him to give up. I close my eyes and pray he will lose strength and let me go.

'Can you hear me? Wake up!'

The muffled male voice pulls me into consciousness, though my eyes are heavy and I can barely open them. I hear the loud crashing of the sea next to me and feel intense fear that I do not know where my baby is. I left her in the cave, I try and tell them, but I am so cold I cannot speak.

I am near the edge of the water; it is rushing under me then pulling away. The tide is pulling me back towards the sea. I hear my baby cry and look inland. There is no one on the beach, there is no one there with her. She is alone, in the cold, dark cave.

I close my eyes again. The man shouts at me and I turn my head away, fighting my nausea. Then I feel a hard slap across my cheek which stings me awake. I open my eyes.

The man is standing over me. It is dark but the moon is bright and I look up at him. He has a round face, dark hair and a thick moustache. I recognize him. He was in the water with me.

'Can you hear me? What is your name?' His breath smells of beer and my nausea increases.

My eyes feel burnt with the salt. The water pounded at both of us, so peaceful below the surface, so violent above it; forcing itself down our throats, into our ears and eyes, as he lay me on my back and dragged me slowly and painfully back to shore.

'Hold on! There's an ambulance coming.' He is coughing violently and bends over, resting his hands on his knees as he gasps for breath. I look up at him. I know it is my fault that he nearly drowned, but I didn't ask him to come after me. I wish he hadn't. I wish he had left me be.

I look away from him and try to take in my surroundings. I feel confused and unsure where I am. My skin is ice cold to the touch and my clothes are torn, but I feel warm.

'Who are you? What the hell were you doing out there?' He spits the words out. His breath is thick and he is shaking.

I am screaming for him to help my baby, but nothing comes out and I only vomit seawater. I close my eyes again so he takes me by both shoulders and shakes me until my neck hurts. He is shouting at me, telling me to talk to him, but I don't know the answers. I wish he would go away. I wish he hadn't come in after me. I can hear my baby's cry.

'Please get my baby, she's in the cave,' I whisper, but he doesn't hear. He is shouting for help.

My thoughts grow tentacles, tangling together. I went to Seaview with my baby. I stood on the balcony holding her and my mother called to me from the sea. I left my baby in the cave. I was going to go back for her.

As I waded in, I saw my mother up ahead, waving at me. But the water looked strange, it moved differently, like thick black tar that would pull me under. It scared me. I looked back at the cave, I didn't want to leave my baby, but then my mother called out to me, beckoning me in deeper. I wasn't holding my baby. I didn't take her with me.

She was safe in a blanket in the cave.

'She's freezing! Get a blanket! Someone get a bloody blanket!' I look up at the man. He is paler now. He is looking up at the lights coming towards us, then down again at me. A whistle blows, long and continuous. People are running towards us. Scurrying like ants. Go the other way, I think. Help my baby. She is all alone. It's too cold for her.

I turn my head and look at the silhouette of the cliffs, lit up by the moonlight. The lights are moving closer and closer.

Nausea overwhelms me and I turn and vomit on to the

gravelly sand. I hear the man shout again, this time with more urgency. As he runs away from me, towards the lights, his voice becomes fainter. I retch seawater. My tummy is in spasm; it hurts, but I don't care. Somebody appears next to me and holds me as I jerk violently. I push them away, but I am too weak and they still have their arms around me. It seems you have no right over your own body when you are dying.

A woman's voice pierces my waterlogged ears. 'Take off your coats, everyone, and lay them on the sand. We need to lift her off the cold ground, we need to get her dry. Where's the ambulance, for heaven's sake?'

'I can hear it. I can hear the siren.' Another man's voice; a crowd is gathering around me. I don't look up but I see several pairs of shoes – red, black, brown. Someone wraps their coat around me but I push them away.

'My baby is in the cave,' I say. 'Please help her.'

I try to stand. I need to get to my baby. I want to cry, but I don't have the strength. I don't have a voice, I don't have anything. A woman in a woollen hat appears next to me. Her eyes sparkle as they catch the moonlight. She has crooked teeth and a kind face, but it blurs out of focus. I point to the cave, but she is looking up at the blue lights.

'The ambulance is here. They're bringing a stretcher for you now. What were you doing in the water, and on such a freezing night? Why would you do that to yourself?'

The whistles continue to blow. People are shouting. I lie on my side and watch the water. I see my mother and me as a child, holding hands, running into the waves, screaming with delight at the waves as they crash into us. She takes my hand to make me brave, the waves crashing, higher and higher until we dive in. She is swimming fast. I can barely keep up. I call out to her. She turns and holds out her hand. Hurry!

'Over here!' I hear running feet over the shingles. They skid to a halt, showering me in tiny pebbles.

'Who is she?' They place me on a stretcher and carry me back up the beach. I am heavy and the sand is soft. They stumble twice and nearly fall. I am struck by blind panic that they are taking me away.

'Nobody knows who she is.' It's the woman in the woolly hat again. 'Who found her?' The sea is still so loud. It roars and everyone has to shout.

'I did.' The man's who pulled me out of the sea is next to me. 'I was walking home from the pub along the cliff path and I saw her walk into the water. I ran down as fast as I could to get to her, but she was already a long way into the water.'

'Heavens, she's bleeding!' The woman's voice again. 'Her legs are covered in blood – look.' As she says it I feel my stomach cramp and I cry out in pain as I realize for the first time that my insides are burning. As we reach the ambulance I hear another siren and turn my head slowly to see a police car pulling up on the cliff edge. Its blue lights twist and turn like a shark's eye watching me.

As the ambulance doors close I catch a last glimpse of Seaview. I grab the man in the ambulance with me, beg him not to leave her, but I am shaking too much to be understood and he plunges a needle into my arm.

With the sound of her cries in my ears, they turn over the engine, the sirens begin to wail, and we start to move.

Chapter Twenty-Four

Rebecca

Friday, 14 November 2014

Jessie looked down at the scrapbook on her lap and slowly turned the page. Rebecca watched her daughter's face as she read.

HOUSE OF HORRORS, the headline of the *Daily Mirror* screamed.

Jessie started to read one of the articles out loud: 'An idyllic seaside cottage became the stuff of nightmares when a war veteran beat his wife to death, then committed suicide all as their young daughter slept just feet away.'

When she had finished she looked up. 'I can't believe you had to stay at Seaview Farm, so close to where it happened. It must have been like re-living it every day.'

'I never went back to Seaview Cottage. Besides, I was only thirteen,' said Rebecca. 'I could stay with Harvey and his dad or go into care. I couldn't bear to be apart from Harvey, and Ted wanted me to live with them. I think he might also have felt guilty,' Rebecca added.

'What do you mean?'

Rebecca wanted nothing more than to close the scrapbook. She felt that the newsprint was crawling across the sofa towards her, like spiders. But Jessie was staring at her, clutching the faded articles as if they were a lifeline, so she forced herself to continue. 'I was lying in bed the night my parents were killed. There was a terrible storm in the bay. The cottage was very exposed, the single pane windows used to rattle so hard you'd think they were going to smash at any moment. I'm sure I heard someone at the door. Whoever it was came into the house and an argument started. I never saw who it was and by the time I went downstairs they were gone, but I'm convinced it was Ted or Harvey. I'd visited Harvey that day where he worked and told him we were leaving Seaview. I thought one of them had came to ask my father if I could stay behind at Seaview Farm with them. It made sense to me that it would cause a row. My father knew that Ted was in love with my mother, he would have been furious.' Rebecca paused at the memory of the rat-tat of the door knocker as she lay in bed. 'Harvey swore it wasn't him or his dad though, and the police confirmed they both had alibis in the pub. Maybe it was the storm, and I imagined it, but it's always bothered me.'

Jessie bit her lip. 'I keep thinking of you walking downstairs and finding your mum. You were thirteen. Did the police offer you any kind of counselling?'

Rebecca shook her head. 'No, it was a different world back then, they interviewed me at the police station right after it had happened, without a chaperone even. The policeman, Detective Gibbs, wouldn't even let me use the bathroom. I was sick all over him in the end.'

'But that can't have been police procedure. It was 1960, not the middle ages,' said Jessie.

'What could I do? I had no one. Ted Roberts was a nice man, but he was an alcoholic, he wasn't about to start complaining to the police.' Jessie was looking at her intently. Rebecca no longer feared that she would walk out at any minute but this moment of togetherness she had craved all her life was taking its toll on her.

'I'm just going to get myself a glass of water. Would you like one?' said Rebecca.

'No, thanks,' said Jessie, and returned her attention to the cuttings.

Rebecca stood and walked through to the kitchen, running the tap to fill a glass then splashing some cold water over her face. She took a few deep breaths, and caught her reflection in the mirror. She felt and looked exhausted.

When she returned to the sitting room, Jessie looked up. 'So when you had me, and you started to hear the voice of this policeman, Detective Gibbs, what did the staff at the hospital say?'

Jessie had obviously moved on from that night and was keen to talk about what had happened when she was born. Rebecca's brain felt like it was going into shock, being made to recall events she normally forbade it to remind her of.

'The hospital didn't know. Nobody knew, except Harvey.'

Jessie frowned. 'You hid how you were feeling? From the midwives and everyone?'

Rebecca nodded. 'It's one of the dangers of psychosis – you don't know you have it. You're convinced you are the only sane person and that everyone else is out to get you. Everyone is a danger, a threat. It's incredibly frightening.'

'But Dad said he knew about you seeing the policeman.'

'Harvey wanted to call the doctor and have me admitted to a psychiatric hospital but, luckily, a friend of mine – well,

John, my late husband, actually – paid me a visit. We worked together. I think he knew I'd been very worried about the pregnancy and he thought he might be able to help. He could see what a terrible state I was in and prescribed some anti-psychotic medication and persuaded Harvey to give it to me.'

'But you needed professional help. You didn't speak to anyone?'

'Jessie, if I had been officially diagnosed, I would have been sectioned. I would have been separated from you and I would never have worked as a doctor again.'

Rebecca watched Jessie take this in, feeling her heart quicken. 'Hang on? So you could have got proper help but you chose not to, for the sake of your career?'

'Well, mainly because I didn't want to be separated from you. Jessie, I didn't need professional help. John gave me the medication I needed. I took it and the hallucinations stopped.'

'How can you say you didn't need professional help? After everything you've just told me?'

'Jessie, you're choosing not to listen to what I'm telling you. I would have been separated from you, my baby. They didn't keep mother and baby together in those days. I was in a complete panic about something happening to you, the thought of you being out of sight for more than a minute sent my anxiety into overdrive. I was not prepared to be apart from you.'

'Then why did you say that about never working as a doctor again? It didn't really matter to you that you'd lose it all?'

'It was a factor but what I cared about most was staying

with you. I was psychotic. I got better. It was tough, I'll admit, but I was coping.'

'But you weren't. Which is probably why Dad had to get Liz. And you try and paint him out as the bad guy in all this.' Jessie's mood had changed, and her eyes glared at her mother. 'You needed help, Mum. You never dealt with what happened to you, you still haven't.'

'Jessie, I think you need to calm down,' said Rebecca. 'It isn't good for you to upset yourself. Please, let's just back up a bit. I'm sorry if I've said the wrong thing. I'm very tired and this is a hard conversation.' She walked towards Jessie and put her hand on her shoulder.

Jessie pulled herself away. 'Yes, you keep saying that. How hard it is for you. What about me? Your baby? Your child? Surely getting better should have been the only thing that mattered. So that you could take care of me?'

Jessie stood up, the cuttings scattering on the floor. 'And what about John?' Jessie continued. 'You talk about Liz already being on the scene, as if she ruined everything, broke up our little family, but he was already sniffing around then, was he? Making sure you didn't get off track with your precious career. Were you seeing him when you conceived me?'

'No, I wasn't! And I think this conversation is getting into dangerous territory. I told you that I would have to say some things that would upset you. About Liz and your dad. Why are you always so determined to trip me up? To back me into a corner so there's nowhere for us to go? I love you, Jessie. I want you in my life.'

'I don't believe you! You've never done anything to make me feel that you've got me, that I can rely on you. That you won't let me down. You always pull the rug just when I'm starting to trust you.'

'Jessie, what are you talking about? Please, don't go like this.'

Jessie walked to the door, but paused for a moment. Tears were pouring from her emerald-green eyes. 'Giving me up was easier than getting proper help and facing your demons.'

'It wasn't like that!'

'Yes it was. You say your mother wanted you to have choices and freedom. But you're as trapped as she was. The fact is that you're both the same, you and Harriet, all she did was teach you how to be a victim and live a lie. I don't want my daughter growing up exposed to that kind of fear and dishonesty. It wasn't your fault, Mum, what happened to you, but still carrying it is.'

Jessie picked up her bag and yanked open the front door.

'I love you. You're my blood, but I can't do this any more. It just hurts me too much.'

And with that, she slammed the door behind her, leaving Rebecca all alone with nothing but ghosts.

Chapter Twenty-Five

Iris

Wednesday, 19th November 2014

Iris finished reading Dr Hunter's notes on his meeting with Harriet Waterhouse in April 1953 and let out a heavy sigh.

Jacob Waterhouse had been desperate to leave Greenways, but his multiple attempts to take his own life, coupled with their inability to track his wife down, meant he had to be detained. It was something he had no control over. According to Dr Hunter's report, Jacob's only comfort lay in talking therapies, particularly art therapy, and during his incarceration he rediscovered a talent for painting and drawing, submitting his work to the patient magazine, *The Wishing Well*. Iris couldn't help lingering over Dr Hunter's closing comment in response to Harriet's asking about Jacob's propensity to violence, with five-year-old Rebecca in mind: *It is not unusual for relatives of a cantankerous patient to expect 'recovered' to mean that the patient is now a much nicer person. Treatment can only treat specific problems; it does not transform anybody. You can't make a silk purse out of sow's ear.*

'We are closing shortly. If you could start to gather your things.' Iris seemed to be the last person there.

Iris looked up at the woman, her cardigan buttoned up

to her neck, her hair parted neatly in the middle and scraped back into a bun, not a hair out of place, then down at her mother's statement, staring up at her from the desk. She imagined her mother as a thirteen-year-old girl, tucked up in bed, oblivious to the horror that was about to unfold in the living room below.

There was a storm that night and as I lay in bed, I thought I heard a knock at the front door and someone else in the house. My father's shouting became louder and I heard my mother screaming. I was normally too frightened to go downstairs when my father was angry but when I heard the gunshot I ran downstairs. I found my mother lying in the front room. Her face was very swollen, she was bleeding from her ear and eye. I called 999 and sat with her. She died a few minutes later. I did not go to my father . . . I could see that he was dead. There was no one in the house. Perhaps I imagined it from the knocking and whistling sounds the storm made at the doors and windows.

'Can I ask a quick question? These notes from my grand-mother's inquest, they mention a patient magazine at Greenways called *The Wishing Well*. Do you know if any copies were kept?'

'Yes, I believe we have a few. If you could come back in the morning, we can get them for you.'

'Is there any chance I could see them now? Please? I don't have to read them now, maybe I could photocopy them quickly?' said Iris, her eyes pleading up at the woman.

The woman looked up at the clock, then smiled at her. 'I'll see what I can find.'

Ten minutes later, Iris left the office clutching a sheaf of photocopies of *Wishing Well* magazines from 1947 to 1952 and a list of Greenways patient admissions for the entire duration of Jacob Waterhouse's stay.

As she ran out into the rain, with the bundles of papers in one hand and her phone buzzing in the other, she waved frantically at a taxi and jumped in.

Chapter Twenty-Six

Harvey

5 p.m. Wednesday, 19 November 2014

'What are you talking about? Rebecca's mother died when she was thirteen.' Harvey had walked up the beach and called DI Galt back.

Harvey looked up at Seaview. He could feel the wind rushing past his ears, the sea thrashing behind him, and he felt like he was being pulled into a black hole. Sucked back in time.

'That's what we need your help with.' DC Galt's voice was faint against the thunder of the sea. 'She says she's Rebecca's birth mother.'

'I can't hear you,' said Harvey. 'Hang on.' He began to walk with heavy footsteps back towards the car park. Away from the wind, he tucked himself in the cave underneath the cliff edge. 'What the hell is going on? Rebecca's mother died when she was thirteen. What has this woman got to do with finding Jessie?'

'We can't prove it at the moment, but she's saying she's Rebecca's birth mother, that Harriet Waterhouse stole her when she was a baby. We have reason to believe Jessie may have known about this, as she tried to visit Cecilia in the days before her disappearance.'

'What? What do you mean, visited her? When?'

'A carer at the home where Cecilia lives, Grace House, recognized her. She went a few days ago and asked to see Cecilia, but she was asleep so she left again. She didn't leave her details but the carer recognized Jessie from the pictures in the *Chichester Evening Herald*.'

'Okay,' said Harvey, not knowing what to think. 'Who is this woman, Cecilia?'

'She's an elderly lady who was brought into St Dunstan's Hospital in Chichester this evening. She's dying, Mr Roberts, and she wants to find her daughter before it's too late. She saw you on the news today and she says you knew her daughter, who she lost as a newborn – Rebecca.' DC Galt paused. 'And Rebecca is obviously Jessie's mother's name. We think it needs looking into, and you may be able to help work out if there is any validity in her story, or any reason for Jessie to contact her, if you would be willing to come and speak to her.'

'Why would Jessie have contacted her? It must be a mistake. I don't want to leave the beach. The window to find Elizabeth alive is closing. If Jessie's here, we should be trawling the coastline until we find her. You should be here with torches looking through the dunes for them. We're running out of time.'

Looking down the beach, he could picture tomorrow if they didn't find Jessie tonight. Imagine the fleet of police cars rushing to Wittering Bay, forensic teams, their tents erected on the dunes, the bodies of Jessica and Elizabeth being examined for evidence of when exactly they died. Probably right this moment, as he stood, on this beach, being asked by the police to leave them behind. Right now, there was still a chance. Where were they?

'We've had confirmation from the bus driver that it was definitely Jessie and Elizabeth on the bus. We are briefing a search party at 5 a.m., ready for first light at Wittering. In the meantime, there are ten police officers patrolling the dunes and coastline tonight.'

Harvey looked up to scan the dunes and saw torchlight moving in the distance. 'If you could come into St Dunstan's Hospital to speak with her, it might help us to work out why Jessie tried to contact her. It's a long shot but possible she may have some information that could help us work out where Jessie's gone. Her visiting Cecilia is too significant to not act upon.'

'Can't Rebecca do it? If it concerns her?' Harvey let out a heavy sigh.

'We'd rather you spoke to her first. Her connection to Jessie, rather than to Rebecca, is the most pressing issue. You know Jessie better than anyone, by all accounts, so it needs to be you. You're the most likely person to be able to work out why she tried to visit Cecilia.'

'Fine.' Harvey ended the call and backed out of the cave, looking up at Seaview as the moon appeared from behind the clouds. The cottage lay in darkness, the lights turned off since the police had left, yet it still glowed on the cliff edge, its white walls catching the moonlight, its black windows making it look like a dice waiting to roll off the cliff and seal his fate.

The drive to St Dunstan's Hospital was a blur of distant memories returning to haunt him. It was the same road he had taken the night Rebecca's parents had been killed.

When he had sat in the back of a police car on the way to Chichester police station.

Through the pouring rain, he had seen the faint brake lights of the police car in front of them, the car containing Rebecca. By the time they reached the police station, she was gone.

When he arrived he had called out for her, desperate to see her and make sure he was okay. After he had caused a scene at the station looking for Rebecca, they had held him and his father in a holding cell all night, finally taking their statements at dawn, as they both sat bleary-eyed and shocked. 'The daughter of Harriet and Jacob Waterhouse is saying that someone knocked on their front door last night, that whoever it was started an argument that led to their deaths. Was that one of you two, by any chance?'

'No, we were in the King's Head all evening – there must have been a dozen witnesses. The first I knew of any of this was when I saw the police lights as we came into Seaview. I need to speak to Rebecca, please. I'm begging you.' The duty officer had just looked away, making painfully slow notes, never replying to his increasingly desperate request to see her.

'She's adamant she heard someone at the door. Who else could it have been?'

'How should I know!' he had snapped.

'Look, laddie, I'm not sure I'm liking your tone.' The policeman leaned forward, beads of sweat forming on his brow. 'It's clear for me to see that Mr Roberts here is inebriated, so perhaps I should lock the pair of you up until he's sobered up and can think a bit more clearly about the events of last night, because he's not able to corroborate your story at the moment.'

'I'm sorry, sir, I didn't mean any disrespect. I want to help you with your enquiries. Please just let me speak to her.' Harvey had tried to stay calm, knowing that he needed to keep the police on side, that if he lost his temper he would never get to Rebecca.

At dawn, with no reason to hold them and their sworn statements signed, they had been released and he was told that Rebecca had left. He raced back to Seaview Cottage to try and find her. But it was cordoned off with police tape, two policemen milling around drinking cold cups of tea and trying to shelter from the fierce wind from Wittering Bay. He sat in the truck, not knowing where she had gone, and then went frantically driving around the town looking for her, asking if anyone had seen her. Finally he went home, fell through the front door, exhausted, and found her fast asleep in a chair in front of the fire.

As Harvey pulled up outside the hospital he could see the throng of reporters milling around in the drizzling rain and a policeman waiting at the entrance to the car park waved him in. The rain pelted at his windscreen as he pulled into the same parking space he had pulled out of just under twenty-four hours before to leave Jessie.

Harvey took several deep breaths and looked up at the group of reporters at the entrance to the hotel. Shaking away the tears, he opened the car door and walked towards the pack.

'How are you feeling, Mr Roberts? Is there any news from Jessie's partner?' They rushed at him, and he bowed his head. 'Have there been any developments since the press conference this afternoon? Do you fear that time is running out for baby Elizabeth?'

They all shouted at him as he passed, their questions bleeding into one, louder and louder.

Then silence as the doors closed behind him. The policeman stretched out his arm towards the long, empty corridor ahead and said, 'DC Galt is waiting for you on Churchill Ward.'

The clicking of the policeman's shoes in front of him rang in his ears as Harvey followed him along the corridors, the endless red signs directing them to Churchill Ward. The last few days had felt like a never-ending car crash, with him, Jessie and Elizabeth skidding towards a collision that was yet to happen. He was exhausted from the lack of sleep, from the worry, from the constant pumping of adrenaline.

The policeman pressed the buzzer on to the ward, they turned the corner and the sound of beeping machines began to bounce off the white walls. Harvey's eyes scanned the corridor, along which a row of wheelchairs were backed up. Beyond it a desk with three nurses on the telephone or writing on a whiteboard. DC Galt was walking towards him, holding out her hand for Harvey to shake.

And behind her, the open door to a private hospital room containing an elderly woman who, as DC Galt gently eased him forward, stared at him intently with her emerald-green eyes before the door slammed shut behind him.

Chapter Twenty-Seven

Harriet

July 1952

Harriet stood in the cool surf in Wittering Bay and clapped her hands together in happiness as her little girl swam towards her for the first time, her blonde curls tumbling in front of her emerald-green eyes which fixed on her with sheer determination.

'You did it, my clever girl!' she said as Rebecca fell into her, her tiny bronzed arms wrapping themselves around her neck.

'I can swim, Mummy!' said the little girl, looking up at her and laughing. Harriet waded back to a spot where Rebecca could stand, and as the sunshine danced on the surface, walked backwards several feet along the seabed and opened her arms to her.

Again, the little girl began swimming towards her enthusiastically, her smile beaming, and as she reached her, Harriet showered her with kisses and pulled her in tight. As she stood with the child in her arms, seawater dripping from their tanned bodies, the warm sea air from Wittering Bay blew past and goosebumps danced up their forearms.

As they looked to shore, they could hear the sound of children laughing and the surf rushing at the golden sand of the bay. A fishing boat chugged across the horizon. Harriet inhaled the sea air, kissed Rebecca's sea-drenched cheeks. At moments like these, it was hard to believe that the picture-postcard scene surrounding them was the same hostile place which had greeted her that fateful night.

Five years had passed since she had found Rebecca freezing to death in the cave, since she had staggered and tripped along the cliff face, hammering frantically at the door of Seaview Farm until Ted Roberts let them out of the bitter night and into his life.

Unable to return to Northcote with baby Rebecca, she had made a new life for them both. Ted Roberts, a recently widowed farmer, was happy to take in Harriet and the baby he believed to be hers, and for her to run the farmhouse and look after his little boy, Harvey. She spent her mornings cooking and cleaning and her afternoons playing with the children. Though the happiness of her days distracted her, when she climbed into bed at night her guilt returned in earnest. As she lay in the dark, she lived the day that she lost Cecilia over and over in her mind. Her body still moved along with the rattling train on the painstaking journey from Northcote to Seaview, she could still feel her panicked heart and the fierce winter wind as she stumbled across the beach in the darkness looking for them. In her dreams every night she heard Rebecca's faint cry guiding her into the cave and her own desperate cries for Cecilia as she stood at the sea edge in the moonlight.

Time did nothing to heal the guilt of what she had not done to save her; that she had not told the police about Seaview as they questioned her relentlessly; not got to Cecilia in time. And as Rebecca grew, the beautiful, fair-haired child

227

looked more and more like her mother every day. To Harriet, despite the untold happiness that Rebecca brought to her life, when her baby's green eyes locked on to hers, it was like Cecilia's ghost coming back to haunt her. At first, she had held out hope that Cecilia was alive, prayed night after night that news of her would surface. Too afraid to go to the police and ask about her for fear of drawing attention to herself, she had accepted Ted's offer to stay at Seaview and work on the farm in the hope that if Cecilia did ever return, she would be able to find them.

All she could do was take care of Rebecca, love her as her own. And wait.

It was spring 1947 when, three months after arriving, she had walked into Wittering with Rebecca in her pram and seen the headline screaming at her from the newsagent's window.

BODY OF UNKNOWN WOMAN
WASHES UP AT WEST WITTERING

Harriet's hands had immediately begun to shake and, stopping in her tracks, she had wheeled the pram slowly towards the glass to read the front page of the *Chichester Evening Herald* on display.

> The body of woman was discovered by fishermen close to the shore on the morning of 10 April.
>
> The woman's body was recovered by Lifeboat teams and is severely decomposed, the Chichester inquest heard.
>
> The coroner said, 'The body was badly degraded. It's impossible for me to state when she entered the water. I would not suggest there's any evidence of third-party involvement.'

Anyone with any information about the woman, who is believed to be aged between twenty and forty, five foot six inches tall with green eyes should contact Sussex police.

Harriet had turned and walked back to Seaview, closing the front door before breaking down. Her worst fears had been realized: Cecilia was dead. Finding her shoes at the shore of Wittering Bay the night she found Rebecca was evidence enough. But this proved it to her beyond a doubt.

The body of a woman? Why hadn't Charles come forward to claim her? He must have read the papers, heard about a body washing up or been notified by the police. Perhaps he thought the body was too far away to be Cecilia. Or perhaps he just didn't care. She couldn't bear to think of Cecilia's body, unclaimed, in an unmarked grave somewhere.

Several times after that she had plucked up the courage to go to the police and tell them what she knew, but every time the thought of Rebecca being taken away stopped her.

Rebecca was Jacob's little girl, her responsibility. Rebecca was a scandal Charles wanted to bury and he would ensure Rebecca was sent away somewhere she would never return from. It wouldn't bring Cecilia back to tell the police that she knew who the unidentified woman was. She owed it to Cecilia to be strong, to raise and love Rebecca as her own.

'Can we see Harvey now, Mummy?' Rebecca said, holding her mother's face in both hands and turning it to meet her eyes, as she always did when she wanted her full attention.

Harriet smiled at the little girl's words. *Mummy*. She still remembered the first time she had said it but like the day Rebecca had taken her first steps, instead of the warm feeling it should have given her, Rebecca's first words – and steps – acted as a reminder of time passing, of the gaping black hole since Cecilia had fled Northcote, left her baby to die and taken her own life in the cruel January sea.

'Yes, we should go or we'll be late!' said Harriet, and Rebecca wrapped her little body around Harriet's as she waded through the water towards shore.

When they reached Seaview, their bodies dripping sea-water all through the cottage, Harriet smiled at the little girl and then walked across the cool stone floor to the dresser and pulled out the drawer containing Rebecca's colouring book. As the heavy drawer fell forward and her red leatherbound diary slid from the back, where she had hidden it from sight on the day Ted gave them the keys to Seaview. She had not looked at it since. She couldn't bear to read it, to think of Cecilia and Northcote and what she had done. Her diary and her post-office savings book were the only things she had as a reminder of the life she'd had before.

Rebecca had been a newborn when she had last poured out her heart on to its pages, sitting at the kitchen table at Seaview Cottage on the first day of their new life at Wittering Bay. Harriet slowly reached in and pulled the diary out and then handed Rebecca her colouring book and crayons which the little girl pounced on happily. As she did so, Cecilia's gold locket, which had been around Rebecca's little neck, fell onto the floor. She picked it up and examined it, the Northcote family coat of arms engraved on to its now dull surface.

Harriet looked up at the clock: ten minutes until she needed to be at Seaview Farm to take over from Ted. She could picture him now, rushing around looking for his boots, which Harriet always put neatly by the back door, a piece of toast in his mouth, butter in his beard, shouting at Harvey to move his toy cars before they found their way under his shoes and sent him flying. Even though she had turned the small Georgian farmhouse around, from the chaos she had found when she'd first arrived to the organized, tidy home and farm office it was today, Ted and Harvey still managed to leave a trail of destruction in their wake.

'Right, little one, let's go,' she said, returning the locket and diary to the drawer. She pulled Rebecca's hand-knitted cardigan on, buttoning it up before opening the front door of Seaview Cottage and stepping out on to the cobbled stone pathway that led along the cliff edge to the farmhouse.

As Harriet pulled the door shut, Rebecca darted past her and skipped along the path they had trodden a thousand times over the past five years. As Rebecca performed her usual trick of walking too near to the edge to wind her mother up. Harriet looked down at the sun-kissed little girl, who smiled back at her, delighted with herself. Harriet reached out and clung to Rebecca's hand, which she held high over her head, inviting Harriet to tickle her under her arms.

'Good morning, Matilda,' said Rebecca, pointing into the distance, where several fat hens were thundering towards them across the courtyard.

Rebecca opened the gate and let her mother through before the gaggle of hens made their escape. The clucking birds surrounding them, and Rebecca started to giggle. 'It's not lunchtime yet,' she said, as the hens trotted along beside them, pestering them for food.

'Will there be any eggs left?' said Rebecca, pointing to the chicken coup at the far side of the courtyard.

'Ted and Harvey have probably gobbled them up already for breakfast, but we can try,' said Harriet, lifting open the lid of the coop and smiling at Rebecca's glee as she spotted a single egg nestling amongst the hay.

As Rebecca retrieved the egg and beamed up at her mother, Harriet looked over at the Georgian farmhouse, from which Ted Roberts was emerging. Set back from the limestone courtyard, two narrow pillars framing the blue front door, wisteria taking over its symmetrical form, it was a pretty house, perfect but for the telltale signs of jobs she still needed to get to despite her best efforts; peeling paintwork on windowsills and windows greying with dirt. As Ted opened the door and waved at her, his blue eyes squinting in the summer sunshine, she smiled and waved back.

'Shall we tell Ted about your swimming?' said Harriet, so that Ted could hear.

'You're not swimming, are you, Miss Waterhouse? You could teach my wimp of a son a thing or two. Harvey, get out here!' he said, leaving the front door ajar as he crossed over to them with his lolling walk. Ted lifted Rebecca up and blew a raspberry on the little girl's cheek as they turned to see a seven-year-old boy with blond hair and wearing dungarees appear at the door. 'Miss Rebecca here is swimming, Harvey Roberts, and she's two years younger than you!'

As Ted picked the little girl up and threw her into the air, Harriet heard the familiar sound of the postman's bicycle bell and she looked up to see him cycling towards the gate.

'I'll get that,' shouted Ted, as he headed through the gate on his way out. 'I need to get up to the top field and mend the electric fence. I'll see you at lunchtime. Are you okay to take the truck to Mr Tucker with the littles and get feed?'

'Something for you this morning, Mrs Waterhouse,' said the postman as Ted passed him, and he and Harriet exchanged looks once his eyes fell on the envelope being passed to her.

Harriet smiled at the postman and took the letter. Her heart raced and her cheeks flushed as she felt Ted watching her. There was only one person who knew where she was – Jacob's doctor at Greenways. She had written to him just the week before, after wrestling with her conscience.

What he had done to Cecilia was unforgivable, but he had been in the grip of battle neurosis. Jacob was a good man, she loved him and he was Rebecca's father. The little girl could never know her mother, but she was his child, Jacob was her husband and he needed them. She could not just abandon him.

She looked down at the letter. The stamp was punched with a Chichester postmark and as she turned it over to open it she looked over at Rebecca sitting on a hay bale and laughing as Harvey chased the hens around the yard. Watching her daughter's happiness, she wished she could freeze the moment in time, as if the envelope were a bomb about to explode in their lives and change everything. As she carefully slid the typed letter from the envelope, she saw that her hands were shaking.

Greenways Psychiatric Hospital, Chichester

18th July 1952

Dear Mrs Waterhouse,

Thank you for your letter dated 14th July notifying us of your new address.

As you know, we have been treating your husband as an inpatient on the Battle Neurosis Ward at Greenways since January 1947. Mr Waterhouse was originally admitted suffering with acute states of neurotic disturbances or battle fatigue, and he had to be heavily dosed with lithium carbonate. Electro-convulsive therapy has proved to mechanically lift Mr Waterhouse's depression, and after a year he was able to leave the locked ward and for the past three years has been on the open ward. He is for the first time showing signs of wanting to reintegrate himself back into society and is able to go for a half a day or a single day excursion before returning to the safety of the ward. Lastly Jacob has particularly benefitted from the talking therapies, especially art therapy.

I am happy to say he is no longer at risk to himself or others and is making progress. I feel the time has come where it would be beneficial for him to see his family. It is my hope that, with your support, he will be able to return home for weekends before his formal discharge. You mention in your letter that you have a five-year-old daughter at home and we would need to ensure you are happy for him to live with you and that you have community support for your husband before he is fully discharged.

In the hope of rehabilitating him and enabling him to come home to his family, I would appreciate the opportunity to discuss his behaviour towards you and any triggers which you found brought on the flashbacks to his experiences in Normandy. We would need to work together to make sure that you understand how the triggers for Battle Neurosis work and how best to avoid them at home, particularly as you have a young child who could potentially make loud noises and startle him.

If possible, I would like to meet with you on Thursday of next week, and as this doesn't leave us much time, I would be grateful if you could reply to me at your earliest convenience. If you would like to bring your daughter, I know that Jacob is very keen to meet her, and we could arrange for your husband to take your daughter to the farm here at Greenways in order to make it as relaxed as possible.

Jacob speaks of you often and I very much look forward to meeting with you,

Yours sincerely,
Dr Philip Hunter

Harriet let out a sigh, returned the letter to its envelope and pushed it into her pocket.

'Come on, little ones, in the truck. We're going to get some feed.' As she reached down to lift Rebecca up in her arms, she looked out at the sea beyond Wittering Bay, which was starting to churn. The bright sunshine of the morning had faded, the temperature had dropped and it was beginning to cloud over. As she started up the engine in the truck, little spatters of rain began to tap at the windows and she knew in her heart that a storm was coming.

Chapter Twenty-Eight
Harvey

6 p.m. Wednesday, 19 November 2014

Harvey Roberts stood at the door of Cecilia Barton's quiet side room and looked in at the elderly lady. Her eyes were closed and the head of her bed was elevated, her faded hospital gown hung from her frail shoulders and her long grey hair fell around her sunken cheeks. From her laboured breathing it was clear that she was struggling to hold on to whatever life she had left. Her cheeks were deathly pale and a mask sat over her mouth. A nurse was at her side, reading the monitor which beeped next to her.

DC Galt stood too close to Harvey at the door's entrance, breathing heavily, so that Harvey had to inch forward to get some space. She made her way over to Cecilia's bedside and fixed her gaze on Harvey. He stayed where he was, rooted to the spot. He was still not sure what was required of him; what this woman wanted from him on her death-bed was not a priority to him. He had enough grief of his own to deal with, enough pain and regret, without having to deal with hers too. He wished he hadn't come here, he should have stayed at Wittering Bay, looking for Jessie. There was a repugnant smell in the air, a stale odour which made him feel as if death were close. He could taste it and it made him feel nauseous.

'What are we doing here?' he asked. 'I've never seen this woman before. It feels wrong – she should be with her loved ones, not us, not strangers.'

'That's what we are trying to help her with. She wants to find her daughter before it's too late. As you can see, she doesn't have long.'

The woman stirred but didn't wake. DC Galt leaned over and whispered in her ear. 'Cecilia, can you hear me?'

As the woman began to stir, Harvey winced. He didn't want this, he didn't want to talk to her, he didn't know who she was. What he did know was that she represented the past, a past he didn't want to wake.

The old woman began to cough, deep, rumbling, hacking coughs. Her shoulders heaved as the phlegm in her lungs tried to fight its way up and out of her. Slowly, she looked around the room and her emerald-green eyes fixed on him. She pulled off her mask and the oxygen coming from it hissed like a snake set for battle.

'Hello, Harvey,' she said.

'Why don't you come and sit here?' suggested DC Galt, pulling up a chair next to the bed. The words were gentle but her tone was assertive.

Slowly Harvey inched across the room.

'I'm sorry about your daughter,' the woman said, coughing again. Harvey waited, expecting another bout of uncontrollable hacking – but it didn't come.

'Thank you. I'm not sure how I can help you,' said Harvey, but he already knew his words were a lie. Her green eyes didn't leave him: eyes he recognized, eyes he knew.

'I think you knew my daughter, Rebecca.' The woman spoke painfully slowly, as if every word took the effort of climbing a mountain. 'She lived at Seaview Cottage, as a child.'

'Yes,' said Harvey. 'I knew Rebecca, but she was Harriet and Jacob Waterhouse's daughter.'

Cecilia's eyes sparkled with tears. Every breath now was a struggle. 'She's my daughter. Harriet stole her from me.'

Harvey shook his head, 'That can't be true – Harriet could never do that, the woman was a saint, she practically raised me after my mother died.' He looked at the clock, imagining Jessie and her baby in the dunes, freezing, alone. He needed to go to them, he needed to leave. His feet were tapping under his chair, he couldn't be here. He needed to go.

'I'm sorry you and Rebecca aren't together any more. You loved her very much. I saw you together, that day she visited you at Greenways. The day her parents were killed.'

As the weight of Cecilia's words hit, it all stopped: his determination to get away from her, his racing thoughts of Jessie and baby Elizabeth, the beach, the cold, the ticking clock. 'What did you say?' Harvey said, his complete attention on the elderly lady now.

She looked at him. 'I saw you that day, with my baby.'

The day Rebecca had visited him there came back to him in flashes. They were leaving Seaview, she'd said, she had come to say goodbye. He had walked her to the gate, past Ward B, the locked ward.

'Why were you at Greenways?' Harvey said slowly.

Cecilia took several slow breaths before carrying on. 'They locked me up for drowning my baby.' She closed her eyes and paused before she continued. 'Jacob raped me, during the time he and Harriet worked at Northcote, and I fell pregnant with Rebecca. We were a scandal my husband wanted to get rid of. And Harriet helped him make it happen.'

'No, you're wrong. I don't know why you would do this and I'm sorry you're suffering, but you're lying, Harriet would never steal another woman's child.'

An image of Harriet in the farmyard came to Harvey's mind. The woman who had devotedly looked after their home. Fed all the farm workers, taken care of him and Rebecca, played with him, made him clothes, fed him and loved him, unconditionally.

He stood up, the scrape of his chair on the floor echoing loudly.

'You were the reason I found my way to Harriet and Jacob the night they died.' Harvey stopped. She paused for a moment, gathering her breath. 'Seeing Rebecca gave me the courage to escape. It had been a long time since I'd last tried to take my own life, so I wasn't on the supervised ward at night.' Cecilia started to cough. Harvey stood over her, waiting for her to continue. 'I stole a key from a junior nurse to get out of the ward. I knew that as long as I was back by dawn they would never know I had gone.'

Harvey's mind raced. 'It was you at the door that night. You started the argument between Harriet and Jacob.'

Cecilia nodded. 'Jacob didn't know that Harriet wasn't Rebecca's mother. I tried to calm him down, but there was nothing I could do. He wanted to kill her.' Cecilia's voice started to tremble and tears trailed down her pale cheeks. 'I just wanted to see my little girl.'

Harvey's heart ached. For this woman, for Harriet, for Rebecca. But mostly for Jessie, for the pain this woman lying on her deathbed in front of him now had unwittingly inflicted on his little girl by causing her mother so much trauma all those years ago.

'What do you mean there was nothing you could do, why didn't you run and get help?' Harvey felt his eyes sting with tears.

Cecilia's eyes fixed on Harvey. 'I tried, I knew Seaview Farm was close, I ran through the rain across the cornfield and hammered on the front door, but there were no lights on, no one came. And as I ran back I heard the gunshot.'

Harvey hung his head, 'So you ran away and left Rebecca all alone?' he said quietly.

'No, I ran back, but when I got to the window I saw her.' Cecilia paused. 'She was crouched over Harriet's body and she was screaming. It was the first time I'd seen my little girl in thirteen years. And I had caused that pain. My baby, my child, who I'm supposed to protect.' Cecilia was crying again now. 'They'd told me so many times that I'd drowned her, it was like seeing a ghost. She was so beautiful.' Rosie leaned forward and wiped Cecilia's tears away. 'Then I heard the police sirens and I panicked. I hadn't set foot outside Greenways for thirteen years and I was terrified of what they would do to me if they found out.'

Cecilia started to cough again, her chest gurgling and wheezing as she gasped for breath. Rosie leaned her forward and rubbed her back until it slowly subsided.

'I know I can't ever expect her to forgive me,' Cecilia said. 'I just want to tell her that I'm sorry.'

Chapter Twenty-Nine
Harriet

July 1952

Harriet Waterhouse sat on the bus to Greenways Psychiatric Hospital clinging tightly to her daughter's hand. Occasionally, Rebecca looked up at her and smiled broadly, her green eyes sparkling, her long, fair hair pulled back from her porcelain skin with a cream ribbon.

The middle-aged woman in the seat next to them smiled as they got on. 'What a beautiful child,' she commented, staring at Rebecca, as people often did. Harriet smiled self-consciously. She always knew what people were thinking: how can such a plain woman have produced such a beauty? At only five years of age, Rebecca was the image of her mother, with her piercing green eyes, heart-shaped face and bee-stung lips. She moved with the same grace and spoke with a smile on her lips, as if everything she discovered filled her with wonder and joy. Standing behind Rebecca in front of the mirror, doing her hair, as she'd done Cecilia's, listening to her contented chatter, it was like going back in time. Harriet looked lifeless in comparison; her pale skin flat, her mousy hair lank, her grey eyes sullen. Rebecca shone, as Cecilia had done, and Harriet would forever be in their shadow.

The bus conductor announced the stop and Harriet swallowed down the butterflies in her stomach. She stood up and Rebecca followed. Stepping on to the pavement, Harriet looked up at the red-brick building behind the wrought-iron gates, then down at Rebecca. Every part of her was screaming to run, that crossing the threshold to Greenways with Rebecca was a mistake she would never be able to undo. But Jacob was her father. She had known that their time would run out, that one day the past would catch up with them and she would have to answer questions about her little girl. But it had still been a shock when that moment suddenly came, in the form of Miss Clara and Miss Ethel as they walked into a tourist shop in Wittering Bay earlier that summer.

8th June 1952

Dear Diary

I had always known the past would catch up with us, that we couldn't hide away forever. As with all the most crucial moments in one's life, it so nearly didn't happen. We had just paid for our ice creams in Barney's and as Rebecca and I were walking out, Miss Clara and Miss Ethel walked in. I saw them before they saw me and tried to pass them quickly, but I knew they had seen us and, my heart thudding loudly in my ears, Miss Clara called out my name.

I smiled politely, my mind racing. 'How are you, Harriet?' they said, looking at Rebecca whose entire focus was on her ice cream. My mind scrambled. If I'd wanted no one to find us, I should have moved further away. But we had no money and nowhere to go. Mr Roberts taking us

242

in at Seaview Farm was a small miracle, and one I felt Cecilia had a hand in. I sensed her spirit at Seaview. Though I knew she was gone, it seemed fitting to raise her child in the place she loved more than any other. I felt tied to it, bonded, unable to leave. But in that moment, looking down at my little girl, with Miss Clara and Miss Ethel's eyes boring into her, I wished I had run far away with baby Rebecca that day and never come back.

'A little girl, how lovely,' said Miss Clara. 'What a beautiful child,' said Miss Ethel. They spoke almost over one another. They had witnessed two of my miscarriages, and called the doctor for the latter as it had been so dreadful. They had shown me great kindness and I didn't want to lie to them.

Ted Roberts had always assumed Rebecca was mine and I had never thought to correct him. Cecilia was dead – what would be the point? I told him only that my husband had been taken away to the local psychiatric hospital having suffered a nervous breakdown and that I had lost my lady's-maid position as a consequence. My story was that we had come to Wittering Bay looking for work and I had got off the bus just as the storm came in. But telling my story to Miss Clara and Miss Ethel then, I felt my face burn.

'How old is she?' they asked, as I clutched Rebecca's hand a bit tighter and pulled her to me. 'Five,' I answered, not wanting to say more. 'And where are you living now?' Miss Clara was wearing too much rouge; she reminded me of the wife in the Punch and Judy show we had just watched on the beach. 'We heard that you were no longer at Northcote but we didn't know where you'd moved on to,' said Miss Ethel. 'Yes, a policeman came to the house looking for you, but we weren't able to help him.' Miss Clara spoke over Miss Ethel in a hurried way that made me think they had fretted a lot over the visit.

'A policeman?' I had whispered the words, trying to subdue the panic in my voice. 'Yes,' said Miss Ethel. 'Apparently, a doctor at Greenways Asylum has been trying to find you. Your husband was admitted to his care.'

'Yes,' said Miss Clara. 'He left his number. I think I still have it at home on the mantelpiece.'

I pictured Miss Clara scribbling the number down and propping it up on the gold-leaf mirror on the mantelpiece I had dusted every day for nearly a decade. Imagined Miss Clara and Miss Ethel coming home after their day on the beach, talking about our meeting all the way home on the train, deciding in the end to call the local policeman to say they had seen me. 'She was acting rather suspiciously,' they would say. 'Not like her at all, and she had a little girl with her. Yes, that's right. Wittering Bay.'

'So where are you residing now?' Miss Clara wiped a bead of sweat from her forehead and I watched it drip down the back of her hand.

'Seaview Cottage, just in the bay,' I said, forcing the words from my mouth. There was no point lying. It was over, we had been found, and if I tried to run it would only arouse suspicion. 'I'm surprised they went to the trouble of sending a policeman,' I said, stumbling over my words. 'I'm sorry he had to trouble you.'

'Well, he said he'd tried Northcote, but that you'd left there in rather a hurry.' Miss Clara's eyes were piercing into me, looking for the truth.

244

'I'll call Greenways and let them know where I am. It was so lovely to see you,' I muttered, smiling, and I took Rebecca's hand and led her from the shop and out into the baking afternoon sun.

'Why are you sad, Mummy?' It was the morning of their trip to Greenways, and Harriet had been dressing Rebecca, lost in thought about the day ahead.

'You are such a darling girl,' said Harriet, thinking of Cecilia's soft-heartedness, something Rebecca had clearly inherited. 'I'm not sad. I'm thinking about how grown-up you're getting. You look pretty as a picture, sweetheart,' she said, kissing Rebeccas's rosy cheek. She had used the wages she had saved to buy her a smart black woollen coat and new patent shoes especially for the occasion, and as she fastened the shiny brass buttons that morning she explained to the little girl where they were going. 'Today we are going to meet your daddy,' she said, smiling as best she could.

The little girl had been cautious in her response, staring at Harriet for a long time before answering. 'Why doesn't he live with us, like Harvey's daddy?'

'Because he's been very poorly, so he needed to be in hospital.'

'Did he hurt himself?' The little girl's green eyes spar-kled as she spoke, though Harriet could sense her apprehension.

'In a way. The war made him very unhappy. He saw lots of his friends getting hurt and it really upset him.' Harriet pushed two kirby grips either side of the ribbon in Rebec-ca's hair.

'Like when I got upset because Harvey cut his hand on the barbed wire?' Rebecca frowned.

'Just like that. But he's better now and he wants to come home. Would that be all right with you?'

'I don't know,' said Rebecca quietly. 'I like it just the two of us.'

'You'll like it with Daddy too. He loves you very much and he's really missed you.' Harriet clutched the little girl's hand tight.

'How can he miss me when he's never met me?' Rebecca looked up at her with her mother's questioning look.

'I loved you before I met you,' Harriet said, before she could stop herself.

'When I was growing in your tummy?'

Harriet nodded at the little girl. 'Go and put your shoes on. We don't want to be late.'

She had asked Dr Hunter several times about taking Rebecca along on their first meeting. The last time Harriet saw Jacob had been five years ago, when he was being taken away from Northcote by ambulance. The same day, Cecilia had confessed to her that Jacob had raped her, and that Rebecca was his child.

'Are you sure it's a good idea to bring Rebecca?' she had said to Dr Hunter. 'Wouldn't it be better if it was just me?'

'Jacob talks about Rebecca a lot,' Dr Hunter had said. 'I think it would lift his spirits to meet her. After all, you are a family now, and he needs to understand what he is coming home to. This isn't a frightening place for a child. There's a farm we can show Rebecca round, and we can take her for a walk in the grounds with Jacob while we discuss the future for you all. This is going to have a huge impact on Rebecca and we need to try and give her some idea of what this means. You can't hide Jacob's illness from her, so it's better if she's encouraged to ask questions and feels included.'

Now, Harriet and Rebecca climbed through a small door beside the gates. They approached a wooden hut with a man sitting in it reading the paper.

'I'm here to see Dr Hunter about my husband, Jacob Waterhouse.'

The man called through to reception and pointed her in the direction of the main building.

The grounds were manicured and fruit trees lined the driveway. Harriet tried not to catch the eye of any of the patients who were wandering around. Rebecca smiled and pointed at the stables. As they reached the imposing building, Harriet saw a sign with arrows pointing to the printing shop, the chapel, shop, bakery, cobbler's shop – a self-contained village you'd never have to leave, she thought. They walked to the reception.

'Can I help you?' said a bespectacled young woman behind a glass panel.

'Yes, I'm here to see Dr Hunter. My name is Harriet Waterhouse.'

'You need to go out, turn right and follow your nose along the shingled path. You'll see a sign for Summersdale Wing. It's just past the art block.'

'Oh right, he said he'd come and meet us. I've never been here before, I don't know my way around,' Harriet said nervously.

'It's easy to find. Dr Hunter has just been held up in meeting, his secretary will meet you.'

'I don't want to walk any more, my shoes are rubbing,' said Rebecca, who was used to running around barefoot on the beach.

'It won't be far, darling.'

'I'm hungry, will the doctor have any biscuits?' said Rebecca, stopping and pulling her tights up.

'Darling, please don't whinge, this is an important day. We need to be happy for Daddy.'

Harriet started to feel her mood bristle. Rebecca hadn't slept well, woken in the night by a bad dream, and then hadn't eaten much breakfast, as Harvey ran around making her laugh. The bus journey had taken much longer than Harriet had anticipated. She had noticed Rebecca nodding off at times on the bus, and had tried to get her to sleep a little but it was too noisy and she had jerked awake every time. It wasn't a good start and she had relied on Dr Hunter being there to greet them and ease her nerves. A feeling of apprehension started to overwhelm her.

'Where are we going?' said Rebecca. 'My feet are really hurting, can we sit down?'

'Okay.' Harriet stopped and looked around. They had been walking for nearly ten minutes along the shingled path they had been directed to, and with no sign of an art block they appeared to be heading out towards some farm buildings.

The sunny start to the day had clouded over and Rebecca's mood started to darken with it as they set off again. After ten minutes they seemed to have lost their way.

Harriet felt a drop of rain, just as a man dragging a trolley of neatly folded linen walked towards them on the path. 'Can you direct me to Dr Hunter's office please?' she said, trying not to sound anxious for Rebecca's sake. 'Apparently it's next to the art block.'

'I'm not sure where Dr Hunter's office is, but the art block is this way, follow me.' The man hurried off as Harriet looked down at Rebecca who had taken off her shoes and was rubbing her feet.

Harriet picked up the little girl, and grabbed her shoes in the other hand. She began to walk as briskly as she could, struggling to keep up as the man walked ahead.

The rain began in earnest and as a crack of thunder rumbled in the distance, Rebecca started to cry. 'It's all right, darling. We're nearly there.' Rebecca was struggling to carry the little girl on her hip and hoisted her up with a groan. As rain dripped from her hair into her eyes the little girl clung to her nervously and her apprehension slowly turned to anger.

She had known all along it was a mistake to bring Rebecca to Greenways. 'Could you slow down please?' she called out to the man as she hurried to catch up. A nurse scurried past holding hands with a patient in a white coat who was enjoying the rain; her black hair was greasy and limp, her teeth yellowing as she tipped her head up, smiling at the sky. As they passed her, the patient stared at Rebecca, stopping in her tracks to touch the little girl's hair as they passed. Rebecca pulled away and let out a whimper, clinging to Harriet tightly.

'It's all right, darling, she won't hurt you.' As the rain started to fall harder, the man broke into a run, clearly anxious that the linen in his charge wouldn't get soaked. 'It's through there,' he said, running ahead, as Harriet looked at him and towards a building flanked by wooden huts with steps up to the entrance. ART THERAPY read the sign on the door. Harriet put the little girl down on the bottom step, took her hand and together they ran up.

At the top of the steps, they looked around. 'Mummy, can we go inside?' said Rebecca, shaking from the cold. Harriet reached for the handle of the art block door and turned it. The door creaked open and they stepped inside.

Despite it still being the middle of the afternoon, the blinds at the windows were pulled and the room was in darkness. It smelt musty, like damp wood burning, and she could make out a row of desks and in front of her a wooden easel. She hunted for a light switch.

She found one and flicked it on. Rebecca stood next to the easel, now illuminated, and was staring at it. Harriet had to cover her mouth to stop herself screaming.

It was a painted portrait. The same green eyes, the same long blonde hair, the same beautiful face as the little girl standing next to it. Harriet knew immediately that the woman staring back at her was Cecilia Barton.

As she drew closer, she saw the initials in the corner: J W. Dr Hunter's words came racing back to her: *Jacob has particularly benefited from the talking therapies, especially art therapy.*

She couldn't breathe and rushed to the window to open it. 'What's wrong, Mummy?' asked Rebecca, her green eyes wide.

Harriet's mind spun. Why was Jacob painting portraits of Cecilia? Was he still obsessed with her, after all these years? What hope was there for them as a family if she was so indelibly ingrained in his mind?

'Mrs Waterhouse? What are you doing? This area is staff

only. You aren't supposed to be in here.' A voice brought her out of her thoughts.

'Dr Hunter? Did my husband paint that picture?' snapped Harriet, already knowing the answer. 'What is the point of all this art?' she cried, her eyes full of tears. 'Are you trying to torture these poor men?'

'Torture them?' Dr Hunter shook his head. 'Mrs Waterhouse, art therapy has been extremely beneficial for you husband. It helps patients to express the things they cannot talk about and can unlock painful memories, which we can then help them to process.'

'Painful memories?' Harriet repeated. 'Does he blame himself for Cecilia's death? Is that why he's drawing her?'

'Her death? I don't understand what you mean, Mrs Waterhouse. Cecilia Barton is alive.'

'What?' said Harriet. 'I don't understand. She drowned.' Harriet stepped back from him, as Rebecca clung to her tightly. 'I know she did.'

Dr Hunter frowned and shook his head. 'No, she tried to drown herself and her child. Her baby's body was never recovered, but she was rescued. She is here, Mrs Waterhouse. Cecilia Barton is a patient at Greenways.'

Chapter Thirty

Iris

6:30 p.m. Wednesday, 19 November 2014

'Are you sure you want to keep waiting, love? This is going to cost you quite a bit.'

'Yes, boss's instructions,' said Iris, looking down at her watch.

It had been an hour and a half since Miles had called her with the address of Jane Trellis, the midwife charged with taking care of Jessie and her baby when she had snuck out of the hospital that morning.

Miles had texted regularly over the past hour since they'd arrived at Jane's house, which lay in darkness. He truly had the bit between his teeth now; there was no way this was going to end well, thought Iris.

Iris closed her eyes for a moment in an effort to try and calm herself down and collect her thoughts, but an image of Jessie walking into the sea at Wittering Bay holding baby Elizabeth in her arms kept playing on repeat in her mind. She had no plan of what she would say to Jane Trellis, if she was home even. And from the state Miles was in, Iris knew it had gone well beyond the point of being able to fob him off. He wanted an exclusive, and from what Mark was saying, the hospital wanted a scapegoat. Iris could imagine the article now, 'Exclusive interview from the midwife who let Jessie Roberts go!' Iris took a deep breath and turned her attention to the papers in her bag.

She started to read the first *Wishing Well*, dated December 1947. It opened with a Christmas message from the medical superintendent congratulating everyone on the success of the magazine and encouraging patients to continue sending in their contributions. There followed pages of beautiful poems and short stories written by the patients, about their experiences of war, of mental illness, of visitors they longed to see who never came, of summer trips to the beach in their childhood. The final pages had news of a dance that was shortly taking place and information about a new wing. Nothing about Jacob Waterhouse. She looked through the others. Again, nothing.

Her phone beeped with a text from Miles. *How's it going?*

Iris cursed at her phone and thought long and hard before typing out her reply. She looked at her watch. *Ten minutes away.*

Miles didn't respond and Iris read on, flicking through the issues, one after the other. No sign of Jacob's name anywhere. Iris read back to make sure she hadn't mis-read Dr Hunter's statement.

I told Mrs Waterhouse that Jacob is benefitting from the talking therapies, particularly art therapy, and has re-discovered a talent for drawing and painting; even submitting some of his work to our patient magazine, *The Wishing Well*.

Iris felt her stomach knot as she carefully turned each

page. 'Come on, where are you?' she muttered to herself as she reached the end of each issue. Lifting the last one from the pile, she turned the first page, then the second – then she saw it. A beautiful single-line sketch of a woman, her profile, looking down, the curve of her nose, her chin, her shoulder, her hip. It was entitled simply '*CB by JW*'. 'CB by JW – Jacob Waterhouse,' muttered Iris. She referred back through the pages: Jacob had been the only patient with the initials JW.

Iris took a sharp intake of breath and reached for the patient notes next to her on the seat.

She scanned the pages, running her finger down line after line of names. Then, finally: Cecilia Barton. CB. The initials on the sketch and the only CB in the entire patient list.

'Cecilia Barton,' said Iris out loud.

'Sorry?' said the driver.

'Oh, just ignore me, I'm talking to myself,' Iris said, frowning down at her paperwork.

'First sign of madness that is,' said the driver, chuckling to himself.

She pulled out her phone and googled the name, added Chichester and a match came up. Archives from a National Trust website.

A black-and-white photograph of a couple at what looked like a party. The man was tall and handsome, with a narrow face, and he was looking at the woman who was staring at the camera smiling. She was wearing a heavy fur coat and wore a locket around her neck. The caption read, 'Charles and Cecilia Barton, Northcote Manor Boxing Day Hunt, 1944.'

Iris zoomed in. The woman's face, her body and the way she held herself were immediately familiar to her. The woman in the photograph was the image of her mother. Goosebumps prickled up Iris's arm as she scrolled down looking for further proof. Another photograph, this one colour. A portrait of Cecilia Barton dressed in a green evening gown. Her blonde hair was tied up away from her face and her green eyes stared out at Iris. Emerald green eyes, exactly like Rebecca's. Tears stung Iris's eyes, as she frantically tried to think back to the documents she had read that day in the County Records Office. *Mr Jacob Waterhouse was first admitted to the Battle Neurosis ward here at Greenways in January 1947 when he was employed at Northcote Manor as head groundsman.* Iris looked up from the pages now swimming in front of her. The truth was impossible to ignore, thought Iris. Cecilia Barton and Jacob Waterhouse had had an affair when he was employed at Northcote – and Rebecca was the result.

Not only that. But because of her refusal to ever discuss that night, and her desperation to keep the past locked away, her mother didn't know – and probably never wanted to know – the truth.

Iris was so engrossed that she didn't notice a young woman approaching until she was almost at her front door.

'I think she's back, love,' said the driver as Iris looked up to see a young woman with a child walking down the path of number fifteen Wilson Road.

'Christ!' said Iris, springing into action and throwing all the papers onto the seat next to her. 'Do you mind waiting here for a few more minutes?' She said, snapping herself back to the present.

'Sure,' said the driver as Iris pushed open the car door.

Iris opened the gate just as the woman was putting her key in the lock.

'My name is Iris Waterhouse,' she said. 'I'm Jessie Roberts's half-sister.'

Jane Trellis shook her head. 'I'm sorry but I've been told not to talk to anyone about her.' The woman was at her door now and opened it to let the child through.

'I'm really sorry to bother you, but I'm desperately trying to find out any information about where Jessie might be.'

'Well, I've told the police everything I know. I can't talk to you,' said the woman, easing her daughter through the front door.

'I'm sure you have, and I realize this must be very difficult for you. It's just that as her family we are desperately worried about her.'

'Well you should be talking to the police. How did you get my name and address?' she said, frowning.

'I'm a journalist,' Iris confessed. 'I have a contact at the hospital who is also an old friend.'

'For God's sake!'

'But all I care is about is finding my sister. Please, Jane, I know the baby has an infection and time is running out for her. I just wanted to ask you one specific thing and then I'll go. Please.'

'I can't talk to you, I'm sorry. You'll get me in trouble. I've told the police everything I know.' Jane turned to close the door.

'I know, but they won't tell us anything. They're keeping us in the dark. Did she mention her family at all? Our mother Rebecca maybe? They don't see each other very often, but Jessie went to see her, on Friday. She had psychosis when Jessie was born, did Jessie say anything about it?' It was starting to rain again. Jane looked shattered as if she had been up all night.

The young woman's eyes filled with tears, her face pale and drawn. 'She didn't say anything about her mother.'

'Okay, thank you.' Iris turned to go.

'But she did mention her grandmother.'

'Her grandmother?' Iris frowned.

Jane nodded. 'Yes, she said that her grandmother had psychosis when she had her mother, that the child was taken away and she was put in an asylum. We talked briefly about how much times have changed, how they do everything they can now to keep mother and baby together. I didn't realize how bad she was feeling, and I'll never forgive myself for not giving her more time. I'm sorry.'

'You've got nothing to be sorry for. You've been really helpful, thank you, Jane,' said Iris, still reeling from what Jane had told her. How could Jessie have known about Cecilia? It was impossible. As she walked back towards the cab 'Miles' flashed on her phone.

'Tell me what I've just been told isn't true!' he roared. 'Jessica Roberts is your half-sister?'

'Miles, I—'

'I don't appreciate being lied to. Go home, Iris. Come in first thing tomorrow. I think we need to have a chat about your future. I'll send one of the other reporters over to speak to Jane Trellis.'

Miles hung up the phone and before she had a chance to catch her breath, her phone rang again.

'Mum Mob' flashed on the screen. Iris had so much to

257

tell her mother she had no clue where she was going to begin. She felt absolutely wrung out. It now appeared that she had lost her job, as well as her husband and her house all in a day.

'Hi, Mum, are you okay?' She got back into the cab and closed the door.

'Where to, love?'

'Mum? Is there any news about Jessie?' Iris panicked, 'Mum?'

'No, darling, not really. I've just been asked to go to St Dunstan's Hospital to meet an elderly lady who is claiming to be my mother. It's ridiculous! And so hurtful. It's probably someone who has called in after the news conference, a crank caller, and I've got to deal with it, when we should be focusing on Jessie.'

Iris took a deep breath. 'Is her name Cecilia Barton?'

There was a long pause. 'How did you know that? What on Earth's going on, Iris?!'

'Mum, you have to go to her.'

'Iris, Jessie is missing!'

'Jessie knew about this woman, Mum. She talked about her in the hospital. To the midwife. Cecilia Barton had postnatal psychosis and was put in Greenways Asylum. Jacob worked for her at a place called Northcote House. Mum, she looks just like you,' said Iris gently. 'I know Harriet brought you up, but I think it's possible she wasn't your birth mother.'

Rebecca paused. 'Iris, please, don't do this to me now.'

'Mum, you have to go to Cecilia.'

'No, Iris! This whole thing is bloody ridiculous!' Iris could hear her mother breaking down on the end of the line.

'Mum, it's okay,' said Iris.

'It doesn't make any sense. Harriet would never have done that to me, lied to me my whole life,' said Rebecca.

'Mum, Jessie was talking to the midwife about her grandmother being put in an asylum. That she had psychosis after you were born and that Harriet took you away from her. Is there any way you can think of that Jessie could have found out about it? Anyone that Harriet might have confided in?'

There was a long silence. 'No. My mother was a very private person. The only place she might have written about it was in her diary,' Rebecca said quietly.

Iris thought for a minute. Could Jessie have maybe found Harriet's diary? And read about it all? Where would it be?

'I have no idea – unless . . . My mother used to escape to the bomb shelter at Seaview sometimes – that's where we used to go to hide from my father. But the entrance is sealed off. Harvey said we couldn't get access. It belongs to another family now, and I can't imagine it would still be down there. There's no way Jessie certainly could have got in, on her own, with baby Elizabeth.'

'She must have found the diary though. How else could she have known all those things?' Iris was speaking fast, her words tumbling over each other.

'Iris, Jessie said something to me when she saw me. About my mother living a lie. She said maybe I didn't know my mother as well as I thought. That everyone had secrets. Iris, you have to go to Seaview and try and get into that bomb shelter. I'll talk to the police liaison officer about this now.'

'Okay, I'll go now. Mum, you must go to the hospital. Please, promise me,' Iris pleaded. 'For Jessie's sake.'

'Okay, Iris, I promise,' said Rebecca as she ended the call.

Iris leaned forward in her seat. 'Thanks for waiting. Can you drive me to Wittering Bay, please. As fast as you can.'

Chapter Thirty-One

I wake and my lamp gives out a soft glow in my darkened room. From the quiet on the ward it feels like the witching hour. Rosie and Harvey and the police officer have gone and I am alone. I am sitting up, because lying down makes me cough until I can't breathe. The mask is over my face permanently now, the sound of the hissing of the oxygen like the rushing of the sea in my ears. My whole body aches; my legs feel like they are on fire.

I take a slow breath in and my lungs crackle angrily in response to my efforts to stay alive. I know I don't have long, but dying is hard work – it's not something that just happens to you. It's not the physical part but the heart of me – who I have been and how I will be remembered. I cannot go without saying goodbye to my child. Without telling her I am sorry.

We are afraid that talking about death beckons it, that if we don't acknowledge it, death might not notice us. Now it is here, standing next to my bed, I cannot let it take me before I unburden my heart of Harriet.

The door opens and a nurse comes in, wheeling the machine which will tell her that I have a high temperature, that my sweats and crackling cough indicate I have an infection, that the antibiotics they're giving me aren't working.

It is the brisk nurse with dark hair. She starts banging at my pillows with a vengeance to prop me up, then takes off my mask, puts a thermometer in my mouth and wraps Velcro round my arm. As it pinches tighter and tighter, she tells me the doctor will be doing his rounds soon and that they may need to send me down for another X-ray. She is efficient, organized, professional. But where is Rosie? This cannot be the person who is with me in my last moments. My head throbs and sweat gathers under my body so my bed feels wet beneath me.

I doze off and when I wake a doctor with blue eyes behind black glasses is at the end of my bed. He is looking at my notes, talking quietly to his colleague. I breathe in and out, listening to my lungs crackle.

'It seems like the pneumonia is getting worse, despite the antibiotics and oxygen we're giving you. The only other option would be a ventilator in the intensive care unit, but I don't feel that would be right in this case. You are very frail and might not survive it.'

Time stops. I feel emotionally numb, frozen in thought.

The doctor's lips are moving, but I don't hear what he says after that. For as long as I can remember, I have feared life, not death. A constant feeling that my life is beyond my control, passing me by. But I will not die as I have lived. It is too late to change the past but it is not too late to take control of the present.

I pull off my mask and ask for Rosie.

'She's the care worker who has been visiting Cecilia, Doctor. I believe she may have just left.'

The doctor looks into my eyes for a minute and I stare back. He asks the nurse to find out if Rosie is still in the

262

hospital. He tells me they will increase my pain medication and that I must let them know if there is anyone I would like them to call.

They leave and I am alone, drowning in fear that it is too late, that I will never see Rosie – or my daughter – again. I turn my head slowly and look out of the window. I see a woman in a blue coat walking away from the hospital. I know from her walk and her beautiful long hair that it is Rosie, and I am powerless to do anything to stop her leaving. I want to get out of bed and bang on the glass, scream at her to come back. But I can only watch her leave.

Suddenly, I am back at Greenways. Standing at the barred window watching Harriet lead my baby away. I banged on the glass then, as I wish I could today, and as Harriet and my five-year-old daughter turned and looked up at me I knew instantly that I was right and the doctors were wrong. They tried to tell me that I drowned my baby, that I took her into the sea with me and she never came out.

But they were wrong, I left her in the cave. And Harriet found her.

The little girl holding Harriet's hand had my hair. She had my eyes. She was mine.

Chapter Thirty-Two

Harvey

8 p.m. Wednesday, 19 November

Harvey Roberts stood in the silence of the black dunes and yelled his daughter's name into the night.

His voice was hoarse and his legs burned from walking up and down the frozen sand.

His heart was heavy with a creeping feeling that felt all too familiar. The same feeling he'd had the night Liz died. A hopeless inevitability. The fight was lost; there was nothing he could do to stop the tide that was coming in to take his daughter.

'Jessica!' A dozen police officers' voices echoing through the night.

His fury at Rebecca was starting to fade. Perhaps it had something to do with meeting Cecilia. And now Rebecca was on her way to meet her.

Harvey had spent only a few minutes with Cecilia, yet he knew she was telling the truth.

Everything she had said made sense. Rebecca looked nothing like Harriet and they were nothing alike as people. It was something that had always niggled him, but he had never verbalized it.

And she knew so much, her story had to be true. About

264

seeing Rebecca at Greenways, about the night Rebecca's parents had been killed, about Harriet.

Deep down, he suspected that Rebecca had always known that her family was never as it seemed. That the night which blew their lives apart was waiting in the wings all her life. Rebecca had always been lost. It had driven Harvey to the limits of his patience: her inability to sit still, to stop pushing herself, to stop running away from herself and her past.

But perhaps all this time it was he who had been at fault for trying to make her forget, to stop her talking about that night. Convince her there had been nobody at the door. It must have been the storm. You must have imagined it. He had claimed to love her, but it had only ever been on his terms.

Even now, fifty years on, that night was still driving their lives. And never more so than tonight. Cecilia had been gripped by postnatal psychosis. So had Rebecca. Did Jessie now have it too?

It was in Rebecca's DNA, and yet he'd been unable to handle it and had punished her for it. Taken her child away from her.

Liz made it so easy to say 'enough'. To convince him that how things were couldn't be good for Jessie or him. That he had a right to put himself and Jessie first. He was so tired and when Liz wanted to take the reins he let her. Women are women's fiercest critics, as Rebecca always used to tell him.

This isn't fair on Jessie. He could hear Liz's voice now and feel her putting her hand over his. *We need to make some rules. Rebecca can't just turn up here whenever she wants and have us all jump through hoops. It's not good for Jessie to be in the car for two hours a day. To be left in a hospital crèche until it shuts. And then what happens when Rebecca becomes unwell again, and we have to pick up the pieces?* So he had taken the easy route, established routines and rules for Jessie's sake.

Made life harder for Rebecca and easier for him.

And destroyed Rebecca and Jessie's relationship so that history was repeating itself.

But really it was his fear. Of Rebecca's psychosis. Of having to go back to that night. Of watching her re-live it time after time.

The past returned in cycles. And here he was again. Close to midnight. Stormy sea. Frozen night. The sound of shouting. On nights like these he and Rebecca would run to their hiding place, and talk by candlelight, play, laugh. All the world to each other. In a safe place, where no one could reach them.

Harvey heard someone shout his name and at the same moment he knew where Jessie was.

The torchlight which had been moving slowly through the dunes began to move faster.

'Harvey!' Another shout, coming towards him, clearer this time, his name, the torchlight jogging up and down.

Harvey suddenly realized the phone in his pocket was ringing.

It was DC Galt's number. 'Mr Roberts, we've had a call from the officer who is with Rebecca Waterhouse. Is there a bomb shelter under the cottage?'

'Yes, but it's blocked off.'

'Can you get to it from the house?' DC Galt's voice was frantic.

'There used to be an entrance under the stairs, but it's

been screeded over.' But Harvey knew as he spoke the words that Jessie had found a way in.

'There's another entrance in the cornfield,' he said, 'behind the cottage, but it's been shut fast for years.'

Harvey started to run towards the steps up to Seaview. 'It's a vault lock, it was rusted, and it'll be covered in foliage. How could Jessie get down there?

'Apparently Rebecca Waterhouse said Jessie may have got hold of a diary belonging to Harriet Waterhouse and that the only place it could have been was in the bomb shelter. It's possible Jessie may have managed to get access before she had the baby, then returned there this morning with her.'

Taking two steps at a time, stumbling twice, Harvey headed for the field between Seaview Cottage and the farmhouse. His chest hurt from the cold, as he sucked in the freezing night air, pushing himself on. Looking up for a moment, Harvey saw two police officers running towards Seaview Cottage with the owner of Seaview Farm.

'They'll break in under the stairs if you can't find the entrance here,' said one of the police officers who'd followed Harvey.

Harvey felt panic rising in him. Why hadn't he thought of the bomb shelter earlier?

'We planted grass over it,' said Harvey, rushing towards where his memory told him the entrance was, 'so no one would know it was here. Where is it?' His head span, the cold air and all the turmoil of the last few days draining his ability to think.

'Here!' said an officer.

The policeman's torchlight revealed a cement circle with five spokes sticking out from a steel band in its centre.

Harvey leaned in and began to turn the rusted wheel, which squealed until he easily lifted it and revealed the heavy iron steps his father had built down to the shelter in the weeks after the Second World War broke out.

'Jessie, hang on!' Harvey turned to lower himself down.

DC Galt had arrived and now put her hand on his shoulder. 'Harvey, wait! We don't know what we are going to find down there – the baby may be very poorly.'

'I know! That's why I need to get to her,' Harvey said desperately.

DC Galt grabbed Harvey's arm. 'But you need to understand that the baby is our priority. If Jessie is in there and won't hand her over, we'll have to force her. We need to work together.'

Harvey pulled his arm away and started to climb down the wrought iron steps he knew so well as a boy. 'There's a light flickering! I think she's down here!' Harvey called up to DC Galt, his voice cracking.

DC Galt handed Harvey a flashlight. 'Get two ambulances here now!' she called out to her colleague. Harvey looked along the dark tunnel and could see what appeared to be candle light flickering against the curved wall. He could hear her but still he couldn't see Jessie as he crept along, fearful of what he was about to find. He could hear DC Galt's shoes on the rusted steps, following him down. As soon as he reached the bottom, he could make out the faint sound of his daughter crying.

'I can hear Jessie,' he called up. 'She's down here.'

Harvey reached the bottom and called softly, 'Jessie, it's me, Dad. I'm coming, sweetheart.'

'Dad, tell them to go! Please, I don't want them here,

they'll hurt Elizabeth. Dad, please don't let anyone down here.' Jessie's voice was weak.

'Jessie, it's so good to hear your voice. Is Elizabeth okay?'

No reply. Harvey couldn't hear the baby at all. As DC Galt reached the bottom, Harvey called to Jessie.

'Just you! No one else,' she hissed.

'Try and keep calm, Jessie darling. I'm here with a police-woman who has been helping to find you.'

'No, Dad, please!' Jessie sounded hysterical.

DC Galt stepped forward and her torchlight fell on a figure crouched at the back of the small, dank room. The moment Harvey saw Jessie his heart broke. Her face was white and covered in dirt, her clothes filthy. She held her hand up to her face to protect her from the bright light and he saw that baby Elizabeth lay limp in her arms. She was sitting on what looked like a turned-over bookcase, and on the floor in front of her was an open tin and a bottle of water. A single candle burned on a pile of books next to Jessie. There was a damp smell in the air, and various bits of junk furniture scattered around.

'Oh God! Jessie!' he said.

Jessie pulled Elizabeth to her. 'Get away from us. The medicine they gave her has made her sick. Look at her! I'm not letting anyone near her!' Her screams thundered around the walls of the shelter as baby Elizabeth's body hung limp like a rag doll.

'Jessica, your baby's very poorly and we need to get her to hospital as quickly as possible.' DC Galt's voice was calm.

'No, no hospitals! They were trying to kill her!'

DC Galt signalled to Harvey and they hurried back to the ladder. 'This isn't working,' she said. 'The baby is unconscious. I need more people down here. Try and keep her as calm as possible. We'll have to restrain your daughter, I'm afraid. Do you understand? We need to get that baby to the hospital now.'

At that moment they heard the ambulance sirens.

'I'll help to hold Jessie,' Harvey said firmly.

DC Galt paused for a moment. 'Okay, but she will fight, hard. We can take an arm each. You have to hold her tight. Just keep telling her that she will be okay and to trust you. We'll get her to release her grip on the baby. Okay, Harvey?'

'Daddy, where are you?' Jessie started to cry, howling sobs of fear and desperation. 'Don't let them take her, Dad.'

'Ready?' asked DC Galt as three more officers appeared beside her.

'Okay,' said Harvey.

Harvey walked slowly back towards his daughter.

'Daddy, what are you doing? Don't let them come any closer.'

'Darling, give me the baby, please. They'll have to restrain you if you don't give her to me. Please, Jessie. You've got to trust me, I won't let them hurt Elizabeth.'

Jessie began scuttling towards the corner of the bomb shelter like an animal who had been tortured and trusted no one. Harvey felt hot tears falling down his wind-burnt cheeks and he struggled to speak.

He sank down on the floor next to her. 'Sweetheart, please give her to me. Please.'

'Why are you on their side? They'll kill her, Daddy.' Tears were streaming down Jessie's dirt-covered face.

Harvey looked to DC Galt who nodded and as Harvey

270

grabbed Jessie's left shoulder and arm, DC Galt launched herself at Jessies's right side.

'Take the baby,' DC Galt directed the policeman next to her.

'No!' Jessie spat at the man as he reached for the child and kicked out frantically.

The second policeman put his arms around the baby and pulled her away gently as Jessie fought with everything she had to get away. Harvey watched as a paramedic rushed forward and the baby disappeared out of sight.

It had all happened in five seconds, but Harvey knew those five seconds would be etched in his mind for the rest of his life. He clung to her daughter as Jessie thrashed, spat and screamed for her baby.

'It's okay, Jess,' said Harvey.

'You let them take my baby!' Jessie broke free and Harvey watched helplessly as she curled up into a ball and sobbed in the corner of the bomb shelter. He couldn't bring himself to go closer, to try again. His legs wouldn't move, he had nothing left.

'I'm her sister.' Harvey heard a voice he recognized and looked up to see Iris coming along the tunnel towards him.

'It's happening all over again,' he said quietly, burying his head in his hands. As Iris focused on her sister and slowly moved towards Jessie, the paramedic spoke to her.

'Jessie, we need to give you something to help you feel a bit calmer,' he said.

'Stay away from me!' spat Jessie, now crouching in the corner of the room.

Iris stood up. 'Can I talk to her?'

'Can she be with her baby?' Harvey pressed.

'The baby will have gone ahead, but depending on how she is doing, there's talk of putting them in a mother-and-baby unit.'

Iris was crouching down now, a few paces from her sister. 'Jessie, it's Iris. Can I come over, please?'

'They're going to lock me up. I'll never see my baby again!' Jessie sobbed, backed against the wall. Iris looked down and saw the diary, covered in black dust, on the ground next to Jessie.

'Jessie. They want to take you to the same hospital as your baby, but they need to give you something to calm you down so you can go in the ambulance. Is that okay? I'll stay with you. I promise.'

'They took my baby,' said Jessie, but she was crying more softly now.

'Everyone wants to get you back together. Please trust me.' Iris couldn't help crying at the state Jessie was in as she collapsed into Iris's arms. She clung to Jessie.

The paramedic approached Jessie and whispered to her as they gave her an injection in her hip before wrapping a blanket around her. Slowly Iris laid Jessie down in her lap as the sedative took effect.

'Look, Harvey,' said Iris, pointing to the book laid on the dust-covered floor next to where Jessie had been.

Harvey picked up the red leatherbound book and saw the words 'Five Year Diary' embossed on the front.

'That's how me and Mum knew she was here. Harriet's diary is the only way Jessie could have found out about Cecilia.'

'They stole her baby,' whispered Jessie, as Iris stroked her hair and looked up at the book in Harvey's hands.

Chapter Thirty-Three

Harriet

July 1952

'I need to see Cecilia.' Harriet glared at Dr Hunter.

'I'm afraid that won't be possible.'

'Why not?'

'She's on a secure wing. She isn't allowed visitors.'

'Why? She isn't a danger to anyone. Cecilia wouldn't hurt a soul.'

'I'm sorry, Mrs Waterhouse, but it is out of the question.'

'Does Charles Barton know Cecilia is here?'

'I'm not at liberty to discuss another patient's treatment with you, Mrs Waterhouse. I believe you came here to see your husband.'

Harriet glared at the man. The warm, comforting voice she had heard on the phone was gone.

'Mummy, I'm hungry. My belly is making grumbling noises.' Rebecca tugged at her.

'Cecilia is my friend and ex-employer. Mr Barton wants Cecilia here to lock away a scandal. If I don't help her no one will!'

'Mummy, what's wrong?' said Rebecca, stroking her mother's hand. Harriet crouched down and picked the little girl up, making a barrier between her and Dr Hunter.

'I don't know what you are implying, Mrs Waterhouse. Two doctors have to certify every patient based on evidence and behaviour – it's not enough for the family, however influential, simply to declare someone insane.'

Harriet pressed on. 'I know how hard it is to get out of here once you are in. You need family support, and she has no one. If Mr Barton wants her in here, she'll be here for the rest of her life.'

'I'm sorry, Mrs Waterhouse. You still can't see her. You aren't family and I would lose my job if Mr Barton found out.'

'Fine, then I'll go to the papers. I know how the law works. Charles needed to have Cecilia certified insane so he could remarry and he wants her to stay in here. He never loved her; she was just a child. It's wrong and, as God is my witness, I will do the right thing by her.'

'You need to be very careful, Mrs Waterhouse,' said Dr Hunter. 'You are playing with fire.'

Harriet looked at Rebecca then back at Dr Hunter as her eyes filled with tears. 'Her baby is alive, Dr Hunter. She didn't drown her. You can't keep her in here for something she didn't do'. Tears slid down Harriet's cheeks as Dr Hunter looked at Rebecca.

As realization dawned, Dr Hunter finally spoke. 'If what you are implying is the case, that the child is hers, there will be consequences. You could go to prison for abduction, and the child taken away.'

'Let me see her, Dr Hunter, or I will blow this scandal wide open and drag your name through the mud along with Barton's!'

'Dr Hunter, there you are!' A nurse burst through the door. 'You're needed in the day room urgently.'

Dr Hunter stared at Harriet for a moment, then spoke. 'Nurse, take this young lady to Burnham Wing and tell the receptionist to tell Sister Julia that she is allowed five minutes with Cecilia Barton. And take the little girl to the canteen and arrange for her to have some tea and stay with her until I meet you there.'

The walk to Burnham Wing was the longest of Harriet's life. Her wool coat was soaked from being in the rain and her body began to shiver despite the warm July day as Rebecca walked solemnly beside her. The child had run out of energy to complain, the promise of a hot meal keeping her going.

After a few moments they reached a Victorian building coated in thick green ivy. Over the heavy white-painted door with its polished brass door handle was a sign saying BURNHAM WING. PERMITTED STAFF ONLY. The nurse buzzed the door open.

Inside was silent, in stark contrast to the elements outside. The hall and corridor were laid with a soft bright red carpet and the lower half of the walls was papered in a wood grain.

Behind the glass panel signposted 'Enquiries' was a telephone switchboard kiosk. Inside on the immediate right behind a reception desk sat a prim-looking young woman with a starched white shirt and a red alice band. Her long dark hair hung down in a bob around her face.

'Please could you call up to Sister Julia on Abbey Ward and tell her that Cecilia Barton has a visitor? And that she is to stay five minutes and no longer.'

'Cecilia Barton is on the locked ward. They aren't supposed to have visitors this late in the day, it unsettles the whole ward before supper.'

'Sister Julia. Visitor for Celia Barton. Dr Hunter's instructions. Five minutes only.'

'Come on,' the nurse said to Rebecca, and as Rebecca left, Harriet felt all her strength go with her.

'Go down to the bottom of this passage,' barked the woman at Harriet. 'Turn left. And then first right, you'll see a set of stairs. Climb up to the second floor and you will find it half-way down that corridor on your left.'

The long passage was coated in thick white linoleum with shone like a conker and had a smell which made Harriet feel queasy and claustrophobic, a mixture of bleach and extinguished fire. There were no windows and only a series of closed doors with 'No Entry' written on them.

As Harriet climbed the stairs her legs began to feel heavy, as if they had suddenly realized where she was going and what it meant. She had to tell Cecilia about what she had done. About the lie she had been living for the past five years while Cecilia had been locked up at Greenways. She had no idea how Cecilia would react. All she knew was that she had to see her and tell her the truth.

Eventually she reached a heavy iron door painted white with a small glass window with bars covering it. To the right was another brass bell which she pressed. It was eerily quiet and as she peered through the window she saw a nurse dressed in white walking towards her.

'Yes?'

'I've come to see Cecilia Barton. Dr Hunter sent me.'

'This really isn't a good time. She's just had an incident and it will unsettle the other patients even more to have a stranger on the ward. Miss Barton hasn't seen anyone for months. I don't think it's a good idea to have a visit sprung on her.'

'Dr Hunter made it clear I was to be allowed on to the ward. I will only be five minutes, then I will go. Kindly open the door.' Harriet glared at her through the hatch.

'Very well. If the doctor said so.' The woman slowly stood aside and Harriet stepped on to the ward.

Harriet stopped, her heart beating so fast that it was making her feel nauseous. She looked around the room, her eyes darting for any sign of Cecilia, but there were none. The room was cold and draughty and Harriet noticed that each bed only had a thin blanket on it. Harriet pulled her coat tightly around her and looked at Sister Julia.

'Follow me,' said the nurse as she set off down the ward.

'This really is most unfortunate timing.' She turned back momentarily. 'It's nearly bathtime and we're all needed. We can't leave them, not for a minute. The last time we made that mistake a patient drowned herself. Any momentary opportunity.'

'That's terrible.' Harriet looked around, drinking in her surroundings. She hadn't known what to expect, but she could feel the misery housed within the room's green walls; it seemed to radiate from every surface, from each poor soul sprawled on their bed or slumped in an armchair. Harriet was struck by the silence. There were no screaming idiots or signs of lunacy; instead, apathetic patients, lost in their sadness. A rotten-egg odour hung in the air, making Harriet feel even more queasy.

'What's that smell?' Harriet wondered out loud.

'Paraldehyde,' answered Sister Julia. 'Cecilia needed a shot to settle her. There really is no point in you seeing her now.'

'Did you see my wife on your way in?' a male voice called out to Harriet as they passed.

'Pardon me?' said Harriet, pausing momentarily as Sister Julia stormed on ahead down the long ward.

'My wife and children, they just visited me, brought all sorts of goodies, I'm a lucky man. Did you see them? When you came up the stairs?' The man spoke quickly, in fits and starts, and looked to be in his fifties, with grey hair and wearing brown pyjamas. He had a warmth to his voice and a twinkle in his eye.

'How nice,' said Harriet. 'I'm sorry but I didn't.' She hurried to catch up with Sister Julia who had reached the end of one room and was pausing at a locked door to the next.

'It doesn't sound like I have been the only visitor this afternoon. That man said his wife and children had been.' Harriet was slightly out of breath from hurrying to catch up.

'Did he also tell you that it was 1936 as he believes it to be? Or that his wife died over ten years ago and that nothing is known about his children as no one ever comes to visit him?' Sister Julia let out a heavy sigh and raised the keys on her belt to the lock.

'You are about to enter an acute ward for the sectioned and most disturbed patients. Only senior staff have a master key, and there will be a senior nursing colleague waiting by the door while you speak with Cecilia. I will also be right next to you.'

'I don't understand why Cecilia is in here,' said Harriet, trying to mask her anxiety.

'Stand well back from her, don't touch her in any way and no sudden movements. Five minutes, and then we leave. Have I made myself clear?'

Harriet nodded. The door creaked open and she felt a raging heat coursing through her body and up into her face, as if she were a wild animal trapped in a burning forest, knowing her fate was coming.

It looked like a hurricane had hit. Tables and chairs had been thrown about, and torn books and broken glass littered the floor.

'Cecilia had an episode. Her inner voices were overwhelming her. It took three of us to hold her down.' The nurse spoke with little emotion, well versed in the private agonies and inner torment of those in her care.

'Where is she?'

The nurse indicated a figure in a high-backed chair. Harriet caught her breath. She recognized the shape of her immediately. Her long blonde hair, her narrow shoulders.

Harriet inched forward so that she was standing directly in front of her friend. Harriet gasped at the vision in front of her. Cecilia was unrecognizable. Gone were the sparkling green eyes, the thick mane of blonde hair, the sun-kissed skin, the permanent half-smile on her rose-coloured lips. In her place, a ghost. Pale, emaciated, her hair brittle, her skin translucent. She appeared to be staring straight at her, but when Harriet moved Cecilia's eyes didn't follow her. She was slumped, her ear resting on her shoulder. A trail of drool escaped from her mouth.

Through force of habit, from years of tending to Cecilia's every need, Harriet leapt forward to wipe it away.

'Get away from her! What do you think you are doing? I thought I made myself very clear.'

'What on earth have you done to her? Why is she slumped like that?'

279

'I told you, she had an injection to calm her down.'

'And she had a treatment this morning, they are always sleepy for a couple of days afterwards,' added the nurse.

'What treatment?'

'Electro-convulsive therapy,' said the nurse matter-of-factly. 'And before you start complaining, contrary to popular belief, the patients queue up to receive it, because it mechanically lifts their depression. Cecilia's illness is far more unpleasant than the treatment. There is a danger of serious or permanent memory loss but, unfortunately, for Cecilia, that doesn't seem to be the case.'

'What do you mean, unfortunately?' Forbidden to touch Cecilia, Harriet stood back. 'What is she supposed to forget?'

'Her baby,' said the nurse, shaking her head. 'She drowned her, but she refuses to admit it. I find that patients can never hope to get better when they are in denial about what has made them unwell in the first place. Cecilia doesn't make life easy for herself.'

'If she would cooperate, they would go easier on her,' the patient piped up.

'Cecilia can be a handful, she fights the staff and she spits and bites. We have to find ways to control unruly patients, for the sake of everyone else on the ward.'

'So you do this to her because she fights back? She doesn't belong here!'

'I'm not sure I appreciate your tone. Cecilia was psychotic when she was brought in and continues to be to this day. She hears voices. She is a danger to herself and others and tries to take her own life practically every week.'

'Of course she does, she's locked up in hell. She would

never hurt anyone. I have to get her out of here. Cecilia, listen to me. Rebecca is alive, and you have to get better. We are at Seaview. You have to come and find us.'

Suddenly Cecilia looked up at Harriet and launched herself forward, locking her hands around Harriet's neck. Harriet couldn't breathe.

'Cecilia! Let go, Cecilia!' The nurse leaned over and began to pull at Cecilia's elbows. But they were locked rigid.

'Nurse!'

A young girl came hurtling towards them, preparing a syringe, her hands shaking in the panic.

As Harriet's world began to blur, Cecilia pressed harder, her green eyes piercing now. 'You were my friend,' she hissed. 'You stole my little girl.'

Slowly Cecilia released her grip as the injection took hold and as she slumped forward, the tears trickling down Cecilia's face dripped onto Harriet's cheek.

'Please help me,' Cecilia whispered, as Harriet clung to her friend's broken body and wept.

Chapter Thirty-Four
Rebecca

9 p.m. Wednesday, 19 November 2014

'Jessie's alive, Mum. They've just taken her off in an ambulance with Harvey to St Dunstan's Hospital.' Iris was barely audible through the wind on the beach.

'Oh thank God! And the baby?' said Rebecca, unable to stop the emotions she had been bottling up inside from spilling out.

'I didn't see her. They took her off first, in another ambulance. She's alive but Harvey said she's not good.'

'Do you know any more than that? Did you see the baby? Where were they?' Rebecca sunk her head into her hands and began to cry. Jessie and Elizabeth were alive.

'They were in the bomb shelter. Apparently the baby was unconscious. Jessie was in a terrible state. They had to sedate her. Where are you, Mum?' Iris asked.

'I've just got to the hospital. I was going in to see Cecilia, but I might wait for the ambulance to arrive with the baby in. I might be able to help.'

'Okay,' said Iris. 'But I spoke briefly to Harvey and I know Cecilia doesn't have long, Mum.'

'Harvey knows about her?'

'Yes, the police took him to see her in the hospital. He says she is telling the truth,' said Iris.

Rebecca, feeling dizzy, put her head back and took a few deep breaths. 'Well, I know Harvey won't want me anywhere near the baby.'

'I'm sure the baby is in good hands. My friend Mark works as a consultant in A&E. I know he's on duty at the moment, he'll take good care of her,' said Iris. 'You don't want to get to Cecilia too late. I'm on my way, Mum. I'll meet you at the hospital.'

Rebecca could hear the anxiety in Iris's voice. 'Okay, darling. I'll see you soon.'

Rebecca got out of her car and tried to compose herself. She looked at her watch. 9 p.m. It had been thirteen hours since the baby had been given her last shot of antibiotics. Her tiny body would be shutting down. She pictured the little girl in the ambulance now, an oxygen mask over her mouth. The first few minutes after they arrived at the hospital would be crucial.

Rebecca tried to compose herself but the thought of Cecilia Barton in the building behind was bearing down on her.

Unable to sit still, she began to walk towards the entrance of Accident and Emergency, straining to hear the sound of ambulance sirens to signal that Jessie was near. Rebecca looked up at the hospital, picturing Cecilia Barton in a bed somewhere, waiting with all of her secrets that Rebecca didn't want to hear. Harriet was her mother. She loved her; that love had been the only thing that was good about her childhood. The thought of it being built on a lie was too painful to bear.

Rebecca began to feel a strange sensation creeping over her, a fear she hadn't experienced for fifty years. As she looked up, the faint lighting in the hospital ward above her created a shadow-like silhouette of a woman. It looked as if the woman was looking down at her, banging on the glass, her shouting silenced by the distance between them. Then she blinked and the figure was gone.

She knew she needed to go to Cecilia, but she felt torn about leaving the location where baby Elizabeth would soon arrive. She waked into reception and up to the desk. 'Hello, I was wondering if you could tell me which ward Cecilia Barton is on please.'

'Are you a relative?' said the woman. Rebecca stared back at her, then slowly nodded.

Rebecca looked down the long corridor. The memory of her and her mother's outing to Greenways when she was five years old started to trouble her as her heartbeat hammered in her ears. She could picture the bespectacled young woman behind the glass panel. She could hear the words she had spoken to her mother as Rebecca had clung to Harriet's hand.

'You need to go out, turn right and follow your nose along the shingled path. You'll see a sign for Summersdale Wing. It's just past the art block.'

Rebecca imagined her beloved mother standing next to her, as she had done that day when they took the long bus ride from Wittering out to Chichester. She could still feel her new wool coat, too tight around her waist, the cream ribbon in her hair, the coarseness of her patent-leather shoes. See the worry etched on her mother's face. 'Today we are going to meet your daddy . . . He wants to come home. Would that be all right with you?' Her mother had smiled in a way Rebecca hadn't seen before. Her eyes didn't light up and sparkle as they usually did at Seaview.

'I don't know. I like it just the two of us.'

She started to make her way to the ward. The black night was giving way to moonlight.

It had started to rain, and they had got lost. Running through the thundering rain, up the steps and into the musty room. Her mother fumbling for the light switch and flicking it on.

The painting had been on a stand. The woman with the green eyes had stared back at her. *'She tried to drown herself and her child. Her baby's body was never recovered, but she was rescued. She is here, Mrs Waterhouse. Cecilia Barton is a patient at Greenways.'*

'Excuse me?' said a young woman's voice. 'I hope you don't mind, but I heard you asking for Cecilia Barton. Are you Rebecca?'

Rebecca looked up at her, too lost in thought to respond.

'My name is Rosie. I work at the care home where Cecilia lives. Are you on your way to see her?'

'I don't know,' said Rebecca. 'I don't know if I can.'

'She just wants to meet you. It would mean everything to her if you went. I'm sorry to say this but she doesn't have long. Would you be able to come now?'

Rebecca stared at the woman, then turned back to the entrance of Accident and Emergency: no sign of the ambulance yet.

Rebecca reached into her pocket and pulled out the gold locket which she had shown to Jessie just days before, and which her mother had been holding the night she died.

'I think this might be Cecilia's,' Rebecca said quietly.

The locket caught the moonlight as Rosie looked at it and smiled. 'Shall we go and find out?'

Chapter Thirty-Five

Harvey

9.30 p.m. Wednesday, 19 November 2014

Harvey watched the father of Jessie's baby run down the corridor towards him and tried to keep his composure.

'Harvey!' said Adam, launching himself at Harvey and throwing his arms around him. Harvey forced himself to hug Adam back.

'I'm sorry you've had to deal with all this on your own. I got back as fast as I could, they couldn't get me on a bloody flight.' Adam looked tanned and healthy and Harvey felt like punching him.

'You should never have gone away when she was so close to her due date, Adam,' Harvey said as calmly as he could manage. 'You're a father now.'

'I know, it just never occurred to me that she'd have the baby nearly a month early. I really am sorry.' To Harvey's shock, Adam started to cry. 'I screwed up, I know I did. I really love her, Harvey. I was going mad on that plane. I don't want our baby to die.'

Harvey felt his shoulders soften. He had never seen Adam show any emotion at all and he had no idea how to react. 'Well, you're here now, and Jessie seems to be doing okay by the looks of things.'

'What about the baby?' Adam asked.

'We don't know yet, she's pretty poorly,' said DC Galt, looking at Harvey.

Adam nodded, his eyes red from crying. 'Where is Jessie now?' he asked the police officer.

'She has been sectioned, and she is sedated. She's peaceful. I'll get my colleague to take you to her now.'

'Where is the baby? asked Harvey.

'She's in Accident and Emergency.'

'I'll go and be with Elizabeth, Adam. You go to Jessie. I'll let you know as soon as I hear anything.'

'Thank you, Harvey,' said Adam, 'for everything.' A policeman followed Adam as Harvey began to walk at speed with DC Galt towards Accident and Emergency.

'I haven't been down there yet, but it might be better if you waited in the relatives' room and I get you an update,' said DC Galt as they passed through the busy waiting room.

'No, I want to be with my granddaughter,' said Harvey.

'It could be distressing. There are going to be a lot of people working on her.'

'I don't care. She needs me. Does Rebecca know that Jessie is okay?' said Harvey.

'Yes, and we've contacted her about Cecilia. I believe she's at the hospital and on her way up to see her now.'

Harvey nodded. He could hear the commotion going on at the far end of the room before they reached the end bay which held his granddaughter. A tall, blond man in jeans with his shirt rolled up to his elbows was addressing a team.

DC Galt introduced herself. 'This is the baby's grandfather, Mr Roberts. Is it okay for us to be here?'

287

'Yes, but if you could stay back a little,' said the doctor, before turning to address his team.

'Okay, baby girl, born yesterday, taken from hospital by her mother. Mum is psychotic; she's with the police now. Baby's airway is clear, she's tachypnoeic – respiratory rate is 80. We couldn't get a BP but there's a faint brachial pulse, slow, at 68. She's unresponsive and her temp is down at 35.7. We couldn't get venous access so she has an interosseous in the right proximal tibia; we've given her 100mils of saline.'

The group of medics started talking over one another, and as Harvey stood watching he could feel the sense of panic coming from the small group.

'I can't hear much breath sound in the left lung at all. There's a lot of wheezing and creps. And I can't hear much air entry in the right side.'

'I can't get a blood pressure. She's completely shut down peripherally, her cap refil is more than three seconds.'

'Pupils are sluggish, she's not responding.'

Harvey moved closer and saw someone push a tiny needle into baby Elizabeth's hand.

'Is the paeds consultant on her way in, Polly?' said the doctor to a young woman in scrubs.

'No, Mark, I was going to wait and assess the baby.' The woman knew from the look on his face that she had made a misjudgement.

'He's ten minutes away,' said a junior doctor in scrubs. 'I can call him now.'

'Do it. Tell him there's a very sick baby here. We may not have ten minutes.' Harvey saw the panic in the doctor's eyes as he worked out his options. 'That should have been done already,' he muttered to himself.

Harvey looked on helplessly, then turned to DC Galt as realization dawned. 'Did you say that Rebecca was in the building?'

DC Galt frowned. Harvey had spent the entire day keeping Rebecca at arm's length.

'She's a paediatrician. Should we get her here?' said Harvey.

DC Galt stepped forward and put her hand on the doctor's shoulder. 'The baby's grandmother works in paediatrics. She should be in the building, shall I try and get hold of her?'

Mark looked over at Harvey. 'Rebecca Waterhouse?' Mark asked. 'I know of her through her daughter. Yes, that would definitely be a good idea. Can you get her here right now?'

DC Galt nodded and ran off down the corridor. As Harvey stood, helplessly, he realized that having kept Rebecca at a distance all day, he was now praying that she would be able to save their granddaughter's life.

If it wasn't for him, Rebecca would already be where she should be, next to him, saving Elizabeth. It wasn't the night when Rebecca's parents were killed, or her postnatal psychosis, or her career that had torn Rebecca and Jessie apart. It was him. Not only was he not helping, he was the problem – and always had been.

'Can I help?' Harvey knew it was Rebecca's voice before he looked up and saw her face. She stood panting by the trolley which Elizabeth lay on, having hurried from where she had been.

'Definitely,' said the doctor, holding out his hand. 'Mark Hathaway, A&E consultant. Our paeds consultant is ten minutes' away and we don't have any time to lose. I know you're family, so it's not ideal, but we don't have any choice.'

'Okay.' Rebecca took off her coat and threw it on a chair. 'Shall I run it?'

'Please do.'

Harvey stood watching Rebecca get to work. Her blonde hair falling around her face, determination in her emerald eyes. He had loved her so much growing up. It had been his sole purpose to do everything he could to keep her close, where he could protect her – where they were once happy, at Seaview. But all those years he had fought who Rebecca was, punished her for wanting so desperately to do something special with her life, to spread her wings, something her mother had been unable to do. And now, in this moment in time, Rebecca had stepped up to try and save baby Elizabeth's life. She was the one they were all relying on.

'Okay. Have you got blood and peripheral access?' Rebecca continued.

Harvey moved forward and stood at the foot of the bed saying nothing, watching the team work on Elizabeth's tiny body, which was completely still, an oxygen mask over her little face. Polly, the junior doctor, looked over at Rebecca. 'She's got an interosseous in her right tibia hip and she's had 100 mils of normal saline through it but I can't get a line in.'

Rebecca leaned forward and looked at Polly trying to put a canula in the baby, near her tiny elbow. Harvey could see Polly was getting flustered. He looked down at Elizabeth's lifeless body and up again at Rebecca. While all the doctors rushed around, Rebecca was watching Elizabeth intensely, as if trying to figure out a puzzle.

'Mark, please tell me what you're doing. Talk me through the ABCs – what's the airway like?'

'Seems clear.' The doctor pressed his stethoscope on to the baby's chest. 'There's a lot of crackles on the left chest and wheezes all over the lung fields.'

'Can we get a probe on her finger, we're not picking up any SATS,' said Rebecca, looking up at the monitor next to the bed where baby Elizabeth lay.

'The probe isn't picking up SATS peripherally,' added Polly, looking at Rebecca. 'I'm trying to get bloods. There's no veins now. There's nothing because she's shutting down,' said the junior doctor.

'Do a femoral stab then,' said Rebecca. 'I'm worried about her chest – the movement isn't symmetrical. Can I have your tubes?' She reached out for Polly's stethoscope. 'Quiet, please!'

Harvey watched as Rebecca listened to the baby's chest. 'She's breathing, but she's very tachypnoeic – she's struggling. There's not much movement on the right side of the chest. And no air entry on the left. She's got a pneumothorax, she needs a drain.'

'But there's no signs of trauma,' said Mark.

'Look at the chest wall – it's not moving,' said Rebecca. 'Trauma's not the only cause of a pneumothorax, it's a neonate with pneumonia – and her chest is not moving. This baby needs a drain in the right lung. I'll do it. Get me some gloves and a chest drain now!'

'Her heart rate has just dropped through the floor,' said Mark. 'We need to start chest compressions.'

'We need to intubate her,' said Rebecca. 'Where's the paeds anaesthetist?'

'On his way,' said Mark.

'Hold the airways open.' Rebecca started to feed a thin tube down the baby's throat. 'We need a chest X-ray now!' The monitor let out a long, loud beeping sound.

'She's crashing,' said Mark.

'Start the chest compressions,' said Rebecca, moving back from the baby once the tube was in place.

Harvey stood watching as Mark started the compressions and Polly hurtled towards Rebecca with the equipment she had requested. Rebecca swiftly pulled a tiny needle from the packet and placed it against the baby's skin.

'Reduce the pressure of the compressions,' she said to Mark. 'Put an ECG on so I can see her heart rate.'

The room fell silent. Harvey held his breath and through the sea of bodies watched Rebecca's fixed concentration: the fierce determination he'd witnessed so many times as they grew up together. Something flickered on the monitor and there was a high-pitched beep.

'She's back in sinus, she's got a pulse, she's got some colour back,' said Mark.

Harvey realized he had been waiting until Elizabeth started breathing again before he allowed himself to. He watched the baby's chest begin to move up and down.

'We need to move her to ICU,' said Rebecca. 'Keep her intubated. We still need to do some work on her. Tell the paediatric consultant to meet us in ICU and I'll do a handover.'

Mark nodded. 'Thank you for stepping in,' he said, turning to Rebecca, relief etched on his face. 'It's good to finally meet you, I've heard a great deal about you.'

'You must be Mark,' said Rebecca. 'Iris mentioned you'd be here. Thank you for getting me.'

They began to walk away. 'I don't think Iris would ever have forgiven me if I'd lost her niece. Anyway, it wasn't my idea to find you, I'm ashamed to say,' said Mark, looking over at Harvey.

Harvey looked at Rebecca, his face white with relief. 'Thank you for coming,' he said.

'No problem,' said Rebecca. 'Let's go.'

As Rebecca walked past Harvey she gripped his hand briefly. 'She'll be okay now,' she said quietly.

Chapter Thirty-Six

Harriet

July 1952

Harriet Waterhouse stepped off the morning bus at the top of Seaview Lane and hurried as fast as her exhausted body would carry her towards the courtyard of Seaview Farm.

Before she even reached it the front door opened and Ted Roberts stood there, his wind-beaten skin pale, his tall frame wilting, the tinge of a morning shadow starting to emerge.

'Where have you been, love?' His words were warm but he looked tense, biting at his lip, black shadows under his eyes.

'I'm so sorry, Ted, is everything okay? Was Rebecca upset when I didn't come home last night?'

'Not half as much as I was,' said Ted, forcing a smile.

'Where is she?' Harriet rushed past him into the kitchen. She had only been gone twenty-four hours but the kitchen reflected how much had changed in that time. The room was littered with used pots and pans, the sink overflowed with plates, and children's toys and chunks of mud and hay were scattered everywhere.

'She's fine. They're playing in Harvey's room. I should have been out at dawn – we're doing the fence up at the ridge today. What happened? You said you'd be back by teatime at the latest.'

'I had some business to take care of and it took longer than I expected.' Harriet turned to face him, his whisky breath filling her nostrils.

'What business? I was worried about you.'

'I can't tell you, Ted. It hurts me to say that, but I can't. You're just going to have to trust me. Go off to work and I'll bring lunch up to you all just after midday.'

'I have a right to know while you're living and working at Seaview. Sam Connors said he saw you go into the police station.'

'Please, Ted, let's leave it. I've barely slept. I just want to see my little girl and get this place straightened out.' She turned and called out to her daughter, leaving Ted, hands on hips, glaring at her.

Harriet walked through the house, calling out Rebecca's name, but there was no reply. She started climbing the stairs, two by two. She began to feel panicked. Where was she? She needed to see her daughter, to hold her tight. For Rebecca to give her strength. 'Rebecca! Come out now!'

Through the painful silence at last she heard the faint sound of giggling and found the two children, both of them a mass of blonde curls, hiding behind some curtains. She held out her arms for her daughter and the beautiful little girl fell into her. Harriet inhaled her – she smelled of spring.

'Darling, I've missed you,' she said, her voice breaking. 'Have you been playing outside this morning?'

Rebecca looked up at her and her eyes filled with tears. 'We fed the lamb whose mummy died last night. She doesn't have a mummy so we have to give her milk in a bottle.'

'Oh, sweetheart, don't cry. I'm sure she'll be fine.' Rebecca squeezed her daughter's hands tight.

'But who will put her to bed at night and read her a story?'

Harriet held her daughter's face in her hands. '*You* can, my darling. Is she in the barn?' She looked at Harvey, who nodded. 'We'll all keep her warm and fed and happy.'

'But she'll always know that we aren't her mummy. She'll miss her for ever.' Rebecca let out a wail. Harriet could see she was exhausted. If Ted had been dealing with a fox attacking one of the ewes in the fields last night, then the children had probably put themselves to bed only when they passed out, around midnight, she guessed.

'Shall we have a play at Seaview Cottage? And maybe you two can have a little nap? I can make the workers' lunches there. I haven't had a chance to wash and change yet today.' She needed to get back to Seaview Cottage, to feel grounded, to think. She could clear up the farmhouse later. The two children nodded and after she grabbed the bread and cheese from the pantry they made their way through the corn-fields and along the cliff path towards the cottage.

As the children skipped along ahead, Harriet felt a little nauseous. She could barely keep her eyes open, and the view brought to mind the night she had found Rebecca. She looked out into the bay and pictured herself, five years before, on the beach below, the wind howling. She could feel still the rain lashing at her face, the desperation to find Rebecca, and hear the faint sound of a baby's cry.

She stopped and looked down the bay to the jagged cliff edge, to where she'd read in the newspaper that the woman's body had washed up. The woman who was not Cecilia.

Cecilia was alive. It still seemed like a dream. She had

296

washed up on the beach in Wittering Bay and been found by a stranger walking home from the pub. A stranger who had handed her over to Charles, who had consented to her being locked away until he decided to release her. Cecilia had lain in the freezing surf in the bay Harriet looked down on now, barely alive, as less than a mile away she and Ted gave her baby whisky by the fire, fighting to save her life.

The pain of what had been done to Cecilia stabbed her stomach and she bent over, retching up bile. Trying to gather herself, she took in deep breaths of sea air. She heard the scrunching of stones as Rebecca rushed to her.

'What's wrong, Mummy?'

'I'm fine, darling, it's just a bit of tummy ache. Let's just get to the cottage.' She needed to put pen to paper and get the night she had just been through out of her system.

'Hold my hand, Mummy,' said Rebecca, and together they walked towards the safety of the cottage.

After putting Harvey and Rebecca down for a nap, she walked over to her dressing table, pulled out the diary from the drawer and began trying to extract the sleepless night she had just endured from her mind.

Saturday, 26th July 1952

Dear Diary,

I discovered two days ago, on my visit to Greenways to see Jacob, that Cecilia did not drown, as I had convinced myself was the case – she is alive. She is locked up in a high-security wing at Greenways, because she is suicidal in the belief that she drowned her baby.

I cannot live with myself knowing this, that I may have played a part in the hell that has been bestowed on her because I found her child and raised her, thinking it was what Cecilia would have wanted – with the beliefs and passion for life that made me see the world differently.

So yesterday, armed with this new-found knowledge, I went to the police to tell them that Cecilia's baby is alive. That I found her and raised her, believing that Cecilia was dead.

I left my child, who I love more than I thought it was possible to love a person, and went to turn myself in. Knowing that in all probability I would have Rebecca taken away from me and returned to Cecilia. And that I would never see my baby again.

On the long, painful bus journey to the police station in Chichester, I went over the facts again in my mind. Trying to decide if I had convinced myself that Cecilia was dead for my own purposes. Because I longed so desperately for a child.

But I have not slept, or rested for a moment, since I discovered the truth. And I know that if I even suspected, had been given any clue, I would have immediately done what I did yesterday.

What other conclusion was I supposed to have reached? Cecilia's shoes lay by the water on the night I found baby Rebecca frozen and close to death. The sea was raging and the temperature icy. Not only this, but within months village gossip told me that Charles Northcote had remarried and I read in the newspaper of a woman's body found washed up on the beach. Was it so wrong of me to reach this conclusion?

I torture myself that I didn't try harder to find out for certain what had happened to her, but I would have found it nearly impossible. Charles has kept the baby's existence a secret, since Cecilia ran away with her when she was five days old. And I have enabled him to keep that secret in the five years since, for fear of Rebecca being taken away and sent overseas for adoption. But at what cost to Cecilia?

Rebecca is Jacob's child, so she is my responsibility. I love her as I would love my own blood, as I loved my mistress. I was sure Cecilia was gone. But still I will never forgive myself.

When I reached the station my legs were heavy and I had to force myself to walk through the front door and ask to speak to the detective in charge about a missing person. The room started to spin as I sat and waited, my hands shaking so much I had to hide them in my coat pockets.

Eventually a man with a heavy black moustache and a long face appeared in the waiting room.

'Mrs Waterhouse? I'm Detective Inspector Gibbs. Please come with me.'

I recognized him immediately; he was the man who had interviewed me at Northcote the day Cecilia went missing. He knew I was holding something back then and he'd looked angry. I hung my head and tried to block out the bright lights and sounds that were overwhelming me – the ringing telephones, the clacking typewriters. I watched his shiny black brogues clicking on the floor in front of me, and it was all I could do to put one foot in front of the other and not turn around and run. I knew that as soon as I told this man the truth he would send someone to Seaview to take my beloved Rebecca away from me.

We entered a small room with no windows and he told me to take a seat. I did so, resting my bag on my lap, and tried to stop my legs trembling with fear under the table.

'So, you have some information about a missing person, I understand?' He spoke slowly, in a way that unnerved me, leaning back in his chair and lighting a cigarette. He threw his packet of Woodbines on the table and pushed his chair back so the legs gave a loud screech and made me jump. He didn't seem trustworthy somehow. I didn't want to tell this man the depths of my pain. But I didn't want to tell anyone. I wanted to turn and walk away, knowing every beat of my heart in that room would be my last as a mother.

I pictured Cecilia sitting next to me, holding my hand, and I told him my story. That I had suspected Cecilia had gone to Seaview, as it was where she holidayed as a child. I told him I found her shoes by the sea, and that I found her baby. I said that Rebecca had been close to death and that the owner of Seaview Farm had saved her life. That he had given us a place to stay and that I had lived there for the past five years, raising Rebecca.

He took a statement from me, which took nearly two hours for him to type up, and when it was finally over and the truth was out, I expected a sense of freedom, some sort of release. But I felt worse than I ever have in my life. Sadness to the pit of my soul at all the memories of my little girl, of the day she was born, of finding her in the bay, of all our years together at Seaview, of the happiness she has brought me. Her skin, her face, her touch – she is my life and without her I am nothing.

Detective Inspector Gibbs took a final drag on his cigarette and stared at me for a long while and then stood up and told me to follow him. Which I did, down a long corridor and set of stairs, to the holding cells, where he unlocked one of the cell doors and told me that they would be charging me with child abduction, that I would be held until my case could be heard before a judge.

I walked into my cell and the door slammed. There was a thin mattress on a metal-slatted bed and a bucket in the corner. It smelled of vomit and urine. I sat on the edge of the bed, my knees hugged to me, and stared at the heavy door with the slit to pass food through. I thought of Rebecca at Seaview Farm, a police car pulling up into the courtyard. Two men getting out, and walking into the house to rip Rebecca from Harvey's grip. I had no idea where they would take her. I couldn't bring myself to think about how frightened she would be. I had no choice, I told myself. I had no choice.

I thought of Cecilia. Of her life, a life behind bars. No escape from the physical and mental prison which she is made to endure every day. I thought of Ted, his kindness to us. His sweet smile, his laugh, and him drinking whisky by an open fire and telling the children stories. I thought of Harvey, how he would never understand where his little friend had gone. I pictured Jacob in the art room at Greenways, painting Cecilia in all her raw beauty. I pictured the painting that brought me here. At dawn I began to cry until eventually I fell asleep.

When the key turned in the lock I didn't know what time it was, but it still felt like night. I was offered no food or water. My body ached and throbbed from sleeping on the thin mattress. I knew only two things for certain, as I sat up and tried to shake myself awake: that

I was going to prison and that Rebecca would be taken away from me.

As the door opened a figure appeared in silhouette and I looked up to see a man I hadn't set eyes on for nearly five years. Charles Barton.

He asked if he could come in, and sat on the bed, requesting that I be brought a cup of tea and a blanket immediately. He said nothing, smiling at me, until Detective Inspector Gibbs returned with them and handed them over and then went out. I couldn't move, I was so frightened, and so Charles Barton wrapped the blanket around me and put the tea down beside me on the floor. Then he began to speak, slowly, as if he were giving a sermon in church. His voice had an edge to it, as if he were presenting me with the facts in a court of law. I drank in his appearance – his suit was freshly pressed, his shoes shining. I had no idea what time it was, or if I was in fact asleep and in the midst of a nightmare.

'We have ourselves a little problem, Harriet. It was a shock to get a call from Detective Inspector Gibbs here, telling me that after all this time of believing she was drowned, Cecilia's baby is alive. I know the child is not mine, and that Cecilia got herself in the family way after casting her spell over your husband. It is very commendable that you took it upon yourself to take care of the child while both its parents were somewhat indisposed.'

I was frightened to look away, but the hatch was open and I could see Detective Inspector Gibbs standing on the other side of the door. The other cells were silent; everywhere else was quiet.

'I have spoken with my lawyer and given it some thought. If you are willing to stay quiet about all this and officially adopt the child by way of a closed adoption so that Rebecca and Cecilia are unable to find any trace of one another, I am willing to drop the child abduction charges. But you will leave this cell and never speak of this business again.'

I couldn't believe what was being said. 'But what would happen to Cecilia?'

Barton looked at me, long and hard. 'Cecilia remains very unwell. If you were to decline my offer, the child would not be returned to her. She needs to stay where she is, for now at least. It would be too confusing for the little girl to be reunited with her mother, then for Cecilia to fall ill again and the two of them to be separated for a second time.'

'But she is unhappy because she is not with her little girl.'

'Now, now, I don't think it is for us to decide why Cecilia has been certified insane. But it is certainly not something that can be cured overnight. Now, I am not an unreasonable man, hence why I am making you this offer – against the advice of my sisters, I might add. But I would say that if you don't sign now, I would have to have the child removed from your care immediately and sent for a closed adoption abroad, so as not to cause any confusion. I presume you haven't told Jacob that the child isn't yours?'

'No, Mr Barton,' I said, my voice a whisper.

'Good, good, I think it's best to leave it that way. He is the child's father, after all. And I understand he is due to be released soon. I think this could all work out for the best for everyone.'

'I don't see how this has worked out well for Cecilia. She loved you, Charles. We cannot leave her in that place. I can't live with myself.'

'She had an affair with your husband. I think you are being far too generous. She has been certified insane by two psychiatrists. I think you have been a very good friend to her, but if we let her out now she will most likely kill herself. At least this way there is a chance she can get better, in the hands of doctors who know what they are doing. So, do I have your word?'

What was I to do? If I declined and handed Rebecca over, they would send her away, Cecilia would not have her and Rebecca would go to a stranger in a foreign country, far away from everyone and everything she loves. I cannot punish Rebecca because I cannot live with myself.

My mind raced as I sat there, thinking of how a powerful man can decide to keep a woman locked up in an asylum for his own personal gain. How someone admitted to an insane asylum could be left there dwindling for the rest of their life.

'Perhaps it has become too much of a burden for you. Would you prefer that we take the child?'

I decided that I had to do right by Rebecca, that all I could do was hope that Cecilia would come one day and find us at Seaview. I am forbidden to tell anyone about Cecilia's existence. As of this moment, I am Rebecca's mother.

I looked him in the eye and said, 'I love that child with everything that I am.'

'Then she is a lucky little girl. I am not a monster, Harriet, which is why I am not pressing charges of child abduction. But my family cannot allow a scandal of this magnitude to get out.'

Detective Inspector Gibbs came into the room and handed him a piece of paper and a fountain pen.

'We have a document here which, if you sign it today, means that we relinquish care of the child to you. Rebecca is Jacob's child. Her care can be transferred to him, if he is living with you.'

He handed me the pen and, after looking up at Detective Inspector Gibbs, I signed my name and sealed my place in hell. As he stood up and buttoned his coat, Barton said, 'The sealed records effectively prevent the adoptee and the biological parents from finding, or even knowing anything about each other, so you have nothing to fear. No one will ever know and, as of this moment, Rebecca is officially yours.'

'Cecilia will know,' I said, before Charles Barton turned on his heels and left.

Chapter Thirty-Seven

Iris

10.35 p.m. Wednesday, 19 November 2014

Iris Waterhouse paused at the door of the relatives' room at
St Dunstan's Hospital, where her mother was sitting alone
in the dark, her head bowed over her lap.

'Are you okay, Mum?' she asked.

'Not really.' Rebecca didn't look up as Iris sat beside her.

'They said baby Elizabeth is going to be okay, that you
saved her life.'

'Well, I don't know about that.' Iris watched her mother
wipe away tears.

'What do you mean?'

'I mean, I've sacrificed so much to do what I do. And at
what price?'

'Mum, she would have died without you.'

'Without me, Jessie wouldn't have been in that state and
none of this would have happened. I should have been
there all along, not just to snatch my grandchild from the
jaws of death.' Rebecca's voice was quiet.

'Mum, I don't know much about psychosis, but I'm
pretty sure it can happen to anyone. It was in Jessie's blood –
you had it.' Iris paused. 'And it sounds like your mother had
it too.'

'I'm scared of what is waiting for me in that room. Harriet is my mother. Everything I've done is for her, because of her. I can't live with that being a lie.'

'Just because she wasn't your birth mother doesn't change who Harriet was, and who you are. And she would be incredibly proud of you – she *was* incredibly proud of you. I know she was.' Iris put her head on her mother's shoulder.

'I don't think she would have been proud of how I've treated Jessie. Harriet gave up everything to raise me. So much so that I felt the overwhelming burden of living for both of us – it was always what drove me on. Every beating she took, I swore it wouldn't be for nothing.'

'And it wasn't. Look what you've done, what you've achieved.'

'But if you aren't there for your family – your blood – what does any of that matter?'

'Mum, you can't say that everything you have achieved is for nothing. You've helped so many people, saved so many lives. And you're a wonderful mother. I should know.'

Rebecca smiled weakly at her daughter. 'I'm sixty-seven years old. I need to slow down. I've just been too frightened to stop because then I would have to think. What Harriet and I went through together – it has haunted me every day of my life.'

Iris slowly pulled the diary out of her bag and pressed it into her mother's lap. 'Harriet was very proud of you. And she didn't steal you from your mother, she had no choice.'

Rebecca looked over at Iris, then down at the red leather-bound book on her lap. 'Is this Harriet's diary? Where did you get it?'

'It was in the bomb shelter. Jessie must have found it. I haven't had a chance to read it all properly, but it was Cecilia's husband who made sure she stayed locked up. He told Harriet that, even if Cecilia got out of Greenways, she wouldn't get you back. And that he'd have you adopted abroad if Harriet ever told anyone. He was a very powerful man and wanted to keep the scandal under wraps, and in those days you could have your wife incarcerated. Harriet loved Cecilia. She stayed at Seaview in the hope that one day Cecilia would get out and come and find you.'

'So, by scandal, you mean my father and Cecilia had an affair?' Rebecca looked up at Iris.

'I haven't read it all, but, yes, it sounds like Jacob was your father.'

Rebecca looked at Iris, her eyes shimmering from the tears waiting to fall. She stroked the cover of the diary. 'Will you come with me, to meet Cecilia?'

'Of course I will.' Iris stood and held out her hand.

DC Galt and Harvey were waiting in the corridor for them and said nothing as they emerged.

'Where's Jessie?' Rebecca asked Harvey, who was looking grey with exhaustion.

'She's with Adam. She's doing okay. They're hoping to get them a place in a mother-and-baby unit at Brighton.'

'That's a relief to hear. I'd like to see her later, if that would be okay?'

'Of course. She's sleeping now, but she knows you saved Elizabeth's life and we are . . . we wanted to say thank you. I'll never be able to repay you for what you did.'

'Harvey, she's my daughter. It's not a case of repaying me.'

'I know, and I owe you an apology, Rebecca. I feel very responsible for so much of this mess.'

'I just want to be in Jessie's life, and in my granddaughter's life. We both do,' said Rebecca, looking at Iris, who smiled gently at Harvey.

'Although I'm going to need an exclusive from you if I'm not going to lose my job over this,' said Iris to Harvey, winking.

Harvey let out a weary laugh. 'I think that's the least I can do.'

'I think there's someone you need to meet, Rebecca,' said DC Galt gently. 'I'm afraid we don't have long. She's struggling to talk, so you may not be able to say much to one another. She has a carer with her called Rosie.'

Rebecca nodded. 'I met her,' she said quietly as they walked along the corridor.

Finally they reached the door of Cecilia's room and DC Galt knocked softly and opened it.

In the bed, sitting up, was a woman with long grey hair falling down around her shoulders. She had an oxygen mask over her face and her eyes were closed.

The elderly woman opened the green eyes and stared at her. Slowly she pulled down the mask and smiled gently.

'Hello, Rebecca, I hear you got called away. Thank you bringing me my necklace.'

Chapter Thirty-Eight
Rebecca

10:45 p.m. Wednesday, 19 November 2014

Rebecca stood at the door. As she walked towards the bed she felt a strange sense of calm. The room had an air of peace about it, and she felt instantly relieved that she had got to Cecilia in time.

The girl who had been sitting in a chair next to the bed stood up. 'Do you want to sit here?' Rosie asked Rebecca quietly. 'They gave Cecilia a shot of morphine a few minutes ago so she's quite sleepy.'

Rebecca sat down. For a moment all was quiet. Cecilia's chest rumbled with every breath as she closed her eyes again. The machine beeped quietly in the background as the hiss of oxygen filled the room.

Rebecca looked at Cecilia, absorbing every inch of her face for the first time. Trying to take in as much as she could all in one moment. Cecilia's skin tone was olive, just like hers, despite her fair hair. And her narrow frame and pronounced cheek bones felt familiar to her. Rebecca could see that, even lying on her death bed, Cecilia had been a beauty.

Slowly, Rebecca reached out her hand and slid it into Cecilia's. Immediately the woman's hand closed around hers.

When she spoke, her voice was gravelly and slow, but loud enough for Rebecca to hear. 'I've waited a long time to hold your hand again,' she said, air catching in her struggling lungs.

Rebecca smiled at Cecilia, then turned to Rosie. 'Do you think we could be alone? Just the two of us.'

'Of course,' said Rosie, as Iris smiled at her mother and the two women left the room. Finally, the door closed.

Rebecca was the first to speak. 'I'm sorry it took us so long to find each other.'

'I hear you saved your granddaughter's life.' Cecilia smiled as she gazed at Rebecca. 'I'm so proud of you, Rebecca.'

'I don't think you would be if you really knew me,' said Rebecca, as one of her tears splashed on to Cecilia's hand.

'I know you better than you think I do,' said Cecilia. She began to cough again. Rebecca waited for her to gather her strength and continue. 'I carried you for nine months, remember, I know what a fighter you are. It's time to forgive yourself.'

Rebecca frowned and looked up into her mother's emerald green eyes.

After taking a deep breath the old woman continued. 'I'm sorry for what you had to witness that night, Rebecca . . . And for what you had to do.'

Rebecca looked at her in shock. 'You saw what happened?'

'Yes, I was at the window, I saw it all. You must never blame yourself.'

Rebecca shook her head in confusion. 'You saw me shoot my father?'

She stood suddenly and walked over to the window.

'Yes, and I was incredibly proud of you. I was there when he was beating Harriet. I was a coward not to try to stop him myself. I hate that I left you alone but I heard the sirens and I panicked. They had broken my spirit at Greenways and I was terrified of what they would do to me.'

'How can you be proud of me for killing someone?' Rebecca turned back and looked at Cecilia. 'There's never a time, even when I'm laughing at a party – or saving my granddaughter's life – that I'm not thinking about it. I have always thought that something would happen to someone I loved as some kind of payback. That's why I went into medicine, to make up for what I did. Because I am a bad person, not a good one.'

'No, that's not true. You were a child. And you had been subjected to years of living in fear and witnessing terrible violence towards Harriet,' said Cecilia.

Rebecca looked out onto the night. 'He was beating her so ferociously that he didn't even see me walk into the room. His gun was on the desk. He'd showed me how to use it in case we ever had an intruder. I didn't even hesitate. He was leaning over her, sweat dripping from his forehead from the exertion of what he was doing to her. I walked over to him and held it to his temple and pulled the trigger.'

Rebecca looked at her reflection in the hospital window. She could still feel the force of it knocking her back. The smell of the gun firing. The blood. So much blood.

'I didn't mean to make it look like he did it, but the pistol fell out of my hands. All I cared about was getting him away from her. But it was too late.' Rebecca's face fell into her hands.

'I'm so sorry,' Cecilia whispered.

'I've never told anyone that before. I need to tell the police.' Rebecca looked at her mother anxiously.

'Well, you can. If that's what you want. But you were trying to save your mother. She should have taken you away from him, and Seaview.'

'I think she stayed because she wanted you to be able to find us.' Rebecca turned back and sat back down next to Cecilia. 'There's something you should know. Harriet didn't steal me from you, she had no choice. Charles forced her hand. I know now that she loved you very much.'

Cecilia looked up to the ceiling as a tear ran down the side of her face. 'And I loved her.'

Rebecca leaned over Cecilia, their green eyes meeting, and wiped the tear away. 'I wish I had known you.'

'You did. My heart was always with you at Seaview. And it is where I'm going now,' she said, struggling to get the words out.

Rebecca started to cry, unable to slow the emotions that had been held in for as long as she could remember.

Cecilia managed a small smile. 'I love you, my darling, I'm so sorry I left you, my baby, my beautiful Rebecca.'

Rebecca watched her mother taking her final breaths.

'Promise me you'll forgive yourself and I will do the same. Promise me, Rebecca. It's time to move on now and allow yourself be happy.'

'I promise.' Rebecca clutched Cecilia's hand.

'I love you,' said Cecilia.

'I love you too,' said Rebecca quietly, unable to stop the tears now.

'Will you read Harriet's diary to me?' said Cecilia. 'I would love to hear my friend's voice again.'

Rebecca opened the door and asked Iris for the red leatherbound book. Opening it at the start, she sat down and, taking her mother's hand, she began to read.

Epilogue

June 2015

Rebecca Waterhouse wrapped her thick woollen cardigan around herself, took a breath and walked slowly into the cave at Wittering Bay.

Though it was a warm June day, the sunlight had left its comfort at the opening of the cave, and she found herself alone in the cold, damp space where her mother had left her as a newborn sixty-eight years before.

As her eyes adjusted to the lack of light, Rebecca scanned the cave which, only an hour before, had been filled with water before the tide started to go out, and ran her hand over the slippery rock. She took a breath and went in deeper, carefully trying to avoid the pits of sea water under her feet, until she reached an algae-covered shelf at the back.

The sounds of the children playing on the beach and the honking horns of summer traffic faded away, replaced by the faint sound of her own cries as an infant through the thick fog, as she pictured Cecilia laying her down, alone, before turning away towards the grey, freezing sea.

'Mum?' Iris's voice echoed through the cave. 'I've been looking for you. Are you okay?'

Rebecca slowly pulled herself from her trance and turned round to see her youngest daughter at the mouth of the cave, the sunlight causing a perfect silhouette around her pronounced bump.

'I'm fine, darling, thank you,' said Rebecca after a long pause, glancing back one last time before retracing her mother's steps out of the darkness into the June sunlight.

'The scan is at midday, so I need to get going,' Iris said, putting her hand on her mother's shoulder. 'Are you sure you're okay?'

'Of course, you must go. I'll come and see you off. Are you sure you don't want me to come?'

'No, I just want to go and get it over with. But she's been kicking me this morning, so perhaps this time . . .'

Rebecca took her daughter's face in her hands and kissed it. 'She'll be fine.'

Iris nodded. 'I just feel a bit sad I've been too anxious to enjoy any of it.'

'I know.' Rebecca linked her arm through her daughter's and they began walking across the bay towards the bottom of the steps which led to the car park.

Rebecca was grateful that her daughter didn't try and fill the silence as they fell into pace with one another and crossed the golden sand. As they passed the cliff face, Rebecca looked up at Seaview Cottage and pictured her younger self and Harvey running down the steps to the beach, with Harriet walking behind them holding a picnic basket.

Yet, since meeting Cecilia that night and discovering the truth, the bay that had felt so familiar all her life now felt like a stranger; as if it were a friend she were trying to forgive for keeping a deathly secret from her.

'I wanted to tell you something, Mum. I hope you don't mind.' Iris kept walking, using their lack of eye contact to give her the strength to continue. 'Jessie has asked me to move in to her flat for a week when she and baby Elizabeth come home from the unit. Adam has to work for some of it and she's scared to be on her own.'

'Why would I mind?' said Rebecca, feeling her heart skip a beat. 'That's wonderful. It's so lovely that you've been spending so much time together.'

Their reflections from the seawater under their feet sent their distorted silhouettes back up to them as Iris tightened her grip on her mother's arm.

'Well, I know you'd like to see more of Jessie,' Iris continued. 'I don't want you to feel hurt.'

'I don't feel hurt, these things take time.' Rebecca took Iris's hand. 'Harvey is making a big effort to be friendly so I'm just relieved we're all talking for the first time.'

Rebecca smiled at Iris. She was her father's daughter. She had John's heart which was why she was always so quick to forgive. Whereas Jessie was like her; they clung to the past, held on to it with every breath, unable to let go.

'She's very grateful for everything you did to save Elizabeth, she's just still struggling with her anxiety. She really loves you, Mum.' Iris's eyes brimmed with tears.

'I know, and I know Jessie's doing her best. She's been through a bad time. We'll get there. I'm really pleased you're building some bridges for us both. I really don't want you to worry about me. I'm fine, honestly, darling. You need to think about yourself, Iris, and the baby. You will text me after the scan?'

Iris nodded as they started to climb the steps slowly, leaving the fierce wind from the beach behind them.

'I heard back from DC Galt,' said Rebecca, eager to change

the subject. 'She's had confirmation that there isn't going to be any further investigation into my actions that night.'

'That's great news, Mum,' said Iris, pulling her mother into her.

'Yes, I must say I was slightly surprised. I suspected at least some sort of consequence for killing my own father, but apparently too much time has passed for them to do anything about it. There are no witnesses, no evidence. It's just my word, and it's not enough. They have kept my statement on file, but I haven't had so much as a ticking off.'

'Have you been back to Seaview since that night, Mum?' said Iris as she struggled to catch her breath climbing the last of the steep steps up towards the car park.

'No, I think it would be too much.' Rebecca shook her head.

'I can come with you, if you want me to,' said Iris.

Rebecca squeezed her hand. 'I know you would. But it doesn't feel like something I want to hold on to any more.'

'I think houses can hold too many memories sometimes,' said Iris, waving at Mark who was leaning against the car and pointing at his watch.

'So has your house sale has all gone through okay?' said Rebecca.

'Yep, it turns out that clinging for dear life to a past that doesn't want you isn't the nicest feeling in the world. It's a bit alien to be with someone who really loves me. And who won't be disappointed in me if I lose our baby.'

Iris paused and Rebecca smiled gently at her daughter, as she continued, 'And I guess I feel relieved that Jessie is in our lives and we can finally talk about what happened to you that night. The secret is out there rather than rotting inside us, taking its toll. But I know it hasn't been easy for you, Mum.'

'I don't know really. I'm glad we're where we are but if I'm honest, I really wish I could understand why Harriet hid so much from me. But maybe she planned to tell me, we just obviously never got to say goodbye.'

'Well, it's all here. I've said before, I really think you should read her last entry.' Iris reached into her bag and pulled out the red leatherbound diary.

'Thank you for looking after it for me,' said Rebecca, taking the book carefully. 'It was a bit too raw for me to cope with before.'

'I really think it will help,' said Iris, waving up at Mark as he sat in the car. 'I'm gonna have to go. I'll call you afterwards.'

Rebecca nodded and held her daughter tight. 'I'll be thinking of you, darling. I'm here for you.'

'I know,' said Iris, walking slowly away from her mother.

Rebecca looked out at the children below, running across the sand into the warm, turquoise sea. The same sea which had taken Cecilia away from her that fateful night. She turned and walked along the path towards Seaview Cottage, and pictured her five-year-old feet in her favourite red leather sandals.

It had been nearly fifty-five years since she had last walked the stony sand-covered link between Seaview Farm and the cottage where she had spent the first thirteen years of her life and yet she knew every kink and bump so well that she could have walked it blindfolded, even now.

When she reached Seaview Cottage, she sat down on the top step, laid Harriet's diary on her lap and took a deep breath. Slowly, she turned to the final pages and began to read.

319

Today is the day Jacob comes home from Greenways. I can already feel the atmosphere in our little cottage has changed. I am carrying my fear from room to room and filling the house with it.

How wicked of me, that I am dreading my husband – whom I loved so much, and who has suffered beyond human endurance – coming home. I keep thinking back to that day on the station when Jacob returned from Normandy, as I waited for the troop train on the crowded platform.

I could feel the electricity from the crowds of people shouting excitedly at the soldiers hanging out of every window, most of them wearing bandages or slings on some part of their poor bodies. I will never forget the silence that fell as the doors opened and they began to unload the stretchers, carrying the badly wounded, men with stumps for legs, who would never walk again, and then the stretcher bearers shouting 'Clear the way' at the stampede of families desperate to get to their men.

A woman with a small child came rushing past me over to a man with terrible scars on his face and only one leg, which he managed to walk on with the help of crutches. The little blue-eyed boy the woman was holding started to scream with fear when he saw his father for the first time. There was such an outpouring of emotion it was hard to stay composed and I just focused on trying to find Jacob in the crowd. But he was nowhere. I searched up and down the platform and eventually he emerged, thin and pale, blinking in the sunshine as if he had risen up from hell, and when he saw me he began to cry – as if the relief of it being over was too much for him to contain.

I ran to him and held him but I had the overwhelming feeling that this wasn't the end, quite the opposite in fact. It felt like the start of whatever was coming next. As the train pulled out of the platform, leaving us alone, it felt like it was taking my happiness with it, that we would never be the same again. The war in Europe was over, but ours was just about to begin.

As I write this I am sitting on the rocking chair on the balcony of my bedroom, watching the sun come up over Wittering Bay. The dawn is spectacular, and as I look at my little girl asleep in my bed, I can only hope that I have given her the strength to survive the changes ahead. This is my cross, which I must bear. I feel nothing for my own suffering because I have the greatest gift I could ever have wished for: my beautiful Rebecca. But I feel terrible guilt that she will now suffer for my sins. I can only hope that in raising her at Seaview, as Cecilia would have wished, she will be strong enough to survive the storm ahead. I will do everything I can to protect, and love her.

I hope that if one day she discovers the truth, she will forgive me. I loved Cecilia. It was only ever my intention to save Rebecca, as she has saved me. Rebecca may not be my flesh and blood, but I would give my life for her.

As Rebecca looked through a fog of tears at the sun setting over Wittering Bay and pictured her five-year-old self swimming in the surf towards Harriet, her phone beeped into life. Her heart in her mouth she reached into her bag and opened the text from Iris.

'Baby doing well. He waved hello! I love you, Mum xx'

Acknowledgements

The Lost Child involved a lot of frantic notetaking whilst chatting to a great deal of extremely clever, kind people, who then put up with me texting them 'One last question, sorry,' so many times.

In no particular order, thank you to Alexis Strickland, Midwife, who spent hours talking to me about her experiences on postnatal wards and her fascinating insights into postnatal psychosis. Thank you to Lorraine Lindsay-Gale for help with my research. Thank you also to the lovely and patient Katie Alexiou, clearly a totally brilliant Divorce Consultant and definitely the first lady you would want on your side if making your husband your ex.

Thank you to the totally wonderful David Williams, better known as Handsome Legend Dave the Wave Williams, for the hours of phone calls and emails and fact-checking on all things paediatrics – I am forever in your debt. To the very charming Barone Hopper, who kindly invited me to his home to discuss his work as a psychiatric social worker at Greenways Psychiatric Hospital in Chichester in the 1960s. As always, thank you to my wonderful mother-in-law Sue Kerry for sharing her extensive experience as a police detective, for her love of research and also for her patience – of which I am severely lacking – for detail.

Thank you to the wonderful Dr Jan Kohler, retired paediatric oncologist, who often had me in tears during our phone calls about the stories of her incredible career working tirelessly to save the lives of children with cancer. As with all angels, Jan thought nothing of her heroics (the greatest of which, in my eyes, was that she was the first female consultant in Southampton in paediatrics, whilst still managing to juggle motherhood and breastfeed).

Huge heartfelt thanks go to Sue Stapely, lawyer/reputation manager, who sent me endless emails in answer to my queries about marriage and women's rights in the 1950s. It was an eye-opener to discover how hard it was to obtain a divorce between the late 1940s and the 1970s, and the lengths people went to in order to get out of an unhappy marriage. I am also very grateful to Dr Alain Gregoire, Consultant Perinatal Psychiatrist, who kindly told me about the harsh treatment a new mother with postnatal psychosis would have received in the 1940s. And to Hannah Perrin at the Royal College of Psychiatrists for putting me in touch with Dr Alain Gregoire and helping me to pin him down! Thank you to the brilliant Dr Claire Emerson, who painstakingly discussed all things Accident and Emergency, pneumonia and hypothermia with me – you definitely get the prize for receiving the most 'Sorry, just one more question,' texts. Thank you also to Jessica Webb for educating me about the world of Art Therapy, and also for always being such a lovely and supportive friend. A huge thank you also to Aimee de Marco for patiently reining in my far-fetched ideas of life on a hospital ward and carefully picking apart what bits of them might happen in real life. Many thanks to the wonderful Dr Nadine Keen, Consultant Clinical Psychologist, for educating me as extensively as her hectic schedule would allow in Postpartum

Psychosis, and also about the systems in place in the modern day to protect mother and baby. As always, thank you to the wonderful Vicky Seal, Paramedic, for talking me through endless procedures and blue light scenarios and for being basically a fab human and mum to beautiful Olivia. My endless gratitude goes to the gorgeous Michelle Ball for having a seemingly unlimited supply of contacts to put me in touch with and for being so generally large-hearted.

Thank you to my wonderful agent Kate Barker for all your navigation in helping me to get my dreams off the ground. To all the wonderful team at Headline: Sherise Hobbs, for all your patience, kindness and brilliance, Phoebe Swinburn, Georgina Moore, Olivia Allen, Vivian Basset, Jennifer Doyle, Rebecca Bader and Nathaniel Alcatraz-Stapleton for always giving it your all. To my incredible sisters Polly, Sophie and Claudia for always being there, and to my girls, Sophy Lamond, Claire Quy, Clodagh Hartley, Kate Osbaldeston, Harriet De Bene, Suzanne Lindfors and Rebecca Cootes. To Esra Erdem and Laura Morris for being lifesavers. Last but not least to my (hell's) angels Grace and Eleanor. I have no clue what it is like to experience the hell that is postnatal psychosis but suffice to say I'm so glad the baby years are over, and I now get the privilege of watching you grow into the brave, kind, funny, stunningly beautiful girls you are becoming.

Finally, thank you to my rock, my husband Steven, who has held my hand through every crisis, character arc and chapter. I love you, more than any of my lame efforts could begin to describe.

Read on for an extract of the
heartrending novel by Emily Gunnis

The Girl
in the
Letter

Prologue

Friday 13 February 1959

My darling Elvira,

I do not know where to begin.

You are just a little girl, and it is so hard to explain in words that you will understand why I am choosing to leave this life, and you, behind. You are my daughter, if not by blood then in my heart, and it breaks to know that what I am about to do will be adding to the mountain of hurt and pain you have had to endure in the eight long years of your short life.

Ivy paused, trying to compose herself so that the pen in her hand would stop shaking enough for her to write. She looked around the large drying room where she had hidden herself. From the ceiling hung huge racks crammed with sheets and towels meticulously washed by the cracked and swollen hands of the pregnant girls in St Margaret's laundry, now ready to go down to the ironing room and out to the oblivious waiting world. She looked back down to the crumpled piece of paper on the floor in front of her.

Were it not for you, Elvira, I would have given up the fight to stay in this world much sooner. Ever since they took Rose away from me, I can find no joy in living. A mother cannot forget

*her baby any more than a baby can forget her mother. And I
can tell you that if your mother were alive, she would be thinking of you every minute of every day.*

*When you escape from this place – and you will, my darling –
you must look for her. In the sunsets, and the flowers, and in
anything that makes you smile that beautiful smile of yours.
For she is in the very air you breathe, filling your lungs, giving
your body what it needs to survive, to grow strong and to live
life to the full. You were loved, Elvi, every minute of every day
that you were growing inside your mother's tummy. You must
believe that, and take it with you.*

She tensed and stopped momentarily as footsteps clattered
above her. She was aware that her breathing had quickened
with her heart rate, and underneath her brown overalls she
could feel a film of sweat forming all over her body. She knew
she didn't have long before Sister Angelica returned, slamming shut the only window in her day when she wasn't being
watched. She looked down at her scrawled letter, Elvira's
beautiful face flashing into her mind's eye, and fought back
the tears as she pictured her reading it, her dark brown eyes
wide, her pale fingers trembling as she struggled to take the
words in.

*By now, you will have in your hands the key I enclose with this
letter. It is the key to the tunnels and your freedom. I will distract Sister Faith as best I can, but you don't have long. As soon
as the house alarm goes off, Sister Faith will leave the ironing
room and you must go. Immediately. Unlock the door to the tunnel at the end of the room, go down the steps, turn right and out
through the graveyard. Run to the outhouse and don't look back.*

She underlined the words so hard that her pen pierced a hole in the paper.

I'm so sorry I couldn't tell you face to face, but I feared you would be upset and would give us away. When I came to you last night, I thought they were letting me go home, but they are not, they have other plans for me, so I am using my wings to leave St Margaret's another way, and this will be your chance to escape. You must hide until Sunday morning, the day after tomorrow, so try and take a blanket with you if you can. Stay out of sight.

Ivy bit down hard on her lip until the metallic taste of blood filled her mouth. The memory of breaking into Mother Carlin's office at dawn was still raw, the anticipation of finding her baby's file turning to shock as she discovered no trace of Rose's whereabouts. Instead, the file contained six letters. One was to a local psychiatric unit, the word 'Copy' stamped in the corner, recommending she be admitted immediately; the other five had been written by Ivy herself, begging Alistair to come to St Margaret's and fetch her and their baby. A rubber band was wrapped tightly around these letters, *Return to sender* written in Alistair's scrawl across every one.

She had walked over to the tiny window of the dark, hellish room where she had suffered so much pain and watched the sunrise, knowing it would be her last. Then she had slotted Alistair's letters into an envelope from Mother Carlin's desk, scribbled her mother's address on it and hidden it in the post tray before creeping back up the stairs to her bed.

Without any hope of freedom, or of finding Rose, I no longer have the strength to go on. But Elvira, you can. Your file told me that you have a twin sister named Kitty, who probably has no idea you exist, and that your family name is Cannon. They live in Preston, so they will attend church here every Sunday. Wait in the outhouse until you hear the bells and the villagers begin arriving for church, then hide in the graveyard until you see your twin. No doubt you will recognise her, although she will be dressed a little differently to you. Try and get her attention without anyone seeing. She will help you.

Don't be afraid to escape and live your life full of hope. Look for the good in everyone, Elvira, and be kind.

I love you and I will be watching you and holding your hand for ever. Now run, my darling. RUN.

Ivy XXX

Ivy started as the lock to the drying room where she and Elvira had spent so many hours together clicked suddenly and Sister Angelica burst through the door. She glared at Ivy, her squinting grey eyes hidden behind wire-framed glasses that were propped up by her bulbous nose. Ivy hurriedly pushed herself up and stuffed the note into the pocket of her overalls. She looked down so as not to catch the nun's eye.

'Aren't you finished yet?' Sister Angelica snapped.

'Yes, Sister,' said Ivy. 'Sister Faith said I could have some TCP.' She buried her trembling hands in her pockets.

'What for?'

She could feel Sister Angelica's eyes burning into her. 'Some of the children have bad mouth ulcers and it's making it hard for them to eat.'

'Those children are of no concern to you,' Sister Angelica replied angrily. 'They are lucky to have a roof over their heads.'

Ivy pictured the rows of babies lying in their cots, staring into the distance, having long since given up crying.

Sister Angelica continued. 'Fetching TCP means I have to go all the way to the storeroom, and Mother Carlin's dinner tray is due for collection. Do you not think I have enough to do?'

Ivy paused. 'I just want to help them a little, Sister. Isn't that best for everyone?'

Sister Angelica glared at her, the hairs protruding from the mole on her chin twitching slightly. 'You will find that hard where you're going.'

Ivy felt adrenaline flooding through her body as Sister Angelica turned to walk back out of the room, reaching for her keys to lock the door behind her. Lifting her shaking hands, she took a deep breath and lunged forward, grabbing the nun's tunic and pulling it as hard as she could. Sister Angelica let out a gasp, losing her balance and falling to the ground with a thud. Ivy straddled her and put one hand over her mouth, wrestling with the keys on her belt until they finally came free. Then, as Sister Angelica opened her mouth to scream, she slapped her hard across the face, stunning her into silence.

Panting heavily, with fear and adrenaline making her heart hurt, Ivy pulled herself up, ran through the door and slammed it shut. Her hands were shaking so violently, it was a struggle to find the right key, but she managed to fit it into the lock and turn it just as Sister Angelica rattled the handle, trying to force the door open.

She stood for a moment, gasping deep breaths. Then she unhooked the large brass key Elvira needed to get into the tunnels and wrapped her note around it. She heaved open the iron door to the laundry chute and kissed the note before sending it down to Elvira, pressing the buzzer to let her know it was there. She pictured the little girl waiting patiently for the dry laundry as she did at the end of every day. A wave of emotion crashed over her and she felt her legs buckling. Leaning forward, she let out a cry.

Sister Angelica began to scream and hammer on the door, and with one last look back down the corridor that led to the ironing room and Elvira, Ivy turned away, breaking into a run. She passed the heavy oak front door. She had the keys to it now, but it led only to a high brick wall topped with barbed wire that she had neither the strength nor the heart to climb over.

Memories of her arrival all those months ago came flooding back. She could see herself ringing the heavy bell at the gate, her large stomach making it awkward to lug her suitcase behind Sister Mary Francis along the driveway, hesitating before she crossed the threshold to St Margaret's for the first time. Hurrying up the creaking stairs two at a time, she turned as she reached the top and pictured herself screaming at the girl she once was, telling her to run away and never look back.

As she crept along the landing, she could hear the murmur of voices coming towards her and broke into a run, heading for the door at the foot of the dormitory steps. The house was deathly quiet, as all the other girls were at dinner, eating in silence, any talk forbidden. Only the cries of the babies in the nursery echoed through the house. Soon,

332

though, Mother Carlin would know she was gone, and the whole building would be alerted.

She reached the door of the dormitory and ran between the rows of beds just as the piercing alarm bell began to ring. As she reached the window, Sister Faith appeared at the end of the room. Despite her fear, Ivy smiled to herself. If Sister Faith was with her, that meant she was not with Elvira. She could hear Mother Carlin shouting from the stairway.

'Stop her, Sister, quickly!'

Ivy pulled herself up onto the ledge and, using Sister Angelica's keys, opened the window. She pictured Elvira running through the tunnels and out into the freedom of the night. Then, just as Sister Faith reached her and grabbed for her overalls, she stretched out her arms and jumped.

Chapter One

Saturday 4 February 2017

'Have you cracked it yet?'

Sam pulled on the handbrake of her battered Vauxhall Nova, wishing it was a noose around her news editor's neck.

'No, not yet. I've only just arrived. I had to drive all the way from Kent, remember?'

'Who else is there?' barked Murray down the phone.

Sam craned her neck to see the usual suspects standing in the drizzling rain outside a row of pretty terraced cottages set back from the road in perfectly manicured gardens. 'Um, Jonesey, King . . . and Jim's at the door now. Why am I even here if Jim's already on the case?' She watched one of Southern News Agency's most experienced hacks trying to get his foot through the door. 'Won't he think I'm treading on his toes?'

'I thought this one might need a woman's touch,' said Murray.

Sam glanced at her watch. It was 4 p.m. – close to cut-off time for the national press going to print – and she could picture the scene in the office now. Murray on his mobile, shouting orders at everyone whilst admiring his reflection in the glass of the framed covers of Southern News scoops. Koop would be typing, pulling anxiously at his unkempt hair, surrounded by cold cups of coffee and wilted sandwiches, while Jen chewed on her Nicorette gum and

334

frantically made calls to contacts trying to fill in gaps in her copy. After he'd hung up on her, Murray would be straight on the phone to the *Mirror* or the *Sun*, lying through his teeth and telling them Sam was already on the case and to hold the press for her.

'I'm really not sure I'm the right person for this,' she said, studying her reflection in the rear-view mirror and catching sight of her grandmother's birthday flowers wilting on the back seat. She was supposed to have been at Nana's flat an hour ago to take over with Emma and cook Nana her birthday dinner.

'Well, the cream of the bunch will have already left for the Press Awards tonight. You'll have to do it.'

'Great. Good to know I'm considered the dregs of this agency,' mumbled Sam.

'Call me when you've got something.' Murray hung up.

'Wanker.' Sam threw her battered phone onto the seat next to her. She was pretty sure that the hours she'd worked that day on her tiny salary amounted to slave labour, and now she was expected to pull off a death knock.

She pressed her fingers into her eyes, massaging the sockets. She'd thought she knew what tiredness was before she became a mother. People lied to new parents, telling you to hang in there, that babies slept at six weeks, which was patently a lie. Then it became once they were weaned, then when they were a year old. Emma was four now, and it was still a miracle if she slept through. Before, Sam would complain of tiredness after getting six hours' sleep instead of eight, dragging herself into work in a haze of hangover after a night out clubbing. Now, at the grand age of twenty-five, she felt like an elderly lady; the four years of accumulated sleep deprivation had infected every muscle in her body, altering her brain and dragging her down so that some days she could barely form a sentence. On Ben's days with Emma, she could at least sleep until seven. But now that he had whittled that down to two days a week, on the pretext of needing more time to job-hunt, she had to be up at six most days to get herself and her daughter up and out of the door in time for nursery drop-off.

She sighed as she watched a dejected Jim walk back down the uneven stone pathway to join the other reporters under a golf umbrella. She knew the game, knew door-stepping was a necessary evil of her trade, but it was the worst part of being a reporter. Though she liked every one of the hapless gaggle standing at the end of this poor woman's pathway, they always looked to her like vultures circling their stricken prey.

She adjusted the mirror, pulled out her make-up bag and assessed how much of her face was salvageable. She would need a trowel of foundation to fill in the scowl-induced dent in the middle of her brow. As she dabbed at it, she closed her eyes and images of the fight she'd had with Ben the night before rushed back. It was always tense when she collected Emma from Ben's flat, the two of them trying not to snipe at each other in front of their daughter, but yesterday hadn't gone well. The fight had been a bad one, she knew that much, but as usual the exchange of insults had become a blur that had ended with them shouting so loudly they'd made Emma cry. Sam hated herself for dragging Emma into their arguments, and hated Ben for not trying harder to hide his disdain for her.

Recoiling at the sight of her frizzy hair, she reached for the portable tongs in her bag. In between getting Emma dressed and pouring breakfast down them both, she had little time for pampering in the mornings. Her red cork-screw curls were usually scraped back from her face, and the five minutes she had spare were given to blow-drying her heavy fringe. Heels were her uniform, and on her wages, eBay was her best friend. Days never went right without Louboutin or Dior to prop her up in a man's world, and she often found the pack sniggering at her as she made her way across muddy fields or flooded car parks in killer heels.

'Hey, Sam!' called Fred as he turned and spotted her, breaking free from the pack and tripping on the edge of a paving stone in his rush to get to her. He laughed in embarrassment, pushing his floppy fringe back and adopting the lovesick gaze he usually reserved for her.

'Hey, yourself. How long have you been here?' Sam pulled the passenger seat forward to grab her coat, bag and Nana's flowers from the back seat.

'Not long. It's my day off and I was rock-climbing in Tunbridge Wells so I've only just got here.' Fred's waterproof waxed jacket made him look like he'd just come from a pheasant shoot, Sam thought, pulling her black mac tightly around her.

'Why has Murray called you in on your day off? That's not fair,' she said, checking her phone as she walked.

'I know, I was a bit gutted. The friction was sick,' said Fred, smiling.

'You were sick? Oh dear.' Sam moved away slightly.

'No, it was good; sick is good,' said Fred, embarrassed.

'Sick is never good when you've got a four-year-old. How long have the others been here?' Sam asked as they approached the pack, huddled in a group.

'Hours. She's a tough one; we've all tried. The *Guardian* and *Independent* have been and gone too. Don't think even you can crack this one, Samantha,' said Fred in the public-school accent that earned him merciless teasing from the troops at Southern News.

Sam smiled back at him. At twenty-three, Fred was only two years younger than her, but as a commitment-free, fresh-faced graduate full of heroic ideals, he seemed part of another generation. It was obvious to most at Southern News that he had a huge crush on Sam. Despite the fact that he was tall, good-looking and accidentally amusing, with an endless supply of blue suede shoes and rainbow-coloured glasses, she found it hard to take him seriously. He was obsessed with climbing, and as far as she could gather spent every weekend scaling mountains and then getting drunk with his friends. She had no idea why he was interested in her. She was an exhausted, joyless grump whose greatest fantasy in the bedroom was eight hours' uninterrupted sleep.

They reached the back of the press pack. 'I'm not sure why Murray's sent you,' Jim called over his shoulder at Sam. Sam smiled politely at the Southern News old-timer, who found it hard to hide the fact that he thought she should be back at the office making tea.

'Me neither, Jim! Am I passable?' she said, turning to Fred.

Fred flushed slightly. 'Yes, definitely. Look out for the old witch next door,' he added hurriedly, keen to change the subject. 'She looks like she's going to attack us all with her Zimmer frame.'

All eyes were on Sam as she walked past the pack and down the path, clutching the bouquet to her chest like a terrified bride. As she reached the front door, she caught sight of an elderly lady at the window of the house next door. She had her net curtains pulled back and was staring intently. Fred was right, she did look like a witch. She was wild-eyed, her long grey hair loose around her shoulders and her bony fingers white from gripping the curtain so hard. Sam took a deep breath and pressed the bell.

It was a good two minutes before Jane Connors opened the door, ashen-faced.

'I'm so sorry to bother you at this difficult time.' Sam looked directly into the woman's reddened eyes. 'My name is Samantha, I represent Southern News. We wanted to offer our sincere condolences—'

'Can't you just leave us alone?' the woman snapped. 'As if this isn't hard enough. Why won't you all just go away?'

'I'm so sorry for your loss, Mrs Connors.'

'You're not sorry! If you were sorry, you wouldn't do this . . . at the worst time in our lives.' Her voice trembled. 'We just want to be left in peace. You should all be ashamed of yourselves.'

Sam waited for the right words to come, then hung her head. The woman was right. She should be ashamed, and she was.

'Mrs Connors, I hate this part of my job. I wish I didn't have to do it. But I've learnt from experience that some-times people wish to pay tribute to their loved ones. They want to talk to someone who can tell the world their story. In your case, you could talk about how brave your father was trying to save your son.'

Tears sprang into the woman's eyes as she moved to close the door. 'Don't talk about them like you knew them. You don't know anything about them.'

'No, I don't, but unfortunately it's my job to find out. All these reporters out here, myself included, have very tough bosses who won't let us go home to our families until you speak to one of us.'

'And if I refuse?' Mrs Connors peered round the half-closed door.

'They'll talk to other members of your family, or local shopkeepers, or write features based on potentially inaccurate information from well-meaning neighbours.' Sam paused. 'That would be a lasting memory for readers that you might find even more upsetting than all this in years to come.'

The woman was looking at the ground now, her shoulders sagging. She was broken. Sam hated herself.

'These are for you.' She laid the flowers on the doorstep. 'Well, they were actually for my grandmother – it's her birthday today – but she'd want you to have them. Please accept my sincere apologies again for intruding. That white Nova is my car, and this is my card. I'll wait for half an hour and then I'll go. I won't bother you again.' She started to make her way back down the cobbled pathway, hoping she wouldn't trip in her heels in front of the bored pack.

'Would I get to check what you wrote first?' Mrs Connors' voice was faint.

Sam turned round. 'Absolutely. You can read every word before I send it off.' She smiled gently at the woman, who examined the sodden handkerchief squashed into her palm.

Sam had noticed that the elderly woman in the house next door was standing at her open door now, still staring. She must be in her nineties. What must it be like to be so old, to have lived through so much? The woman was almost bent double over her Zimmer frame, an age spot like a large bruise on her hand. Her heart-shaped face was pale apart from the dark red lipstick she wore.

'Well, I suppose you'd better come in then,' said Mrs Connors, pulling her door open wide.

Sam glanced back at the pack, then at the old lady, who had fixed her with her pale blue eyes. It wasn't uncommon for neighbours to become involved when the press were out in force, but their presence was usually accompanied by a great deal of swearing. She offered the woman a smile that wasn't returned, but as she turned to close the door behind her, she looked up and their eyes met.

Keep in touch with

EMILY GUNNIS

Join the community on Facebook
f @EmilyGunnisAuthor

Connect on Twitter
🐦 @EmilyGunnis

Follow on Instagram
📷 @emilygunnis